'This is my home.'

'Where else would I have brought you?'

Disconcerted, Tamsin bit her lower lip.

'My dear young woman, in case you haven't noticed it is nearly midnight. No doubt I ought to place you in the care of some respectable dame, but I am damned if I am going to stir myself to try and find you a chaperon tonight.'

Lysander took a deep breath and reined in his temper. 'Instead of talking, would you prefer to go straight to bed?'

Tamsin's pulse began to race. Did he really mean to let her sleep undisturbed? He'd denied any interest in her, but could his word be relied upon?

Gail Mallin has a passion for travel. She studied at the University of Wales, where she gained an Honours degree and met her husband, then an officer in the Merchant Navy. They spent the next three years sailing the world before settling in Cheshire. Writing soon became another means of exploring, opening up new worlds. A career move took Gail and her husband south, and they now live with their young family in St Albans.

Recent titles by the same author:

THE ELUSIVE HEIRESS

THE RELUCTANT PURITAN

Gail Mallin

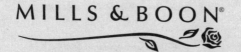

MILLS & BOON®

First published in Great Britain 2000
Harlequin Mills & Boon Limited,
Eton House, 18-24 Paradise Road, Richmond, Surrey TW9 1SR

© Gail Mallin 2000

ISBN 0 263 82330 X

Set in Times Roman 10½ on 11 pt.
04-1200-87986

Printed and bound in Spain
by Litografia Rosés S.A., Barcelona

Chapter One

1660

'Dover ahoy!'

Lysander Saxon's fair head whipped up at the cry floating from the crow's-nest.

'At last!' he breathed, a vivid smile lighting up his fine-boned face. Breaking off his conversation with a sailor coiling rope, he hurried across the empty deck to the ship's rail and scanned the horizon, his heart thumping.

There! Where the sun had pierced the veil of early morning mist he could see white cliffs gleaming in the distance.

'Can you see anything, lad?'

Lysander turned as a stout middle-aged man clad in burgundy satin came hurrying up to him, puffing in breathless anticipation.

'Aye,' he replied, his smile broadening. 'We're home, Tom. Home!'

'God be praised!' An answering exultation lit Lord Treneglos's face. 'It's hard to believe our long exile is over!'

It had been eleven years since the canting Puritans had cut off King Charles the Martyr's head and rendered his son homeless. Eleven bitter years of poverty and cruel, unfulfilled hope.

Lysander shook off unwelcome memories, determined not to let them spoil this longed-for homecoming. The Civil War, which had torn the country apart, had robbed him and many other Royalists of their youth and inheritance, but today was not a day to dwell upon wrongdoings. Today the King was restored to his own again.

'I'll wager Charles means to make up for lost time,' he said, a glint of amusement brightening his cool green eyes as he surveyed the deck of the *Royal Charles,* now alive with people shouting and gesturing excitedly towards the distant shore. 'And every man jack here will gladly follow him in his pleasure-seeking.'

'I suppose so.' Lord Treneglos's smile faded. 'For myself, my first aim must be to seek news of my daughter.' He sighed heavily. 'If she still lives.'

'God willing, you will find her, Tom!' Lysander gave the older man's shoulder a swift squeeze of encouragement.

'It's been a long time, Lysander. She was only a baby when I saw her last.'

'Don't fret.' Lysander spoke firmly and the sound of his deep voice seemed to steady his companion. 'You will succeed in your quest and be reunited with her.'

'I hope so,' Tom replied softly, gratefully patting the elegant, long-fingered hand which lay upon his shoulder.

Deciding Tom might appreciate a moment to recover his composure, Lysander stepped back and turned his attention seawards. Staring absently at the waves, now sparkling in the late May sunshine, he became aware of an increase in the hubbub fermenting on the quarterdeck.

He turned and saw that the King had emerged from his cabin. Charles was surrounded by a crowd of chattering gentlemen, but his great height gave him an uninterrupted view across the oaken deck.

'Lysander. Tom. Can we see the town yet?' Waving away his companions, Charles strode over to join them at the rail.

Bracing himself against the roll of the ship, Lysander

bowed with his usual easy grace. 'There, Sire,' he said, pointing.

Someone sprang to hand the King a telescope. Charles raised it to his eye. For a moment he stood quite still and then he lowered the instrument.

"Odsfish, and there was I beginning to think I should never set eyes on old England again,' he murmured lightly, handing the telescope back to the waiting naval officer and dismissing him with a sweetly careless smile.

Lysander knew Charles too well to be deceived by this show of humorous nonchalance. Charles was good at hiding his feelings, but they had been friends for too long.

Ten years, in fact, Lysander thought, remembering how he had finally persuaded his father to allow him to join the court in exile just a few weeks after his eighteenth birthday.

Sir James had not wanted his only remaining son to uproot himself from Melcombe. Both of Lysander's older brothers had been killed during the war and he felt that Lysander's place was at home with his mother. However, in 1650, when Charles decided to try and recover his throne by force of arms, he had reluctantly given way to Lysander's incontrovertible argument that the King needed every man he could muster.

Bidding a jubilant farewell to his mother and little sister, Lysander had ridden with all haste north to Scotland where Charles was gathering support. There was less than two years in age between him and the King and they had developed a swift rapport. Lysander had sometimes wondered if their friendship would have ripened quite so rapidly if the circumstances Charles had found himself in had been less dire. As it was, surrounded by gloom and endless sermons as the Scots harangued him to meet their stringent demands, Charles was in sore need of someone to confide in.

'You are looking very serious, Lysander,' said the King in a teasing tone. 'Are you having second thoughts about leaving that pretty little Dutch widow of yours behind?'

'Aye, she was a cosy armful, lad,' Tom chimed in.

Lysander quirked one eyebrow upwards in a characteristic gesture. 'And never so cosy as when she was trying to persuade me to wed her,' he retorted drily.

Charles grinned. 'But I thought you said you planned to marry and settle down?'

Lysander shrugged. He had made this rash avowal over supper last night. 'I may have said something of the sort,' he murmured evasively.

'Just the Rhenish talking, eh, lad?' Tom teased.

Lysander shook his dark blond head. The generous amount of wine he had consumed may have prompted the idea, but, now he came to consider it, it was a sound one. 'I have it in mind to find myself a rich heiress to swell the empty family coffers.'

''Odsfish, no doubt I shall have to do the same!' Charles laughed. 'But not yet a while. I think a little enjoyment is in order before I settle to that particular duty.'

His dark eyes twinkled with anticipation and Lysander flashed a grin at Tom at this confirmation of his earlier prediction.

'God knows, after all we have been through, gentlemen, only the harshest Puritan would deny us a taste of pleasure,' Charles continued.

The laughter faded from his voice and a small sigh escaped him. 'I only wish, Lysander, that your father and all those other gallant gentlemen who died fighting for my cause could be here to share this day with us.'

Sir James Saxon had fallen at Worcester, the battle which had seen the end of that campaign begun in Scotland, a campaign which had been beset with trouble from the start.

Lysander's mind flew back to that bright September day when he had first fought for Charles. It had been a hard fight. Cromwell had 30,000 seasoned soldiers compared to Charles's force of 16,000, but Worcester had a good defensive position and it was a city renowned for its loyalty to the crown.

He had been at the King's side as they rode out of the

Sidbury Gate in a daring attack on the parliamentary forces to the south-east. At first they had been successful and hope had flared in his youthful heart that they might snatch victory after all. This hope was cruelly dashed when Cromwell had launched a counter-attack, forcing them to beat a bloody path back into the dubious safety of the city.

Sir James met his death in the bitter hand-to-hand fighting which filled the narrow streets after this withdrawal. Lysander saw his father fall, but was unable to force a way through the carnage to his side. Wild with despair, he had redoubled his efforts to kill the enemy.

All around him other Royalists were fighting with the same fierce abandon, including the King himself, who could not be persuaded to withdraw to safety.

The very gutters of Worcester had run red with blood, but in the end their courage was not enough.

Lysander felt the old familiar sadness well up in his heart. For a moment his joy in the day was vanquished and then common sense reasserted itself.

'I'm sure my father and the others would want today to be a day of celebration,' he said quietly, but with such conviction in his deep tones that his listeners nodded.

'Aye, you are right.' The King's sober expression lightened. 'Come, let's go and break our fast. We'll raise a cup of ale to their memory and our happy homecoming!'

He turned away from the rail and Tom followed, but Lysander lingered a moment longer, his gaze fastened on the white cliffs gleaming in the distance.

What would London be like after all this time?

The smell hit Tamsin like a blow to her stomach. It seemed to be composed of dirty water, fish and tar overlaid with a ripe stink of manure. She choked, took a deep breath and then wished she hadn't as she almost gagged.

'London not to your liking, eh, mistress?' A cackle of laughter escaped the waterman as he skilfully brought his skiff alongside the steps so that his youthful passenger could disembark.

Tamsin gave him a haughty look copied from Aunt Deborah's repertory and, bundling up her dusty skirts, prepared to exit from the boat, nose in the air. Unluckily for her dignity, the skiff suddenly bobbed about in the wash from other traffic on the river and she had to make a mad leap, nearly tumbling to her knees in the process.

Recovering her balance and with the waterman's mocking laughter still ringing in her ears, Tamsin picked up her cloth bundle and climbed on to the quay. She stood looking about her, trying to quell a sense of panic.

Well, at least she had got here in one piece! And she knew where some of the stink was coming from.

Heaps of dung gathered in piles littered the wharf, steaming in the June heat. Tamsin's nose wrinkled. No doubt it was collected from the streets to be shipped off to some of those elegant gardens she had glimpsed from the river on the last part of her long journey.

She took a few steps forward and then hesitated. Which way had Sam said? Maybe she ought to ask—?

'Get out of my road, you stupid doxy!'

With a squeak of fright, Tamsin jumped aside and the waggon bearing down on her rattled past with a scant foot to spare.

The noise was unbearable. Waggons were rumbling everywhere along the wharf and every single driver seemed to be yelling for right of way. Dockers shouted, cranes creaked, sails flapped and boatmen were bawling enticement to passers-by.

Dazed, Tamsin sought to gather her wits.

Cousin Samuel had tried to warn her. 'Thee cannot imagine it, Tamsin. London is vast. Thee could put all of Chipping Sodbury in one single parish and still have room to spare.'

'I've no choice. I have to go. If I stay here at Whiteladies, your mother will force me into obeying her. You know what she is like!'

Since Samuel Barton knew only too well the strength of his mother's inflexible will, he had abandoned his protests and consented to helping Tamsin escape.

Putting aside the comforting memory of Sam's homely face, Tamsin firmly told herself to stop dithering like a lack-wit and ask the way. Unfortunately, she couldn't spy anyone respectable.

There were plenty of sailors and dockers about, but she was wary of approaching such rough-looking men on her own. If she hadn't been so travel-stained, she might have appealed to that high-born lady waiting in a gilt carriage over there, but after a single step her nerve failed her.

The only other women Tamsin could see were clad in gowns of such shamelessness that a bright blush rose to her cheeks as she stared at them.

You could see most of their breasts and they were wearing paint upon their faces. Could they be...? Surely not? Not walking around in broad daylight!

Subduing a sneaking envy of their gloriously untrammelled curls, Tamsin tucked a stray lock of her own unruly hair firmly back within the confines of her white linen cap and, Aunt Deborah's thunderous admonitions concerning the ungodly ringing in her ears, decided to ask for information once she was safely away from the wharf.

Choosing a direction at random, she soon found herself in a maze of narrow streets. Her brisk pace slowed and her eyes darted from side to side, trying to take everything in at once. Truly, this was a different world!

At home at Whiteladies, she'd only had to lift up her head to see the distant horizon. Here, there didn't seem to be any open spaces at all. Buildings crowded in on her, cutting off the afternoon sunshine. Carved woodwork and time-worn gargoyles flaunted themselves before her bemused gaze while, overhead, painted sign-boards swung in the warm breeze.

'You may send the rest on.'

A loud voice caught Tamsin's attention and she stared across the street.

The woman, who was most respectably dressed in a long dark cloak and a velvet hood, was standing at the doorway of what Tamsin thought must be a pewterer's shop since there was a variety of pewter plates and dishes set out on the narrow stall-board that protruded into the street. She was talking to a stout man whose long holland apron proclaimed him to be the shopkeeper or perhaps his assistant.

Tamsin was just wondering if she could interrupt their conversation when the man handed over the small parcel he held and with a low bow disappeared into the dark interior of his realm.

The woman began to walk away.

'Wait! Oh, please wait!' Tamsin darted after her.

Her quarry halted abruptly and Tamsin, her left boot suddenly slipping on a piece of rotting cabbage-leaf, was unable to stop and cannoned into her.

'God-a-mercy!' The woman emitted a squawk of surprise and dropped her parcel.

'I beg your pardon, mistress,' Tamsin gasped and made a hasty dive to recover it.

Shyly, she held it out to her victim, a rosy blush of embarrassment mantling her cheeks.

The woman stared up her and down and then, to Tamsin's relief, her angry frown eased.

'And where were you going in such a hurry, child?' she asked, taking back her property.

'I...I wanted to speak to you, mistress.'

'Indeed? What about?'

There was a note of intense curiosity in the woman's flat nasal voice, but Tamsin scarcely noticed it as she explained that she needed to find St Mildred's church. 'Which I do believe is in Bread Street.'

'Are you a newcomer to London, my dear?'

Nervous under the woman's sharp scrutiny, which was somewhat at odds with her dulcet tones, Tamsin hesitated.

She had been taught to be polite to her elders, but an innate caution warned her to be wary of tattling her business to all and sundry.

'Oh, come.' The rather hard features softened into a coaxing smile. 'If you are new to town, it's hard for me to know how best to direct you. You see, the shortest way is not always the easiest.'

Deciding that there could be no harm in admitting it, Tamsin confessed she had just arrived in town.

'But you have a place to go to? And people expecting you?'

'Oh, yes, I have a friend who lives near St Mildred's.' Tamsin nodded vigorously.

'Is that so?' The woman's grey gaze became even sharper.

'Aye, indeed. She…she knows I am to arrive today,' Tamsin fibbed hastily, hoping her face didn't betray her nervousness.

She was worried it might because she lacked experience in deception. Aunt Deborah had always punished her and Sam with a whipping whenever she found them out in a lie, so it paid to be honest.

Still, what she'd told her new acquaintance was near enough the truth. Martha Shore had been one of the maids at Whiteladies before she had wed Ned Croft and gone off to live in London. She had been Tamsin's nurse and, after her mother died, she had been very kind to her, so Tamsin was sure there would be no difficulty in staying with the Crofts.

Anyway, with luck, she wouldn't need to impose upon them for long. Once she found her father, everything would be all right.

The woman eyed her in silence for a moment longer and then gave a brisk nod as if coming to a decision. 'As it happens, I'm going that way myself,' she said, a smile curling up her narrow lips. 'You can walk along with me.'

'Thank you, mistress. 'Tis mighty kind of you.'

They fell into step and Tamsin's new acquaintance, who

was called Mrs Cole, kept up the conversation, as seemingly
oblivious of the din made by street vendors crying their wares
as she was of the muck that littered the narrow lanes and
gloomy alleyways. Even when they emerged on to a much
broader thoroughfare, the situation didn't improve. In fact,
with the addition of carriages and more folk on horseback,
the chaos was worse!

Tamsin found the noise and bustle bewildering. She had
never seen so many people all together in her life! Unable to
concentrate, she returned unwittingly revealing answers to the
questions fired at her by her companion.

'Look, there's a hackney for hire.' Mrs Cole suddenly took
Tamsin by the elbow and propelled her across the cobbles.
'We'll ride the rest of the way.'

Tamsin, who was hot and longing to rest, had no objection
to this plan. However, when she climbed up into the carriage,
she was shocked to find how dirty it was. It smelt of ancient
sweat and the thin leather pad which covered the wooden
seat was cracked and torn.

It was also very uncomfortable. There were no springs to
cushion them from the jolting as they rattled over the cob-
blestones and, since the driver seemed intent on going as fast
as he could, Tamsin had to put down her bundle and cling
to the seat to prevent herself from being bounced on to the
filthy floor.

'Never mind, my dear.' Ill-concealed amusement flickered
over Mrs Cole's expression. 'You'll get used to riding in hell-
carts after you've been in London for a while.'

Tamsin didn't believe it, but she nodded politely, anxious
not to seem ungrateful.

She glanced out of the open window and wondered where
they were. Surely they must be almost there?

Perhaps her sense of awe had distorted her perceptions, but
this drive was taking much longer than she had expected.
According to Sam, Martha didn't live too far from the river.

'Take a boat upriver when you part company with Master
Latham and tell the waterman to set you down at Queenhithe.

Bread Street is only a few minutes' walk from there,' he'd said to her on that last morning at Whiteladies.

He had attempted to give her a few more directions, gleaned from the single visit he had paid to the capital with his father, and then held out a small leather purse to her. 'Here, take this,' he'd added gruffly. 'It's not much, but there should be enough to see you safely to Martha's.'

Tamsin, knowing how short of money his mother kept him, had been touched by his generosity.

Without Sam's help, her escape from the awful match Aunt Deborah had planned would have been impossible!

One day, when I am reunited with my father, I will find a way to repay Sam...aye, and Master Latham too, she vowed silently.

If she found him...

Tamsin swallowed hard and tried to quell the anxious churning in her stomach, a queasiness which had nothing to do with the lurching motion of the coach or the humid warmth of the day.

'Ah, here we are!'

The hackney was slowing to a halt even as Mrs Cole made this announcement.

Somewhat to Tamsin's surprise, when she descended from the malodorous vehicle she found herself in a handsome street, containing many large houses.

'Are you sure this is Bread Street, mistress?' She could see no sign of the church Sam had described.

Mrs Cole was paying the driver and didn't seem to hear.

Tamsin glanced about her, feeling suddenly uneasy. Ned Croft had been fortunate enough to inherit his uncle's shoe-making business, said to be a more prosperous concern than his own little cobbler's in Chipping Sodbury, but she couldn't believe he and Martha could afford to live in such grand surroundings.

'Come, my dear.' Mrs Cole had finished with the driver. She beckoned to Tamsin.

Tamsin stood her ground. 'This isn't the right place.'

'Of course not.' Mrs Cole gave a cheery laugh. 'I've brought you to my own house.' She walked over to the nearest dwelling and knocked briskly upon the door. 'I thought you might like to freshen up your appearance before presenting yourself at your friend's. You can stay to supper and then I'll take you round there.'

Tamsin hesitated. ''Tis very kind of you, but it is growing late and I think—'

'Oh, don't tell me I've done the wrong thing!' Mrs Cole put an apologetic arm around Tamsin's shoulders. 'Only you look tired, my dear and…' her voice dropped to whisper '…very dirty.' She smiled coaxingly. 'Surely you don't wish your friends to see you in such a state?'

Tamsin bit her lip. Perhaps Mrs Cole was right. She did feel hot and sticky and her clothes were streaked with dirt and dust from the journey.

Scenting victory, Mrs Cole drew her forward towards the house and, before Tamsin could say yea or nay, the door opened and she was whisked inside.

It slammed shut behind them and Tamsin found herself standing in a large, well-swept hallway.

'Ah, Peg, show our guest into my closet and then fetch a jug of small beer.' Mrs Cole spoke to the fleshy maid who had let them into the house and then turned back to Tamsin. 'I'll join you in a moment, my dear, when I've removed my cloak and tidied myself.'

Without waiting for Tamsin's reply, she walked off towards the flight of stairs leading up from the centre of the hallway.

'This way.'

Tamsin followed the maid's squat figure down a short corridor and entered Mrs Cole's closet, a small room which was sparsely furnished with two cupboards, a few plain stools and a desk tidily arranged with a sharpened quill, ink-pot and neat piles of papers and ledgers.

Late afternoon sunshine slanted in through the window, which was hung with green serge curtains. The golden light burnished the oak panelling the walls and shone on the well-polished floorboards, but Tamsin owned to a slight sense of surprise. She had been expecting something more luxurious. Instead, this impersonal room reminded her of Aunt Deborah's private parlour, where her aunt did the household accounts, a place of business with everything lined up in its appointed place!

'Sit down.' Peg, who was eyeing her with open curiosity, pointed to a stool. 'I'll fetch your ale.'

She went out and Tamsin sat down, clutching her bundle in her lap. For some unknown reason she couldn't relax.

A moment later a loud shriek of laughter coming from somewhere on the floor above made her jump.

Nervously, Tamsin settled back on to her seat, wishing her benefactress would hurry up. Crazy as it seemed, all she wanted to do was to thank her for her kindness and get out of here!

A few more minutes ticked by. What was taking Mrs Cole so long?

Tamsin was on the point of leaving when she heard footsteps in the corridor. 'Oh, it's you,' she murmured as the stout, middle-aged maid entered. 'I thought it was Mrs Cole.'

'Madam will be busy getting changed for the evening.' Careful not to disturb the papers on the desk, Peg set down the tray she carried.

'Do you know how much longer she will be?' asked Tamsin.

Peg shrugged, plainly indifferent to Tamsin's anxiety. 'Help yourself.' She gestured at the jug and mugs she had brought in and turned to leave once more.

'Please don't go. I…I can't—'

Peg halted, but her lined face wore an impatient frown. 'I ain't got time to wait on the likes of you, lass.'

There was a note of rough sympathy in her voice which puzzled Tamsin. She opened her mouth again.

'Nay, save your questions for Madam. I've too much work

to do. At this rate, the first customers of the evening will be here before I've got the gooseberry tarts out of the oven.'

She hurried out of the room, leaving Tamsin more confused than ever. Customers? What customers?

Tamsin realised that she had made the assumption that Mrs Cole was wealthy because her clothes were of good quality and she had a big house in a fine neighbourhood.

'Maybe she has to earn her living running this place as an eating-house,' she murmured to herself, getting up and moving towards the desk.

Too thirsty to ponder the puzzle any further, Tamsin poured herself a mugful of the weak beer and drank it down quickly. It was cool and refreshingly tart upon the tongue, but her stomach rumbled, reminding her she hadn't eaten since she had shared a morning draught of ale and mutton pie with Master Latham. They had parted company soon after and she'd had no money to spare for buying herself any dinner.

'Good. You've helped yourself. I meant to tell you not to wait for me.'

Tamsin turned at the sound of Mrs Cole's voice and almost dropped her empty mug in surprise.

Mrs Cole had removed her hood and her dark hair now rioted in wanton curls about a boldly painted face. Gone too were the respectable brown camlet skirts, swopped for an extremely low-cut gown of crimson silk.

Scandalised by the acreage of flesh on show, Tamsin's fingers itched to pull it up.

'Pray don't look so shocked, my dear.' Mrs Cole walked up to Tamsin and calmly removed the mug from her nerveless fingers and set it down. 'Under that dirt you're quite a pretty little creature.' Her appraising gaze flicked to an unruly lock of apricot-gold hair which had escaped Tamsin's cap. 'I'm sure we can do business if you are sensible.'

Tamsin got a whiff of her strong musky perfume and sneezed. 'What…what do you mean?' she sniffed.

Mrs Cole's look of amusement intensified. 'Lord, what an

innocent you are! I was sure you would have guessed by now.'

Without knowing precisely why, the uneasiness which had been haunting Tamsin ever since she got of the hackney cab suddenly doubled. 'I don't understand what you are talking about.'

Mrs Cole sighed. 'You told me that you intended to look for work,' she said impatiently, aware that there was little time for explanations.

'Aye.' Tamsin vaguely remembered admitting she was short of money.

'I can offer you work. Well-paid work with good lodgings thrown in.'

'What kind of work—?'

'Madam.' Peg stuck her head round the door. 'Sorry to interrupt, but Betty wants a word with you. Says it's urgent.'

'Where is she?'

'In the salon. Moaning about Annie pinching her new necklace.' Peg rolled her eyes heavenwards. 'I can't do anything with her.'

'Very well. Leave her to me and get on with organising supper, Peg.'

Peg nodded and withdrew.

Mrs Cole turned to Tamsin. 'Come with me.'

She swept from the room in a rustle of skirts and Tamsin, who was feeling more bewildered than ever, decided that she had better follow.

The salon was a large room. Held up by several gilded pillars, the ceiling had been painted with garish scenes of half-naked gods and goddesses whose amorous cavorting made Tamsin blush to the edge of her cap. She eyed the furniture with equal disapproval. Low tables, fancy-looking chairs and several couches scattered with gaudy cushions.

It was all very odd!

A blonde girl was lolling on one of the couches. She jumped up at their entrance and Tamsin saw that she was wearing a gown that made Mrs Cole's look modest.

'That cow Annie has pinched m'necklace,' she shrieked, the thin blue taffeta which veiled her plump charms threatening to give up the struggle altogether as she waved her arms in agitation. 'The one Sir Harry gave me last week. It ain't bloody fair! I had to work hard enough for it, it ain't easy pleasing that old goat.' She planted her fists on her hips. 'I wants it back or I swear I'll scratch her bleeding eyes out!'

'Don't shout, Betty.' Mrs Cole's response was cool. 'I'll speak to Annie, but remember, I won't have any brawling. And keep your tongue sweet. Our gentlemen come here expecting a little refinement. If they want vulgarity, they can find it a lot cheaper elsewhere.'

Enlightenment burst in on Tamsin. 'This is a house of sin!' she gasped.

Raucous laughter answered her. 'Gawd, who dragged you in?' Betty eyed her up and down, contempt obvious in her blue gaze. 'Look at them clothes! Right little Puritan, ain't she!'

She laughed again. 'Skinny, too. Why, she hardly looks old enough to—'

'That's enough, Betty. She'll clean up nicely and some of our customers prefer them young.'

Mrs Cole glanced at Tamsin with a proprietorial smile. 'One of them will be willing to pay me a handsome sum for the privilege of deflowering such a fresh little virgin.'

There was no time to berate herself. It didn't matter whether it was her sheltered upbringing or sheer idiocy which had landed her in this mess. Nothing mattered…except getting out of here as fast as her legs could carry her!

Tamsin whirled and ran out of the salon, racing towards the front door.

'Jenkins!'

A thick-set man moved into view, blocking her escape.

Tamsin dodged to one side. If she could reach the stairs, there might be a way out through one of the upper windows…

She screamed as she felt his hand catch in her skirts and heard the cloth tear as he hauled her back towards him.

'Take your hands off me, you brute!'

Struggling wildly, Tamsin wriggled in his grasp and one of her flailing fists made violent contact with his ear.

'Let her go, Jenkins. I don't want her marked.' Mrs Cole's sharp voice cut across his growl of anger.

He stepped back, his small eyes promising revenge as he released Tamsin.

Tamsin shuddered.

'Come, child. There's no need for such dramatics.' Mrs Cole sighed impatiently. 'Accept your fate gracefully and I'll make it worth your while.'

'I won't become a…a whore!' Tamsin spat the word out as if it burnt her lips.

Betty laughed. 'You ain't got a choice, Mistress Puritan.'

'Be quiet, Betty!'

Mrs Cole turned her hard gaze back to Tamsin. 'I meant what I said earlier about being able to provide you with employment.' A note of pride entered her nasal voice. 'This is one of the best brothels in the city. My prices are high, but my girls are pretty and I serve only the finest wines and ales.'

Her frown softened. 'Be sensible, my dear. Now that the Cavaliers have returned, we are busier than ever and I need new girls. You will live in comfort and have fair wages, I promise you.'

'I won't do it!' Fear was making Tamsin's knees shake, but her expression was defiant. 'No, not even if you beat me!'

A grim smile touched Mrs Cole's thin mouth. 'Oh, don't worry! If necessary, I shall have you whipped senseless.'

'Will you have done, Jack! I told you, I'm in no mood tonight to visit a brothel!'

'Great Jove, Lysander! Anyone would think you had turned Puritan!' Lord Fanshawe cried.

Lysander Saxon laughed. 'That's the first time anyone has accused me of *that* particular failing!'

He set down his empty wine glass and stretched his long legs, settling more comfortably into his chair. 'However, I do have an important appointment I must keep in the morning. To meet Mistress Godolphin.'

Jack Fanshawe whistled. Jane Godolphin was a wealthy young widow, newly come to town. 'I've heard she is in search of a new husband.'

'So have I.' Lysander's tone was dry.

'And you want to keep a clear head for tomorrow.' Jack nodded his understanding.

'Another time, perhaps.' Lysander smiled to soften his refusal.

'Truly, Lysander, you would enjoy it.' Jack's brown eyes shone with enthusiasm. 'The wine is excellent and you can play a hand of cards if you tire of the wenches, though I promise you they are uncommon attractive.'

'No doubt.' Lysander inclined his dark blond head in acknowledgement. 'However, I've no mind to sample their charms this evening.'

'Or any other evening, if I know you!' Jack snorted. 'Too much success with ordinary women has given you a peculiar aversion to consorting with whores!'

Lysander shrugged his broad shoulders, not troubling to deny the accusation.

Jack poured himself another glass of sack and sipped it, his normally cheerful face gloomy. 'It won't be as much fun without your company,' he complained.

Lysander eyed him thoughtfully. Jack Fanshawe was a cousin on his mother's side, another of the down-at-heel Royalists who had flocked to London in King Charles's wake. A few years younger than Lysander, they had played together as children before the war had put an end to visits between their two families.

They had met again in exile when they had both served under the Spanish flag. Charles had sent a force commanded by his brother, the Duke of York, to help his new ally, Spain, fight the French. As Jack's elder and his senior officer, Lysander had slipped into the habit of looking out for his cousin, a habit which lingered when they had rejoined Charles's court after Marshal Turenne had defeated Spain at the Battle of the Dunes in the summer of 1658.

Perhaps he ought to go along to this place in Lime Street. Although they were not much alike, he counted Jack as a good friend and his cousin had spoken of gambling for high stakes there. Unfortunately, Jack had little skill at either cards or dice.

S'death, he had better check it out! By nature, Jack was too trusting and he had a poor head for drink. Worse, he couldn't afford a fleecing. Like most of the returned Cavaliers, he was already deep in debt and living on borrowed credit.

Since their arrival in London three weeks ago, life had been a whirl of celebrations and entertainments. Everyone Lysander knew had spent freely, buying new clothes, new furniture for their rooms, horses, carriages and every other kind of luxury.

He surveyed the littered table, spread with the remains of a dozen dishes. He was as bad as the rest. He had rented this stylish house in Wych Street, situated in the fast-growing suburbs to the west of the city, and purchased a smart new coach. He'd even had tonight's supper sent in from Chatelin's, the fashionable French eating-house patronised by the royal household, when the cookshop round the corner could have furnished a good meal at a quarter of the price.

And his purse was as near empty as Jack's!

Mentally shrugging off his vexing lack of fortune, Lysander gestured towards a platter which held a few remaining venison pasties, Jack's favourite, and said, 'Are you still hungry, coz?'

'Nay, I've done.' Jack shook his brown head mournfully and pushed aside his plate.

Lysander stood up. 'Then let's be off.'

'You'll come to Madam Sarah's?' Jack's expression brightened instantly.

Amusement gleamed in Lysander's green eyes. 'Aye, providing you buy the first drink, dear coz!'

The warm summer twilight was fading as Lysander's coach with its four matched greys drew into Lime Street.

Lysander tossed his coachman up a coin. 'Have yourself a drink, Nat, and then wait for me here. I won't be long.'

Nat, a burly-shouldered individual with a tender love of horses, gave him a broad, disbelieving grin. 'Aye, sir.'

They entered the house and, by the time they had handed their cloaks to the waiting attendant, a dark-haired woman in her late thirties was hurrying into the hallway to greet them.

'Lord Fanshawe.' She swept a curtsy, her crimson silk skirts rustling.

'Good evening, Madam,' Jack responded with a flourish and promptly introduced Lysander.

'I am delighted to make your acquaintance, sir.' Sarah Cole dipped another curtsy. 'You are most welcome.'

Lysander nodded silently, noting her hard eyes. She had a veneer of polite manners, but he'd wager she could be a harpy if crossed.

She led the way into the salon. 'I'll have one of the girls bring you some wine, my lords, and then, if you wish, we can discuss what entertainment might best please you tonight,' she said and quietly withdrew.

Lysander's left eyebrow quirked.

'Not as bad as you feared, eh?' Jack wore a smug grin.

It was true. The place was decorated with a florid abandon that offended his discerning eye, but the atmosphere was surprisingly restrained. A fiddler was playing discreetly in one corner and several men and women stood or sat in small groups, drinking and chatting. It could have been any ordinary party, except for the extremely revealing outfits the girls were wearing.

'The gaming tables are through there.' Jack indicated a curtained alcove. 'Do you fancy a hand of cards?'

'Why not?'

They took their places at one of the tables and Jack asked a serving-wench to bring them wine. A game of tarocco was in progress. Lysander kept a close eye, but could detect no cheating. During his wanderings, he had struck up a friend-ship with a French highwayman who knew all the tricks of palming, slurring, and knapping. Thanks to François, he could spot a swindler at fifty paces.

Jack, as usual, lost.

'Damme, Lysander, how is it you always win?' he de-manded when Lysander picked up the twenty pounds which intelligent concentration had brought him.

'I have the Devil's own luck,' Lysander replied sweetly.

Even more importantly, he knew how to stop before it ran out, though it didn't seem politic to say so to his reckless cousin.

They returned to the salon and Lysander called for a bottle of claret. The same attractive serving-wench brought them an excellent Haut Brion.

'I commend Mrs Cole's taste,' Lysander remarked, sipping it appreciatively.

A full-bosomed redhead wearing naught but a wisp of green silk came up to them. 'Evening, milords.'

Jack greeted her by name and with a cheeky grin she sat down in his lap.

Lysander came to the conclusion that he could safely leave. Jack had no further need of a nursemaid.

He set down his glass and rose to his feet. 'I'll see you tomorrow, perhaps.'

Jack tried to persuade him to stay. 'Some of the girls are going to perform an Eastern dance.' He winked. 'Without their clothes.'

Lysander grinned. 'Too much excitement for my old bones, coz! I'll leave such delights to you young lads.'

Accepting defeat, Jack laughed and bade him farewell.

In the hallway, Lysander asked the attendant to bring him his cloak.

'Leaving so soon, my lord?' Sarah Cole appeared at his elbow.

'I'm afraid I have an early appointment tomorrow, Madam.'

'Are you sure I can't tempt you to change your mind?' She smiled at him ingratiatingly. 'My girls cater for all tastes.' Her nasal voice dropped to a whisper. 'No matter how…unusual.'

Lysander shrugged. 'My taste does not run to whores.'

Surprise registered upon her face.

A flicker of amusement flowed through Lysander. 'And no, before you ask, I don't want a boy.' He collected his cloak and tipped the attendant. 'Goodnight, Madam.'

It was rare in Sarah Cole's experience to find a man so fastidious. Maybe with those good looks he could afford to be choosy!

Her professional pride injured, a determination to get the better of him invaded her. 'Wait! What if I offered you a girl fresh from the country?' A look of sly triumph gleamed in her hard eyes. 'Pretty, no more than sixteen and innocent as a newborn.'

'Madam, I ceased to believe in fairy stories at my nurse's knee.'

'I don't cheat my customers, sir!' Stung by the lazy amusement in his deep voice, Mrs Cole drew herself up. 'I warrant you she's a virgin. So, if you baulk at other men's leavings, why not walk up those stairs and enjoy her maidenhead? It will cost you only ten pounds.'

Lysander laughed. Ten pounds would pay his household expenses for a month!

Not that he had any desire to accept her outrageous bargain. 'Thank you for the offer, Madam, but I should not like to take advantage of the poor creature.' His velvet voice hardened. 'You see, I prefer my women willing.'

'Oh, you needn't worry, sir. She's obedient, I promise you—'

A loud shriek of defiance cut off the rest of what Mrs Cole had been about to say.

Looking up, Lysander saw a young girl struggling with a thick-set man in a doorway on the upper floor. Suddenly, she broke free and ran for the stairway.

'Come back here, you little minx!'

Ignoring the cry, the runaway flung herself down the stairs, taking them two at a time in her haste.

Halfway down, she suddenly seemed to become aware of their presence near the foot of the stairs and froze, a look of horror on her pale face.

Even at that distance Lysander could see she had the most amazing turquoise blue eyes.

'Come back, or it'll be the worse for you!'

Casting a look over her shoulder, the girl saw her pursuer closing in. With a little cry of despair, she resumed her flight.

'Take care!'

Lysander leapt forward just in time to break her fall as she missed her footing and tumbled to land in a heap of white petticoats at his feet.

Chapter Two

'Allow me to help you.'

The sound of a deep but gentle voice penetrated the numbing fog of terror which surrounded Tamsin. Gathering her courage, she lifted her head and saw that the man who had broken her fall was holding out his hand to her.

She stared at him, her heart pounding. His dark blond hair fell in gleaming waves to his broad shoulders and he was dressed more finely than any man she had ever seen. The short jacket of his dark-blue velvet suit permitted a glimpse of snowy white linen and it was trimmed with costly silver braid. Expensive lace foamed at his neck and wrists and a sword hung at his hip. Silver buckled shoes and a wide-brimmed hat, decorated with swirling feather plumes, completed his elegant appearance.

With a jolt, Tamsin realised he must be a Cavalier. Perhaps he even knew her father!

Hope flooded her veins, drowning out her terror, and, eagerly, she put her hand in his and allowed him to draw her upright.

'Ouch!' She winced involuntarily as a twinge of pain shot through her left ankle.

'Are you hurt?' the deep voice enquired.

Gingerly, Tamsin wriggled her foot and then, realising it was only bruised, denied any injury.

'Good.' He released her hand, but remained close.

A moment ago Tamsin had been inclined to put his impressive physique down to the fact that she was viewing him from an odd angle. Now, standing next to him, she realised he was even taller, and broader in the shoulder, than she had first thought.

She'd heard it said that the new King was over two yards high. Surely this man must run him close? Certainly, he was much taller than any of the men she knew back home and she suspected he might outmatch them in strength, too, for his lean figure was superbly muscled.

He was smiling at her. Tamsin caught her breath. Gemini, but he was handsome!

She stared at him with frank curiosity. His features were clear cut and regular with a deep brow, arrow-straight nose and a firm, strong chin. He must have spent a lot of his time outdoors for the sun had darkened his skin and there was a thin scar running along his right cheekbone, which only added to her impression of uncompromising masculinity.

In contrast, his well-shaped mouth held a hint of tender sensuality and his vivid eyes were framed by long black lashes any girl would have envied.

Against his bronzed skin, their colour was that of spring leaves in the forest.

Tamsin was unable to understand why she suddenly felt so hot and giddy. What was the matter with her? She couldn't stop staring at him, although she knew he was bound to think her mannerless.

'I'm glad to hear you are all right.' His deep voice, tinged with a note of amusement, interrupted her agitation. 'It would have been a pity to injure such a pretty ankle.'

Coming to her senses, Tamsin blushed the colour of a corn poppy. How could she have forgotten her state of undress? Peg had wrestled her black bodice and skirt off her. All she was wearing was her linen shift and a petticoat, which must have flown up to reveal her legs when she had fallen!

The laughter in his green eyes vanished abruptly as she

hurriedly crossed her arms in front of her bosom to cover herself. 'Pay my thoughtless remark no heed, young mistress.'

Tamsin wondered if he was sorry for having teased her, but before she could decide Mrs Cole intervened with an angry snarl.

'It would have served you right, you stupid jade, if you had broken your neck!'

Tamsin's stomach gave a sickening lurch.

Incredibly, for a brief moment, the stranger's smile had made her forget her dreadful predicament, but now she could feel her skin begin to crawl with fear again.

'Let me take her back to Peg, Madam.' Jenkins had reached the foot of the stairs. 'I'll see to it she does as she is told this time.'

His piggy little eyes glared at Tamsin and with a shudder of revulsion she shrank back.

'You'd better.' Sarah Cole's tone was still sharp with annoyance. 'And no more mistakes. Make sure Peg dresses her in the green satin.'

'No! I won't wear that lewd garment!' Tamsin let out a shrill protest.

'Be quiet or I'll whip you myself!'

Her mouth drying with fear, Tamsin fell silent.

The brothelkeeper withdrew her basilisk glare and waved her henchman forward. 'Hurry up!' She flicked a glance towards the salon. 'I don't want a scene in front of the customers!'

Jenkins took a step towards Tamsin. Instinctively, she turned towards the man at her side, her expression pleading.

'Hold back, you rogue!' Damning himself for a fool, but unable to resist the look of appeal in those lovely turquoise eyes, Lysander put out an arm to bar the other man's advance.

Jenkins growled threateningly. Lysander ignored him and directed his attention towards the brothelkeeper. 'I've changed my mind.'

His announcement wiped the frown from Sarah Cole's

face. With an air of satisfaction, she gestured her henchman
to back off.

'Shall we adjourn to my closet, my lord, while my servants
make her ready for you?' she invited, giving Lysander a hon-
eyed smile.

'As you wish.' Lysander nodded carelessly. 'Though I've
no desire to dawdle all night, settling terms with you.'

Mrs Cole let out a bawdy laugh. 'Jenkins, tell Peg to forget
about the green satin. Just clean her up. His lordship is in a
hurry!'

Tamsin gasped aloud as the implication of this order sank
in. Flinching away from the man at her side, she exclaimed,
'You want to…to… Oh, you are as bad as all the rest!'

She swallowed down the tears of disappointment which
were rising in her throat. Lack-wit, why else would he visit
a brothel except to satisfy his lusts! Just because he had
shown her a moment's kindness, there was no reason to suppose him a paragon.

'Don't worry. I promise you it will be all right.' Lysander
injected all the reassurance he could muster into his voice.
'Just go upstairs for now.'

The turquoise eyes widened.

Watching the jumble of emotions chasing each other across
her expressive little face, Lysander knew she was trying to
work out if she could trust him.

'Very well.' Coming to a decision, she gave an abrupt nod
and began to mount the stairs.

Jenkins turned to follow her.

'Leave her be.' Lysander rapped out the order and, re-
sponding to the authority in his crisp tone, Jenkins came to
a swift halt.

He threw an uncertain look at his employer.

'Go back to your post.' Mrs Cole nodded affirmation. 'I'll
ring for you if I need you.'

She led the way into her closet. 'Be seated, my lord.' she
said, waving Lysander towards a stool. 'May I offer you a

drink?' She fluttered her eyelashes at him, her expression flirtatious. 'I have a fine French brandy that you might enjoy.'

'Thank you, but no,' Lysander replied coolly, making no attempt to sit.

Sarah Cole shrugged. 'To business then,' she said, abandoning her attempt to charm and becoming brisk. 'Hand over the ten pounds we spoke of and the wench is yours for the next hour.'

'I want more than that.'

'Several of my gentlemen like to hire the services of their favourites for a whole night.' An avaricious smile curled the thin mouth. 'I'm sure we can come to some arrangement.'

'You misunderstand me. I want to buy her from you.'

The brothelkeeper emitted a low whistle of amazement. 'Do you, indeed?' She moved to seat herself behind her desk. 'May I ask why?'

Lysander smiled, but the warmth did not reach his eyes. 'That's my business, ma'am.'

'Of course.' Mrs Cole decided it was futile to attempt to pursue her curiosity. 'You do realise, however, that I won't give her up unless you can make it worth my while?'

'Naturally.' Lysander pulled out a leather purse and, loosening the drawstring which held it shut, tipped out a pile of gold coins on to the surface of the desk.

Mrs Cole eyed it greedily.

'Twenty pounds,' Lysander said.

It was the money he had won at the gaming-table an hour ago. A much-needed windfall he'd had plans for until he'd let foolish sentiment get the better of him!

'A handsome sum.' Sarah Cole couldn't resist reaching out to touch the gleaming heap. 'However, it's not enough.' She withdrew her hand and sat back in her chair, her expression hard. 'I want fifty.'

A frown tugged Lysander's brows together. 'I think you jest, ma'am.'

'I never make jokes about money!'

An unwilling laugh escaped him at her shocked tone. 'Somehow that doesn't surprise me!'

She gave him a puzzled look and, sobering, Lysander decided to try another tack.

'Has it occurred to you that you might get into trouble by keeping the girl here against her will?' he asked silkily.

'I have friends in high places,' she retorted, unperturbed by his veiled threat.

Lysander's patience snapped. 'Much as I hate to boast, I think you will find my influence outweighs your own. Unless you count the King amongst your protectors?'

It wouldn't have surprised him in the least to learn that she had supplied Charles with a pretty slut or two, but to his relief she let out a gasp of dismay and turned pale beneath her rouge.

'Come, let's not brangle.' Satisfied she had taken his point, Lysander allowed his harsh tone to soften. 'Sell me the girl and I promise you there will be no trouble. Of *any* kind.'

The threat of violence hung unspoken in the air and a cold shiver ran down Sarah Cole's spine as she met his unwavering gaze.

'Twenty pounds, you said?'

'Aye.'

She rubbed her neck, thinking rapidly. It irked her to be outsmarted, but he was offering a fair price. More than fair, in fact, for she'd lay odds that the wench wouldn't make a good whore. Some women never did.

What's more, to judge from that glint of steely determination in those cool eyes, he'd make good his threats if she refused!

'Well, mistress, what say you?' Lysander demanded impatiently.

With a quick movement of her hand she swept the coins towards her. 'She's yours.'

Lysander acknowledged her capitulation with a brief nod and, strolling over to the bell-pull, rang it. Jenkins appeared with such suspicious promptness that he suspected the fellow had been listening outside the door.

'Fetch the wench.'

'Do as he says.' Mrs Cole endorsed Lysander's order. 'But tell Peg she's to wear the clothes she arrived in.'

She wasn't going to waste good silk on the little baggage. Let her new protector trick her out in fancy duds if he'd a mind to!

'Make sure you return all her belongings,' Lysander added in a manner that brought an obedient mumble from Jenkins.

When he had lumbered out, Mrs Cole rose to her feet. 'Will you take that glass of brandy with me now, my lord?'

There was a placating note in the nasal voice and, hearing it, Lysander hid a smile. 'Aye, I'll drink to our bargain.'

Her jaw clenched at his pointed remark, but her unctuous smile remained in place as she moved to one of the cupboards and extracted a bottle and two glasses.

She didn't like him any more than he liked her, Lysander mused, watching her pour the brandy. Not that it mattered. She had the wit to realise that a dispute would be in nobody's interest.

Although he had been quite prepared to use force to wrest the girl from the brothelkeeper's clutches, Lysander was very well aware that he had let a momentary impulse, and his innate dislike of being beaten, lead him into folly.

Looked at logically, his behaviour tonight had been absurd. What the devil was he to do with the wench? He didn't want her maidenhead!

'Your good health, sir.' Mrs Cole handed him a glass and raised her own to her lips.

'And yours, ma'am,' Lysander responded with equally insincere civility.

They drank in silence for a moment and then Mrs Cole said, 'When you tire of her charms, my lord, and wish to be rid of her, I might see my way to taking her off your hands.'

'I'll bear your offer in mind,' Lysander retorted drily,

knowing he would roast in hell before he allowed such a thing to happen.

Goddamn it, those lovely turquoise eyes must have him bewitched!

Why else did the idea of that skinny little waif earning her bread as a whore disturb him so much? Or perhaps it was her youth which aroused his pity? For certes, she didn't arouse him in any other way! His taste in women ran to ripe brunettes, not underdeveloped adolescents!

The door opened and the cause of his uneasy reflection entered, clutching a cloth bundle to her thin chest.

'This gentleman has bought your freedom. You are to go with him,' Mrs Cole announced as her captive advanced into the room with wary caution.

The wench gasped aloud. 'You have no right to sell me to anyone! You don't own—'

'Silence!' Mrs Cole ignored her protest. Flicking a malicious glance at Lysander, she added sweetly, 'I wish you joy of your purchase, my lord.'

Lysander scarcely heard her mocking gibe.

The startling apricot hair had vanished into the confines of a chaste white coif and her slight figure was robed in coarse black homespun, its austere severity relieved only by a broad white collar: the dress of his former enemies.

'You are a Puritan!' Lysander stifled a groan of dismay.

This impulsive rescue was turning into an even greater act of folly than he had imagined!

'Wake up, young mistress. We've arrived.'

Reluctantly, Tamsin opened her eyes. For an instant she stared sleepily at the man seated opposite to her and then, memory returning with an appalling clarity, sat up in haste.

'I'm…I'm sorry.' Hopefully, the interior of the coach was too dark for him to discern her embarrassment. 'I didn't mean to fall asleep.'

'No matter.' He waved aside her apology and, opening the carriage door, jumped down. 'Come, let's go in.'

Tamsin remained frozen to her seat, a dozen alarming images racing through her brain.

'My dear young woman, this is no time to be having second thoughts!' Impatience fringed the velvet tones.

'What do you intend to do with me?' In spite of her best efforts, Tamsin's voice shook.

If only she wasn't so tired, perhaps she could think straight! But it was very late and she had been up since dawn. Relief on escaping from Lime Street had buoyed her up for a while, but she had been unable to resist the rocking motion of his comfortable carriage.

'Don't fret. I mean you no harm.' In the light shed from one of the nearby windows Tamsin saw his impatient frown soften.

'But I don't know if I can trust you,' Tamsin blurted.

'Rest assured that I have absolutely no interest in making love to you.' There was a ghost of amusement in his voice.

Tamsin remained where she was.

'Come,' he repeated. 'Nat needs to put the coach away and see to the horses.'

Knowing she had little alternative other than to hope her instincts were correct, Tamsin clutched her bundle to her and rose. In the doorway of the coach she hesitated. It was too dark to see the ground clearly. The last thing she needed was to trip and make a fool of herself for a second time that evening.

He muttered something inaudible under his breath and, clasping her around the waist, lifted her out of the carriage and began to carry her towards the house.

His unexpected action caught Tamsin by surprise and her senses reeled from the sudden impact of his nearness. The warmth of his tall body, the masculine smell of him and the controlled strength in his arms were so strange and alarming it took her a moment before she recovered herself enough to snap, 'There is no need for this, sir!'

He shrugged. 'I'd no mind to wait all night,' he retorted,

continuing to hold her with one-handed ease whilst hammering on the door for admittance.

Deciding it would be undignified to struggle, Tamsin contented herself with glaring at his averted profile.

The door opened. 'God save us, Master Lysander, what's to do? Banging fit to wake the dead—*what have you got there?*'

A middle-aged man dressed with sober neatness stood open-mouthed on the threshold. Under his shocked scrutiny, Tamsin strove for composure and tried not to think about her dirty face.

'And a good evening to you, too, Matthew.' There was a wealth of irony in Lysander's tone as he greeted his faithful manservant.

Matthew Cooper sniffed, disapproval writ plain on his blunt features as he ushered them inside.

Lysander hid a grin and, cheerfully bidding his long-time mentor to go and light the withdrawing-room candles, deposited his burden upon the black and white marble tiles of the hallway.

'Thank you!'

Disregarding this pleasantry, Lysander called after Matthew to fetch them some wine as soon as he'd finished.

Tamsin hugged her bundle anxiously to her. Wine? Why was he asking for wine at this late hour? He…he didn't mean to try and get her drunk, did he? According to Aunt Deborah, it was a favourite ploy of the wicked to debauch a girl by first fuddling her wits with strong liquor!

'This way.' Lysander gestured her to accompany him.

Tamsin shook her head. 'Nay. I will not budge from this spot until you agree to tell me why you have brought me to this place.'

'This is my home. Where else would I have brought you?'

Disconcerted by this unexpected reply, Tamsin bit her lower lip. Was he mocking her?

'My dear young woman, in case you hadn't noticed, it is nearly midnight. No doubt I ought to place you in the care

of some respectable dame, but I am damned if I am going to
stir myself to try and find you a chaperon tonight.'

Lysander took a long breath and reined in his temper.
'Look, we can't stand here arguing all night. If you insist on
cross-examining me, at least do it where we can be comfortable.'

He strode off and, her knees quaking, Tamsin followed.

The man named Matthew had been generous with the candles and the withdrawing-room was near as bright as day.
Tamsin had never seen anything like it. In spite of the anxiety
churning in her stomach, she couldn't help goggling at the
splendid yellow brocade panelling the walls and the deep blue
sarcenet curtains hanging at the tall windows. A brightly pat-
terned carpet covered the centre of the floor and there was
an ornate gilt-framed mirror above the carved marble fireplace.

Awed by such luxury, Tamsin kept silent as she watched
her host divest himself of cloak, sword and hat and toss them
casually on to a velvet-upholstered couch.

'Would you care to sit down?'

Lysander, who thought she looked weary enough to col-
lapse, was surprised to have his offer refused with another
vehement shake of her becapped head.

Good manners kept him standing. 'Then, instead of talking, would you prefer to go straight to bed?'

Tamsin's pulse began to race. Did he really mean to let
her sleep undisturbed? He'd denied any interest in her, but
could his word be relied upon? Aunt Deborah vowed that all
Cavaliers were liars.

She had to make sure!

'I cannot rest, sir, until I know your plans for me.' Tamsin
met his gaze resolutely, unaware that her fingers were clench-
ing her bundle so tightly that her knuckles shone white.

Lysander, who had noticed, was impressed by her determination. She was obviously scared and exhausted, which
was why he had offered her the chance to postpone this discussion, but she was sticking to her guns.

'To be honest, I haven't given the matter much thought,' he confessed gently.

Tamsin gulped. 'Mrs Cole said that you had bought my freedom,' she managed, her voice shaking. 'What exactly did she mean?'

'I paid her twenty pounds to secure your release.'

Twenty pounds? It was a fortune!

'But why? I don't understand.' Tamsin could feel her heart hammering fit to burst. 'You just said you didn't want to bed me!'

'I don't!' Lysander's control slipped. 'You are much too young and skinny!'

Tamsin swallowed hard. Did he have to be so *brutally* frank!

She has a very expressive little face, Lysander thought, running a hand through his hair in a gesture of suppressed irritation at his own ineptitude. 'I'm sorry, I didn't mean to be rude. I know this is difficult for you, but, really, you must stop imagining that I am about to pounce on you!'

He essayed a slight smile. 'It is quite insulting, you know, to keep on implying my efforts to help you are motivated by lust.'

Abashed, Tamsin hung her head and mumbled something that might have been an apology.

To her relief, his servant arrived at this point with a tray of refreshments.

'I took the liberty of bringing some milk as well, sir,' he announced. 'I thought the young person might prefer it.'

He placed his burden down carefully upon a small oak side table. 'And a little food in case either of you were hungry.'

There was a note of curiosity underlying Matthew's helpful efficiency and Lysander knew he would be lucky to escape an interrogation before he retired for the night.

That was one of the troubles with employing servants who had known you since you were in swaddling clothes!

'Thank you, Matthew, that will be all for tonight. You can go to bed.' Lysander dismissed him firmly.

Matthew gave him a baleful look and withdrew.

Tamsin hardly noticed this exchange. Her attention was fixed upon a plate of cold chicken and, seeing her longing look, Lysander said lightly, 'I'm famished, but unless you agree to sit down and share some of this with me, manners will oblige me to return it untouched to the kitchen.'

Deciding that there was nothing to be gained by cutting her nose off to be revenged upon her face, Tamsin graciously consented to put her bundle down and take a seat near to his.

'Here, try one of these.' Lysander handed her a venison pasty which had escaped Jack's ravening appetite.

Tamsin took a hungry bite. It was delicious!

For the next five minutes she ate with gusto, savouring the rich savoury tastes on offer, so different to the plain fare she was used to at home, and then, remembering her manners, blushed crimson.

He would think her a greedy savage!

Such criticism was far from Lysander's thoughts. He had gone hungry himself too often not to recognise her need and, besides, there was something quite charming about her silent, childlike appreciation of his hospitality.

Tamsin put down her empty plate and tidily brushed the last lingering crumbs from her chin and fingers. 'Thank you. I feel much better now.'

Her frank admission amused Lysander but, wary of spoiling their current harmony, he kept his smile to himself and said easily, 'Then it seems a good time to introduce ourselves.'

Tamsin nodded shyly. She had been so anxious about his motive in rescuing her that his actual identity had seemed immaterial.

'Lysander Saxon. At your service.' He raised his wine glass to her with a flourish.

Tamsin scrambled to her feet and bobbed a curtsy. 'Tamsin Barton, sir.'

'And where do you come from, young Tamsin?' Lysander waved her to resume her seat. 'I'll warrant you are no Londoner.'

There was a slight soft burr to her speech which made him suspect she was from the West Country. He was also convinced she had run away from home, but, rather to his own surprise, he wanted to hear the story from her own lips.

For some strange reason, she intrigued him!

Tamsin hesitated. He had been amazingly kind, but he was a stranger. Until she had some idea of how he might react to her confession, it might be better to keep her reasons for coming to London to herself.

'Did that grasping harpy discover you were a runaway and promise you a good home?' Lysander asked and Tamsin stared at him, her eyes widening.

He seemed to have the uncanny knack of hitting on the truth!

'Come, you can tell me.' Lysander injected a jovial note into his tone. 'I won't scold, no matter what you've been up to.' He grinned. 'I only eat country maidens for breakfast.'

Tamsin was aware of a flicker of resentment. He was treating her as if she were seven years old!

'I may be fresh up from the country, sir, but I hope I am not so green as to be taken in by such an obvious trick!' she asserted indignantly. 'No, Mrs Cole cozened me by offering to show me my way when I asked her for directions. Instead, she took me to her own house and…well, you know the rest,' she finished, her voice dwindling to a whisper.

'Does it bother you that I was a witness to your humiliation?'

Lysander put the question carefully, feeling as if he trod on eggs. She had glared at him like an angry cat a moment ago when all he'd meant to do was put her at ease.

She nodded wordlessly, a bright shine of tears glittering in her eyes.

Lysander's irritation vanished. 'Then we shall not speak of

what happened tonight again.' He smiled at her reassuringly. 'There is no need. You are safe now.'

Tamsin swallowed her tears. 'Thank you,' she muttered, knowing that the matter could not be so easily dismissed. She owed him a great debt and not only for his kindness in helping her. Somehow, she would have to find a way to repay him the money he had spent to secure her release.

The thought was so daunting that she took a hasty sip of milk to distract herself. Finishing it, she set her empty mug down.

'Would you like some more?'

Tamsin shook her head. 'Thank you, but my hunger is quite satis—' To her dismay a sudden urge to yawn swallowed up the rest of her polite disclaimer and she was forced to cover her mouth to try and conceal it.

'I think it's time we found you a place to sleep.' Lysander rose to his feet, a faint grin playing about his well-cut mouth.

Tamsin gave an embarrassed murmur of assent and, collecting her bundle, followed him from the room.

They mounted the main staircase to the next floor and traversed a long corridor. At its end, Lysander halted and threw open a door.

'We don't use all the rooms in the house,' he remarked. 'But you should find this one reasonably clean and well aired.'

He held up the candlestick he carried to illuminate the bedchamber and Tamsin got a shock. Her benefactor might have spoken in a somewhat disparaging tone, but the room was many times more luxurious than her own tiny Spartan chamber at Whiteladies.

'Gemini, everything is as fine as fivepence!' she exclaimed. Having expected to sleep in a garret, she couldn't keep a delighted grin from her face.

Her enthusiasm made him smile in turn. 'I'll leave you the candle. Is there anything else you need?'

He looked much younger when he smiled like that with

real warmth in his eyes and no cynicism spoiling the curve
of his mouth.

'A nightshirt, perhaps?' Lysander prompted. 'Mine will be
too big for you, but you are welcome to borrow one.'

Tamsin pulled her idiotically wandering wits together. 'I
have a night-rail of my own.' She indicated her bundle.
'However, if it's not too much trouble, do you think I could
have some hot water?'

He eyed her dirty face. She could certainly do with a wash!

'I'll see what I can do.'

He turned and strode off, seemingly oblivious to the darkness which filled the corridor beyond the candle's reach.

*He must have eyes like a cat. They are certainly green
enough…and unusually compelling. Just like his voice, they
add to the magnetism of his personality.*

Becoming aware that her thoughts were meandering again,
Tamsin gave herself a reproving mental shake and entered
the bedchamber.

It was a large room, half-panelled in some dark wood, with
the walls above painted in a warm shade of ochre which
glowed where the candlelight caught it. Tamsin set down her
candlestick on a candlestand by the bed and closed the rasp-
berry-red calico curtains at the window.

Turning round, she studied the bed. It was enormous and
the mattress, which she proceeded to test with an experimen-
tal hand, seemed twice as thick and soft as the simple pallet
on which she slept at home. A tester, supported by four posts,
towered up towards the ceiling and was finished with red
embroidered curtains.

A pair of simple back-stool chairs, a carved chest and a
small oak clothes-press completed the furnishings.

Tamsin unpacked her bundle. In addition to her night-rail,
it contained a clean smock, a spare pair of stockings, a clean
white cap and collar, a little pot of toothpowder and her
comb: her mother's pearl necklace and her few remaining
coins were safely stowed in the pocket hanging beneath her
petticoat.

She placed everything on the bed and surveyed her belongings with a wry smile. Pitifully little with which to start a new life, but she didn't have much else to bring! Indeed, the only thing she regretted having to leave behind was Sam's cheerful face.

'Here's your water. It isn't very hot, I'm afraid. The kitchen fire was almost out.'

Tamsin whirled round and beheld her host standing in the doorway. He was carrying a jug and there was a linen towel tucked beneath his arm.

'I've also brought you some soap.' Lysander advanced into the room and set the jug and towel down on top of the oak chest. He fished the bar of Castile soap from a pocket and laid it on top of the towel. 'You'll find a basin stored away in the press.'

'I...I didn't expect you to bring...I...I thought you would send a servant,' Tamsin stammered.

'Matthew has gone to bed. Apart from Nat and a woman who comes in to do the cleaning, I don't keep any other servants.'

'Oh, I see!' Tamsin nodded in belated comprehension. It seemed a rather odd way of running a household to her—Aunt Deborah had always kept plenty of hired help—but perhaps city dwellers had different ideas? Not that she was in any position to question his domestic arrangements!

'I'm sorry to have put you to so much trouble,' she continued shyly. 'You must be wishing me at Jericho.'

Lysander denied it.

There was a slight awkward silence.

'Well, if you have everything you need, I'll say goodnight.' Lysander fought a ridiculous urge to stay.

'Goodnight, sir.' Tamsin dipped a respectful curtsey.

Lysander moved to the door. 'Sleep well, little mistress.'

The door closed quietly behind him and Tamsin collapsed in a boneless heap upon the bed, feeling strangely forlorn.

It was foolish of course, but she hadn't wanted him to go!

* * *

In spite of her exhaustion, sleep eluded Tamsin; when it finally came, she was plagued with bad dreams. The result was that she overslept, waking much later than usual.

Bright sunlight filtered in through the curtains and for a few seconds she lay there, groggily confused, before sitting up with a gasp as memory returned. Flinging back her coverlets, she jumped out of bed and hurried to the window. A glance at the sky confirmed her fear that the morning was well advanced.

They would think her a slug-a-bed!

Biting her lip in vexation, she dipped the end of the towel into the remaining inch of water in the jug and hastily scrubbed her face and hands. Fortunately, she had managed to remove the worst of her grime last night.

Before retiring, she had also done her best to shake the dust and creases from her clothes. Scrambling into her sole remaining smock and clean linen thread stockings, she pulled on her bodice and then her skirt before turning to the problem of her hair. As usual, it was a tangled mass of rebellious curls and her eyes were watering by the time she had subdued it with her comb and bundled it safely beneath a clean cap.

Her boots were scuffed, but she lacked the means to polish them, unlike her teeth which she rubbed vigorously with a fingerful of toothpowder. Scorning to buy such an item from an apothecary, Aunt Deborah made it herself from salt, ground cuttlefish bone and orris-root and insisted that the whole household use it daily, claiming that it kept the teeth white and healthy. Since Tamsin's teeth were excellent—she had never been pained with toothache in her life—she thought her aunt must be right.

She was ready to brave the world, or at least as ready as she ever would be, she decided, trying in vain to crush the butterflies swarming in her stomach.

The house seemed very quiet as she emerged from her room. Perhaps it wasn't as late as she had feared and her rescuer was still a-bed? He had indicated his room last night as they had passed it by, but Tamsin, who had no intention of knocking on his door to find out if he was in, gave it a wide berth.

Descending the stairs, Tamsin peered nervously into the withdrawing-room. It was empty. So was the smart dining-room, panelled in gilt leather. Beyond this lay a small closet, which bore the hallmarks of being the private retreat of the master of the house, where she drew another blank.

She was just pondering her next move when she heard a door slam somewhere down below on the ground floor.

'Hello, is anyone there?' Tamsin, who had followed the sound, stuck her head round the door of what turned out to be the kitchen and was rewarded with an answer at last.

'Don't just stand there, young woman. Come in.'

Tamsin obeyed, a little scared of the testy snap in Master Cooper's voice.

'I suppose you want some breakfast?'

'If it's not too much trouble, sir.' Tamsin bobbed an apologetic curtsey.

She risked a glance from beneath her lowered lids and saw that he was frowning. A tremor of dismay quivered down her spine. She had wanted to make a good impression!

'Do you know what the time is?' Matthew sighed impatiently. 'Sir Lysander left hours ago and I'm too busy to wait on table twice in a morning.'

'I'm very sorry. I overslept.'

Something in his shrewd hazel eyes and upright bearing warned you that Master Cooper was not a man to be trifled with and Tamsin was so busy trying to apologise that it took her a moment to register exactly what he'd said.

Sir Lysander. It seemed her rescuer was a gentleman of title!

'Aye, well, I suppose you were late to bed so I'll make an exception this once.' Appeased by her meek apology, Matthew gestured towards the large scrubbed deal table which occupied the centre of the room. 'Sit yourself down, lass.'

Tamsin drew out a stool and, while Matthew bustled about fetching her bread and cheese and a mug of small beer, she glanced around the kitchen, admiring the pristine limewashed walls and the bright pots of aromatic flowers which adorned each window-sill. They used the same device at home to discourage flies and Tamsin thought they gave the kitchen a cheerful air.

She began to eat her simple meal with relish, but her appetite disappeared when Matthew said, 'My lord told me something of what happened last night. He said you might be staying with us for a while. Is that right?'

Tamsin set down her mug. 'I'm not sure,' she murmured hesitantly, hoping desperately that her befriender had not revealed how he had found her in a brothel.

In fact, much to Matthew's aggravation, Lysander had been deliberately vague in his explanation of how their unexpected visitor had come into his care.

'Don't fuss, Matt,' he'd said cheerfully when his mentor had demanded to know what they were to do with the wench. 'I'll speak to her when I get back. Until then just treat her as you would any other guest.'

A guest, forsooth! Matthew frowned. The lass was a Puritan and, unless he was very much mistaken, penniless to boot. Her manners were pretty enough, which indicated good breeding somewhere in her background for all her current friendless state, but she didn't belong here.

Matthew knew Lysander too well to imagine that he intended to debauch the girl. Beneath that mask of rakish cynicism the lad had a heart of gold. It was typical of him that he should befriend a waif in distress, but in his opinion it could only lead to trouble.

'I've finished, thank you, sir. Shall I clear these pots away and wash them?' Tamsin asked nervously, wary of intruding on his brooding silence.

'Nay. Mrs Finch can deal with them when she comes in.' Matthew forced a smile. 'Go sit yourself down in the parlour. Sir Lysander ought to be back soon.'

Feeling distinctly in his way, Tamsin removed herself with all possible speed.

She was just crossing the hallway when she heard a knock at the front door. Not wishing to appear forward, she hesitated. Master Cooper might object to her taking it upon herself to answer this summons, but when the knock sounded again, more urgently this time, and still he did not appear, she opened the door.

'Can you tell 'em Mam can't come no more?' A ragged urchin of some eight summers stood hopping impatiently on one leg, his grimy face anxious. 'She's sick.'

'Is your mother the cleaning woman here?' Tamsin asked, struggling to understand his strong London accent.

'Aye. Mrs Finch.'

'And she's too ill to work, you say?'

He nodded. 'Midwife says she must stay a-bed.'

'She's having a baby?' Tamsin exclaimed.

He nodded, but before she could question him further he darted off.

Tamsin debated running after him. Coming to the conclusion it would be a waste of time, she closed the door.

However, instead of continuing on her way, she stood stock-still, her mind busily turning over the information she had just received.

That young boy had given her an idea!

Chapter Three

By the time Lysander returned it was almost noon and Tamsin was in a fever of impatience. Hearing his footsteps in the hall, she rushed into the hallway.

He was speaking to Matthew, whom he dismissed as he caught sight of her hovering expectantly.

'Good day to you, Mistress Barton. I hope you slept well.'

'Yes, thank you, my lord,' Tamsin answered with more politeness than truth.

She thought he looked rather preoccupied, but found it impossible to contain her eagerness. 'May I speak with you?'

'What…now?' After a morning spent paying elegant compliments to Mistress Godolphin, Lysander was sorely tempted to refuse.

'Oh, please! It's very important.'

Lysander thought he could guess what she wanted to talk about. 'Very well,' he agreed, deciding obligation took precedence over inclination. 'Let's go into the parlour.'

Less fashionable than the withdrawing-room, it had a cosy air with its set of verdure tapestries, some well-polished furniture and a matted floor. Since it faced south, it also caught the sunlight.

'I think this is the nicest room in the house in which to sit during the day,' Lysander remarked lightly, breaking the silence which had fallen once they had sat down. 'And one can always admire the tapestries if the conversation falters.'

Aware that she was annoying him with her dithering, Tamsin gathered up her courage. 'I have something to ask of you, sir, only I cannot think how to phrase it.'

'Spit it out.' Charmed by her candid confession, Lysander felt his scratchy ill-humour fall away. 'I promise I won't shout at you.'

Now that her face was clean, he could see a spattering of tiny freckles across the bridge of her neat little nose. Most people would regard them as a blemish on her otherwise clear skin, but his sister, another redhead, had freckles too and he rather liked them.

She was younger than Corinna, of course, but occasionally something in the way she moved, all coltish grace and energy, reminded him of his sister. The resemblance was slight and totally irrelevant. Yet, oddly enough, it had niggled at him last night when he had retired to bed, depriving him of sleep until he had solved the puzzle.

'Your maid is ill. She can't come in to work.' Tamsin paused and then added in a rush, 'I wish to take her place.'

'The devil you do!' Lysander abruptly collected his wandering thoughts. 'What maggot put such an idea in your head?'

'I owe you twenty pounds, but I have no money.' Tamsin gestured apologetically. 'I thought I could repay it by working for you.'

'Your desire to pay your debts is laudable.' Lysander's frown faded and a gleam of amusement lit his green eyes. 'You do realise, however, that you would have to act as my servant for the next seven years?'

Tamsin's mouth fell open.

'Mrs Finch gets three pounds a year. Oh, and a daily meal and her aprons, I believe.'

A rosy blush mantled Tamsin's thin cheeks. How stupid of her not to have thought of this difficulty!

'Matthew tells me that it is the going rate.'

The deep voice was level, but Tamsin sensed his underlying amusement and resentment flared in her breast.

'You think me a fool, sir,' she exclaimed hotly.

He shook his head. 'Not at all. However, you are young
and inexperienced. Too young, in fact, to be let loose on the
world at all.'

'I am sixteen!' Tamsin bridled. 'Many girls are married at
my age and mistress of their own households.'

'True,' Lysander agreed. 'My own mother was no older.'

Appeased by his admission, Tamsin's voice resumed its
usual soft tones. 'I can handle your housekeeping.'

'No doubt,' he retorted drily. 'But I don't believe you have
been bred to the life of a servant.'

Tamsin bit her lip, wondering how to answer him without
giving away too much. 'You are right in thinking my station
up to now has been higher than a servant's,' she admitted.
'My family is a well-respected one, but…' She paused uncertainly.

'Go on,' Lysander encouraged gently.

Tamsin took a deep breath. He deserved an explanation
and she didn't want to lie to him. 'As you guessed last night,
I am a runaway. You see, my mother died when I was a
small child. My uncle and aunt became my guardians, but
my uncle died three years ago.' She shrugged awkwardly.
'My aunt and I don't see eye to eye. In the end, I had no
choice but to run away!'

Lysander's flicker of satisfaction at having his suspicion
confirmed was rapidly replaced by consternation as he realised that her confession presented him with a moral dilemma.
The proper course, undoubtedly, was to return her immediately to her rightful guardians.

'Did you leave without warning?' he asked thoughtfully.

'My cousin Samuel knew, but he will not betray me.'

'Do you think your aunt will search for you?'

Tamsin nodded. 'But not for long. I wrote her a note saying I preferred to seek my own fortune rather than accept her
plans for me. She will be furious.' She shrugged. 'Not that

she cares for me. All that will really concern her is silencing any wagging tongues.'

Whether or not she was correct in thinking that her aunt disliked her, Lysander decided it was not his place to interfere. He could claim no authority over her—sheer chance had brought them together.

The chiming of the walnut longcase clock, which stood near the window, as it struck noon pierced the tense silence which had fallen.

'I dare say you thought you had just cause for escape.'

There was a somewhat mocking edge to his tone, but to Tamsin's relief he did not appear to be disgusted by her confession.

'I believe I had, sir,' she answered quietly. 'I know my behaviour must seem disgraceful, but I beg that you will not let it influence your decision. I was brought up to know the value of work. I *can* keep a house clean.'

She met his gaze with a challenging look. 'And I don't like being obligated to strangers.'

Lysander rose to his feet and took a swift turn about the room. Coming to a halt by the fireplace, he rested one elbow upon the carved wooden mantelpiece and surveyed her with an exasperated expression.

'I salute your determination,' he said at last. 'However, in this case, you are mistaken. You owe me nothing. I undertook your rescue without your knowledge or consent.'

'But it cost you a fortune!' Tamsin protested.

A wry smile twisted his mouth. 'True, but it would have left a more costly stain on my self-respect to leave you there.'

Tamsin realised that honour was important to this gentleman. Smoothing her skirts with a mechanical gesture, she tried to regroup her arguments.

'It isn't that I am ungrateful, sir,' she said shyly. 'I appreciate your kindness more than I can say, but it seems very odd that you should be willing to spend all that money when you didn't know anything about me. You didn't even know my name!'

Bewilderment troubled the turquoise eyes fixed on his and Lysander curbed an urge to curse.

How on earth was he to answer her when he himself didn't truly understand the impulse which had driven him?

'I didn't need a formal introduction to realise that you didn't want to become a whore,' he replied slowly. 'And, as someone who was until recently trapped in a hateful exile, I suppose I felt a kindred sympathy for your plight.'

It was as good an explanation as any.

Tamsin nodded her understanding, but her expression remained unconvinced.

'Do you have friends here in London you could go to?' Lysander decided it was time to change the subject.

Surreptitiously crossing two fingers beneath the concealments of her skirts, Tamsin shook her head.

'I thought you said you were entrapped by Mistress Cole when you were asking for directions?'

Tamsin's pulse skipped a beat. 'I wanted to know the way to the nearest church. I intended to ask for help there,' she fibbed hastily, inwardly praying that her distortion of the truth would be forgiven.

She would have to be more careful. He was too quick!

'So you always intended to seek work?'

Knowing that it might not be easy to find her father, Tamsin had indeed planned to find employment to avoid becoming a drain upon Martha's purse, so she was able to answer with a clear conscience, 'I did, sir.'

Lysander stroked his chin thoughtfully. The fact that she was completely friendless put an entirely different slant on the situation. He could hardly turn her out into the street!

'Wouldn't you prefer to go home?' he asked hopefully. 'I'm sure your aunt will welcome you back. Your absence is bound to have given her a fright and she might be willing to overlook whatever quarrel caused you to leave.'

Tamsin shook her head so hard several unruly curls escaped the confines of her cap. 'I will not go back! She wants me to marry a man I detest!'

Lysander let out a low whistle of surprise. She had reminded him just now that she was well past the age of consent but, for all that a girl could be legally married at twelve, she didn't seem old enough to him to wed.

'I am going to stay in London.' Tamsin's voice was filled with determination. 'Whether or not you let me work for you.'

'Are you trying to blackmail me, young woman?' Lysander demanded.

The turquoise eyes widened. 'I…I wouldn't dream of such a thing, sir.'

Her stammering reply held a note of true conviction and Lysander's sudden anger cooled as rapidly as it had arisen.

Too long an association with the ladies of the court had rendered him unfit for the company of an innocent, he reflected ruefully. He was used to women lying and scheming to get what they wanted!

'Forgive me,' he said lightly. 'I should have known better.'

Tamsin didn't entirely understand him, but she was so pleased to see his frown disappear that she gave him a sunny smile and exclaimed, 'I am so glad you aren't cross with me!'

'I'm glad too, Mistress Barton.' He laughed before continuing firmly, 'However, I'm not going to let you persuade me into agreeing to your scheme. If you don't want to go home and you haven't any friends here, I shall have to think of another solution. A bachelor's residence is no place for any gently born maiden.'

An ironic curl twisted his mouth. 'Particularly when the bachelor in question is a member of his Majesty's court, a court not noted for its morals as I'm sure you must have heard.'

Tamsin had. Aunt Deborah and the other respectable matrons of Chipping Sodbury had lately engaged in numerous whispered discussions about the depravity of King Charles and his followers. Tamsin rather thought they all enjoyed being shocked by such wickedness!

'I'd already guessed you were a Cavalier, sir,' she declared eagerly. 'But do you really know the King?'

Lysander ignored the awe which rounded her eyes. 'Aye, but that's not the point at issue,' he retorted, doing his best to make his expression stern. 'It is not seemly for a young unmarried girl to live without a chaperon. You will have to leave.'

Tamsin's face fell and his tone softened. 'There's no need to fret. I'll find someone to look after you properly.'

He straightened and briskly shook out the cuffs of his dark green moire coat. 'I'll begin the search this afternoon after I have dined. Now, is there anything else? Dinner must be almost ready.'

Recognising her dismissal, Tamsin swallowed her protests and rose obediently to her feet to pay him the respectful farewell curtsy good manners demanded.

On the point of leaving the room, Lysander suddenly changed his mind. 'Should you care to join me?'

Tamsin was startled. She had expected to eat in the kitchen. 'Are you sure that's wise, sir? After all, I'm not a proper guest,' she blurted.

Lysander's brows rose. 'I think I am the best judge of what is proper in my own house,' he replied with an unconscious arrogance.

'Of course, my lord,' Tamsin apologised hastily. He had been so kind to her that she had almost forgotten his rank!

Lysander wasn't entirely sure why he had invited her to dine with him. It went contrary to all he had just been saying! The absurd idea having entered his head, however, he was determined not to be thwarted.

'I'll give you that the situation we find ourselves in is somewhat awkward,' he announced with a faint smile. 'But no matter how you came here, you *are* my guest for now and it would delight me to have your company over dinner.'

Tamsin coloured, flustered by the unexpected compliment. 'I should be honoured, sir,' she murmured, bobbing another curtsy.

'Good. Matthew will summon you when it's time. Now pray excuse me.'

Tamsin sank weakly into a chair after he had gone.

Trying to ignore the tingle of excitement that thrilled through her veins at the thought of him wanting her company, she forced herself to concentrate. The interview had not gone as she had hoped and she must think of a way to reverse his decision.

It was all very well for Sir Lysander Saxon to say in his high-handed way that she owed him nothing, but she hated the thought that she was the one responsible for him losing such an enormous sum. She simply had to find a means to pay him back!

But how was she going to persuade him into letting her stay? He was intent on packing her off to lodge with a more respectable chaperon.

Tamsin chewed her lower lip, a frown tugging her copper brown eyebrows together. She had the depressing feeling that it wouldn't be easy to find an inducement which would change his mind.

It might have been better if she had been honest and explained that she had friends in London who would take her in. Instead, she had denied Martha's existence in the hope of coaxing him into allowing her to remain in his house. The ploy had failed and she had landed herself in a worse mess!

Aunt Deborah always said that liars suffered for their sin in the end!

They sat down to dinner in the elegant gilt-leather panelled dining-room. The long table was covered in a fine white damask cloth and laid with delicate glass goblets and silver spoons and knives. Forks had been set out too, a novelty they had lacked at Whiteladies. Tamsin had no idea how to use one and decided she would have to try and copy her host.

She was amazed too at the number of dishes on offer. A leg of roast mutton, beautifully carved into neat slices, a loin of veal, a dish of pullets, a neat's tongue, a sallet and several vegetables. Even on feast days the table at Whiteladies had never been so lavish!

'For the second course, there's a baked marrowbone pie, a cheese, a dish of prawns and some sweetmeats,' Matthew announced with a low bow.

Lysander thanked him. 'We shall serve ourselves, Matt,' he added, correctly guessing from her expression that his guest was feeling rather overwhelmed and would prefer as little ceremony as possible.

'Just try what you fancy, Mistress Barton,' he said gently as Matthew bustled out. 'You aren't expected to eat everything.'

Tamsin grinned. 'I don't think I could!'

She cast him a sparkling look, her turquoise eyes brimming with laughter, and Lysander caught his breath. She had a lovely smile!

Startled by his own reaction, Lysander reached hastily for the bottle of wine that Matthew had placed within his reach. What the devil was the matter with him? Why should he suddenly notice how sweetly red her lips were? She was just a child!

'Can I offer you some of this claret?' he asked without thinking.

Tamsin hesitated. She had never touched anything stronger than small beer which, given that water was often tainted, everyone, even fervent Puritans like her aunt, drank.

Her silence brought Lysander's mind back into focus. 'Would you prefer something else? I don't want to offend your principles.'

'You think me a Puritan, don't you?' Tamsin watched him pour the wine into his own glass. It was a lovely rich red colour and she wondered what it would taste like.

Lysander eyed her thoughtfully. There was an oddly strained note in her soft voice. 'I made that assumption. Was I wrong?'

Tamsin stared down at the tablecloth. What would he think

of her if she told him the truth? Lifting her gaze to his she
met his enquiring look with a perplexed frown. 'Yes and no.'

'What a very enigmatic answer!' Lysander replied lightly.
He picked up the nearest dish, the carved mutton, and held
it out to her. 'Would you care to elaborate?'

Tamsin helped herself to the meat, her appetite sharpened
by its rich aroma. 'It's complicated,' she prevaricated.

He quirked one eyebrow at her and Tamsin suddenly realised how rude her reluctance to answer must seem. It was
cowardly of her to hedge just because she was afraid of losing
his good opinion!

'I come from a Puritan family, but I must confess I am
not a good Puritan,' she announced rather breathlessly.

'How so?' Intrigued, Lysander paused in the act of spoon-
ing peas on to his plate.

'I am too vain, too fond of pretty things and I don't pay
enough attention in church.' A rosy blush coloured Tamsin's
face.

Lysander struggled not to laugh. 'Who told you this?' he
asked gravely.

'My aunt.'

'She sounds a most disagreeable woman.'

'She is…I mean…oh, I know I should not say so, but you
are *right,* sir!'

'Is this the aunt who wishes you to wed a man you detest?'
he asked curiously, ignoring his food.

Tamsin nodded. 'She says marriage to Master Hardy will
steady me.' A glum sigh escaped her. 'He is a neighbour of
ours and a strong Puritan.'

'Older than you, I suppose?' Lysander hazarded.

'By more than thirty years.' Tamsin took a bite of her
mutton. It seemed petty to mention that she found the man
ugly, but something about his broad, florid face and bulky
figure repelled her.

'He's a widower twice over with nine children, some of
them older than I am. He beats them if they disobey him.'
The mutton seemed to stick in her throat as Tamsin remem-

bered how savagely Gideon Hardy had punished his youngest son, a boy of only seven, for taking an apple without permission.

She set her cutlery down abruptly, her appetite vanishing at the thought of little Robert's bruises. It wasn't so much her suitor's age or looks which bothered her as his merciless streak!

'For all his talk of God, I think Master Hardy a hard man with little kindness in him and I refused his suit when he first asked for my hand in marriage last March,' she continued, unconsciously lifting her chin with remembered defiance. 'Unfortunately, he proposed again a few weeks ago and this time he offered to take me without a dowry.'

A wry twist distorted Tamsin's pretty mouth. 'Aunt Deborah insisted I accept him. She said I should be grateful for my good luck.' Tamsin hastily pushed aside the memory of the other announcement her aunt had blurted in her fury and finished by saying lightly, 'She is always reminding me, you see, that I live by her charity since God has sought fit to render me a penniless orphan.'

Lysander was silent for a moment. It was not unusual to find a big difference in age between a groom and his bride, but it wasn't ideal in his opinion, particularly if the man was as insensitive as this fellow sounded.

As for Aunt Deborah, he had met her like before, all canting piety and a spirit meaner than a heathen Turk's!

'I am beginning to see why you felt you had to run away,' he commented, an unspoken sympathy in his eyes.

Tamsin gave him a grateful smile, her spirits rising. 'I was worried you might think me an undutiful ingrate,' she murmured shyly.

'Duty works both ways.' Lysander took a sip of his wine. 'Your aunt should have found you a better match.'

'She just wanted to be rid of me.' Tamsin shrugged and then suddenly grinned at him. 'Even as a child I always had the impression that she regarded me as a thorn in her side.'

'Were you a saucy brat?' Lysander grinned back.

Tamsin confessed it. 'I'm sure her arm must have ached from punishing me!' She saw a frown touch his brow and added scrupulously, 'I was only beaten when I had done wrong and never worse than her own son. She is very strict, but not needlessly cruel.'

'I dare say her motto is spare the rod and spoil the child.' His tone was ironic.

Tamsin giggled. 'In that case I must be a paragon of virtue!'

'Undoubtedly!'

The glint of answering laughter in his eyes convinced Tamsin that he did not censure her for refusing Gideon Hardy and, her appetite restored, she picked up her cutlery again.

Lysander copied her. However, as he chatted lightly of the sights of London, he was assimilating what he had learnt of her history.

It was good to have his gut instinct that she was no fanatical Puritan confirmed. Brought up by her strict aunt, she was bound to have been infected by their ideas, but her independent streak would make life easier if she was to share his house.

Despite his confident words earlier, Lysander had a feeling it might take some time to find her a suitable chaperon. For one thing, the respectable matrons of his acquaintance would look askance at his patronage of the girl. Even if they didn't suspect his motives, it would take a liberal donation, which he didn't have, to soothe their ruffled sensibilities.

He might have better luck asking Nat, who was familiar with half the shopkeepers and traders in London, if he knew anyone suitable who might be prepared to take her in.

To Lysander's surprise, distaste flickered through him and he realised that particular solution disturbed him.

Sheer sentimental folly! It was the only sensible way to deal with the dilemma. Such an arrangement would not strain his purse and, while life in a tradesman's household might not be what she was used to, she would at least be safe.

And yet…no matter how much he told himself he was not

responsible for the girl, that indeed he scarcely even knew her, the thought of her in some cheap lodgings was abhorrent.

Maybe it was because of her elusive resemblance to his sister or, more likely, because his sympathies had been engaged by her story. She hadn't sounded in the least bit sorry for herself, but to his ears it had been clear that her life up to now had not been an easy one.

It was a tribute to her resilient nature that she was not bitter. Instead, she seemed to possess a cheerful, determined optimism, which was as admirable as it was attractive.

'My lord.' Her softly accented voice interrupted his musing. 'Did you hear something?'

Lysander shook his head.

'I thought I heard…there it is again!'

This time the faint cry reached Lysander's ears and he sprang to his feet. 'That sounds like Matthew. Something must be amiss.'

Tamsin followed as he raced from the dining-room. Hampered by her skirts, she was slower and by the time she reached the kitchen he was already bending over the supine form of his servant, who lay sprawled upon the stone floor.

'Is he all right?' she gasped, hurrying forward to see if she could help.

'He's lost consciousness.' Lysander finished running his hands over Matthew. 'No bones broken that I can tell.' His eyes narrowed. 'See that nasty bump on his forehead? I suspect he fell and banged his head.'

Tamsin knelt down at Lysander's side, carefully avoiding the scattered pastry crusts oozing gravy all over the floor. 'He must have been carrying the marrowbone pie at the time,' she said, pointing to a broken china platter at Matthew's feet.

'He's coming round.' Matthew's eyes opened and he let out a groan. 'Easy, old friend.'

'What…oh, my head!' A spasm of pain crossed Matthew's blunt-featured face as he struggled to rise.

'Can you recall what happened?' Lysander asked, surveying his servant carefully as he assisted him into a sitting position.

'I think I slipped. I remember noticing earlier that there was a patch of grease on the floor.' Matthew's clouded gaze grew clearer as he spoke, relieving Lysander's anxiety. He touched the bump on his head gingerly. 'Serves me right for not cleaning it up.'

'You have too much to do without taking on the task of cleaning as well.' Lysander sat back on his heels, a flicker of guilt creasing his brow. Sometimes, without even realising it, he took his hard-working retainer for granted!

Matthew bridled. 'I hope you aren't saying that I am getting too old to look after you, lad!'

'I'm sure Sir Lysander meant nothing of the sort, Master Cooper,' Tamsin intervened gently. 'He is merely anxious about your welfare.'

'Aye, let's get you up off that cold floor before you catch an ague,' Lysander said, hastily seizing this olive branch.

Tamsin hurried to pull out one of the stools from beneath the kitchen table and Lysander helped the older man to his feet.

'There. You rest a moment, Matt,' he ordered, settling him onto it. 'I'll fetch you a cup of ale to restore you.'

Matthew grumbled, but since his fall had shaken him more than he was willing to admit, he was quite happy to obey.

While Lysander disappeared in the direction of the larder, Tamsin decided to make use of a broom lying propped in one corner and began sweeping up the broken china.

'You don't have to do that!' Lysander exclaimed as he emerged carrying a mug of ale.

'Who else is going to do it?' Tamsin cocked her head to one side, amused by the look of consternation which appeared on her host's face.

'She's got you there, lad.' A burst of gruff laughter from his servant made Lysander swing round and glare at him.

'Well, shall I carry on or not? Or do you intend to sweep this floor yourself?'

A cheeky grin robbed her words of their sting and Lysander laughed, his exasperation vanishing. 'Please do,' he invited cordially. 'I'm sure you'll make a better job of it than I could.'

Keeping out of her way he went to hand the ale to Matthew. 'Here's your…damn!' Lysander made a quick lunge and caught the heavy mug as it slipped from Matthew's hand.

'I'm sorry!' Matthew had gone white. 'I couldn't hold it.'

'No harm done.' Lysander brushed splashes of ale from his moire breeches. Luckily, he'd been quick enough to prevent most of the contents from spilling. He set the mug down. 'Let me see your wrist.'

Matthew extended his right arm and Lysander carefully pushed up the sleeve of his serviceable brown stuff jacket. 'I think you may have sprained it.' He turned his blond head and called over his shoulder to Tamsin, 'Do you have any knowledge of healing, Mistress Barton?'

'A little, sir.' Tamsin came hurrying to join them and inspected Matthew's wrist. 'It looks like a bad sprain to me,' she murmured, echoing Lysander's diagnosis.

'I'll fetch a doctor,' Lysander announced, but before he could make a move Matthew spoke up.

'I'll have no damned leech prodding and poking around me,' he exclaimed vehemently. 'I will do well enough if you strap it up, Master Lysander.'

'But—'

'Nay! Let be, lad! I don't want a fuss.'

Lysander bit back an expletive and nodded curtly. It was no use arguing. Matt hated doctors and it would probably do more harm than good to insist.

'I'll need something to strap up your wrist and make you a sling.' He turned to Tamsin. 'Can you fetch a clean sheet while I escort Matthew to his room?' he asked.

'Of course.' Tamsin dusted her hands against her skirts, glad to help. 'Where will I find the linen-press?'

The next half an hour was busy as they endeavoured to make Matthew comfortable. He objected to wearing the sling

Lysander fashioned for him and then refused to lie down upon his bed and rest until Lysander swore at him, causing Tamsin's eyes to almost pop out of her head.

Deeming it best to remove herself, she escaped back to the kitchen and finished cleaning up the mess left by the ruined pie.

'A difficult patient, our Master Cooper,' Lysander commented drily as he strolled back into the kitchen.

'Indeed, my lord,' Tamsin agreed.

She accepted his invitation to retire to the parlour to recruit their energies after their exertions. Lysander waved her towards the sofa and took a seat nearby. 'The trouble is, Matthew forgets he is almost fifty. He thinks he is still a young man and insists on doing too much. He hates being idle.'

Tamsin nodded. 'Anyone could see that he was in pain, but I thought he would never agree to your suggestion that he take a nap.'

Lysander coughed, suddenly uncomfortable. 'I should not have lost my temper in front of you,' he muttered.

Tamsin coloured. 'My aunt says all Cavaliers curse,' she murmured, staring with rigid concentration at one of the tapestries.

'Doesn't have a good opinion of us, does she?' Lysander's tone was wryly ironical.

'She hates you.' Tamsin shrugged awkwardly. 'When the King's Declaration of Breda was read out in our parish church last month, I thought she would burst with fury.'

Lysander had helped Charles compose this momentous document, named for the town in North Brabant where they stayed during the final days of their exile. It was a statement of Charles's good intentions towards all his subjects, promising pardon and tolerance for everyone except those directly involved in the execution of his father.

Obviously, it had not helped soften some hearts!

'Do you feel animosity towards Cavaliers, Mistress Barton?'

Tamsin hesitated. She had never had occasion to question

her family's views until the day she had learnt that her unknown father had fought for the King. But how was she to
explain her recent change of heart without revealing the
shameful secret of her birth?

'Well, I dare say you have your reasons.'

He had misunderstood her silence. 'I don't hate anyone—'
Tamsin began anxiously, but was swiftly interrupted.

'Don't apologise. You have every right to your opinion.'
Lysander's tone was careless, but a strange disappointment
ran through him.

Tamsin hung her head, her fingers twisting nervously together in her lap. Oh, why hadn't she had the courage to
speak out? Now she couldn't think of a way to retrieve her
mistake without it sounding as if she was trying to curry
favour!

Too flustered to look up, she didn't see how his gaze softened as he took in her agitation.

'Don't be embarrassed.' He left his seat and came to sit
next to her. 'I should not have asked you that question.'

'I...I didn't really know any Cavaliers until I met you, my
lord,' Tamsin whispered, her eyes still fixed on the tips of
her boots. 'I hope you will not think me discourteous.'

Lysander stretched out one long-fingered hand and gently
tilted up her chin so that she was forced to meet his gaze. 'I
think you a brave and honest girl,' he said softly.

Tamsin's heart began to hammer so violently she was sure
he must hear it.

Lysander stared down into the blue-green depths of her
lovely eyes and experienced a fierce urge to gather her into
his arms and kiss her.

Shaken, he released her.

'I fear you flatter me, sir, but thank you.' Tamsin managed
to find her voice.

'On the contrary, it is I who should be thanking you for
your help with Matthew.' Lysander had recovered from whatever madness had afflicted him and his expression was as

smoothly bland as cream. 'And, indeed, for your sterling efforts in setting the kitchen to rights.'

'I enjoyed being able to repay a little of your kindness,'
Tamsin replied simply.

She paused and then, greatly daring, added in a rush, 'You
are going to need assistance in the house now that Master
Cooper is incapacitated.'

'Don't tell me.' A resigned look appeared on Lysander's
face. 'You want to take over Matthew's duties.'

'I know you think it a harebrained notion, sir, but won't
you at least let me try? I could act as housekeeper until Master Cooper is better.'

Lysander considered her request. 'You are right. We can't
manage as things are now,' he admitted slowly. 'Matt and I
contrived perfectly well during our exile without anyone to
wait upon us, but this house is too big to run without servants.'

The house had been understaffed before he lost the services
of Mrs Finch. Matt had exacting standards and it was difficult
to find honest and reliable help who met with his approval.
It was usual to hire servants for a full year, but none of the
applicants had lasted longer than a few days.

There was a shortage of trained servants in London, made
worse by the influx of the Cavaliers wanting staff. Not being
one to stand upon his dignity, Lysander had been content to
manage without the usual plethora of maids, footmen and
butlers demanded by many men of rank. In the end, as there
were other, more pressing, demands upon his attention, the
problem had fallen into abeyance.

'Very well.' Lysander decided that since Fate seemed determined to take a hand in his affairs he might as well give
in gracefully. 'You can stay until Matthew's wrist is
mended.'

Her vivid little face lit up. 'You won't regret it, sir. I will
work hard, I promise you.'

'Remember, this is only a temporary arrangement!' Lysander warned her.

'Of course, my lord.' Tamsin dipped an obedient curtsy, her expression demure.

Predictably, Matthew objected when Lysander informed him later that evening that they had acquired a housekeeper.

'I'm not saying the wench isn't up to the job,' he grumbled, twitching at his bedclothes. 'She seems capable enough, but we don't need her. I'll be up and about tomorrow.'

'Nonsense,' Lysander retorted briskly. 'You are staying in bed for the next couple of days at least, Matt, and that's an order.'

'My wrist will feel better in the morning,' Master Cooper protested indignantly.

Lysander fixed him with a disbelieving look. 'Even if that were true, you still need to rest. You took a nasty knock to the head and I don't want you collapsing on me like young Coyle.'

Ensign Coyle had served under Lysander's command when the English Royalists had fought on the side of Spain against the French. During an engagement to defend the town of Mardyke from Marshal Turenne's forces, the ensign had suffered a blow to the left temple which had rendered him unconscious.

Lysander had rescued him from the field and the young man had later recovered his senses. He had seemed perfectly fit and healthy, apart from complaining of a headache, but two days later, without any warning, he had suddenly dropped down dead.

'Aye, well, but—'

'No more arguments, Matt. Mistress Barton stays. Now, eat your supper and go to sleep.'

Lysander thrust out the soup spoon he was holding and with a sigh Matthew abandoned his objections and opened his mouth.

The next morning Lysander took his new employee on a tour of the house. 'If there is anything you require, now is

the time to tell me,' he informed her as they descended the
main staircase after their inspection of the upper floors was
completed.

'There seems to be a sufficient quantity of bed-linen and
towels, sir, but I shall need to visit an apothecary's and purchase some oil of spikenard to deter the moths or else all
those woollen hangings will be ruined,' Tamsin replied
gravely.

Lysander hid a grin. Her solemn air put him in mind of
his sister playing house with her dolls in those far-off child-
hood days at Melcombe.

Not that he doubted his new housekeeper's competence.
She had made several sensible suggestions already and
seemed to know exactly what ought to be done to keep a
home running smoothly.

They entered the kitchen, the final call on their tour of
inspection.

'We need to order more sand for scouring the pots and I
noticed that the broom I was using yesterday could do with
new bristles. Oh, and we require some horsetail. Most of the
pewter is sadly in need of a good burnishing.' Tamsin stood
in the middle of the room, ticking off items on her mental
list.

'I think you can buy all of those things from the street
vendors. They'll come to the back door if you hail them.'

Tamsin was impressed. London had advantages in the war
against dirt, which Chipping Sodbury lacked.

Mind you, she reflected, the inhabitants of this city needed
all the help they could get. When she had opened her bedroom window this morning there had been a pall of grimy
smoke hanging in the air.

'It's from sea-coal,' Lysander had explained in response
to her mentioning this disagreeable cloud to him when he
had strolled into the kitchen soon after six in search of a
morning draught.

'Why do people use it?' Tamsin had sprung up from her

stool to pour him some ale from the jug she had been consuming for her own breakfast. She set the tankard down on the table-top. 'It leaves sooty black smudges everywhere.'

With the casual informality Tamsin still found slightly shocking, Lysander rested his lean hips against the edge of the table, stretching his long legs out in front of him, and picked up his tankard. 'There's not enough wood to go round these days,' he answered.

He declined the offer of food. Tamsin, who was always hungry, had already eaten, but she hadn't finished her drink. She reached for her mug, careful to avoid tripping over her employer's outstretched legs.

They were clad, she noticed, in a pair of knitted silk hose and garnet-red farandine breeches. A gold-laced coat in the same material completed his outfit and Tamsin thought he looked wonderful, if wildly out of place.

'I have never cooked on a coal fire before.' A faint look of alarm creased Tamsin's brow as she contemplated the prospect.

'I'm sure you'll manage,' Lysander replied blithely.

Tamsin wished she shared his confidence. 'Will you be home for dinner today, my lord?'

He shook his head. 'I have arranged to meet a friend of mine this morning at Whitehall. He is leaving London tomorrow and we will probably dine at a tavern.'

Lysander firmly dismissed a foolish impulse to change his mind and stay at home to keep an eye on his protégée.

Tamsin experienced a faint flicker of relief. His absence would give her a chance to get settled in before she had to produce a meal for him. After yesterday's magnificent feast she didn't want to let him down.

'Or I could bring Lord Treneglos home with me instead,' Lysander continued casually.

Tamsin's gaze flew to his.

'Don't look so worried. I'm only teasing.' Lysander grinned at her. 'You will be too busy, I expect, to bother preparing very much today.'

Tamsin thanked him coolly for his consideration, a militant gleam in her eyes.

'Of course, if I ever do spring unexpected guests on you,' Lysander offered repentantly, 'you can always send out to a cookshop.'

'Cookshop, sir?' Tamsin stared at him. 'You mean you sometimes *buy* your dinner?'

Her scandalised tone revealed how shocking she found this notion.

'It's a common practice in London, I'm afraid,' Lysander replied meekly.

Tamsin's face took on an expression of suspicion. 'Did Master Cooper cook that lovely meal for us yesterday or not?'

This time Lysander couldn't restrain a chuckle as he shook his head. 'Matt can manage a few plain dishes. For that matter, so can I. Life as a soldier in exile teaches you self-sufficiency, but neither of us have the talent to create fancy fare.'

He took a swallow of his ale. 'Just do your best, Mistress Barton. We won't complain if on occasion you serve us bread and cheese.'

Tamsin silently vowed to do better if it killed her.

'Would you like me to show you around the house? Normally, Matthew would do it, but he is still asleep and I needn't leave just yet.'

Tamsin had accepted his offer with alacrity.

Now, remembering their earlier conversation, she glanced around her new kitchen, relieved to note that it was very well equipped. The windows faced north, giving excellent light, and a big fireplace, flanked by two brick ovens, took up most of one wall. There were brine-tubs, a dough trough and a salting-table all handily placed while a multitude of pans, kettles, skillets, skewers and trivets hung up in gleaming readiness.

She would have no excuse to blame her tools!

'Do you want to inspect what's available in the larders?'

Lysander asked. 'Matthew usually orders the provisions, but it might be better if you took over for the moment rather than bothering him.'

A thoughtful look passed over his handsome features. Matthew also managed the day-to-day household expenses and Lysander knew him well enough to be sure that his faithful retainer would be indignant if he asked anyone else to handle the task. On the other hand, the wench wouldn't be able to obtain everything on credit.

'Remind me to leave you some money before I set out for Whitehall,' he announced. 'You might need to buy something urgently.'

Tamsin swallowed hard. She wasn't used to handling coin. 'Yes, my lord.' She would manage somehow!

They examined the larders. Ale, wines, milk and butter were kept in one and in the other joints of meat and fowls were hanging up in the chilly air. Tamsin was delighted by the unexpected plentifulness of the provisions, but she was puzzled by the cold until she realised it was coming from the mouth of a large well.

Lysander grinned at her exclamation of surprise.

'The well at home is some twenty yards from the house,' Tamsin murmured, colouring slightly. He would think her a complete rustic!

Still, she wouldn't have far to carry water here and even more conveniently, the house had its own privy out in the walled garden, which lay to the rear of the property.

Tamsin had already discovered that most inhabitants of the city had to rely on laystalls for disposing of their various household wastes. These basket tubs were dotted about the streets and their stench was overpowering, to say nothing of the way they encouraged flies, rats and scavenging cats.

Lysander led the way back into the main kitchen. 'I think that's everything,' he said, preparing to depart. 'If you have any questions or need advice, ask Matthew.'

Tamsin hadn't realised that the tour was over. 'Where is

your laundry, sir?' she asked, puzzled. 'And your brew-house?'

'The laundry is sent out and we buy our ale in,' he replied.

Tamsin felt more like a country bumpkin than ever. It was rapidly being borne in on her that her new life was going to be very different from her previous existence at Whiteladies.

'Don't worry. You'll soon get used to city ways.'

Tamsin nodded, her faltering confidence restored by the warmth of his encouraging smile.

'I am determined to do so, sir,' she said firmly.

The sooner she found her feet, the sooner she could begin searching for her father.

Chapter Four

The sound of laughter reached Lysander long before he arrived at the palace tennis court.

'Come and watch with us, Sir Lysander,' a dulcet feminine voice invited as he joined the spectators. 'The King is thrashing Lord Buckhurst.'

Lysander strolled over to the speaker, a tall, full-bosomed brunette. 'Your servant, Mistress Godolphin.' He bent with elegance over the hand she extended to him.

'I see I need not ask how you are keeping this fair morning,' he said, straightening up to gaze into her eyes. 'Your radiance outshines the sun.'

Jane Godolphin laughed and ran her fingers lightly over the bodice of her bright yellow silk gown. 'Why, thank you, sir, but I fear you are mistaken. It is only the colour of my gown that shines so brightly.'

Playing in accordance with the rules of flirtation, a game as intricate as the one taking place on the court before them, Lysander promptly shook his head. 'Nay, lady, even a blind man could discern your beauty. It needs no aid to dazzle the eye.'

'Marry, come up, sir! You flatter me.' She rapped him lightly on the arm with her painted fan and gave him a roguish smile. 'Still, you do it so prettily I feel obliged to forgive you.'

Lysander returned her smile and turned to greet her companion, an elderly man with a surprisingly foppish mode of dress.

'My uncle was just saying that we must invite you to dinner. Weren't you, Uncle Edward?'

Lysander saw the warning glance she flicked at Edward Fielding. So, the wealthy widow was interested, was she?

Mr Fielding took the hint and immediately claimed that nothing would give him greater delight than to welcome Sir Lysander to the house they had taken in Lady Court, off fashionable King Street.

Wryly aware that the man could say little else, Lysander thanked him. 'I should be honoured to dine with you,' he said with a graceful inclination of his head that set the red-dyed feathers on his wide-brimmed hat a-tremble.

The tennis match was reaching its climax.

'Oh, we must stop talking and watch now!' Jane exclaimed.

She made a pretty show of cheering on the King, but Lysander was conscious of the covert glances she threw in his direction when she thought she was unobserved.

Satisfaction flickered through him. At their first meeting yesterday he had done his best to make a favourable impression and it seemed he had succeeded.

The match ended and the players came off to receive the congratulations of the crowd.

'Ah, Lysander.' Charles hailed him with one of his lazy smiles. 'I am glad you are here. I want to show you the newest addition to my collection of timepieces.'

'I should be delighted, Sire.' Lysander shared his friend's taste for horology.

'If I had known you meant to visit the palace this morning, I should have challenged you to a game instead of Buckhurst,' Charles said easily. 'He is out of practice.'

Lysander grinned. 'You usually beat your opponents.'

Charles laughed. 'Not you, my friend.' They were so evenly matched that few would wager on the outcome.

An attendant hurried to hand the King his hat and coat, which he had removed to play tennis. Charles donned them, his manner as informal as ever, but there was a lively curiosity in his black gaze as it swept over his friend's handsome companion.

'My reason for coming to Whitehall, your Highness, was to meet Lord Treneglos,' Lysander explained. 'Unfortunately, he seems to have been delayed.'

'Poor Tom. He is fair distracted over this quest of his, I fear,' Charles replied with a sympathetic sigh.

Lysander nodded and then, aware of the tense anticipation vibrating in the woman at his side, continued in an apparently casual manner, 'May I present Mistress Godolphin to you, Sire? Her family were ever loyal to your father's cause.'

Jane immediately sank into a deep curtsy. 'Your Majesty!'

Charles flashed Lysander a knowing grin, which quickly vanished as she rose from her obeisance. 'Let me welcome you to Whitehall, Mistress Godolphin,' he said affably. 'I am always pleased to meet those who support the Crown.'

'My first husband was killed at Naseby,' Jane murmured a little breathlessly.

Charles, who had already grown weary of petitioners clamouring for reward for past services, adroitly changed the subject. 'I understand you are newly come to London. Is this your first visit?'

Jane quickly denied it, but Lysander noted that she was careful not to mention that her previous trip to the capital had been undertaken in the company of her second husband, a former major in Cromwell's Ironsides.

From the gleam of amusement in Charles's dark eyes it was obvious that he knew all the gossip and had spotted this omission too. Not that Lysander blamed Jane for her discretion. She wasn't to know that Charles was a tolerant man. It wasn't in his nature to be vindictive.

'Be sure to come to Whitehall again.' King Charles's glance was admiring as he brought the conversation to an end. 'It is always a pleasure to see lovely ladies gracing the court and I'll warrant Sir Lysander would be happy to escort you here whenever you wished.'

He turned to Lysander to arrange a time for his friend to inspect the new clock and gave him a secret wink.

With a final smile for Jane he moved on. The crowd eddied in his wake, all eager for a crumb of royal attention, and Lysander's small group was left behind.

'Thank you for the introduction.' Jane Godolphin's rather narrow grey eyes were brilliant with triumph.

'Aye, it was well done of you, Sir Lysander,' Edward Fielding chimed in excitedly, breaking his awed silence.

A member of the Sussex gentry, he had accompanied his niece to London to lend his support to her venture. They had arrived a week ago, knowing no one of influence, but already Jane's money had opened several doors. One of these new acquaintances had suggested they visit Whitehall, the place to be seen for any social aspirant.

It had proved an easy matter to gain admittance to the palace, the guards allowed any well-dressed person to enter, but mingling with the fashionable crowd was not the same as being part of it. Without connections at court, it was difficult to gain the introductions necessary for advancement.

Well aware of this, Mr Fielding had been impressed by the friendship shown by the King to his niece's new suitor.

'His Majesty liked you, niece!' he exclaimed. 'Your social success is assured!'

'Indeed.' Jane's expression was smug. She glanced at Lysander hopefully. 'I would be even more grateful, sir, if you could bring yourself to follow the King's advice and offer me your escort here one evening.'

'I would be happy to be of service,' Lysander answered sweetly. 'There is a reception on Sunday. Perhaps you would care to attend?'

'I should like that.' Jane paused and added in a slightly nervous tone, 'Will you come to dinner with us beforehand?'

'Gladly, ma'am.'

Surer now of her conquest, Jane patted her elaborately

curled ringlets with an air of satisfaction she didn't trouble to hide.

When a woman was looking thirty in the face she was a fool not to know her own mind. Lysander Saxon was one of the most handsome men Jane had ever met and, since he seemed as agreeable as he was well born, she had decided to encourage his suit. True, he had no fortune to recommend him, but few of the newly returned Cavaliers were rich. More importantly, he had the friendship of the King and could offer her entree into the elevated circles of society she craved.

After two forced marriages, neither of which she had found congenial, she was determined to make her own choice this time!

'My uncle and I are going to take a dish of syllabub at Harper's before returning home,' she announced, mentioning a fashionable tavern in King Street. 'Can I tempt you to join us, Sir Lysander?'

Her bold invitation confirmed Lysander's instinctive feeling that she found him attractive. He was not coxcomb enough to imagine his looks alone had ignited her interest. Their acquaintance had been short, but he already knew there was a ruthless side to her nature. He thought her perfectly capable of using him merely to further her social ambitions. However, unless he had mistaken his guess, she genuinely liked him.

'It would give me great pleasure to accept, Mistress Godolphin,' he replied, allowing a note of regret to seep into his tone. 'However, I am promised to Lord Treneglos.'

'But he isn't here.' Jane cast him a languorous look, fluttering her eyelashes in her most seductive manner.

At that moment, as if to give lie to her words, there came the sound of heavy footsteps hurrying up the path towards them.

'Lysander! I beg pardon for my tardiness. I hope you haven't been waiting long.' Lord Treneglos halted, panting a little, the high colour in his plump cheeks vying with the orange tabby of his fashionably beribboned suit.

'Tom.' Lysander greeted him with a warm smile. 'There is no need to apologise. My time has been most pleasantly occupied.'

Jane acknowledged this compliment, hiding her disappointment behind a polite smile as Lysander proceeded to introduce her and her uncle to Lord Treneglos.

After a few minutes of affable conversation she noticed that the Cornishman was beginning to look restless. Having no desire to outstay her welcome and spoil the good impression she had made, she judged it time to make her exit.

'Until Sunday then, my lord,' she said, holding out her hand to Lysander.

He kissed it, his lips lingering just long enough to invest the formality with significance. 'I shall count the hours, Mistress Godolphin.'

He stood and watched her walk away on her uncle's arm, her elegant bell-shaped skirts swaying gracefully.

'A handsome piece.' Lord Treneglos's tone was approving. 'And they say her fortune is enormous. You could do a lot worse, my boy.'

The faint smile curving Lysander's well-cut mouth grew cynical. 'I know, which is why I intend to snap her up before some other rogue beats me to it.'

Tom laughed. 'I wish you a fair wind to speed your courtship!'

Lord Treneglos had bespoken dinner at the Turk's Head in New Palace Yard. 'How say you we go by river? I know it's only a short walk to Westminster, but I fancy some clean air. These damned smoky streets do my chest no good at all.'

Lysander readily agreed. Tom suffered from a wheeziness in his lungs and his condition had become worse since their return home. London was a great city—to Lysander's knowledge, only Paris and Constantinople were bigger—but it was a dirty place.

A faint smile touched his mouth as he remembered his little waif's complaints about sea-coal, but household fires weren't the only source of pollution. Small businesses abounded cheek by jowl with ordinary houses in the narrow city streets. Brewers, soap-boilers, glue-makers—he could think of a dozen noisome trades which belched forth clouds of foul smoke.

Small wonder, then, that Tom's cough was more trouble-some lately!

They began to stroll in the direction of the river and Ly-sander said, 'Speaking of fair winds, how goes the prepara-tion for your journey?'

Tom shuddered, his heavy jowls quivering in mock horror. 'I am beginning to wish I had elected to travel overland. The *Venus* leaves for Bristol on tomorrow's early tide and I still haven't found a suitable present for my daughter.'

He sighed. 'I wish I had some idea of what she liked, but I know nothing about her.'

'How old will she be now?' Lysander asked gently, careful not to question Tom's optimistic assumption that the girl was still alive.

'Sixteen,' Tom replied with a promptness that revealed how often he had thought about it. 'Her birthday was in Feb-ruary.'

A reminiscent smile softened his gaze. 'She was a pre-mature babe. At first we didn't think she would live, but she was a tenacious little thing.'

He shook his iron-grey head with a sudden violence. 'God, how I wish I had not sent her to my wife's relatives! I thought an army camp was no place for a newborn, but I should have kept them both with me!'

'You were wounded at Marston Moor, Tom.' Lysander had heard the whole story from his father, who had been one of Lord Treneglos's closest friends in spite of the twelve-year age gap which separated them. 'You were too ill to protect anyone and the situation was dangerous. You did what you thought was best.'

'Aye,' Tom agreed heavily.

He fell silent and, reluctant to break in on his thoughts, Lysander held his tongue as they crossed the palace grounds and made their way towards the Garden Stairs, but anger on his friend's behalf stirred in him.

The damned war had torn Tom's life apart as it had so many others. With no close relatives of his own in Cornwall to look after his wife and infant daughter, Tom had been forced to send them to Bristol to seek refuge with Lady Treneglos's family, who, unfortunately, abhorred his support of King Charles.

The ravages of war and the duty he had unfailingly rendered to the royal family had prevented Tom from reclaiming his womenfolk before he had been forced into exile. Then, one day in Paris, the latest of his endless letters to his wife had found its way unopened back to the dire lodgings he was sharing with Lysander's father. A brief note from his in-laws had accompanied it, a few brutally curt lines declaring that Lady Judith and five-year-old Thomasina had died of the plague.

Devastated, Lord Treneglos had had no suspicion that his sister-in-law might be lying. However, two years later during the ill-fated campaign to recover the English throne by force of arms, a chance encounter with a former servant of Judith's family had revealed that his daughter had survived her illness.

In the disastrous aftermath which followed the battle of Worcester, Tom was unable to discover if the man had spoken the truth. Back in exile once more, he had sent an increasingly furious stream of letters to his in-laws. Every one was ignored.

Was it any wonder, Lysander reflected, that he was anxious to seek out the truth for himself?

They had reached the Garden Stairs and the fresh breeze blowing off the river seemed to disperse Lord Treneglos's anxious melancholy.

'Forgive me,' he said, attempting to look cheerful. 'I wanted us to meet today so I could say farewell, not to burden you with my problems.'

Lysander shrugged. 'What are friends for?' he retorted lightly, masking his concern with his usual veneer of humour.

Tom had known Lysander since he was breeched and he recognised the tactic. During their long exile the boy had grown a hard shell to disguise his emotions, but beneath that protective carapace there beat the kindest of hearts.

A wherry approached the stairs. A single passenger disembarked and Lysander and Tom got in. 'Westminster Stairs, if you please,' Lysander requested.

The waterman grunted and thrust out his hand for their fare, which Lysander, refusing Tom's offer, proceeded to pay.

'Ain't you got anything smaller?' the waterman grumbled, frowning at the coin Lysander had handed him before reluctantly handing over the correct change.

'A surly fellow,' Tom remarked as they took their places.

Lysander shrugged. 'We've been home almost a month now and I have yet to meet a waterman who can smile.'

Tom chuckled. Some things didn't change. Watermen had always been an abusive breed.

The wherry swung out into the river and Lysander sat back to enjoy the view. As usual, the Thames was crowded with small craft and larger boats plying their trade and he thought that they made a brave sight on this sunny morning. In the distance he could see several of the fine buildings which lined the river bank and beyond them, framed against the skyline, the spires belonging to some of London's hundred-and-odd churches.

His spirits lifted. It was good to be alive on such a glorious day!

'What are you thinking about, Lysander?' Tom asked curiously. 'You got an expression on you like a dog in a butcher's yard.'

'I'm counting my blessings,' Lysander replied with a grin. 'One, here we are back home again, a miracle indeed. Two, the would-be-merry Widow Godolphin has taken a fancy to me, which means my prospects are looking up. Three, even a threat of domestic chaos has been averted thanks to a little wench I rescued last night.'

Tom's sandy eyebrows rose. 'I scent a mystery.'

'I'll tell you all about it when we are comfortably settled with a pot of ale,' Lysander promised cheerfully.

Who knows? With one or two name changes to protect Tamsin's reputation, a courtesy she surely deserved, it might divert Tom's mind over dinner and prevent him fretting about his long-lost daughter.

Tamsin hummed an old tune cheerfully under her breath as she laid her spare cap, smock and stockings out to dry, draping them carefully over a rosemary bush in the walled garden at the back of the house. The afternoon was well advanced, but it was so warm that they should be fit to bring in before darkness fell.

Thank goodness she'd had only to wash these few items. At Whiteladies it took all day to do a proper wash. Once a month, weather permitting, the pile of dirty linen would be collected and laid at the bottom of the buck-tub and soaked in a lye of wood ash and urine or bran water. Then the dirty water was run off by a spigot into the underbuck tub and the process repeated until the clothes appeared clean.

Stubborn patches of dirt had to be scrubbed away and then everything could be rinsed, an exhausting business of vigorous shaking and stirring of the water-heavy linen. When it was all wrung out as hard as tired arms could make it, the laundry could then be taken into the garden to be dried.

Today she had been too busy with other household tasks to wash more than her change of underwear. Still, everything had gone well and she felt satisfied with her day's work. Master Cooper had even praised the beef pudding she had served for his dinner.

'If the Devil makes mischief for idle hands, you must be in a state of grace, Mistress Barton.'

Tamsin, who had been too preoccupied to hear him enter the garden, whirled round at the sound of Lysander's deep tones.

'My lord.' She bobbed a hasty curtsy. 'I did not realise you were back.'

Lysander surveyed her. She had discarded the broad linen collar she had worn earlier and pushed up her sleeves, exposing her bare forearms.

'You look uncommon warm. I hope you haven't been working too hard,' he said.

Her cap was awry. Several apricot-gold curls had spilled on to her neck and her thin cheeks were flushed with pink. It suddenly occurred to him that, dressed in more fashionable clothes with her hair properly arranged, she would look decidedly pretty.

It was a disturbing thought.

Tamsin shook her head, laughing. 'I am used to hard work, sir. There is always something needing doing on a farm.'

Lysander suspected her aunt had been a hard taskmaster. 'Aye, but we must find you some help,' he protested lightly. 'This house is too big for you to manage on your own.'

About to object, Tamsin paused. Working hard to pay off her debt was one thing—skimping tasks from sheer lack of time was another.

Much as she hated to admit it, he was right.

'I can manage the cooking on my own, but I could do with someone to help with the cleaning,' she agreed, smoothing down her apron briskly.

'And you'll need a footboy to run your errands and accompany you when you go marketing,' Lysander declared.

'Nat could do that, surely?'

'Not when I need his services myself,' Lysander pointed out. 'And I don't want you going out alone.'

'I'm a servant, not a fine lady,' Tamsin protested.

'Gallants don't always make a distinction.' Lysander's tone was dry. He didn't want to scare her, but it wasn't unknown for a pretty girl to be snatched off the streets by some drunken bucks, raped and thrown back into the gutter when her attackers had done with her. 'It can be dangerous for a woman on her own. Until you are better acquainted with the city and its ways, you must not venture far without an escort.'

Tamsin was accustomed to walking freely anywhere she

wished at home, but her brush with Mrs Cole had already demonstrated the need to be more wary here so she nodded obediently.

Not that she believed she would draw any gallant's eye… Did his warning mean that, despite his avowal that he found her too thin, Sir Lysander actually thought her attractive enough to invite attention?

The thought sent an inexplicable warm glow rushing through her veins and Tamsin almost missed what he was saying about seeing if any acquaintance could recommend a housemaid.

'Beg your pardon, my lord,' she interrupted hastily, 'can we not enquire if Mrs Finch's daughter is free to work for you?'

Lysander's eyebrow quirked. He had been unaware that Mrs Finch even had a daughter. How the devil had she found that out and so quickly?

'Nat told me,' Tamsin answered demurely when he asked.

Lysander had gone by river to Whitehall that morning, leaving the coachman free to help out in his brother's livery stables round the corner in Bell Yard. Nat preferred to live there than lodge in Wych Street, but he was accustomed to eating his dinner in Lysander's kitchen.

Today he had shared the beef pudding with Tamsin. Friendly and loquacious, he was a mine of useful information.

'He also said that they would be hard hit by Mrs Finch losing her position,' Tamsin continued. 'I thought that, if the girl was suitable, it would be a good solution to both problems.' She searched his expression anxiously. 'That is, if you have no objection to the idea, sir?'

'None at all. Hire the girl if you think her capable.'

'And the errand boy, sir? Nat did mention that she had several brothers.'

Lysander laughed, amused by her coaxing tone. 'I leave it up to you. All I ask is that they can do the job.'

'Thank you!' Tamsin beamed at him. 'I shall go to see them tomorrow. Nat knows where they live.'

She rolled down her sleeves and picked up the empty basket wherein she had carried her wet clothes out into the garden. 'I will leave you to enjoy the air in peace, my lord.'

'Wait! Don't go.' Lysander discovered he was reluctant to lose her company. 'Stay and talk to me for a while.'

Tamsin took a step back, clutching the basket tightly to still the sudden trembling of her hands. 'I ought to get on with preparing supper,' she murmured.

'Surely you can spare a few minutes?'

Tamsin hesitated.

'I thought we agreed yesterday that the usual rules did not apply?' Lysander said softly. 'You have offered your services as housekeeper, but that doesn't mean you have to behave like a servant. As far as I am concerned, you are still my guest.'

Unable to resist the smile which accompanied his words, Tamsin nodded and put her basket down again.

'Let's sit over there.' Lysander pointed to a bank of camomile and violets, which had been fashioned into a seat, the latest elegant whim.

Tamsin eyed it dubiously. The weather had been dry, but damp might still linger in such a flower-covered spot. Informal as ever, her benefactor was in his shirtsleeves, both hat and coat removed in response to the heat, but his breeches were made of farandine, an expensive mix of silk and superior wool. 'You might stain your fine clothes, sir.'

He grinned. 'The cost of being fashionable, I'm afraid.'

They sat down and Tamsin cast an admiring glance about her. Although somewhat long and narrow in shape, the garden was a pleasant place. There were formal beds of flowers carved into rectilinear patterns and edged with thrift, paths of gravel, decorative shrubs and elaborate swirls of coloured sand outlined with silver-leaved plants. A small arbour covered in honeysuckle and roses, both red and white, added perfume to the air. There was even a grass carpet-walk for the taking of exercise, although it stood in dire need of scything.

Lysander stretched luxuriantly. 'Long may this fine weather continue,' he remarked with a sigh of content.

'Do you feel stifled being indoors, sir?'

He was surprised by her perceptiveness. For someone so young, she had an unusual ability to show empathy with others. Her championship of Mrs Finch's family revealed the same fellow-feeling at work.

He ought to have thought of hiring the girl himself. He had already sent Mrs Finch the wages she was owed for this week, although, strictly speaking, he need not have paid her anything. Guessing that the family might be in difficulties, he had even added a few extra shillings on top, but Tamsin's solution was a much better one.

A long time ago his father had taught him that a master was responsible for the welfare of his whole household down to the lowliest servant. 'Be firm, but always temper discipline with benevolence, my son,' Sir James had advised. 'The ability to treat people well is one of the signs of a man's inner strength and maturity. Just as a braggart needs to puff himself off, so will a weakling take out his frustrations and fears on those beneath him. A good man thinks of others as well as himself.'

It seemed that his little waif had already absorbed this valuable lesson.

Tamsin coughed awkwardly, wondering if she had annoyed him with her curiosity.

Seeing her discomfort, Lysander made haste to break his silence. 'I do prefer being out in the fresh air,' he said lightly. 'A morning spent paying courtesies at Whitehall tires me more than a day in the saddle. The result of a country upbringing, followed by service in the army, I suppose.'

A look of interest brightened the turquoise eyes fixed on his. 'Did you fight for the late King, sir?'

'I was too young, at least according to my father, but I have fought on behalf of his present Majesty,' Lysander replied.

'Will you tell me about it?' Tamsin begged.

Lysander complied, relating some amusing experiences while avoiding the more unsavoury aspects of a soldier's life.

Tamsin listened avidly and, forgetting all reserve, pelted him with a multitude of questions.

'S'death, perhaps you should have been a boy,' Lysander laughingly exclaimed at last, amused and a little startled by the depth of her curiosity.

Tamsin blushed. 'I would have gone for soldier if I could,' she agreed shyly.

It was on the tip of her tongue to explain that his words had made her feel closer to her mysterious father, but caution intervened. She had already confessed to the shaming fact of being a runaway. What might he think if she told him the whole truth?

Unwilling to dwell upon why his good opinion was so important to her, Tamsin hastily cast about for another topic of conversation.

'This garden is so different to the one we had at home,' she announced brightly. 'My aunt grew herbs and vegetables, not flowers. She said that she had no use for such frivolous things.' A giggle escaped her. 'In fact, I think she found their bright colour sinful.'

'Really? You surprise me.'

There was a wealth of irony in his deep tones and Tamsin giggled again, realising that he disliked her aunt's narrow viewpoint as much as she did.

'I think God was in one of His better moods when He created these,' he remarked lazily, picking a violet from the bank on which they sat and offering it to Tamsin. 'How could anything which smells so sweet be sinful?'

Tamsin buried her nose in the velvet soft petals and inhaled deeply. 'It's lovely,' she exclaimed.

Her uninhibited enthusiasm made Lysander smile. She had an aptitude for enjoyment, at once both refreshingly innocent and curiously sensual, which might explain why she was such a reluctant Puritan!

He found it enchanting.

Tamsin wondered why he was smiling. 'Have I said something silly?' she asked anxiously, putting the flower down.

He shook his head. Sunlight caught in the deep waves of his gleaming hair, turning it to pure gold.

Tamsin's breathing quickened. She became aware of how close together they were sitting. The sunlight seemed to have turned the faint scar on his cheek into a fine ribbon of silver. Tiny laughter lines crinkled up the corners of his brilliant eyes and she could see that his long dark eyelashes were tipped with bronze.

In response to the warmth of the afternoon he had loosened the strings of his neckband so that his shirt lay open at the throat. Against that trimming of snowy Venetian point, his skin was very brown. If she reached out she could touch his flesh…

She jumped up, horrified by her wanton thoughts. Aunt Deborah had often accused her of being a daydreamer, but until this moment her imagination had never led her to wonder what it might be like to be held in a man's arms!

'I had better go and put on that leg of pork I am roasting for supper,' she muttered, panic fluttering along her veins. She scarcely understood what had just happened to her, but she was aware of an urgent need to put distance between them.

'Of course.' Lysander curbed a selfish urge to keep her talking. She was conscientious about her work, which, no doubt, explained why she was suddenly looking uneasy.

Thankful he appeared to have no notion of her inner turmoil, Tamsin dipped a hasty curtsy, picked up her basket and fled.

Tamsin was just drying her hands after washing up the breakfast pots the next morning when she heard Lysander calling her name.

'Are you ready?' he demanded as she hurried into the hallway.

'To visit Mrs Finch?' She stared at him in astonishment.
'I thought Nat was taking me?'

'I need his services.' Lysander clapped his hat upon his
head. 'You'll have to make do with my escort.'

Delight trickled along Tamsin's veins, but she schooled
her expression to neutrality and obediently removed her
apron.

Lysander flung open the front door. 'Come on, we've an
errand to perform first and time is short.'

Grateful that her appearance needed no further tidying,
Tamsin scurried after him. Nat was waiting for them and
Lysander bundled her up into the coach.

'The New Exchange, Nat. As fast as you can.' Lysander
leapt into the vehicle and it rattled off at high speed.

Tamsin clutched the seat in some alarm. 'Do you always
travel so fast, sir?'

'Only when I am in a hurry.' Lysander grinned at her.
'Don't fret. Nat is an excellent coachman. He won't overturn
us.'

To Tamsin's relief, this somewhat alarming reassurance
proved justified. Nat wove skilfully through the heavy traffic
along the Strand and they reached their destination after just
a few minutes.

Lysander jumped out. 'Wait for us here, Nat.'

He took Tamsin by the arm and swept her into the ornate
building, which had been erected some fifty years ago in
imitation of the older Royal Exchange within the city walls.

Inside, there were two long double galleries filled with
dozens of small shops. Fine candles burned everywhere to
better illuminate the items on offer and well-dressed atten-
dants stood ready to lure passers-by.

Tamsin's eyes widened. In spite of the early hour there
were plenty of richly clad strollers. She had never seen so
many fashionable outfits…or such a display of luxury goods
in her life!

Lysander was amused by her shocked expression. 'Don't
you like what they are selling?' he teased.

Tamsin came to the conclusion that she did. 'Though I probably shouldn't,' she added with her usual candour.

'Forget you are a Puritan,' Lysander begged. 'I need your advice in choosing a present.'

'*My* advice, sir?' Tamsin couldn't imagine what possible use her opinion would be.

'It's for a girl of your age. Like you, she is country-bred.' Lysander smiled at her briefly and waved a hand to encompass the gallery. 'Given a free choice, what would you select?'

'I…I don't know.' Tamsin stared in confusion at the nearest stall, which was selling bottles of perfume and elegant vizard masks. Taking a deep breath, she tried to collect her wits. 'Do you know her tastes, sir?'

Lysander shook his head. 'I know nothing about her. She is the daughter of a friend I wish to honour.' There was a slight edge of impatience to his tone. Tom would be leaving his lodgings soon.

'Let's try some of the other shops,' he suggested.

They moved along the gallery and Tamsin tried to ignore both the noisy cries of the shopkeepers puffing off their wares and the disdainful stares she was receiving from other strollers.

This must be a fashionable meeting place, she decided, feeling uncomfortably out of place in her Puritan garb. They probably wonder what I am doing here.

Giving herself a mental shake, she dismissed the harebrained wish that she too might be finely dressed. She had no time for such foolishness, she had to concentrate.

'These perfumed gloves are lovely, but getting the right fit might be difficult,' she murmured, pausing to examine the goods at one stall.

Lysander nodded agreement. 'What about this fan?'

'It is very pretty, but those feathers look as if they might break easily.'

It was hard to decide. There were so many lovely things

on show. She liked nearly everything, but what would the unknown recipient prefer?

The next shop sold jewellery and Tamsin quickly passed it by, her aunt's warnings about Jezebel ringing in her ears.

'We must choose quickly or Nat will miss my friend, who is leaving on this morning's tide.'

Tamsin nodded. Wishing that the gallery was not so noisy and wit-addlingly hot, she cast a last desperate look around.

'Over there, my lord.' She pointed to another stall with a little cry of excitement.

The shopkeeper specialised in cosmetics. Lysander raised his eyebrow. 'I'm not sure if she is allowed to paint and patch,' he commented as they walked over.

Tamsin laughed. 'She might like to try,' she replied mischievously. She pointed to the object which had caught her eye. 'But this is what I had in mind.'

'A most discerning choice, mistress.' The stall's attendant, a smartly dressed young man, picked up the silver toothbrush and held it out to Lysander. 'Newly in from France, sir. The very latest in fashionable novelties, but useful too. It will keep the teeth most excellent white.'

'How much?'

The shopkeeper named a price which made Tamsin gasp.

'We'll take it.' Lysander counted out the money while the young man wrapped it in a square of fine linen.

As soon as the gift was handed over, Lysander took Tamsin by the elbow and swept her out to where Nat was waiting for them.

'Take this to Lord Treneglos at the Mitre in Fenchurch Street as swiftly as you can.' He handed over the little parcel. 'Tell him to give it to his daughter with my compliments.'

Nat grunted acknowledgment. 'And afterwards, my lord? Do you wish me to meet you somewhere?'

Lysander shook his head. 'Return home when you are done.'

Nat acknowledged this command with a flourish of his

whip and, with a cry of encouragement to his horses, set off at a spanking pace.

'I hope your friend's daughter will like the gift,' Tamsin murmured, staring after the coach.

'I'm sure she will.' Lysander smiled at her. 'It was a very clever choice of yours.'

Tamsin basked in his praise, her guilt at the exorbitant cost receding. Having a professional interest in the latest novelties, Master Latham had spoken of these newfangled toothbrushes to her on their journey to London. She doubted if she would have recognised them otherwise, but now she knew why the elderly pedlar didn't carry any himself—they were far too expensive for his humble customers!

'Shall we hire a hackney to visit Mrs Finch?' Lysander enquired, gesturing towards the cabs waiting at the nearby stand for trade.

'I would rather walk an' it please you, sir,' Tamsin replied.

Lysander nodded. 'As you wish.'

He thought she might want to stretch her legs because she missed the exercise she was accustomed to at home, but Tamsin's reason was even simpler. She could see much more on foot than cooped up in a coach and London, for all its noise and stinks, fascinated her.

Luckily, the thoroughfare was wide, making it easier than usual to avoid the evil-smelling open kennel that ran down the street.

'Take my arm,' Lysander instructed, positioning himself so that he stood between her and the wooden posts which separated those on foot from the carriageway.

Tamsin obeyed, swallowing a nervous lump in her throat. Beneath the smooth indigo broadcloth of his coat, she could feel his hard muscles.

Other pedestrians were also trying to hog the space closest to the walls, the safest and driest place, but one look at her protector's broad shoulders prevented anyone from attempting to jostle Tamsin out of the way.

'Am I walking too fast?' Noticing her slight breathlessness, Lysander shortened his long stride.

Tamsin thanked him for his consideration and, made bold by his evident good humour, began to ask him about the handsome buildings which lined their route.

Lysander obligingly pointed out the great houses of the nobility. 'That one is Somerset House. It used to be the official residence of Queen Henrietta-Maria. I expect she will take possession of it again when she returns from France.'

'The Queen is coming to London?'

Lysander heard the uneasy awe in her voice and reflected that she had probably been taught to hate the King's Papist mother, who had possessed such a strong influence over her late husband.

'Aye, she will arrive sometime in the autumn, I understand,' he replied.

Tamsin silently wondered if she would still be in London. Perhaps she would have discovered her father's whereabouts before then.

The first step was to seek out Martha. Her former nurse might have some helpful information. When the new servants were settled in she would ask Master Cooper if he could spare her for an hour or two.

'Can you sew?'

Her benefactor's question roused Tamsin from her speculations. 'Sew, my lord?' she echoed, wondering if she had missed some vital part of the conversation.

'I was thinking of our errand,' Lysander explained. 'It is customary to provide new servants with a set of clothes, but from what I've heard all the tailors in London are snowed under with orders since the King was restored. Everyone wants new outfits to attend all the celebrations.'

Tamsin nodded her understanding of his dilemma. Dinah Finch and her brother could not be expected to possess any garments befitting life in a gentleman's residence. They were too poor.

Clothes were very expensive items. Tamsin knew their

purchase could easily eat up a great portion of even a prosperous family's earnings. Gideon Hardy had paid twelve pounds for a good cloth suit in which to come courting and he boasted an income of one hundred pounds a year.

Only the rich could afford to own an extensive wardrobe. She herself had never possessed more than two gowns to her name at any one time. Admittedly, this had more to do with the fact that her aunt discouraged profligacy than a lack of money at Whiteladies. However, since all her gowns had come in the same plain style and black homespun for the past eleven years Tamsin had scarcely felt her lack.

On the rare occasions she had ventured to ask for something different, Aunt Deborah had tartly pointed out that she was lucky to receive any new garments at all. 'Three pounds and eight shillings I've just paid for a new gown for thee, Mistress Ungrateful,' she had snapped last February when Tamsin had finally grown out of her old winter dress. 'Go and ask in the village if any girl there is so well treated. Bah! They think themselves fortunate to receive old cast-offs! I don't know why I bother to be so generous with thee!'

Tamsin suspected her aunt's motive had been to impress Master Hardy, but she'd had sense enough to hold her tongue.

'My aunt taught me to sew,' she informed Lysander, answering his question. 'I could make their new outfits if your tailor is busy.'

Lysander thanked her. 'I hope I shall not have to trouble you. The fellow may have something in stock which will do.' He saw her look of puzzlement. 'Many tailors keep a selection of made-up garments which need only a few alterations to fit. It's useful if clothes are needed in a hurry, particularly for something like mourning.'

Tamsin had never heard of this practice. 'At home everything was made to order if we could not sew it for ourselves.'

'Patience is not a virtue much praised in London.' Lysander grinned at her.

'You mean you are all too spoilt to want to wait for any-

thing?' Tamsin enquired, widening her eyes at him inno-
cently.

Her teasing sally made him laugh and Tamsin was so
pleased with her success that she forgot to look where she
was going and almost trod on a rotting, squelching onion
which was littering the thoroughfare.

'Careful!' Lysander quickly steered her clear. 'You'll dirty
your gown.'

Lysander eyed Tamsin's modest raiment, his expression
growing pained as a belated realisation hit home. 'You could
do with some new clothes as well.'

Misunderstanding that it had been directed at himself,
Tamsin bridled at his critical tone. 'There is nothing wrong
with this dress!' she declared, coming to an abrupt halt and
removing her hand from his arm.

'That's a matter of opinion,' Lysander retorted with more
honesty than tact. 'It makes you look like a skinny little
crow.'

Tamsin glared at him. 'It is obvious that you do not approve of Puritans, my lord,' she said hotly, 'but I see no
reason for you to be so rude! I know my attire is plain, but
I am not one of your Court ladies, who sit around idle all
day. Or do you expect me to dust the furniture prinked up in
silks and satins?'

Her sarcastic tone brought a flush of annoyance to Lysander's clear-cut features. 'You misunderstand my concern,' he
said coldly. 'It is my duty to provide for you. Board, lodgings
and clothes are a normal part of a servant's wages.'

Tamsin sucked in her breath. So that's what he really
thought of her in spite of his fine words about her being his
guest!

Lysander saw the hurt flickering in her eyes. 'Let's not
quarrel,' he said in a more conciliatory tone, realising his
irritation with his own lack of foresight had led him astray.
'I didn't mean to offend you. You brought so little with you
to London that I thought you would welcome the offer.'

He essayed a slight smile. 'Wouldn't you like a new gown

to wear? Something in a brighter colour, perhaps? You could choose the material yourself.'

'I do not need your charity,' she said through gritted teeth, spurning his olive branch.

Lysander's smile faded. 'No? Then perhaps I should have left you in Lime Street. Your lack of manners might have gone unnoticed there.'

Tamsin paled. 'How…how dare you accuse me of being unmannerly just because I disagree with you!' she spluttered.

'I speak as I find,' Lysander snapped. 'You are behaving like a silly child insisting on taking offence where none was intended.'

Tamsin had the uneasy feeling he was right, but she was too angry and upset to acknowledge it. 'Don't call me a child!' she shrieked furiously.

'Then stop acting as if you were seven years old.' Lysander folded his arms and surveyed her calmly. 'Otherwise, I suggest we terminate this expedition. Mrs Finch has problems enough, I imagine, without having to deal with your tantrums.'

Stung by this accusation, Tamsin blenched. So he wanted to ruin her plan to help the Finch family just because she wouldn't do as he ordered! 'You are nothing but an arrogant bully, sir!'

'If I were a bully,' Lysander retorted, wrath darkening his green eyes at the insult, 'I should turn you over my knee and spank you as you so richly deserve!'

Chapter Five

'May I tempt you to some of this salmon, my lord?' Jane Godolphin smiled at her guest.

'I fear my appetite is unequal to the lavishness of your hospitality,' Lysander declined.

'Perhaps another glass of hock, sir?' Mr Fielding encouraged, directing a slightly anxious sideways glance at his niece.

Lysander forced a smile and allowed the older man to refill his glass. 'Thank you. It is an excellent wine.'

Mr Fielding beamed at the compliment. 'I received a supply of it from my merchant yesterday. You are very welcome to take a cask home with you.'

'You are too kind.' Lysander deftly avoided a more direct reply.

Mr Fielding raised his glass. 'To friendship.'

They all joined in the toast and Jane signalled her steward to remove the mostly untouched dishes of the second course. Nuts, fruits and comfits were brought and fresh wine.

'Shall I withdraw?' Jane enquired with a coy smile that sat oddly upon her strong features.

'No need to be so formal, my dear. Eh, my lord?' Mr Fielding answered with a promptitude that made Lysander think the pair of them had planned the exchange.

'Please stay, ma'am.' Lysander was aware that he was being cynical.

He stirred restlessly in his comfortable chair. Admit it, man, you've been in an irritable mood for the last forty-eight hours!

It annoyed him to concede the fact, but he regretted the quarrel with his little waif. Despite his best intentions, he could not entirely dismiss it from his mind. In the two hours he had sat at this well-polished table, Tamsin's piquant little face had floated through his mind on several occasions, blotting out his hostess's richly clad figure.

Jane had chosen to wear a low-cut gown of vivid red taffeta and a necklace of rubies and pearls blazed around her white throat. Her dark brown hair had been arranged in fashionable ringlets on either side of her head and a star-shaped patch accentuated her grey eyes.

Her uncle had also rigged himself out finely in a handsome coat heavily laced in silver and they had both been extremely attentive ever since Lysander had stepped over the threshold of the smart house they were leasing in Lady Court.

They had plied him with the finest food and drink, but it had been an effort to respond with the correct pleasantries.

'I shall take a glass of Florence wine with you,' Jane announced.

'Allow me.' Determined to shake off his stupidity, Lysander roused himself from his introspection to pour the rich sweet wine for her.

'Thank you, my lord.' Jane fluttered her eyelashes at him.

They sipped their wine and Jane asked Lysander if he had attended the touching for the King's Evil on the previous day at Whitehall. 'Lady Crewe invited us to join her party. Her young nephew is afflicted and she thought we might be interested in the ceremony.'

'Nay, ma'am, I spent the day with my cousin, Jack Fanshawe. He wanted to buy a horse and I promised to give him my opinion.'

'Ah, that explains why we did not see you.' Jane laughed

prettily. 'There were so very many people present I thought we might have simply missed each other.'

'Aye, I heard it said that more than six hundred souls wanted the King's blessing,' Mr Fielding chimed in. 'It was a very impressive service with prayers offered for the sufferers who were each given a golden touchpiece to hang around their necks.'

Lysander, who had no faith in the notion that scrofula could be cured by the royal touch, smiled politely. 'The King believes it is his duty to help his subjects.'

Jane cocked her dark head on one side in a thoughtful pose. 'Do you think his Majesty's sense of responsibility will extend to restoring property which was stolen from his loyal subjects by Parliament?' she asked coolly.

Lysander set his glass down. 'It is difficult to know how the King can satisfy everyone,' he replied smoothly.

'And yet surely there are many Royalists who expect to be rewarded with the return of their lands?' Jane persisted, disregarding her uncle's embarrassed expression.

Lysander wondered what she was leading up to. Her manner had lost its usual veneer of feminine charm.

'Many people were forced to sell their homes to pay the fines imposed by Parliament,' he agreed. 'However, given that some of those properties have changed hands several times since the war, resolution of the problem cannot be simple. No matter how much he would like to, Charles cannot afford to reimburse everyone who suffered for the Stuart cause. There are bound to be losers.'

'You display great stoicism, Sir Lysander,' Jane's bold smile lost none of its determination. 'Or perhaps you have advance knowledge of the solution the King will decide upon?'

'Melcombe Manor was confiscated by Parliament,' Lysander answered, suddenly understanding her purpose. 'In the end I believe that all such properties will be restored to their rightful owners, but I have his Majesty's personal promise that Melcombe will be mine again before the summer is out.'

Jane's smile assumed the contentment of a cat who had got at the cream. 'Thank you for satisfying my curiosity, my lord.'

'I am happy to have been able to oblige you, ma'am.' Lysander hid his amusement.

She could not have made it plainer that she would reject any alliance which would not add to her consequence. Clearly, no matter how much she liked him—and she had made it obvious that she did—she wanted the solid backing of a good estate behind the title her money purchased.

As he had suspected earlier, there was more to Jane Godolphin than first met the eye. She might appear to be a flibbertigibbet, hellbent on pleasure, but, unless he was mistaken, she had a practical mind and firm ideas about what she wanted from life.

'Shall we retire to the withdrawing-room, gentlemen?' Jane rose gracefully to her feet. 'I thought we might have a little music, unless you object to such a pastime on the Sabbath, my lord?'

'Not in the least.' Lysander stood.

'We have several song-books in the house and a pair of virginals, a bass viol and a flageolet.' There was a hint of pride in Jane's voice as she listed this impressive choice of music-making. 'I enjoy singing, but I am more proficient on the virginals.'

'Nay, my dear, you have a great talent for both,' her uncle protested.

Blushing prettily, Jane quickly turned to Lysander. 'Do you play an instrument, my lord?'

'The lute for preference, but I can play the flageolet.' Lysander had attained some competence with this whistle-flute when he was in France. 'Though I must warn you my skill is somewhat rusty.'

'Then, if you prefer, you may turn my music for me.' Jane gave him a caressing smile.

'I should be delighted to do so.'

He met her seductive gaze steadily, his own eyes cool and faintly amused.

Now she was sure of his prospects, it appeared that the lady wanted to encourage his wooing!

Tamsin stretched her arms and yawned. It was gone ten and she was tired. She would be glad to see her bed, but she still had a few tasks to perform.

She bent over the small cooking-pot which she had hung over the kitchen fire to check its contents once more.

'Shall I take that caudle in to Master Cooper for you, Mistress Barton?' piped up an eager voice at her elbow.

'I thought I told you to get off to bed, Dinah.' Tamsin turned round to behold the newcomer, a smile softening her scolding tone.

Dinah Finch bobbed an awkward curtsy. 'Beg pardon, mistress. Only I didn't like to leave you to finish up on your own.'

'Thank you, but I can manage. Besides, you will need to be up betimes in the morning. We have the marketing to do and Master Cooper tells me that it pays to get there early.'

'The first two hours are reserved for housewives before the street traders are allowed to buy,' Dinah confirmed. 'You have to be quick to get the best stuff.'

Tamsin had already learnt that all of London's markets were owned by the City authorities who enforced strict regulations. Only perishable items were sold and produce was segregated so that each market specialised in one type of food.

'I swear I will be up early,' Dinah added earnestly.

Tamsin hid a smile. 'I'm sure you will. You are as good a worker as your mother promised.'

It was only two days since Dinah and her brother Luke had arrived, but Tamsin was already wondering how she had managed without them. At twelve Dinah was as almost as tall as she was herself and, although underfed, her wiry frame was strong and tireless.

Luke, a year younger than his sister, possessed the same lanky body and fair colouring. Tamsin had insisted on both of them taking a bath when they had arrived and to her surprise, once the ingrained dirt was washed out, their hair proved to be corn-yellow. Luke's eyes were a paler blue than Dinah's and his expression was more mischievous, but he was equally eager to prove to his new employer that he was worth keeping on after their trial period ended.

'I shall engage them both for a month,' Sir Lysander had said to their mother. 'Here is ten shillings on it and after that we shall see.'

Mrs Finch, who was desperately anxious that her two eldest should have a chance to better themselves, had nearly wept with joy. In a few minutes best garments were donned, last kisses exchanged and the excited pair were waved off with fervent instructions to behave themselves.

Tamsin could readily understand Mrs Finch's desire to give her children a better life. She had been shocked by the filth and squalor of the narrow alley off Long Acre in which they lived with their parents and seven siblings. There was poverty a-plenty in Chipping Sodbury, but this was much worse than anything she had seen before.

Although only a stone's throw from more respectable areas, Long Acre had gone down in the world since the reign of the last King and brothels, coachmakers and decaying houses abounded in its wide street. The alleyways running off it were worse, full of wretched hovels and tumbledown taverns.

Greasy-haired women clad in tattered gowns stood in the open doorways of some of these dwellings. They turned to stare at Tamsin and her tall companion, muttering to one another. Cackles of laughter from a pair of heavily painted girls who, clad in tawdry finery, lounged on one doorstep taking swigs from a squat black bottle reinforced Tamsin's uncomfortable feeling that her appearance was being discussed in unflattering terms.

Half-naked urchins tumbled in the dust where lean cats

prowled sniffing the heaps of rubbish. There were few men about, apart from one group loitering halfway along the alley. Badly dressed and blue-jowled, their hard eyes followed Tamsin, making her shiver involuntarily.

'Don't fret. They won't bother us.' Lysander's hand touched his sword significantly.

Tamsin gulped and nodded, reassured by the confidence in his voice.

She was still angry with him, but honesty compelled her to admit that she was glad of his company. She wouldn't have felt half so safe under Nat's protection.

Lysander asked an urchin to point out where Mrs Finch lived. He tossed the child a halfpenny and knocked upon the door indicated, which was answered by the same young boy who had brought the message about his mother's illness to Wych Street. Recognising Tamsin, he ushered them inside.

'We lives upstairs,' he announced, leading the way.

The hallway stank and Tamsin was glad to get out of it. She was aware, stepping inside the Finches' two-room apartment, that the air was cleaner and she noted that some attempt had been made to sweep and tidy the main room, but it was dingy and depressingly bare. A rickety-looking table and a few stools were all the comforts on offer.

Their guide's younger siblings stared in silent awe at the visitors until he herded them into the back room. A few moments later Mrs Finch, a faded blonde in her early thirties, emerged.

Timidly, she welcomed her unexpected guests and Tamsin explained their errand. A husband who drank most of his wages as a porter and a baby a year had extinguished her looks, but her weary face had lit up when she had grasped Sir Lysander's generous offer.

'They knows how to behave and they'll work hard for you, sir,' she had promised.

'Will your mother be all right now that you are working here?' Tamsin asked Dinah, remembering the glint of tears shining in Mrs Finch's eyes as she had waved goodbye.

'Don't be anxious on Mam's account, Mistress Barton,' Dinah reassured her. 'We have a good neighbour next door and Audrey, she's the next eldest, knows what to do.'

Carrying the cooking-pot over to the kitchen table, Tamsin reflected that twelve was the normal age for girls to go into service and Dinah had already been working three days a week in the kitchen of a nearby cookshop to supplement the family's income. Mrs Finch must have got used to relying on ten-year-old Audrey to look after the little ones when necessary.

'You can go and visit her whenever I can spare you,' she promised, carefully tipping the caudle, a thin gruel made with wine which was said to aid sleep, into a bowl. 'Now, since you are here, you can fetch me a spoon from that drawer.'

Dinah scurried to obey. Tamsin thanked her and put both items on a wooden tray. She picked it up. 'When I get back I don't want to see you still here.'

A grin split Dinah's face and she nodded happily.

'Come in,' Master Cooper called in response to Tamsin's knock at the door of his chamber.

He had not gone to bed, but had changed into a loose dressing-gown and was sitting in a chair by the window.

'Are you feeling any better, sir?'

'My headache is improved.' Matthew Cooper shrugged. 'I wish I could say the same of my wrist.'

Today he had risen from his bed and attempted his usual routine, but by evening he had been feeling wretched and had retired early.

'I thought you might like this,' Tamsin said, setting down her tray by his elbow. 'You barely ate anything at supper and it's hard to get to sleep on an empty stomach.'

'Thank you, Mistress Barton.' Matthew's stern expression softened.

Wary at first of the waif his master had brought home, Matthew had been impressed by her capacity for hard work. Her efficiency was matched by her unfailing cheerfulness. No matter how difficult or disagreeable the task, she always had a sunny smile.

He had also noticed her kindness to the two youngsters now employed in the house. She never shouted at their mistakes, but encouraged them to do better.

'You know, you are a very unusual Puritan, mistress,' he remarked, leaning forward to pick up the bowl of caudle.

Tamsin blushed. 'I went to church twice today,' she murmured defensively.

It wasn't what Matthew had meant, but she was looking so uncomfortable he decided to drop the subject and spoke instead of the provisions she must be sure to buy in the morning on her trip to the white and herb markets in Newgate Street, which sold poultry and garden produce.

By the time this discussion was over Matthew had finished the caudle, so Tamsin bade him goodnight and carried the tray back into the kitchen.

Drawing a bucketful of water from the well she heated it and washed the last remaining pots. This task finished, she damped down the fire and carefully covered it.

She glanced around the kitchen to confirm that everything was tidy and then checked the hearth a second time, a habit acquired from her aunt. Some years ago there had been a destructive blaze in the parlour at Whiteladies caused by a loose spark flying from the unguarded grate. Afterwards, Aunt Deborah had forcibly instilled caution in the whole household, administering beatings to anyone who showed any sign of carelessness in dealing with candles or fire.

Removing her apron, Tamsin hung it up on its hook by the door and shook out her creased skirts.

'Oh, no!' she exclaimed, spotting a tear near the hem.

She was too tired to sew it now, but she would have to mend it first thing tomorrow. She had spilt something on her sleeve too. Somehow she would also have to find time to sponge it clean. Fresh clothes had been delivered last night from the tailor for Dinah and Luke. They had been thrilled to receive new outfits and worn them proudly all day. She could not set them a bad example by appearing in a stained and torn gown.

'You wouldn't be in the suds if you'd had the sense to accept his offer!' Tamsin muttered to herself with a twinge of exasperation.

It was very irritating to have to admit it, but Tamsin knew she had let temper get the better of her the other day. She had always longed to wear brighter colours and it was only obstinate pride which had led her to refuse a new gown.

She sighed. 'Your feelings were hurt because he called you *a skinny little crow!*'

She ought to confess that she had changed her mind. Unfortunately, the words had stuck in her throat whenever she had tried. Not that she'd had much opportunity to retract her hasty assertion.

If she didn't know better, she would almost think he had been avoiding her!

The banging of the front door roused her abruptly from her gloom. With a start of surprise, she realised that her employer had returned home from the reception at Whitehall.

Indecision held her paralysed for an instant before she made up her mind. Here was her chance to apologise!

'I thought you would be in bed.' Lysander greeted her as she emerged into the hallway.

'I was about to retire, sir.' Her confidence evaporating, Tamsin stared at the tips of her boots.

Lysander nodded. 'I suppose I am back early,' he replied, throwing the bolt which secured the front door.

Tamsin had been attending morning service at St Bride's church with Dinah and Luke when her benefactor had left the house and so had not seen him dressed in his finery for Whitehall. Now she drank in his elegant appearance with eager eyes.

He was wearing a suit in black velvet laced with silver on the deep turn-back cuffs. Its sombre hue enhanced his fair colouring, bringing out golden glints in his dark blond hair and he looked so handsome that Tamsin's stomach somersaulted giddily.

Lysander eyed her warily. Since they had quarrelled they had exchanged words only when necessary, but something in her stance warned him that she nerving herself to speak to him.

'Will you join me in my closet before retiring?' he asked a little awkwardly. 'There's something I wish to say to you.'

The unexpected invitation made Tamsin looked up sharply. Was he still angry with her? Perhaps he intended to throw her out?

'I will only keep you a few moments. I know you must be tired.'

Hearing the sudden warmth in his tone, Tamsin felt a quick rush of hope flood through her veins. 'Very well, my lord.'

Two candles set in brass sticks stood on the hall table, the last of the row which Tamsin had set out earlier to light the household to their beds. Lysander lit them from the branch of candles affixed to the wall, which illuminated the hallway, and handed one to Tamsin. 'Is everything secured for the night?'

'Yes, sir.'

'Then come.' Snuffing out the hall candles, Lysander took the other candlestick and led the way upstairs.

His closet was situated next to the dining-room, a small, private retreat where a comfortable air of disorder reigned. Tamsin had not dared to disturb the riding whip and spurs left lying on a chair or the collection of books and journals littering many surfaces, contenting herself instead with a quick sweep of broom and duster.

'Sit down.' Lysander waved her to a chair and, setting down his candle, strode over to a small oak dresser on which resided an assortment of bottles and tankards.

He poured himself a bumper of brandy and, turning to Tamsin, said politely, 'Will you take a glass of something?'

He'd expected her to refuse, but to his surprise she nodded.

'I should like to try a little wine, if I may, sir,' Tamsin

declared, hoping it would give her courage. Sam had imbibed some hippocras before telling Aunt Deborah that he wanted to become a sailor last year. His mother had refused, of course, but according to Sam the strong spicy wine had helped him to face her wrath!

Lysander poured out a tiny measure of Bristol milk and handed it to her with the advice to sip it slowly.

The sherry sat strangely upon Tamsin's tongue. She hadn't expected it to taste so sweet or to ignite such a glow of warmth as it descended to her stomach!

'Well?' Lysander, who had taken a seat opposite hers, regarded her with a glint of amusement in his green eyes. 'Is the Devil going to snatch you up and fly off with you, do you think?'

Tamsin shook her head cautiously. 'I don't believe so, my lord.' She took another sip and rolled the sherry round in her mouth. 'In fact, I don't see what all the fuss is about. It tastes harmless enough.'

Lysander grinned. 'Drink too much and you'll soon learn that the reverse is true, kitling.'

Tamsin was startled by his use of this term. 'Why do you call me that, sir?' she asked shyly.

'Because you remind me of a kitten,' he answered promptly. 'You have the same expression of wide-eyed curiosity.'

Tamsin coloured. She wasn't precisely sure, but that remark sounded suspiciously like a compliment!

Realising he had inadvertently discomfited her, Lysander pretended an interest in his brandy to allow her time to recover her composure.

When her complexion had returned to normal he said casually, 'How are Dinah and Luke getting along? Are you satisfied with their work?'

Tamsin nodded and, forgetting her unease, launched into an enthusiastic description of her protégés' capacity for hard work.

'I'm glad you find them useful. You were doing too much

before they came.' Lysander paused, the words of the apology he had planned drying up in his throat. God's teeth, but when she looked at him like that with stars glowing in her lovely eyes it was hard to think of anything but an urgent need to kiss her smiling mouth!

'Was that what you wanted to talk to me about, sir?' Tamsin enquired, puzzled by his continuing silence.

Lysander, busy telling himself that he was a fool, nodded in a distracted fashion.

A rush of relief extinguished Tamsin's anxiety. What a noddle she was to have been worried! He wasn't angry with her. In fact, if truth were told, he was treating her with more consideration than she merited.

Tamsin set down her empty glass. With the sherry warming her innards, she felt a surge of bravery revive her earlier decision to beg his pardon. 'About the other day, my lord,' she said, her voice trembling slightly. 'I should not have rejected your offer in such an ill-mannered fashion.'

A faint smile touched Lysander's mouth. 'Is this an apology, Mistress Barton?'

Tamsin nodded earnestly. 'My behaviour was very rude. I must have sounded like a fishwife,' she murmured, her hands twisting together.

'Nay, you had every right. I deserved it.'

Lysander's smile deepened at her open-mouthed astonishment. 'I asked you here tonight so that *I* could apologise. It was unfair of me to try and ride rough-shod over your objections. You are not a servant, I have no right to dictate how you dress.'

'Ah, but you do, my lord. I am living in your house and my appearance reflects upon you,' Tamsin pointed out, her mouth curling into a sudden grin.

Lysander laughed. 'Minx! Do you think me such a coxcomb?'

'Nay, sir!' Her teasing smile fading, Tamsin leaned forward in her anxiety to reassure him. 'You were right. I do need more clothes, but I was too proud to admit it.' Her hands

fluttered in her lap. 'I shouted at you because I was angry
with myself for succumbing to the sin of envy.'

'You wanted to wear bright silks and satins like the other
women at the Exchange?' Lysander grasped her meaning instantly.

Her cheeks reddening, Tamsin nodded.

'No matter what your aunt may have told you, at your age
it's perfectly natural to desire finery and gewgaws,' Lysander
said firmly.

'Do you really think so?'

'Of course.' He gave her an encouraging smile. 'Tomorrow
I shall take you to buy some material for a new gown. There
are several excellent drapers in Paternoster Row. You can
choose whatever you like.'

Seeing the hesitation lingering in her eyes, he continued
lightly, 'The wearing of a pretty gown is no more wicked in
itself, you know, than eating rich food or listening to fine
music. Enjoying yourself doesn't automatically preclude
good morals.'

'I'm sure Aunt Deborah thinks enjoyment is a sin.' A wistful expression flickered across Tamsin's face. 'Even at Christmas she would not permit any carols or games.'

'Then we must ensure you have a chance to celebrate properly this year.' Lysander kept his tone calm and easy, but a
furious desire to strangle the old witch possessed him. The
woman was nothing but a killjoy!

Tamsin's heart skipped a beat. Christmas was many
months away. Was she to be allowed to remain?

As usual, her expressive face betrayed her hopeful thoughts
and Lysander inwardly cursed his carelessness. He had no
business encouraging her to want to stay.

Her presence was rapidly becoming a danger to his peace
of mind!

The following morning Lysander's coach bore them
swiftly towards the city. Passing over the bridge which
spanned the River Fleet, Tamsin discreetly held her nose

against the stench arising from the water, which was foul with rubbish.

At the Ludgate they passed through the walls and their progress was immediately impeded by the heavy traffic which bedevilled London's ancient heart. Tamsin marvelled at Nat's skill as he wove through the tangle of carts, carriages and pedestrians. A flock of geese being driven to market merely added to the confusion and noise.

Paternoster Row, in comparison, was a haven of quiet, its broad thoroughfare lined with handsome buildings. Dinah had told Tamsin that it was famous for its mercers, who sold fine silks and lace. To her relief, Lysander led her into a shop which also sold more modest materials.

Bolts of cloth of every kind lined the shelves and, after listening to her requirements, the master draper, who had come hurrying to serve them himself as soon as he had espied Lysander, lifted down a roll of deep-green say.

'This would suit your colouring, ma'am,' he suggested.

Tamsin was about to protest that such a fine woollen cloth would be too expensive when Lysander said briskly, 'We'll take it.'

'I thought you said I could choose,' she whispered fiercely.

'Don't you like it?'

'That's not the point!' Really, he could be so high-handed sometimes!

Her gaze raked the shelves. 'That dark blue linsey-wolsey would be more suitable.'

'As you wish.' Lysander paused and added wickedly, 'Providing we buy the green as well.'

Tamsin gasped and he grinned at her. 'You really need them both.'

'I can't accept *two* gowns!' she protested.

'I thought you wanted your appearance to be a credit to me?' Lysander smiled at her teasingly.

Tamsin's resistance melted.

Lysander arranged that the draper should convey their pur-

chases to Wych Street later that day and swept Tamsin out
of the shop.

'Are we in a hurry?' Tamsin was surprised by his impatient
refusal to wait for the material to be measured and parcelled
so that they could take it with them.

'I told my shoemaker to visit us this morning.'

She looked at him blankly.

'You need new shoes.' Lysander's tone brooked no argument. 'But, first, I thought to call in on Joseph Moxon.'

Tamsin had never heard of the scientific instrument maker
favoured by the King, so Lysander explained how he had
ordered a pair of terrestrial and celestial hemispheres. 'Moxon
said that they might be ready today.'

Tamsin was of the opinion it would have been quicker to
walk to Cornhill where Moxon had his premises, especially
when an overturned waggon of hay blocked their route, de-
laying them for several minutes while the spilt load was
cleared. However, when they finally arrived at the instrument
maker's, she quickly forgot this minor inconvenience.

'These are wonderful,' she exclaimed, gazing in delight at
the globes which Mr Moxon brought out for his client.
Painted by his own hand, the hemispheres were works of art,
one depicting the Earth in cunning detail, the other the stars
and planets. 'I have never seen their like before. How do they
work?'

Lysander, who had not expected her to exhibit such an
interest in geography, showed her how to find England.

While the globes were being carefully packed up they examined the maps and charts the instrument maker had on
display. Tamsin was fascinated by a beautifully coloured map
of Africa which had a decorative border of wild beasts.

'Very handsome.' Lysander leant over her shoulder to
view what had caught her attention.

Tamsin was suddenly very aware of his nearness. She
could smell the hint of lavender which permeated his linen
and a lock of his dark blond hair had fallen forward to tickle
her cheek.

'You have excellent taste, Mistress Barton. This must have taken many hours of labour.'

'I suppose it is very expensive,' Tamsin blurted to distract herself.

He nodded. 'Too much for my purse,' he admitted and, to the relief of her strained nerves, straightened.

Her heart still thumping, she watched him hand over payment for the globes.

Three pounds and ten shillings. Aunt Deborah would have a fit of the mother to hear of spending so much money on a mere plaything.

The notion of her aunt in hysterics made her think guiltily of Sam. She must keep her promise to write to him!

The globes were taken out to the coach by Moxon's assistant and Lysander said their farewells while Tamsin lingered, apparently still engrossed in the maps, but desperately trying to invent a good reason to remain behind.

'We can come another day if you wish.' He touched Tamsin gently on the elbow to indicate it was time to go.

She couldn't think of an excuse to visit Martha. She was not supposed to know anyone in the city!

Reluctance to re-enter the coach made Tamsin's footsteps slow.

'Is something wrong?'

Tamsin turned to smile at him quickly. 'Not in the least, sir.'

She must take more care to hide her secrets! He was too perceptive!

Tamsin's desire to visit Martha grew stronger as the days passed. Master Cooper's wrist still limited what he could achieve, but as he continued to improve and Dinah and Luke grew more competent the pressure on her eased.

With more time to think, Tamsin's anxieties thrived. She had been in London for almost three weeks and was no nearer finding out anything about her father than she had been on the day she had left Whiteladies.

It was so frustrating!

Her opportunity came one morning when Lysander announced he was to dine with Mrs Godolphin and escort her to a play afterwards. 'And I am promised to my cousins, Lord Fanshawe and his sister, for supper.'

Tamsin had met Jack Fanshawe the previous week. Returning home with Lysander one evening after a visit to a cock-fight, he had greeted his cousin's new protégée with a whistle of surprise. 'God save us and who might you be, sweeting?' He eyed her with cheerful impudence. 'Damme, but you are far too pretty to be wasting your time on m'cousin. Can't I persuade you to favour me instead?'

Tamsin, who had been wearing her new green gown, had been at first startled and then secretly delighted to be paid compliments by this good-looking young man.

'Jack, mind your manners,' Lysander had said repressively.

'Soul of discretion,' Jack replied with a broad wink.

Lysander glared at him. 'You, *mon ami,* are a rattlepate, but heed me well. I'll carve out your entrails and feed them to the nearest hound if you go spreading false gossip about Mistress Barton.' He flicked a warning glance at Tamsin. 'She is a niece of Matthew's, honouring us with a visit.'

'Didn't know Matt had any nieces,' Jack declared suspiciously.

'I am his younger sister's daughter, sir,' Tamsin said, entering into the spirit. 'My mother suggested I act as Sir Lysander's housekeeper while Uncle Matthew was laid low.'

'Why not ask Matt yourself since you are so interested?' Lysander suggested with smooth sarcasm. 'I'm sure he would be happy to give you chapter and verse concerning the ramifications of his family tree.'

Jack sniffed. 'Wouldn't tattle your business in any case, coz,' he muttered, his cherubic features creasing in a reproachful way that made Tamsin want to giggle.

Lysander ignored this remark and strode towards the stairs. 'Let's discuss our plans for tomorrow in my closet. I'll open a bottle and you can tell me who you are backing to win the race.'

Jack nodded, but turned back to Tamsin, his expression brightening as he made her an extravagant bow. 'Delighted to make your acquaintance, Mrs Barton.' His admiring glance swept over her. 'Your presence will cheer this place up and no mistake!'

Jubilant to be addressed as Mrs Barton instead of Miss, a title which was reserved for immature girls, Tamsin had been quite disappointed when Lysander had grumpily hauled his cousin off with a curt admonition not to make an even bigger looby of himself.

However, it was not Sir Lysander's mention of the irrepressible Lord Fanshawe which now caught Tamsin's attention, but his casual allusion to attending the theatre.

'You are going to see a *play!*' she exclaimed.

Her shocked tone reminded Lysander of her Puritan origins, a fact he was finding increasingly easy to forget, especially since she had taken to occasionally leaving off her severe coif and forbidding black.

This morning she was bare-headed, her apricot-gold hair plaited into a thick braid, which she wore twisted up into a bun on the nape of her neck. The gown she had created from the bolt of blue linsey-wolsey was demure, but she looked enticingly pretty in it.

Realising his thoughts were wandering dangerously, Lysander called himself to order and said briskly, 'Have you ever been inside a theatre?'

'Of course not! They are home to the Devil.'

Lysander smiled. 'You sound like your aunt.'

Tamsin flushed to the roots of her hair. 'I'm...I'm sorry,' she muttered. 'I don't mean to appear priggish, but I can't believe you intend to take Mistress Godolphin to a playhouse.'

'You think it an unsuitable entertainment for respectable women?'

Tamsin nodded vigorously.

'It is true that some plays are marred by crudity,' Lysander admitted. 'However, even the poorest often have a redeeming sparkle of wit. The best of them can make you cry with laughter…or weep at the human tragedy unfolding before you.'

Her eyes widened in surprise and he shrugged as if a little ashamed of having dropped his guard for once to reveal his real feelings.

'Then you do not think it corrupts?'

'No more than any other form of story-telling. Why should any sensible person imitate what they see on stage? Surely it is possible to distinguish the difference between a tale told to entertain and real life?'

'I suppose so.' Tamsin smoothed down her apron nervously as another objection occurred to her. 'My aunt says all actors are rogues.'

'Like Cavaliers?' Amusement lurked in Lysander's deep tones. 'Perhaps, but in my experience actors are no different to other people. Some bad, some good, a few lazy.' He shook his head. 'There may be devils among them, but not, I think, on account of their calling.'

He met her perplexed gaze. 'Would you like to see for yourself?'

'*Me?* Attend a play with you?'

'Why not? If you are willing to set aside your prejudices I think you might enjoy the experience.'

Tamsin gulped hard. 'I thank you for the invitation, sir,' she replied shyly, dipping a polite curtsy. 'But I do not think that it would be appropriate for me to accompany you to the theatre. I do not want people speculating about my position in your household and coming up with the wrong answer.'

Lysander was aware of a prick of disappointment. She was right. The Court was extremely fond of play-going and he was too well known for his companion to escape notice. There would be gossip.

Gentlemen did not take their housekeepers to the theatre. Gentlemen did not favour their housekeepers at all, unless, of course, they happened to serve in another, less respectable position.

'Very wise of you, Mistress Barton,' he had murmured and properly changed the subject, instructing her not to wait up for his return.

The part of Tamsin which had always rebelled against her aunt's strictures bitterly regretted having to turn him down. She watched him leave the house with a heavy heart, longing to call him back and rescind her decision, but knowing she could not.

However, when her unruly emotions had settled, she realised that his long absence would give her the perfect opportunity to slip away unnoticed.

'Of course you may have leave to explore the shops, Mrs Barton,' Master Cooper declared. 'As you know, I am to dine at the house of a friend today so you need not worry about cooking dinner.' He smiled at her, pleased to endorse her request.

'Enjoy yourself, but make sure you watch your purse. Speaking of which—' Matthew moved to open the household's strongbox and selected several coins '—Sir Lysander authorised me to give you some money should you express a desire for an outing.'

'I cannot take it, sir,' Tamsin protested, horribly aware of how much she already owed her benefactor.

'You must, my dear, or he will be angry with us both.' Matthew pressed the coins into her unwilling hand. 'Besides, you have earned them twice over these last few weeks.' He nodded at her with formal gravity. 'Indeed, I thank you for your excellent care of me. I doubt if I would have recovered so quickly without your help.'

Unable to explain her reluctance since he did not know the precise circumstances in which his employer had found her, Tamsin accepted the gift with a polite murmur of thanks.

'Now remember, take Luke with you and don't talk to chance-met strangers.'

Guilty at having had to deceive him about the purpose of

her outing, Tamsin promised to heed his advice and return in plenty of time to prepare supper.

She went up to her room to wash her face and tidy her hair. Resisting the temptation to impress Martha, she changed into her old black gown.

'This gown is more inconspicuous if you remove the collar,' she muttered to herself, whisking off the broad linen neckband which was the only trimming her aunt had ever permitted.

A white hood such as the one Dinah wore, instead of her Puritan coif, a clean apron and she looked like every other servant. No one would take any notice of her.

'Would you like to visit your mother?' she asked Dinah and Luke on her return to the kitchen.

This offer was eagerly accepted and, after packing a generous basket of tasty leftovers for Mrs Finch, they set off.

'I have an errand to perform in the city.' At the end of the street Tamsin halted. 'I shall meet you at your mother's later.'

'You ain't thinking of going shopping on yer own!' Luke exclaimed.

'I shall be perfectly all right. I know my way.' Tamsin had discreetly questioned Nat some time ago and discovered how best to get to Bread Street.

Dinah and Luke exchanged doubtful glances. 'You did ought to take Luke with you, Mrs Barton,' Dinah said.

'Nonsense,' Tamsin replied briskly, but a flicker of doubt assailed her.

'I won't get in yer way,' Luke promised, seeing her hesitation. 'I can wait for you someplace if you wants, but Sir Lysander will have m'guts for garters if you goes off alone into the city and any harm comes to you. Told me special that I had to watch out for you, see.'

Tamsin sighed. 'Oh, very well.'

They parted from Dinah with a promise to meet her later and headed east towards the city.

The day was overcast and dull. Tamsin thought it might rain so she had donned her stout boots instead of her new shoes to protect herself from the muck of the road. Luckily, it was only a short journey, barely a mile, and Luke's chatter helped distract the nervous apprehension churning in her stomach.

'That's St Paul's,' he pointed out the city's principal place of worship with pride.

Tamsin nodded, reluctant to spoil his moment by mentioning that Sir Lysander had showed her the cathedral on the day they had visited Paternoster Row.

They had walked around the outside of the old church and she had been surprised and a little saddened by its shabby state.

'It lost its spire when it was damaged by lightning almost a hundred years ago,' Lysander had explained. 'Some rebuilding was carried out by Inigo Jones, but then it suffered insult under Cromwell, who allowed it to be used as a cavalry barracks.'

Tamsin had winced.

'You are not to blame for the past or for the actions of other Puritans,' Lysander said firmly.

To his surprise he found he meant the words he'd offered merely for comfort. She might be of Puritan stock, but she wasn't like the majority of his former enemies. She had a joyousness of spirit far removed from their narrow-minded bigotry.

'The King has plans for restoring St Paul's to its former glory,' Lysander had continued hastily, determined not to let his mind dwell on his waif's attractions. 'He intends to set up a commission when he can find the time to do so.'

This information had pleased Tamsin, but she had no time to think about architecture today. What was she going to do with Luke? She couldn't talk freely to Martha hampered by his presence.

'There's the Cordwainers' Hall.'

Distracted by the worry that Martha might have moved house since Sam and Uncle Daniel had visited her four years ago, Tamsin stared at Luke blankly.

'You know, the shoemakers' guild hall,' Luke explained self-importantly. 'Bread Street is just beyond.'

St Mildred's church came in sight and Tamsin was still wondering how best to get rid of her young escort when she spotted a cookshop.

'Here, take this sixpence and go and buy yourself some dinner, Luke.' She handed him the coin.

Luke's eyes lit up. It was almost noon and, as usual, his stomach was flapping against his ribs, but as he took the money he hesitated. 'What about you? Ain't you hungry?'

Mendaciously, Tamsin shook her head. 'I want to look round the church,' she improvised. 'Off you go. I will meet you outside that shoemaker's shop over there when you are done.'

Luke scratched his head, plainly puzzled by her behaviour. 'You won't go sloping off without me, will you?'

Tamsin promised to wait. 'And take your time, Luke. I want to be on my own for a bit.'

Nodding his corn-coloured head, he skipped off down the street, eagerly following the savoury smells wafting from the cookshop.

As soon as he was out of sight Tamsin hurried over to the shoemaker's. Entering the dim cavern of the shop, she blinked to adjust her eyes and beheld a plump, brown-haired woman neatly dressed in grey standing behind the counter polishing a pair of handsome boots.

'Martha!'

The woman stared at her for a moment and then recognition flared in her dark eyes.

'Lord-have-mercy! Miss Tamsin! What are you doing here?'

Chapter Six

To the astonishment of her husband's apprentice, Martha Croft rushed forward to clasp the plainly dressed newcomer to her ample bosom.

'Let me look at you! It's been all of six years since I've seen you! My, how you have grown!' she exclaimed, at last releasing Tamsin to dab the corners of her overflowing eyes with the edge of her apron.

'Not by so very much!' Tamsin grinned.

Martha laughed, her tears vanishing. 'Get away with you! You have turned into a pretty young lady, just as I always knew you would.'

She conducted Tamsin to the back of the shop where a door led into the family's dwelling quarters.

'Rob, you mind the shop,' she called over her shoulder to the young lad, who was staring after the pair of them in a bemused fashion. 'I am not to be disturbed. Call your mother or my husband if there is any problem.'

'Aye, Mrs Croft,' he replied obediently.

The note of respect in his voice made Tamsin smile. It seemed Martha had not lost her knack of inspiring the best from her charges. That she managed to do so without ever raising her voice was a tribute to her kind and capable nature.

'I missed you when you left Whiteladies,' she said as they entered a small cosy parlour.

'I missed you too, my lamb.' Martha gave her a fond smile.

Master Barton's sister had been frail. When she had parted from her husband and returned home with her baby daughter to live with her elderly mother and brother, he had hired fifteen-year-old Martha to look after the child. Martha, who loved babies, had ignored the gossip about Mrs Penhaligan and happily become part of the household.

Soon afterwards old Mistress Barton had died and, once the period of mourning was over, Master Daniel had wed Deborah Pym, a sour-faced spinster who was lucky to catch such a good man in Martha's opinion. Jealous of her bridegroom's fondness for his sister, the new mistress's constant complaints had made their life difficult.

Loyalty to Mrs Penhaligan kept Martha at her side, even when Mistress Deborah, who nursed grand ambitions beneath her cloak of Puritan piety, persuaded her husband to abandon his family trade of shipbuilding and buy Whiteladies, a small estate which was going cheap because its Royalist owners had been ruined by fines. Unfortunately, Master Daniel was not cut out to be a farmer.

Disappointed that the change did not bring increased fortune in its wake, Mistress Deborah practised strict economies. She insisted that Martha must take on extra duties about the farm without any increase in wages. She was so demanding that Martha had been on the point of giving notice to leave when summer plague had struck the district.

Mrs Penhaligan and Tamsin were amongst its victims. To give the mistress her due she had nursed them well, but Mrs Penhaligan had died. Martha could not bring herself to desert her five-year-old orphan. She had remained, combining her role of Tamsin's nurse with the other duties demanded of her until Ned Croft had asked her to marry him. Even then she might have delayed the wedding had not Ned been offered the chance to better himself, a chance which necessitated his immediate removal to London.

'How have you found living in the city, Martha?' Tamsin asked, as her hostess waved her to be seated. 'You only wrote that once and I have often wondered how you and Ned were getting on.'

'I'm no hand with a pen, Miss Tamsin, you know that,' Martha murmured apologetically. 'But I didn't forget you.'

'I know,' Tamsin smiled warmly at her old friend. 'Uncle Daniel gave me your message and the red shoes you sent.'

Aunt Deborah had put Martha's gift away, declaring it unsuitable. The shoes had stayed in the cupboard and Tamsin had outgrown them, but she had no intention of hurting Martha's feelings by telling her that she had never been allowed to wear her pretty gift.

'What brings you to London?' said Martha, seating herself opposite Tamsin upon an oak settle placed near the hearth. 'How did Sam manage to persuade your aunt? I never thought she would venture so far from home—' She paused abruptly. 'Mistress Deborah isn't here, is she?'

Cursing her revealing face, Tamsin shook her head. 'I came alone, Martha. I ran away.'

'Dear Lord!' Martha gave a gasp of horror. 'What did the old besom do to you?'

Tamsin explained about Master Hardy. 'It was horrible, Martha. I couldn't make Aunt Deborah listen! On the day they called the first banns in our parish church I knew the only solution was to flee Whiteladies. Sam helped me. He got in touch with Master Latham, who agreed to take me with him.'

'Old Peter the Packman? I remember him. He bore a grudge against your aunt after she accused him of trying to cheat her. Aye, and never apologised when it was proved to be her mistake.'

'I know. He told me all about it when we were on the road,' Tamsin replied.

They had waited until Deborah Barton was away for the day. She had gone over to Master Hardy's for a meeting with the lawyers who were drawing up the marriage contract and was not expected back until supper-time, which gave Tamsin a good head start. Sam was to tell her that Tamsin had gone to bed early and then deny all knowledge of his cousin's whereabouts when her absence was discovered the following morning.

'I'll warrant she smoked him for it!' Martha exclaimed.

'Sam said when things got desperate he would say that I had been talking a lot about Bristol.' Tamsin grinned. 'I hoped that she would begin her enquiries there and I think she must have done because we were not followed.'

Master Latham had pursued a rambling roundabout path to London, stopping many times in small villages along the way to pursue his trade. Tamsin, who could not remember having ever ventured beyond the confines of Chipping Sodbury, had relished their journey, although the novelty of sleeping in barns and cooking over a camp-fire had worn off by the time they had reached Chiswick.

'I would escort you into London myself, lass, but I promised my daughter I would bide a few days with her the next time I passed this way,' Master Latham had said on the morning they had parted company. 'Are you sure you will not wait? I'm certain she could find room to put you up.'

'Thank you for your concern, Master Latham, but I'm sure your daughter will want to be private with you.' Tamsin had smiled at him, grateful for all his help and kindness. 'And I am anxious to reach my destination.'

Martha's anxious sigh interrupted Tamsin's memories.

'You took a big risk in running away, my lamb. What if she had caught you? You would have been thrashed for certain!'

'There's not much chance of anyone catching me now.' Tamsin shrugged defiantly. 'Even if Sam eventually admits that I planned to come to London, this city is such an enormous maze Aunt Deborah will never find me.'

'I wouldn't reveal I had seen you if she does come looking here,' Martha reassured her. 'But I must confess your action troubles me.'

'Do you think I should have stayed?' Tamsin ejaculated in astonishment.

'Nay!' Martha shook her head firmly. 'I would not see you wed to that man. He is a brute, but…'

Her voice trailed away and Tamsin finished the sentence for her. 'You think me too young to be on my own in a hard cruel place like London.'

'Something like that.' Martha gave her a faint smile.

To allow them both a breathing space, she decided to offer refreshments to her guest, although it was almost dinner-time. 'There's some cold buttermilk in the pantry and I baked a cherry pie this morning, if you are still fond of it?'

Tamsin accepted with alacrity and Martha got up and went off to the kitchen.

While she was out of the room Tamsin took the opportunity to examine her surroundings. The parlour, which was painted a deep red, boasted several stools and chairs as well as the carved settle and an oaken dresser. A bright rug lay before the hearth and there was a pretty china vase on the mantel-shelf.

Ned's business must be prospering, she thought with a burst of satisfaction.

'Here you are.' Martha returned and, handing Tamsin the plate she carried, set a mug of buttermilk down by her stool. 'You eat and I'll tell you all about my children.'

'Oh, Martha! You always wanted babies of your own!'

For the next few minutes Martha proudly described her offspring while Tamsin sampled the cherry pie and drank her milk.

''Course the four of 'em do make it a bit of a tight squeeze, seeing as how Ned's widowed cousin and her three boys live with us too. Still, it makes sense. Ned needed an apprentice—that's Rob, the eldest—and Nelly had nowhere to go when her husband died.' Martha gave a philosophical shrug of her plump shoulders. 'She helps me with the housework and the children so I can't complain.'

Tamsin nodded, setting down her empty mug. 'I'm glad to hear that things have worked out well for you, Martha.'

Martha beamed at her. 'Aye, they have, thank the Lord!'

Her expression sobered. 'But what are we to do about you, Miss Tamsin? You are welcome to stay here, of course. It isn't what you are used to, but—'

'Oh don't worry about me, Martha,' Tamsin interrupted hastily and launched into an explanation of how she had been tricked by Mrs Cole and the consequences of her unusual introduction to Sir Lysander Saxon.

'So you see, I'm provided for,' she concluded.

'Well! I never!' Martha regarded her open-mouthed.

Tamsin began to laugh. 'Oh, Martha, you should see your face!'

'You were always a handful, Miss Tamsin. I don't know why I am surprised Mistress Deborah failed to make a good Puritan out of you.' An answering grin touched Martha's plump face. 'Housekeeper to a titled gentleman. It sounds as if you have fallen on your feet.'

'I am very happy in Wych Street,' Tamsin agreed.

'I am glad to hear it, but are you sure that this Sir Lysander is no rakehell in disguise?' Martha asked anxiously, her smile fading.

'My virtue is perfectly safe. He thinks me too young and skinny to be of any interest,' Tamsin replied drily.

'That's all right then.' Martha gave a little sigh of relief. 'A pretty young girl like you can't afford to take any chances—'

Just then the door opened and a ginger-haired man with an impatient frown on his face entered.

'Martha, what's all this I hear about you entertaining some servant girl? It's dinner-time and I want my—oh, Miss Tamsin, it's you!'

'Hello, Ned.' Tamsin rose swiftly to her feet and greeted her friend's husband with a shy smile. 'How are you keeping?'

'Very well, I thank you.' Ned Croft's cheeks vied with his fiery hair. He glanced apologetically at his wife. 'Sorry to barge in on you, m'dear. I'll leave you in peace.'

He nodded diffidently at Tamsin and withdrew in haste.

Martha muttered something under her breath and Tamsin announced that she had better take her leave.

'Take no heed of Ned,' Martha exclaimed. 'He didn't mean no harm.'

'All the same, I am holding up your dinner.'

'Stay and eat with us,' Martha urged.

'I can't. I told Luke—he's Sir Lysander's footboy who escorted me here—that I would meet him outside your shop.' Tamsin shrugged apologetically. 'I don't want him to know that I am acquainted with you.'

Martha looked puzzled and Tamsin said hastily, 'There isn't time to explain now, but I will come and visit you again, I promise.'

'See that you do, my lamb.' Martha gave her a hug.

At the door Tamsin paused. 'There's so much else I wanted to talk to you about, but I must ask one thing before I go. Something important.'

Martha cocked her head enquiringly. 'Aye?'

'I know you never met my father,' Tamsin's voice trembled with eagerness. 'But, you see, I hope to find him and I thought that you might be able to give me some clues.'

Martha turned pale. 'Oh, my lamb! I wish I could help you, but it's too late. Your father is dead.'

'Here's a letter come for you, Sir Lysander.'

Tamsin bobbed a curtsy and held out the silver salver she carried.

Lysander, who was seated at his desk, looked up with a smile. 'Thank you.'

He took the letter, but he did not open it. Instead he asked, 'Forgive me if I seem to pry, but is something troubling you? You have seemed rather quiet these last few days.'

Striving to control her dismay, Tamsin shook her head. 'Everything is well, sir.'

It was a lie, of course. Martha's pronouncement had been as devastating as a cannon ball. It had been difficult trying to behave as if nothing had happened, but she thought she had succeeded. Master Cooper, Dinah and Luke had not appeared to notice any difference in her.

She ought to have known it would be harder to fool her sharp-eyed benefactor!

Lysander wondered if he ought to press her for a more truthful answer. She had tried to maintain her usual cheerful front, but there had been a look of distress in her lovely eyes for several days now and it disturbed him to think that she was unhappy.

On the other hand, she clearly did not want to talk about whatever was upsetting her and he had no right to force a disclosure from her.

'Your new hemispheres look very well in here,' Tamsin pronounced hastily, hoping to divert his attention.

Lysander shot her a suspicious look, but decided that her admiration was genuine. 'Thank you. I think so too.'

He had placed the twin globes on either side of the large walnut bookcase which dominated his closet. Tamsin could not resist wandering over to touch one lightly with a careful hand. 'I wish I could travel,' she murmured.

'Why?' Lysander was intrigued by her wistful expression.

'Until I came to London I had never been anywhere further than our village. It must be wonderful to see new sights and meet different peoples.'

'Not half as wonderful as coming home again,' Lysander declared with a wry smile.

Tamsin nodded, understanding that he was thinking of his exile. 'All the same, sir, it must be exciting to visit foreign places and learn new things.'

'You want to broaden your horizons, Mrs Barton?'

Wary that he might be teasing her Tamsin stared at him suspiciously, but his handsome face was serious. 'Aye, my lord.'

'Then why don't you start by reading a few of these?' Lysander waved a hand towards the well-filled bookcase. 'There are volumes of geography which might interest you, and history—' Lysander halted abruptly at the odd expression which appeared on her face. 'You *can* read, can't you?'

Tamsin pulled herself together and nodded vigorously. 'Do you really mean it, sir? You would trust me with your books?' she breathed.

'Of course,' Lysander replied gently, suddenly understanding. 'Don't forget, I've watched you around the house these last few weeks. You are deft and conscientious in the performance of every task you undertake.'

Part of Tamsin's heart warmed with pleasure to think that he approved of her efforts, but she was too excited to dwell upon his praise. 'I swear I shall take the very greatest care of them,' she vowed fiercely.

He smiled and, with a little embarrassed laugh, Tamsin blushingly explained that she had always wanted to read more widely, but all she had been allowed to study was the Bible and a book of sermons deemed suitable by Aunt Deborah.

'Very worthy,' Lysander murmured, his eyes dancing.

Smoothing a crease in the cuff of his dark blue velvet coat, he curbed his unseemly amusement and said, 'I suppose your aunt did not believe in educating girls?'

Tamsin nodded. 'She said it was a waste of time.'

It was a very common view. Lysander, whose parents had been more enlightened, did not share it.

He said so and Tamsin grinned. 'Luckily, my uncle was of the same opinion as you, sir. He taught me to read and write alongside my cousin Samuel.' Her smile faded. 'Sam went on to have further lessons with our local parson. I should have liked to have accompanied him, but my aunt insisted I stay and help at home.'

'Well, you may borrow whatever you like and, if you have any difficulties, come to me and I shall do my best to clarify the problem,' Lysander promised and was rewarded with a dazzling smile of thanks.

'Why don't you choose something now while I read my

letter?' he suggested, trying to ignore the tug of attraction rising in him.

Tamsin hurried over to the bookcase. When she had been dusting this room she had always longed to explore her benefactor's collection, but she had been too nervous. Books were very expensive objects, especially the kind of sumptuous volumes Sir Lysander had acquired since his return home.

The thought of accidentally damaging one was horrifying, but, emboldened by Lysander's faith in her, she began to eagerly investigate the shelves.

'Good God!'

Startled, Tamsin looked up from her contemplation of Alsted's *Encyclopaedia* with a squeak of surprise.

'It's from my sister,' Lysander said apologetically. 'She is coming to visit me.' A broad smile lit up his clear-cut features. 'It will be good to have her here. The last time we were together was at her wedding three years ago.'

The ceremony had taken place in Paris. Lysander had travelled there from Bruges where the court-in-exile was currently residing. It had been a perfect spring day and Corinna had made a lovely bride.

Initially, Lysander had been dubious. The Comte de Montargis was almost twenty years older than Corinna and his reputation was none too sweet.

'He is rich, Lysander. He can give her all the things she has missed,' Lady Althea Saxon had reminded him when he had voiced his doubts the evening before the ceremony.

'I appreciate that, Mother, but will he make her happy?'

Lady Althea had shrugged. 'She will have security, my son, which is more than either of us can offer her.'

Lysander had fallen silent. He was about to go on campaign, wielding his sword in Charles's service. He could not provide Corinna with a home and his mother, who was one of Queen Henrietta-Maria's ladies-in-waiting, was seriously ill. She had a canker growing in her stomach and the doctors had told her they could do nothing.

'I want to see Corinna settled before I die,' Lady Althea murmured. 'That is why I promoted this match. I dare say the Comte will be unfaithful once his passion cools, but I think he will always treat her well.' A proud smile touched her mouth. 'Corinna is a sensible girl. You mustn't think she is unhappy with her lot.'

'I don't like the idea of her marrying a Frenchman,' Lysander said stubbornly.

'Perhaps not, but where are the Englishmen for her to choose from?' Lady Althea retorted tartly. At his stricken look she shook her blonde head wearily. 'It is five years since Melcombe was taken from us, Lysander. We cannot go on living in the past...or surviving on hopes for the future.'

Lady Althea sighed. The match was not ideal, but it was the best she could do. Corinna's dowry was tiny and, with King Charles's fortunes at such a low ebb, few French families wished to ally themselves with a failing cause. The Comte de Montargis, enthralled by Corinna's vivacity and looks, was a notable exception.

'Speak to her yourself, my son,' she suggested. 'I am sure she will tell you she is content.'

Corinna had. 'I don't want you to put a stop to the wedding, Lysander,' she had said firmly. 'I don't pretend to be in love with Pierre, but I do like him. He is kind to me and...and I shall need someone when Mama goes.' Her voice wobbled, but she recovered to smile at him gamely. 'Besides, I shall be twenty in a few weeks, high time I was married!'

'You needn't rush into this marriage because you fear being left to fend for yourself,' Lysander said quickly. 'This alliance with Spain will improve the King's chances and therefore yours of obtaining a better suitor. In the meantime, I'm sure the Queen would look out for you.' He coughed awkwardly. 'I promise I would come and see you as often as I could.'

Corinna shook her head. 'You mean well, Lysander, but your concern is misplaced. I don't want to sit around waiting for the King to be restored. As for the possibility of marrying one of my own countrymen, I feel at home here in France.'

'You may pine for England eventually.'

'I am sure Pierre will let me visit. He is a reasonable man.' Corinna patted Lysander's arm in a gesture of reassurance. 'Marrying him isn't too high a price to pay for being able to resume my proper place in society again. After all these years of existing on the fringes of the Queen's charity, I will have a real home of my own and, quite frankly, the thought of being able to spend as freely as I wish delights me!'

She had tossed back her dark red curls and given him an impish grin. 'I am sick of being poor, dearest brother.'

Remembering her words, Lysander set down the letter he held, a wry expression replacing his smile. How could he criticise his sister's pragmatic decision when he was about to emulate her?

'Shall I leave you, my lord?'

Tamsin's hesitant query captured Lysander's wandering attention and he answered her with a shake of his dark blond head.

Rising to his feet, he strolled over to where she stood. 'What have you got here? Ah, an excellent choice! Now, let me see, yes, this entry should interest you, I think.'

In the agreeable hour which followed as they explored the book's contents it was easy to forget the faint sense of distaste which filled him whenever he contemplated the prospect of marrying merely for money.

In spite of torrential rain, the reception at Mrs Godolphin's house in Lady Court held on the afternoon of the sixteenth of July was well attended. When Lysander arrived the smart crimson-hung drawing-room was already crowded with fashionably clad visitors.

'My lord!' Jane, who was dressed in an eye-catching sapphire gown with a silver lace petticoat, broke off her conversation with another guest and hurried over to greet him.

'I thought you weren't coming,' she murmured, laying her

hand on his arm and looking up into his face with a coy smile.

'I was delayed at Whitehall,' Lysander replied, resisting the urge to free himself from her possessive clasp.

The reproachful expression in her dark eyes vanished. 'You were with the King?'

Lysander nodded. He had gone to the palace to ask for permission to take Corinna down to Melcombe Regis. 'The lawyers are still wrangling about returning the house to my possession so I thought it best to clear the visit with Charles.'

Matthew had counselled this act of prudence and, although it went against the grain, Lysander had taken his advice. 'I don't want anything to spoil Corinna's visit.'

Jane nodded carelessly. She had little interest in his sister. The important thing was that the King had agreed to Lysander's request, a sure indication that his property would soon be restored to him.

'I should like to see the Manor myself,' she announced, fluttering her eyelashes at him. 'It sounds delightful. Perhaps we could make up a party? I'm sure your sister would appreciate another woman's company on the journey.'

'Rest assured, ma'am, that you shall be one of the first to be invited to visit,' Lysander replied with an easy smile. 'Once I am certain that any neglect has been made safe, of course.'

'Do you expect there to be much damage?' Alarm flared in Jane's voice and her hand fell abruptly from his sleeve.

Lysander shrugged. 'After all this time it would be astonishing to find Melcombe in good condition.' His tone was dry. 'Garrison soldiers are not noted for their tender care of other people's property.'

A thoughtful look passed over Jane's face. 'I had not realised the house had been used as a Parliamentary garrison...' Her voice trailed off for a moment and then, assuming a smile, she continued brightly, 'But I am neglecting you, sir! Come, let us procure a glass of wine for you and I will introduce you to some new friends I have made since I saw you last.'

It was some time before Lysander could disengage himself. Electing to go in search of another drink, he was surprised to bump into Lord Fanshawe.

'Jack!' He shook his cousin's hand warmly. 'I didn't realise you knew Mistress Godolphin.'

Jack grinned at him. 'Met her a couple of weeks ago in Hyde Park. We got to talking and she invited me to call on her.' He smoothed back a dark lock of hair with an impudent chuckle. 'Afraid I'll poach your quarry, coz?'

Lysander's eyebrow quirked. 'I didn't know you were in the market for a wife.'

'Thought I'd take a leaf out of your book.' Jack's cherubic features were wreathed in innocence.

For an instant anger ignited in Lysander and then he realised Jack was deliberately teasing him. 'Mind you,' he continued thoughtfully after politely threatening to disembowel his cousin, 'I see that there are dozens of heiress-hungry fellows here.'

This was something of an exaggeration as Jack pointed out, but it was true that several notable fortune-hunters were present.

'Wonder whether Mistress Godolphin knows what a set of rogues she is entertaining,' Jack muttered, half-angrily.

Lysander threw him a surprised look and Jack coloured sheepishly. 'I like her,' he said simply. 'Oh, I know she ain't interested in me. I'm small fry as far as she is concerned, but I wouldn't want to see her taken advantage of.'

He fixed his dark eyes enquiringly on his cousin's face. 'You can tell me to go boil my head if you like, but are you serious about wanting to marry her, Lysander?'

Lysander stared across the room where the lady under discussion was engaged in conversation with her uncle and another guest. Her full bosom was enticingly revealed in her low-cut dress and an attractive smile softened her slightly hard features.

She was lively and intelligent, with the added bonus of the dark colouring and lush figure he had always preferred in women, so why did her charms leave him cold?

His gaze returned to Jack's anxious face. 'You're right. It's none of your business, coz,' he replied coolly.

Jack bit his lip. 'Why can't you stop hiding your feelings and be honest for once?' he blurted.

Lysander shrugged and carefully changed the subject.

He wasn't about to admit it, not even to his favourite cousin, but he was damned if he knew the answer to either of Jack's questions.

The house was quiet as Tamsin slipped out into the rainy street. Sir Lysander was at some reception or other, Master Cooper was busy with the accounts and Dinah and Luke were clearing up after dinner. When they had finished that task, Tamsin had left them instructions to give the furniture in the second-best bedroom a thorough polishing to make it ready for the arrival of the Comtesse de Montargis.

No one would miss her for a couple of hours.

The heavy rain impeded her progress towards Bread Street, but Martha's warm welcome made up for the soaking. Whisked upstairs to her friend's bedchamber and ordered to remove her wet gown, she was soon snugly wrapped in a blanket and sipping a mug of burnt ale.

'How have you been, my lamb?' Martha asked anxiously, sitting down next to Tamsin on the wide bed. 'I didn't like sending you away with such bad news.'

Tamsin quickly reassured her. 'Besides, I've been too busy to brood. We are expecting visitors next week so we have been spring-cleaning, and in my free moments I have been reading one of Sir Lysander's books.'

Martha's mouth rounded in surprise. 'He let you borrow it?' she exclaimed.

Tamsin nodded. 'Aye, and he's helped me understand the bits I found hard.' Her lips curved with reminiscent pleasure. They had spent several agreeable hours in Lysander's closet and his patience had been exceeded only by his talent for making what had been baffling seem crystal-clear.

'But why?' Worry creased Martha's plump face. 'You are gently born, but you are not of his world. What lies behind his kindness?'

'Nothing! I told you before, he isn't interested in me.' Tamsin's eyes sparkled with indignation on her benefactor's behalf. 'I think he rescued me on a whim and let me stay because I am useful.' She shrugged. 'I amuse him, I think.'

Tamsin knew she had no right to complain, but sometimes it rankled that Lysander treated her like a child. He was willing to indulge her, but his reluctance to acknowledge she was a grown woman puzzled her. Sometimes she thought she caught a glimpse of admiration in his vivid eyes, but it always vanished before she could be certain.

Afraid to examine her own feelings too closely, Tamsin had tried to ignore the heady rush of pleasure which filled her whenever he walked into the room. She'd told herself that she liked him in the same way she liked her cousin Sam, but it was growing ever harder to pretend her feelings were so innocent. Day by day the barriers she had erected in her heart were crumbling into ruin.

Soon she would have no defences left at all.

'Just you remember you are more than welcome here if he forgets to behave as a gentleman ought,' Martha said.

Her scolding tone snatched Tamsin from her uneasy reflections. 'Thank you, but I'm sure it won't come to that.'

Martha sniffed doubtfully. 'Perhaps I should have a word with him?' she suggested. 'Set him straight in case he has got the wrong idea about you, my lamb.'

Tamsin stared at her in horror. 'You can't do that!'

'I know he far outranks me, but your mother would never forgive me if I let you be ruined just for the want of speaking up.'

Setting down her empty mug, Tamsin bent all her energies into persuading her old friend to abandon this idea. It took several minutes to convince her and Tamsin felt clammy with relief when Martha reluctantly agreed.

'Can you tell me about my father, Martha?' she said hastily before Martha could think of another reason in favour of accosting Sir Lysander. 'I'd really like to hear anything you can remember.'

Martha smoothed her apron, her expression ruminative. 'There's not much to tell, my lamb,' she warned. 'Your mother rarely spoke of the past.'

Tamsin sighed. 'Didn't she tell you anything about his family or his home?'

'Only that he came from Cornwall and that he was a gentleman.'

'My aunt told me he was a Cavalier.'

'Aye. That's why your mother fell out with her family. She told me that she first met Mr Penhaligan in forty-one when he was visiting relatives who lived near Bristol, but your grandfather couldn't abide the idea of your mother marrying someone outside their own circle, especially someone who didn't support Parliament.'

'Aunt Deborah said Mama ran away with him.'

Martha nodded confirmation and Tamsin stirred restlessly. She had been hoping against hope that Martha would deny it.

'You mustn't blame her, my lamb,' Martha said softly. 'She tried to obey your grandfather, but when the war broke out she knew that he would never accept the man she loved.'

A sigh escaped her. 'You are too young to remember any of it, but the war had a strange effect on us all. Things that had seemed certain were suddenly overturned and people behaved in ways they wouldn't normally have done.' She shrugged her plump shoulders. 'I don't condemn your mother for seizing her chance of happiness.'

'I wish my aunt felt the same!' Tamsin shuddered. 'She said my mother was no better than a whore!'

The memory of that dreadful interview with her aunt was

still strong enough to make Tamsin's stomach churn. Barely able to sit still, she felt as if she was suffocating.

Her agitated movement sent several apricot-gold curls tumbling to Tamsin's bare shoulders and Martha leant across the bed. 'These are still wet,' she said calmly. 'Let me unpin them for you or they won't have a chance to dry before you leave.'

Tamsin stopped squirming, allowing the familiar attention to soothe her distress. How often had she sat like this while Martha tended her hair! It was one of the things she remembered best from the old days when her mother was alive.

'I've been racking my brains, trying to think of everything Mama told me,' she murmured softly. 'All I can remember though is that she said my Papa was handsome and had hair like mine.'

'You were too young for her to try and explain, my lamb.' Martha finished fluffing out the silken curls and sat back.

'Do you think they were married, Martha?'

Martha's mouth fell open. 'Did…did that old besom tell you they weren't wed?' She took Tamsin's hand in her own and squeezed it in speechless sympathy.

Tamsin nodded. 'When I informed her I didn't want to accept Master Hardy, she said I ought to be grateful that he was interested in me because not many men would take on a dowerless bastard.' Tamsin stared down at their linked hands, her voice shaking as she repeated Deborah Barton's pitiless verdict.

The shock of hearing herself declared illegitimate had temporarily overwhelmed Tamsin, crushing her spirit.

'She was always jealous of your mother!' Martha exclaimed in disgust. She shook her head. 'She would never have dared say such a cruel thing to you if your uncle had still been alive.'

'I know this will sound strange,' Tamsin said in a strained voice, 'but I've had time to think on it since I have been in London and I can't help wondering if Aunt Deborah was concealing something. Her manner was…odd!'

Martha hesitated, reluctant to raise false hopes. 'Your mother swore she was wed,' she said at last. 'I believed her, but when she refused to give details of your father's whereabouts Mistress Deborah and many others said he must have abandoned her. They declared that she was lying about being married to try to save her reputation and protect you.'

A sudden chill swept over Tamsin and she clutched the blanket closer to her. 'I don't suppose we will ever know the truth now,' she whispered.

Martha longed to reassure her former charge and save her from heartache, but Tamsin was no longer a child to be shielded from harm.

'All I know for certain is that your mother loved your father,' she announced. 'She cried so much when your aunt told her that he was dead that I feared for her health. Verily, I believe she would have lost the will to live without you.'

'When did Aunt Deborah announce that my father was dead?' Tamsin asked slowly.

Martha blinked at the odd note in her young friend's tone. 'Let me think…you were three. Aye, it was around the end of November. Your mother had been full of hope that the King's cause would take a turn for the better. She'd just had a letter from your father telling her about the King's escape—'

'He *wrote* to her?' Tamsin interrupted, her thoughtful frown vanishing in a flurry of excitement.

'Aye, several times. Don't you remember? She used to read them out to you at night.'

Tamsin cast her mind back and a shadowy mental picture formed of herself lying in bed, with her mother sitting next to her speaking in soft tones. But she couldn't hear the words and the image blurred even as she sought to make it come clear.

'It's no use,' she exclaimed in despair. 'I can't recall what she said.'

Taking a deep breath, she strove to calm herself. 'Do you know what happened to those letters, Martha? My aunt never mentioned them when I asked her if my mother had left me any keepsake other than her pearl necklace.'

'I'm sorry to have to tell you, but she burnt them after your mother's funeral.'

Tamsin's disappointment showed on her expressive face and Martha gave her hand a sympathetic pat. 'Your uncle was furious. It was one of the few times I can remember him berating her.'

Uncle Daniel had been a placid man. Most of the time he'd been content to let his wife rule the roost, but occasionally he had stood up to her when he thought she was behaving unfairly. 'Do you think he believed my mother was married?'

Martha grimaced. 'He took her in when she arrived home with you as a tiny baby and he would never let anyone say a word against her, but he refused to have your father's name mentioned in his presence. He even insisted that you take the name of Barton after your mother's death.'

Martha had heard that Master Barton had been indifferent to politics as a young man, becoming a firm supporter of Parliament only after his sister's disappearance. His own marriage soon afterwards into a fervently Puritan family had encouraged this new trait and his antagonism towards Cavaliers had grown stronger as the years passed, but perhaps its roots lay in what he privately considered a family tragedy.

'I wish there was some proof,' Tamsin sighed. 'I came to London in the hope of discovering whether or not Aunt Deborah was telling me the truth...'

'Tamsin? Are you all right, my lamb? You have gone as pale as a bowl of whey.'

'Maybe Aunt Deborah *was* lying!' The queer note Martha had heard earlier was back in Tamsin's urgent tone. 'Lying on purpose, I mean. You said yourself that she disliked Mama and she hated Cavaliers. What if she told Mama that my father was dead in order to put an end to their relationship?'

About to protest that even Mistress Deborah would not be so wickedly spiteful, Martha paused. 'Your mama was talk-

ing of leaving,' she said slowly. 'You were no longer frail
and she yearned to rejoin Mr Penhaligan. She said it was safe
to take the risk of travelling since the fighting was over at
last and the countryside was quieter.'

Martha gave Tamsin a troubled look. 'Your aunt might
have convinced herself that it was both proper and godly to
stop her.'

'And Uncle Daniel would have gone along with her plan
to prevent further shame being brought on the family.'

Tamsin shivered. It would have been easy for her uncle
and aunt to intercept any letters before they reached her
mother. Perhaps they had even played the same lying trick
on her father!

'What are you going to do, my lamb?' Martha asked un-
easily as Tamsin began to dress. 'We don't know for sure
whether or not your aunt lied; even if she did, it's been a
long time. Anything could have happened to him.'

'I feel in my heart that he is still alive.' Tamsin's face
assumed a stubborn expression.

Unwilling to crush her revived hopes, Martha did not argue. 'Perhaps. But you have very little information to go on.'
Her frown lifted. 'I know! Ask Sir Lysander for help.'

Tamsin shook her head. She was not going to expose her
shame and risk losing his good opinion.

'Then how are you going to set about finding him?'

'I know his name,' Tamsin said grimly. 'If I have to, I
will ask every Cavalier in London whether they can tell me
his whereabouts!'

The conviction that her father was still alive buoyed up
Tamsin's spirits as she walked home. It was still raining
heavily, but she scarcely noticed the downpour as she hurried
past Temple Bar and into the Strand.

There were few people about; the bad weather had discouraged casual strollers. Tamsin quickened her pace. She
hadn't meant to stay so long at Martha's. She was going to
be late!

Ducking her head against the rain-soaked wind, she ran towards Wych Street. Martha had scolded her for venturing out alone, but she hadn't been able to think of a suitable excuse to get rid of Luke and she was sick of telling lies.

More worried that her absence might have been noticed than taking care of where she was going, she hurtled round the corner and instantly collided with a large body coming swiftly in the opposite direction.

'Aaargh!' Tamsin gasped inelegantly, the wind knocked out of her by the force of the impact.

Her nose was squashed up against a rock-hard chest covered in smooth farandine so that she could scarcely breathe, and her first reaction on being thrust free was to gulp down air in noisy pants of relief. On becoming aware that hard hands still held her firmly at arm's length, this response changed to indignation.

'Let me go, sir!' she exclaimed, raising her head to stare up at her captor. 'Oh!'

Sir Lysander Saxon gazed grimly down into his prisoner's flower-like face.

'And where the Devil have you been, you disobedient little fool?'

Chapter Seven

'I will not tell you where I was!' Tamsin glowered at Lysander, her chin held defiantly high as she confronted him across the parlour.

Refusing to release her, he had dragged her home and thrust her willy-nilly into the hallway. Tamsin had caught one brief glimpse of Luke and Dinah's startled faces before her irate benefactor had marched her into the parlour and slammed the door closed.

With a face like thunder he had then flung off his wet cloak and hat and repeated his demand. Tamsin's knees were quaking, but she was so incensed by his high-handed behaviour that she was determined not to answer him.

'Why? What mischief are you trying to conceal?' Lysander returned her angry look with a glare of his own.

'I wasn't up to any *mischief,* as you so charmingly term it.' Tamsin unknotted the strings of her cloak with false calm and let it fall on to the thin woven matting which covered the wooden floor.

'No? Then why won't you answer my question?'

'Because it's none of your business,' Tamsin retorted hotly.

'All that goes on in this house is my business.' Lysander's deep tones had lost their usual velvet smoothness.

'I am not neglecting my duties. I completed every task

before leaving.' Tamsin surreptitiously rubbed her damp palms against her skirts. He was making her nervous! She hadn't imagined his handsome face could look so cold!

'You insult me if you think I would begrudge you time free to enjoy yourself,' Lysander snapped. 'I am well aware of how hard you work, but that is not the point at issue.'

Tamsin took a deep breath. 'I don't understand why you are so angry with me,' she said in a quieter tone.

Lysander stared at her in disbelief. 'You disobeyed me and went out alone.'

'Oh, for heaven's sake!' Tamsin discarded her rain-soaked hood and pushed an irritating stray curl off her face. 'I am not a child. Why do you persist treating me as if I was incapable of looking after myself?'

Lysander stared at her in silence for a moment and then, before Tamsin had time to grasp what he meant to do, he crossed the narrow space separating them in a single rapid stride and grabbed her by the shoulders. Another swift movement and he had pinioned her arms behind her, clipping them into the small of her back with an iron grip.

'What...!' With a gasp of outrage, Tamsin tried to free herself.

Lysander contained her struggles with contemptuous ease. 'Now do you understand?' He held her tight against him. 'What if you had run into someone other than myself, someone who sought to take advantage of you—how could you have stopped him?'

Tamsin's response was to try and kick him in the shin, but he was too quick for her.

'Let me go!' Her attempt to stamp on his foot was no more successful.

'It's no use,' he laughed, his green eyes glittering. 'Admit it. You cannot prevent me from doing whatever I wish with you.'

He was holding her against him so tightly that Tamsin didn't think a pin could have been inserted between them. Breast to breast, thigh to thigh, her body was forced against his and a strange tingling excitement suddenly shot through her angry distress.

His coat was damp where it had escaped the protection of his cloak, but she could feel the warmth emanating from his tall strong body. The blood in her veins began to beat with a hot dizzying languor that made her head swim.

'All right!' Tamsin stopped struggling. 'I admit I cannot defend myself against your superior strength.'

She spat the words at him through gritted teeth. What was the matter with her? His nearness was provoking an onslaught of sensation that destroyed her ability to think. The clean masculine scent of him, mingling with the faint aroma of lavender-fresh linen and cold rain, surrounded her, fanning her confusion.

As soon as the words were out of her mouth, Lysander released his hold on her and stood back. Automatically, Tamsin brought her wrists up and rubbed them to restore the circulation.

'Forgive me. I didn't mean to hurt you,' Lysander said gruffly, a contrite expression leaping into his eyes.

Tamsin's arms fell to her sides. 'It's nothing,' she muttered in a strained voice, her gaze avoiding his.

'Tamsin, look at me.' Urgency filled Lysander's deep tones and he took a step forward, closing the gap which separated them. 'I'm sorry if what I did just now offended you, but I wanted to *show* you what I meant about the streets not being safe for a woman on her own.' He shrugged impatiently. 'Sometimes words aren't enough.'

Tamsin slowly raised her head to meet his gaze and he continued softly, 'Don't be angry. I want to keep you safe from harm.'

'Why?' Swallowing hard to try to dispel the dryness in her throat, Tamsin managed to croak out a single question.

Lysander smiled at her, that heart-stopping smile which always had the power to enthral her. 'I'm surprised you need to ask, kitling. I should have thought it was obvious.'

Slowly, so as not to alarm her, he lifted a hand and gently

ran one long forefinger down her cheek. 'It would grieve me
to see you hurt. Please, promise me to be more careful. You
are too much of a temptation to be let loose without an escort.'

Tamsin blushed. 'You exaggerate, sir.'

'I wish I did.'

There was a note of frustration in his unguarded answer
and Tamsin's pulse quickened. He *did* find her attractive after
all!

A silence fell over the room, broken only by the sound of
their breathing.

Tamsin discovered it was impossible to tear her gaze from
his mouth, which was well shaped with a hint of sensuality
in the lower lip. She was aware of a sudden fierce longing
to know if his kiss would fulfil its sweet promise.

She shook her head, trying to clear it of such wanton fan-
tasies, but it was no use.

Against his bronzed skin the green of his eyes was intense,
like a mysterious forest pool whose cool depths promised
relief from the burning sun. Dizzily, Tamsin swayed towards
him, instinct telling her only his touch could assuage the fire
raging within her trembling body.

Lysander's reaction was swift and automatic. His hands
flew to her slim waist to hold her steady.

A delicious shiver rippled through Tamsin at his touch.
Mindlessly, she lifted her face to his, her eyes closing…and
felt him begin to draw her firmly towards him…

With a supreme effort of will Lysander mastered his desire
and released her.

Tamsin's eyes snapped open and her expression of disappointed bewilderment almost undid Lysander's resolve.

Folding his arms across his chest to better resist the temptation to draw her back into his embrace, he said lightly,
'Now, if I have convinced you of the folly of going out alone,
may I ask what was the purpose of your expedition today?'

Tamsin took a deep breath, struggling to regain her shattered composure. She had been certain he was about to kiss

her! Tears of mortification pricked at her eyelids. Gemini, what he must think of her, throwing herself at him like a harlot!

Had he been right to pretend nothing had happened? He had thought to save her further embarrassment, but ruefully, he acknowledged he was not used to dealing with such an innocent.

However, having chosen his course, there was no option but to continue. 'When I arrived home, the others were worried by your absence,' he said quietly. 'They had no idea where you had gone, so I set out to search for you.'

Trying to ignore the embarrassment heating her cheeks, Tamsin blinked away the threatening tears. 'I don't suppose you'd believe me if I told you that I felt the need of some exercise?' she said with a shaky attempt at humour.

Lysander was impressed by her gallant refusal to use feminine wiles to wriggle out of trouble. Most of the women of his acquaintance would have been watering his coat by now!

He shook his head and waited in silence, hoping she would trust him.

Tamsin heaved a sigh. 'I was visiting a friend.' No matter the consequences, she couldn't go on lying to him.

'I thought you didn't know anyone in London.'

Tamsin's blush deepened. 'I lied,' she said baldly.

Lysander's eyebrow rose and she went on hastily, 'I thought you would send me away if I told you about Martha and I wanted to stay and repay my debt to you.'

'There is no debt to repay!'

His sharp tone made her wince, but she stuck stubbornly to her guns. 'I cannot accept that, sir. It may mean nothing to you, but it offends my pride to think I owe you so much money.'

Lysander was silent. He hadn't realised she felt so deeply about a debt he had long since dismissed from his mind.

'Shall I go and gather my things, sir?'

'What?' Her quiet offer startled him from his thoughts.

'Surely you wish to dismiss me?' Tamsin stared down at

the tips of her boots. They were muddy and the hem of her
skirt was soaking, but her discomfort was more mental than
physical. 'I lied to you and I deserve to be punished.'

'S'death, if we all got what we deserved, life would be
infernally dismal!' Lysander gave a short laugh.

Hope flickered in Tamsin's breast. She had expected him
to be angry, but his expression was amazingly calm.

'You lied to me, but I realise that you believed you had a
good reason.' Lysander shrugged. 'Besides, I don't hold with
your Puritan notions of retribution.'

'You mean I can stay?'

'Aye, if that's what you want.' Lysander ignored the sensible voice of his conscience urging him to send her away.

'Thank you!' Tamsin's eyes lit up. 'I promise I won't disobey you again.'

'See that you don't, kitling.' Lysander's severe tone softened as his gaze absorbed her glowing smile. 'Now go and
put on some dry clothes and then you can tell me all about
this friend.'

Tamsin nodded and, snatching up her discarded cloak and
hood, hurried from the room.

She threw a reassuring glance at Dinah, who was hovering
anxiously in the kitchen doorway, and sped up the stairs.

In her own chamber she stripped off her wet garments and
replaced them with her green say gown. Taking her comb,
she attacked her damp hair, subduing the curly mass until it
was fit to be braided.

Halfway through this task she paused, her busy fingers
stilling as she stared at her reflection in the little looking-
glass that Lysander had presented her with a week after her
arrival.

He had hung it up for her on the wall near the bed, with
a joking comment that now she had no excuse for not setting
her cap straight. Tamsin, who had never owned a mirror before, had been secretly delighted by her new acquisition, although her conscience scolded her on the sin of vanity every
time she looked into it.

Her conscience, honed by a lifetime of Aunt Deborah's homilies, was pricking her now.

She had behaved disgracefully!

'You had no business encouraging him to embrace you,' she whispered to her reflection, trying to dismiss the deep ache of disappointment that still filled her.

It was mere vanity to think he might be interested in her. He was a gentleman of rank, friend to the King himself. Why on earth would such a man of the world bother with a nobody who had neither family nor fortune to recommend her?

Tamsin could think of only one answer to this question. To her shame, a quick tide of excitement ran through her veins as she recalled the look of desire in his vivid eyes.

'You are a fool, Tamsin Barton!' she told her image sternly. 'What do you imagine can come of this wanton behaviour? You are lucky he is too much of a gentleman to take advantage of you!'

But she still wished he had kissed her!

With a quick movement Tamsin turned away from the mirror. She was playing with fire and she knew it. Already, she liked Sir Lysander Saxon far too much for her own peace of mind. To allow her feelings to grow even deeper would be an act of madness.

Only a lunatic would fall in love with a man so far beyond her reach!

'And this is Mrs Barton, who is kindly acting as our housekeeper.'

As her benefactor finished his introduction, Tamsin sank into a respectful curtsy.

The Comtesse de Montargis shot her brother a startled look across Tamsin's bowed head.

'I am pleased to meet you, mistress.' Corinna hastily wiped the surprise from her face as Tamsin rose to greet her with a shy smile. 'My brother told me how you rallied to his aid when Matthew was injured.'

Tamsin hadn't realised that Lysander had mentioned her

in his letters to his sister and, while the knowledge that he thought enough of her to do so delighted her, she also found it disconcerting. What exactly had he said? Pray God that he had not told her of Lime Street and Mrs Cole!

Peeping through her lashes, Tamsin decided that the Comtesse did not have the look of someone who had been told those shocking details. She was smiling, her dark hazel eyes merry as she turned to greet Luke and Dinah who had been summoned to the hall to join the presentation line-up.

At first glance Tamsin had thought the Comtesse beautiful. She was tall enough to be imposing and her elegant figure was clad with great style, but as Tamsin covertly studied her she realised that Corinna's features lacked her brother's clear-cut regularity. Yet somehow it didn't matter that her brow was too wide and her chin slightly pointed. Her vivacious expression conquered these defects and the eye was drawn automatically to her lovely dark red hair, which curled in great rings to her shoulders.

The introductions were concluded and Dinah and Luke scampered off back to the kitchen at a gesture from Tamsin.

'I have lit a fire in the withdrawing-room, my lord,' she announced.

'A good idea.' Lysander threw her a smile of thanks. 'This damp weather is enough to give us all an ague!' He offered his arm to his sister. 'You must be weary after your journey. Come and rest and I'll show you over the house after dinner.'

'I cannot deny it would be pleasant to sit down on something that does not rock or bob about,' Corinna laughed.

'Shall I bring up some tea for the Comtesse?' Tamsin offered and Lysander nodded.

Corinna gestured to her maid, a small dumpy woman who stood waiting in the background. 'Go with Mrs Barton, Marie.'

Lysander swept his sister towards the stairs. They had barely disappeared from sight when the door opened again and Nat and Master Cooper came in with the Comtesse's luggage.

'We'll take this straight up,' Matt said, wiping drizzle from his brow.

Tamsin nodded and beckoned Marie to follow her.

The Frenchwoman spoke little English, but she soon understood that Tamsin wished to offer her refreshment and she happily drank a mug of cider and ate one of Tamsin's fresh-baked sugar cakes while Tamsin prepared a tray of tea for upstairs.

Sir Lysander had informed her that his sister was fond of this newly fashionable drink and he had bought some in preparation for her visit. Tamsin had never tried it. At anything between sixteen and fifty shillings a pound, Aunt Deborah declared it was too expensive and refused to buy it. Unsure how it should taste, Tamsin decided the best course was to let the Comtesse brew it for herself. She was bound to have her own preferences on how to mix the leaves anyway.

With this in mind, Tamsin had already taken the spirit kettle on its elegant little stand up to the withdrawing-room. All that remained was to set out the porcelain teapot and its delicate matching dishes. This done, she took the tiny wooden tea cabinet, which held the precious leaves, and placed it on the tray.

Marie finished her cake. 'Please. For Madame I…I…' She gestured awkwardly. Seeing their looks of incomprehension, she pointed up to the ceiling and mimed a lifting and folding movement with her hands.

'Oh, I see!' Tamsin exclaimed. 'You wish to unpack for the Comtesse?'

'*Oui.*' Marie clapped her hands vigorously.

'Very well. Dinah, will you show Marie to the Comtesse's bedchamber while I take this up?'

Tamsin left the kitchen. Balancing the tray upon her hip, she knocked on the withdrawing-room door and was bidden to enter.

'Let me help you.' Lysander rose quickly to his feet.

'It isn't heavy, sir.' Tamsin thanked him with a smile. She

carefully deposited the tray upon the low table near the Comtesse's chair. 'Shall I light the spirit burner for you, my lady?'

Corinna gave a quick nod of assent and Tamsin moved nervously forward.

Worried she might fumble the task, she lifted up the copper kettle, which she had earlier filled with water, to make the job easier.

Her turquoise eyes widened in consternation as she belatedly realised there was no suitable place to set it down within her reach.

'Allow me.' Lysander took it from her.

Grateful for his help, Tamsin murmured her thanks.

'Don't be nervous. You are doing splendidly,' he whispered back.

Tamsin beamed at him and, her confidence bolstered, proceeded to light the burner with quick efficiency.

Lysander looked up and noticed that Corinna was watching them curiously. Their eyes met and her eyebrow quirked in an interrogatory gesture identical to his own.

'Would you like something to eat, my lady?' Tamsin asked, blithely unaware of the unspoken message which had passed between brother and sister.

Corinna shook her head. 'Nay, or I shall have no appetite for my dinner,' she announced with a smile.

'Thank you, that will be all for now, Mrs Barton.' Lysander nodded dismissal.

Tamsin curtsied and withdrew.

'She's a very pretty little thing,' Corinna murmured.

Lysander coughed. 'Aye.'

Corinna grinned. 'You never mentioned so in your letter. Nor how young she is.'

'Does it matter?' Lysander sat down opposite her.

Corinna smoothed the violet skirts of her woollen travelling gown. 'Aren't you going to tell me all about her?' she invited sweetly. 'You obviously like her.'

'If you are implying that there is anything untoward in the

relationship, you are far out,' Lysander replied with a bland expression that belied the sudden quickening of his pulse.

'Really? Then why haven't you dispatched her back to the country?'

'She doesn't want to go. Her aunt wants to force her into wedding a man she cannot stomach.'

Corinna fell silent. Her curiosity had been intrigued by the orphan her brother had rescued, particularly as she was now sure he hadn't told her the whole tale in his letters. However, she could not help but feel sympathy for the wench if she had run away to avoid an unwanted marriage.

'You needn't worry. I am not such a fool as to lose my head over Mrs Barton.' Lysander gave her a quick smile. 'I feel responsible for her, but, to be honest, I have done well out of my impulsive act of charity. She works hard and she is extremely efficient. The whole household now runs like one of Charles's beloved clocks.'

'How is his Majesty?' Corinna asked, diverted. 'Is he still *épris* with the lovely Barbara?'

For a few moments they discussed Charles's current favourite, the gorgeous Mrs Palmer who had captured his eye at The Hague a few weeks before the Restoration.

'She has a great deal of influence over him. He is deeply infatuated.' A slight frown touched Lysander's brow. Barbara was amazingly beautiful, but she was greedy and had a shocking temper when thwarted. Instead of buying jewels he couldn't afford to decorate her graceful white neck, Charles ought to be spending the money on paying the long overdue wages of his sailors.

'Do you think he will give her husband a title to keep him sweet?' Corinna enquired, unlocking the little tea cabinet.

'I expect so.' Lysander shrugged, suddenly impatient with the conversation. He didn't blame Charles for falling under Barbara's spell. Her sensual beauty was enough to arouse a dead man and she could be amusing company when she wished, but he was disappointed that his old friend was not willing to devote as much time to business as he was to the pursuit of pleasure and bedsport.

'Then no doubt Roger Palmer will think his cuckold's horns worth it.' There was a bitter note in Corinna's voice. She measured out the tea to her satisfaction. 'The pain of adultery can usually be soothed by the application of gifts, or so I'm told.'

Forgetting his disenchantment with the way the Court was turning out, Lysander shot her a questioning look. 'Have you quarrelled with Pierre?'

Corinna bit her lip. She had forgotten how perceptive he was! 'I didn't mean to tell you but, since you ask, that's the reason why I decided to visit London now instead of waiting to sail with Queen Henrietta-Marie in the autumn.'

This had been her original intention, but she could not bear to watch her husband lavishing his attentions upon a new mistress, a lady-in-waiting to Marie-Therese, King Louis's Spanish wife.

'I don't expect perpetual fidelity from him.' Corinna poured the boiling water upon the tea leaves. 'However, to have to stand by and watch that woman crow over me in triumph is beyond my patience.'

Last year, when Pierre had thought himself in love with the Duchesse, she had told herself it was a temporary aberration. She had been able to maintain her composure, secure in the knowledge he would come back to her when the affair fizzled out.

It had helped that the Duchesse, a lady of great charm, was actually older than herself and no particular beauty. Her new rival was young and pretty and she lacked the Duchesse's tact, flaunting Pierre's besotted adulation in Corinna's face.

'Do you want me to—?'

'No! You must not attempt to interfere,' Corinna interrupted, seeing anger flare into his green eyes. 'It is my problem.' Corinna shrugged. 'After all, you did warn me.'

'It gives me no satisfaction to be proved right.' Lysander strove to restrain his desire to break his brother-in-law's neck.

Corinna poured the tea. 'It is my hope that he will miss me enough to abandon her.' A sigh escaped her. At the moment that didn't look likely!

'Did Pierre object to you leaving?'

Corinna shook her head. 'He was as amiable as ever and wished me a pleasant journey.' She handed Lysander the dish of tea.

'But you mean to return?'

'Of course.' Corinna looked surprised. 'I am out of charity with him at the moment, but he is still my husband.'

'You could always come and live with me.'

Corinna smiled at him. 'You are very kind, dear heart, but I have no intention of giving up my position. Pierre would never agree to divorce me.'

Lysander was silent. Corinna would not be free to make a new life for herself while she was legally tied to the Comte and her situation would be dubious.

'If I desert Pierre, I run the risk of being ostracised by society,' Corinna said, echoing his thoughts. 'And I have no desire to lead my life as an outcast.' She took a sip of her tea. 'Sooner or later, he will lose interest in her. I shall just have to be patient. After all, it is a virtue I have managed to learn in other spheres.'

A look of sadness flickered in her dark hazel eyes and Lysander guessed her thoughts. A year after her marriage, Corinna had borne a still-born child. The Comte de Montargis's disappointment had been great and a certain coolness had crept into the marriage. Corinna was desperate to give him a son and her failure to conceive again had been a bitter blow to her hopes.

'We must ensure you enjoy yourself while you are waiting for Pierre to come to his senses,' Lysander said, assuming a deliberately cheerful tone. She had been to several doctors to no avail and he knew she would not discuss the subject of her childlessness.

'I intend to.' Corinna gave him a wicked grin. 'Who knows, I might even take a lover!'

'A somewhat drastic way to teach Pierre a lesson,' Lysander commented drily, raising the dish of tea to his lips.

'Perhaps.' Corinna laughed. 'Shall you take your own vows so seriously, I wonder?'

His frown made her drop her teasing tone. 'Lysander? Has something gone wrong with your wooing of the widow?'

He shook his dark blond head. 'Not in the sense you mean. However, I must admit to some second thoughts.'

'But why?' Corinna gazed at him in surprise. 'You are twenty-eight. High time you chose a wife.'

Lysander knew it. After all, his father had two sons to succeed him before he was twenty.

The thought triggered a flicker of sadness. War had deprived both his elder brothers of the chance to inherit.

Still, Corinna was right. Duty demanded he continue their name.

'Papa was ten years younger than you when he married and he was very happy,' Corinna said encouragingly. 'Besides, you will need a great deal of money if you are to restore Melcombe to its former state and Jane Godolphin is rich.'

'Charles has agreed to pay me a pension in honour of our father's bravery.'

'It's barely enough to support you in the style of a gentleman, let alone refurbish Melcombe.'

'He has many other claims upon his purse.'

'But he would not be here today if Papa had not saved his life at Edgehill,' Corinna retorted.

Lysander admired this piece of feminine logic.

'Do you remember Father telling us about it when he came home on leave that time?' he asked with a sudden grin.

Corinna nodded. She had been barely six years old, but the story of Sir James's daring rescue of the Prince of Wales and his younger brother, the Duke of York, was engraved upon her memory.

It had happened towards the end of the battle when Sir John Hinton, who had been in charge of the princes, had become cut off in the fading light. A body of Parliamentary Horse came riding towards the royal party and, confused by their direction into thinking them friends, Charles and his brother James had moved towards to meet them.

Suddenly recognising them for Parliamentary troopers, Hinton had begged Charles to retreat.

'Papa said he could hear Charles shouting "I fear them not" at the top of his voice as he whipped out his pistol ready to charge them!' Corinna laughed.

'Aye.' Even at thirteen his friend had been brave, if fool-hardy! 'He was lucky that trooper wasn't mounted on a better horse.'

A trooper out for glory had broken ranks and dashed forward to capture Charles. Sir James, coming upon the scene, had immediately galloped to the Prince's rescue. He had intercepted the trooper and pole-axed him, his brave action allowing the royal party time to get away. The subsequent arrival of his own men caused the rest of the Parliamentary troop to change their minds and withdraw.

Corinna's reminiscent smile faded. 'Have *you* changed your mind? About restoring Melcombe, I mean?' she asked uncertainly.

'No!'

'Then how do you propose to go about it unless you marry money?'

Lysander shrugged. This question had been exercising his mind of late. 'As yet, I have not come up with a better solution,' he admitted.

'You sound as if you wish you could!' Corinna's heart-shaped face wore an expression of confusion. 'It isn't like you not to know your own mind, Lysander.'

'I am not quite fool enough to give up such a prize as Jane.' His tone was bitterly self-depreciatory.

'I don't understand,' Corinna said slowly. 'You told me she was an attractive woman. Have you discovered some hidden fault in her?'

'Nay. She is entirely without blame.' Lysander shrugged. 'However, I cannot envisage her as my wife.'

'You have been too long a bachelor, dear heart.' Coming to the conclusion that the problem must lie in his reluctance to lose his freedom, Corinna smiled at him sympathetically. 'Once you ask Mistress Godolphin to marry you, these symptoms will disappear.'

'No doubt you are right!' With an amused shrug that masked his true feelings, Lysander began to talk of the plans he had made for her visit.

The day after the Comtesse's arrival was Saint James's Day and Mistress Godolphin invited Lysander and his sister to supper. They came home late and, while Corinna went straight upstairs declaring her intention of seeking her bed, Lysander paused in the hallway to speak to Tamsin.

'You should not have waited up,' he said to her quietly.

'I thought someone should and Master Cooper was tired.' Tamsin gave a little shrug. 'The gardener you hired did not come so we spent the afternoon weeding.'

Which explained the green stains on her fingers, he supposed. 'Thank you. I shall find out why and hire someone else if necessary.'

'There is no need to thank me, my lord.' Tamsin was tempted to remind him of her indebtedness, but decided not to risk annoying him by mentioning it. There was a faint frown between his brows and she couldn't help wondering if he had enjoyed his evening. 'I like gardening.'

He smiled at her suddenly, his frown vanishing. 'So do I, although I cannot claim much experience or skill.'

Tamsin caught her breath. Oh, why did he have to be so heartbreakingly handsome!

'I...I must lock the front door,' she muttered, suddenly anxious to put some distance between them.

'I'll do it. I can reach the bolt more easily.' Lysander turned at the same time and Tamsin bumped into him.

Her face flamed. 'I'm...I'm sorry.' In a panic she tried to

move away, but her stubborn limbs refused to obey her and of its own volition a slow inviting smile began to curve her lips.

Her skirts were brushing against his thigh and he could smell the rosemary with which she had washed her hair. If he put out his hand the merest inch, he would encounter her warm flesh...

Taking a deep breath, Lysander stepped back. 'You get off to bed, kitling,' he said in his most avuncular tone. 'I'll see to everything down here.'

Sense returned in a blinding flash of shame. With a little gasp, Tamsin snatched up a candlestick from the hall table and fled.

Lysander watched her go, desire tightening his loins.

God's teeth, if she was a year or two older he would have taken her at her word!

An angry frown creased his forehead as he locked the door and blew out the remaining candles. Striding up the stairs, he entered his closet and, throwing off his hat and cloak, poured himself a large bumper of brandy.

He sat down in his favourite chair to drink it, his thoughts seething.

There was a coquettish magic in that warm curving of her lips. Was it as unconscious as it was alluring? Or did she mean what her provocative smile promised? He knew she enjoyed his company—they had spent too much time together for him to be mistaken on that score—but her flirtatious behaviour could be the result of giddy innocence. Girls of her age often wanted to test out their powers of attraction and any man would do as well as another.

Damn it, he must be imagining things! Certes, she liked him, but she was much too young and innocent to want him to make love to her!

The matter settled to his satisfaction, Lysander heaved a sigh of regretful relief and, finishing his brandy, went off to bed.

* * *

The following morning Corinna expressed the wish to visit St James's Fair. 'It is an age since I attended a fair,' she announced with a wheedling smile at her brother.

Lysander gave in. 'You'd better take Marie to attend you. Knowing you, you'll want to buy an armful of fairings and I'm damned if I am carrying them around like a looby.'

Corinna laughed and promised him he should not be called upon to act as her footboy.

However, when she rang for Marie, it was Tamsin who answered the bell.

'I am afraid your maid is indisposed, my lady,' she replied in answer to Corinna's enquiry. 'She has a stomach ache. I think the lamprey pie we had for supper last night disagreed with her.'

No one else in the household had been sick, so Tamsin was sure that the pie could not have been bad. It was just ill luck that it had set the Frenchwoman retching.

'I thought she looked a little green when she brought me my washing-water.'

'I have given her an infusion of dill and peppermint to help settle her stomach, but I think she should stay a-bed, my lady.'

A vexed frown touched Corinna's wide mouth. While she felt sorry for Marie, it was annoying to have her plans upset.

She eyed Tamsin thoughtfully. 'Do you like fairs, Mrs Barton?'

Tamsin had little experience of fairs. She had sneaked off once with Sam to visit one, but they had both received such a thrashing from his mother that they had never dared try again. Unwilling to admit to her ignorance, she nodded cautiously.

'Good.' Corinna's expression brightened. 'Then I want you to attend me today.'

She smiled at Tamsin's astonishment. 'Run along and change out of that working-dress, *petite*. My brother hates to be kept waiting.'

Tamsin's spirits lifted. In spite of her idiotic loss of control

last night, she yearned for Lysander's company and the
thought of spending several hours in his presence was enough
to banish any misgivings.

The fair, which ran for fourteen days after St James's Day,
was held in the road leading from St James's Palace to Ty-
burn. By the time Lysander and his companions arrived it
was in full swing. People dressed in their best swarmed
amongst the booths that had been set up and the noise was
tremendous. Fiddles screeched and drums beat as a stilt-
walker and a fire-eater performed their tricks and the owners
of the booths bawled their wares.

Tamsin stared at a troop of jugglers, her eyes wide with
wonder as their balls and hoops spun up into the warm morning air.

'What should you like to do first?' Lysander asked his
sister, but his gaze strayed to Tamsin.

S'death, her eyes were like stars!

Corinna's glance followed his and she hid a smile. 'I think
I should like to stroll about and see what's here,' she replied.

Lysander offered each of them an arm and, colouring with
pleasure at this unexpected distinction, Tamsin placed her
hand upon his dark broadcloth sleeve.

For once she felt as finely clad in her blue gown as her
companions, who had both taken the precaution of dressing
more plainly than usual. In such a crowd it was easy to spoil
delicate, expensive fabrics and Lysander had no wish to deliberately invite the attentions of cut-purses, who, he had assured Tamsin, were rife at such gatherings.

For this reason he had also advised his sister to leave her
jewellery at home and she wore only her wedding-band and
small pearls in her ears. Tamsin decided, however, that no
matter how plainly he dressed, only a fool would make the
mistake of thinking Sir Lysander Saxon anything other than
a gentleman of high rank.

It was his proud bearing that betrayed him. That arrogant
tilt of his blond head and his innate air of command spoke

of good breeding. Allied to his startling good looks, it was no wonder he drew every feminine eye!

Tamsin restrained a sigh. It wasn't fair! How was a simple country girl to resist such a man?

They paused to watch a puppet-show and Lysander derived more pleasure from Tamsin's enjoyment than the entertainment. When it was finished he bought them all a beaker of julep each to cool their thirst.

The sweet fruity taste lingered on Tamsin's tongue as they strolled on.

'Do you want to see the Celebrated Italian Dwarf?' Lysander asked, stopping outside one of the booths.

Corinna laughingly declined, rather to Tamsin's disappointment, and they moved on to where a row of stalls selling ribbons and jewellery had been set up.

'Those pink ribbons are pretty.' Corinna pointed out a bunch and the stall-keeper, scenting a sale, pounced.

'Cheapest at the fair, my ribbons are, and the best. You'll not find finer anywhere in London, my lady.' She snatched up the bunch Corinna had admired and thrust them at her. 'They suit you, mistress, on my oath!'

'How much?' Lysander enquired.

The woman named a scandalously high price, but when Corinna shook her head and would have walked on she dropped it by half.

'That's reasonable.' Corinna reached for her purse, but Lysander waved her to put it away.

'Thank you, dear heart.' Corinna smiled at him and took the ribbons. She admired them for a moment and then handed them to Tamsin to put in the small basket she carried, which already held some sweetmeats and other fairings.

Corinna began to inspect the goods on the next stall, leaving Lysander to conclude payment. Tamsin moved to follow her.

'Wait.' She turned back and Lysander handed her a bunch of turquoise satin ribbons.

'I'll take both bunches,' he said to the woman on the stall

and Tamsin stared at him speechlessly as he handed over the necessary coins.

He took her arm and urged her forward to rejoin the Comtesse.

'I…I can't take these,' she finally managed to splutter.

'You must. They match your lovely eyes.'

'But…but—'

'Tamsin, it's only a fairing.' Lysander smiled at her gently. 'Surely it cannot offend your Puritan principles to accept so trifling a gift?'

She was silent for an instant and then smiled back at him. 'Thank you. They are lovely.'

Tamsin put the ribbons into the basket, her heart singing. He might have described them as a trifling gift, but she would always treasure them as proof of his thoughtfulness.

And as a reminder of his unexpected compliment!

'Look! There is an astrologer here,' Corinna exclaimed, pointing out a small tent which was decorated with a painted moon, six stars and an outstretched hand. 'I think I shall have my fortune told.'

Lysander grinned at her. Astrology was extremely fashionable and most people believed one's birth chart held all the secrets of the future. Lysander was unconvinced.

'Shame on you, brother!' Corinna laughed when he voiced his scepticism.

Tamsin was rather inclined to agree with Lysander. Her aunt had condemned astrology as a branch of witchcraft and, while Tamsin was more open-minded, she suspected that an astrologer reduced to making his living at a fair might not be the best exponent of the art.

Undeterred, Corinna moved towards the tent. 'Do you wish to consult the stars, Mistress Barton?'

Tamsin was tempted. However, she had very little money left and she did not wish to waste it. Knowing that Lysander would doubtless offer to pay for her if she showed interest, she shook her head firmly.

'Very well. We shall leave you here to wait for us.' Corinna took her brother's arm.

'Don't move,' Lysander commanded. He had no interest in consulting the astrologer, but he did not mean to leave his sister alone with the fellow. In spite of her present high spirits, Corinna was in a vulnerable state of mind and could be easily upset if the rogue started to spout the wrong kind of nonsense about faithful husbands and a quiverful of babies.

They disappeared into the tent and Tamsin set down her basket. It wasn't heavy, but the day had grown very warm and her hand was feeling sticky. She was glad, however, that she didn't have to wear a vizard mask to protect her reputation like the Comtesse—her face was hot enough as it was. Being a servant had a few advantages!

A grimace twisted her lips. Perhaps it was as well she was growing used to the role for it seemed likely it was to be her destiny. She would not, *could* not, return to Whiteladies and she needed employment, especially if she could not find her father.

Nat the coachman, in whom she had partially confided, had advised her to post a notice in St Paul's Cathedral asking if anyone had any information about the man she sought. Tamsin had been surprised at this suggestion, but Nat had assured her that it was one of the best places to garner news.

'Lord love you, Mrs Tamsin, there's any garner of such business goes on there! If you wants a servant, you posts a notice outside one of the small shops between the buttresses. Aye, and the printing-press in the crypt can fix you up with the very advertisement if you've a mind,' he'd said.

Tamsin was debating the idea. She would ask Martha what she thought the next time she saw her. After their talk the other day Sir Lysander had given her permission to visit her former nurse whenever she liked, providing she took Luke with her.

'Help! Thief! Stop, I say!'

A loud feminine voice cut into Tamsin's cogitations and she looked up to see a tall, pock-marked youth hurtling towards her being chased by a dark-haired girl in a vivid red gown.

Without conscious thought, she sprang forward and grabbed the boy by the arm.

'Le' go!' He struck out with his free hand, punching her in the midriff with a force that winded her, but she hung on grimly.

The dark-haired girl's screams had attracted attention. Made desperate by the roar of condemnation that went up, the youth increased his struggle to be free of Tamsin's clinging grip.

'Stupid bitch!' he panted and swung a blow at her head which would have felled her had not a strong hand shot out to prevent it landing.

With a yelp of fright, the youth stared up at the tall man who held his wrist in a grip of steel.

'Scum!' said Sir Lysander Saxon pleasantly. 'Give me one good reason why I should not break your neck.'

Chapter Eight

'Thank you. You were very brave,' the dark-haired girl said to Tamsin as they watched the would-be thief being dragged off.

Corinna, emerging from the astrologer's tent after her brother, had managed to persuade Lysander to release the miscreant into the custody of the law.

Someone in the crowd had obligingly run to fetch a constable. When this well-fed individual had arrived, carrying his staff of office and bristling with self-importance, Lysander had handed the youth over and the crowd which had gathered drifted away.

'And my thanks to you, sir.' Turning to Lysander, the girl curtsied low. When she straightened there was admiration in her coal-black eyes and her smile was warm. 'I don't know what I would have done without your help.'

To Tamsin's surprise, Lysander's well-cut features remained impassive. 'My pleasure, ma'am,' he replied with a cool disinterest.

'Here, this is yours, I think.' Puzzled by his unusual hauteur, Tamsin gave the girl her brightest smile as she held out the purse which the thief had dropped during their struggle. Tamsin had picked it up while they were waiting for the constable. Her hands had been shaking, she'd noticed, but she was glad to see that they were steady again as she dropped the purse into the girl's outstretched palm.

'Thank you again, Mistress…?' Her voice, surprisingly deep and strong for a woman, rose in enquiry.

'Barton. My name is Tamsin Barton.'

'Molly Heron.' The girl touched her own breast lightly.

Her gaze drawn by the movement, Tamsin realised for the first time that her new acquaintance was wearing a very low-cut gown, which revealed a good deal of her voluptuous figure. She had been too preoccupied to notice it before or the paint which adorned Molly's bold-featured face.

'If you no longer need our assistance, ma'am, we will take our leave,' Lysander said in a politely dismissive voice.

Molly Heron nodded silently.

Lysander offered his arm first to Corinna and then turned to Tamsin. 'Mistress Barton?' Impatience fringed his tone.

'One moment, my lord.' Rebellion stirred in Tamsin as she watched Molly walk away. She did not approve of his brusque manner and she didn't care if he knew it!

With a quick movement she darted after Molly. 'Mistress Heron!'

Molly turned round.

'May I call on you?' Tamsin asked shyly.

'On me?'

'I should like to reassure myself that you have not taken any harm from your fright today.'

'I reckon it's me who should be calling on you!' Molly's black eyes twinkled.

Tamsin grinned. 'To tell you the truth, Molly Heron, I am new to London and in sore need of a friend of my own age. I thought that perhaps…' Her voice trailed off uncertainly as she realised how forward her behaviour must seem.

'We could be friends? Aye, I should like that!' Molly's contralto voice was warm.

Her gaze flicked to where Lysander and his sister stood waiting. 'But won't those fancy mates of yours object?'

Tamsin gave a defiant shrug and Molly laughed. 'Like that,

is it? Well, I lodge above Master Wintershall's, the stationers at the sign of the Bible-in-the-Hand in Duck Lane. I am in most mornings. Come any day that suits you.'

'I'll visit you as soon as I can.' Tamsin promised, memorising the address.

'Aye, do, but now you'd best go. He's got a face on him like a thundercloud.' Molly giggled. 'Damn handsome, though! Wouldn't mind dancing Sallenger's Round with him!'

Tamsin wasn't sure, but she rather thought this must be a bawdy allusion. Shock rippled through her, but there was such good humour in the saucy wink that accompanied this bold statement that she couldn't find offence in Molly's frankness.

With a last smile she bade Molly farewell and hurried back to where Lysander and Corinna were waiting.

'Are you ready to leave now?'

A steely coldness froze his voice and Tamsin felt a flicker of trepidation.

By the time they reached Wych Street this emotion had given way to indignation. She had done nothing wrong. There was no reason for him to be so cross with her.

Once inside the house she quickly excused herself and marched off to the kitchen, her back ramrod stiff.

Lysander made a move to follow her, but was forestalled by Corinna.

'Let her go, dear heart.'

He quirked his eyebrow in enquiry and Corinna chuckled. 'Can't you see she is angry?'

'*She* is angry?' A black scowl marred Lysander's handsome features.

Corinna sighed. She could see that he was in no mood to listen to her advice. 'I think I shall go and rest on my bed for an hour or two,' she murmured. 'I don't know why, but I am devilishly sleepy these days.' A wry smile touched her wide mouth. 'It must be all this fresh London air!'

'Do you want Tamsin to hold back dinner?' Lysander asked, his scowl fading.

Corinna shook her head. 'I am not hungry. In fact, I feel quite queasy.'

'Perhaps you've had too much sun,' Lysander spoke lightly, masking his concern. Unlike Marie, Corinna had not eaten lamprey pie last night. In fact, she had sampled very little of Jane's lavish feast, either.

Hoping that her lack of appetite did not signal the onset of some illness, he offered to escort her to her room.

'Nay, I can manage,' Corinna refused him.

Lysander watched her climb the stairs and then turned on his heel.

The kitchen was a hive of activity. All four members of his staff were busily engaged in preparations for dinner and his entrance went unnoticed for a moment.

'I wish to speak to you, Mistress Barton.' Tamsin looked up from the sauce she was stirring. 'Now.'

Tamsin was tempted to refuse, but the look on his face told her he was perfectly capable of dragging her out of the kitchen if she dared.

'Very well.' Beckoning Dinah from her task of chopping vegetables, she told her to stir the sauce until it was smooth.

'And, Luke, make sure you keep turning that spit or the roast will burn. It's nearly ready so be careful.'

Lysander stood waiting for her to finish her instructions, his foot tapping impatiently.

'Don't worry, I'll see that nothing spoils.' Matthew paused in his polishing of the silverware which was to grace the dining-table.

She could see that he had sensed the strained atmosphere and his reassuring smile heartened her as she followed Lysander into the hallway.

Once out of earshot Lysander halted. Tamsin had been expecting him to lead the way into the parlour and her expressive face revealed her surprise.

'This won't take long,' he said tersely. 'You are to have nothing to do with that girl.'

'What gives you the right to dictate my friends?'

Her curt demand made his face darken. 'The fact that you appear to have no sense,' he retorted.

'There is no need to be rude—'

'If you had remained quietly by the astrologer's tent as I ordered, you wouldn't have got into difficulties,' Lysander continued inexorably. 'You could have been seriously hurt.'

Tamsin bit her lip. He was right and she knew it. 'I didn't mean to disobey you,' she confessed. 'I heard Mistress Heron screaming for help and acted without thinking.'

'You have a kind heart, kitling.' Lysander's tone softened. 'And it was brave of you to go to her aid, but you must learn not to act on impulse. It can be dangerous.'

'You acted on impulse when you rescued me,' Tamsin said softly.

Lysander stared down into her lovely face. 'Aye,' he replied, his voice suddenly hoarse.

That impulsive action had proved more dangerous than he could have dreamt!

Tamsin sensed the change in him. His green eyes were glittering and she could see a pulse beating at the base of his throat. Her own blood was racing within her veins and a fierce yearning for his touch exploded in the pit of her stomach.

For a long silent moment the warm still air seemed to vibrate as their gaze locked and the passion they were both struggling to suppress fought for freedom.

Tamsin's mouth was dry with tension. Nervously, she licked her lips.

With an effort Lysander wrenched his gaze from her mouth and crushed the desire rising in him. 'I understand why you put yourself at risk to help Mrs Heron, but you must not see her again.'

'Why not?' Tamsin's anger, which had been temporarily

blocked by the bewildering sensations his ardent gaze had provoked, boiled up again.

'She isn't a suitable companion for you.'

'You *know* her?'

'Not in the sense of having been introduced.' He shook his blond head impatiently. 'I've seen her at the Red Bull Playhouse. She is one of the orange-girls there.'

Seeing she hadn't a clue what he was talking about, Lysander began to explain. 'Various refreshments are sold in theatres. You can get drinks, China oranges, lemons, sweetmeats. The cost is exorbitant—'

'You think her a cheat for overpricing her wares?'

'That's not my point.' Lysander swept aside this interruption with a brusque wave of one hand.

'Then what has her job got to do with anything?' Tamsin demanded in angry confusion.

'Orange-sellers trade on their looks. They stroll among the benches, encouraging men to handle them in whatever familiar manner they fancy.'

Tamsin blushed as the implication of what he was saying sank in. 'You mean...'

'Aye, they sell themselves.' Lysander's tone was curt as he nodded confirmation. 'Most of them are no better than the whores at Madam Cole's.'

Tamsin's hands clenched into fists. 'Maybe some of those women would choose another way to earn their living if they had the opportunity,' she snapped.

'And some women are born whores,' Lysander replied harshly. 'Unless I mistake my guess, your Molly Heron finds it as easy to sell her body as she finds selling oranges.'

'You can't know that for sure!' Tamsin's blush deepened into red flags of temper flying in her thin cheeks.

'What do *you* know of such matters?' Lysander shot back. 'You have no more experience of the world than a new-born babe.'

'I may be young and inexperienced, but I am not stupid!'

'Do not presume to argue with me, my girl. You are to keep away from that tickle-tail!'

His arrogance fanned the flames of Tamsin's fury. 'I will see Mrs Heron whenever I choose!'

Lysander took a deep breath and silently counted to ten. 'You think me unreasonable, but believe me, I have only your best interests in mind,' he said in a quieter tone. 'Even if Mrs Heron is not what I think, she still frequents a world that is wholly unsuitable for an innocent like yourself.'

Why did he keep harping on about her innocence? She had already guessed Molly was no saint! 'I do not intend to patronise the theatre, my lord,' she said in a cool little voice. 'Nor do I intend to mix with Mrs Heron's friends.'

'You may find that more difficult than you anticipate.'

Tamsin shrugged carelessly.

A hankering to wring her neck began to possess Lysander. 'And if I forbid you to see her on pain of leaving this house?' he said roughly.

'You…you wouldn't be so…so tyrannical?' Tamsin gulped.

Gazing down into her wide eyes, Lysander knew his threat to be empty. 'I should,' he muttered. 'But I won't.'

Tamsin heaved a sigh of relief. Shooting a glance at him through her thick lashes, she saw that he was still frowning. 'I'm sorry,' she murmured, surprising herself. 'I don't mean to be such a nuisance to you. It's just that I want to make my own decisions.'

'You are so young.' Lysander said, almost to himself.

A wry grimace tugged at Tamsin's mouth. 'You think me a child, but how am I to learn to stand on my own two feet if I never get a chance to do things for myself?'

Lysander was silent.

Living with her Aunt Deborah, she had never had the opportunity to choose her own path. Now, having had a taste of freedom, the rebellious streak which had enabled her to survive her aunt's harsh dominion was flowering into a yearning for independence.

'Please don't be angry with me. I hate it when we quarrel.'

Lysander's sombre expression gave way to an ironic smile.

Realising what he was thinking, Tamsin continued hastily, 'I know I have rejected your advice before, but I swear I will be careful this time.'

'You promise to take Luke with you?'

Holding her breath, Tamsin nodded.

'Very well. You may call on Mrs Heron, but I don't want you gadding about town with her. Stick to visiting her lodgings if you must.'

Tamsin expelled her breath in a rush of relief. 'Thank you!'

Lysander fixed her with a stern look. 'Above all, don't let her inveigle you into accompanying her to the theatre!'

'Oh, I won't!' Tamsin gave him a sunny smile. 'I am still too much of a Puritan to have any desire to visit a playhouse, my lord!' she announced and, bobbing a curtsy, excused herself to return to the cooking.

Charles Stuart ducked his head as he moved into the shelter provided by the canopy of the shallop. ''Odsfish, what a foul evening!'

Climbing down into the boat, Lysander shook the rain out of his eyes and followed his friend. 'At least the christening went well, Sire.'

Charles grinned. 'The poor brat cried so loud I was a-feared I should drop him!' He beckoned Lysander to join him on the seat beneath the canopy. 'Come and sit down and tell me how goes your wooing of the rich widow.'

They had been to the Tower, where Charles had acted as godfather to Sir John Robinson's child. Robinson, a fervent Royalist, had been a colonel in the Civil War and had played a part in bringing about the Restoration. As a reward he had been given the important post of Lieutenant of the Tower as well as a baronetcy.

A rich man, he had provided a splendid dinner to follow the christening. Lysander had been one of the guests and had greatly enjoyed the occasion. Charles's innocent question, however, had reminded him there was no easy escape from his dilemma.

'The courtship is proceeding as planned,' he replied lightly, masking his inner misgivings. 'I think Mistress Godolphin will accept my suit.'

'I shall expect an invitation to the wedding!' Charles sensed there was something Lysander was not telling him, but decided not to probe. Lysander was a complex man, not given to displaying emotion, and he did not appreciate curiosity, even from close friends.

'Does she accompany you to Melcombe next week?' he continued, raising his voice against the thunder rumbling in the air.

Lysander shook his head, setting the wet feathers on his beplumed hat dripping. 'Nay. Her uncle wishes to return home to Rye to see to some business and I believe Jane may go with him.'

Jane owned a house in Mermaid Street. It had belonged to her family for some generations and she had returned to live there after the death of her second husband.

'I dislike the place,' she had told him when he had asked why she did not live at Thornhill, the estate which had come to her from her first marriage.

They had been strolling arm-in-arm in the Mulberry Gardens enjoying the fresh morning coolness at the time. The gardens had been quiet at that early hour and the peaceful atmosphere had apparently encouraged Jane to confide in him.

'My father was an extremely wealthy wool merchant. I was his only surviving child and he wanted me to marry well. The advent of war hastened the marriage he had arranged for me. I was barely fourteen when Lord Cowley took me to his bed.'

Jane repressed a shudder. Her wedding night had not been a pleasant experience. His lordship, an ardent Royalist, had been forty-five and fat. Luckily, he had gone off almost immediately to rejoin the fighting.

'I shed no tears when I learnt that he had been killed at Naseby a few months later.'

She had barely known Robert, but in becoming his widow she had become a tempting prize. The wide acres of Thornhill and her father's legacy encouraged Major Denham to lay siege to her. His troop of Parliamentary Horse ruled the district and Jane had found herself with no choice but to accept the Major's suit.

To her relief, Joshua proved a better lover, but he was a hot-tempered man, much given to finding fault. Living with him had been a great strain on her nerves.

'I respected Joshua, but I did not care for him. Perhaps if we'd had children I might have been happier.' A sigh shook Jane's shapely shoulders. She had miscarried twice and their only living child had died aged six months of the spotted fever.

Lysander had murmured a few words of comfort and wondered what had prompted Jane to cast aside her usual coquettish manner.

'Uncle Edward was my chief support in those dreadful times. Oh, I know he is vain and inclined to be worldly, but he has always been very kind to me. When Joshua broke his leg out hunting he was there to help me.'

The Major's leg had refused to heal and to everyone's horror the wound had become poisoned. He had died slowly and painfully.

'Whenever I visit Thornhill I can still hear Joshua's screams and curses.' Jane shivered in spite of the warm sunlight now bathing the grass walk. 'I could not live there.'

After a moment's silence she continued, 'That's one of the reasons why I reverted to using my maiden name. Both my marriages were unhappy and I want to forget the past.' She turned her grey eyes on Lysander. 'Indeed, I hope to sell Thornhill.'

Lysander nodded, understanding dawning on him. Her future husband might think to inherit a handsome estate and feel peeved to find it sold. She was warning him what to expect.

'If you detest the place, then selling is the best course,' he replied firmly.

The tension evident in Jane's buxom frame relaxed. 'I knew you would understand!' she exclaimed. 'Uncle Edward said I should tell you and he was right.'

'Your uncle is a shrewder man than he pretends.'

Jane laughed. 'He has been enjoying our stay in London so much! He is very sad that he must leave.'

She quickly explained that urgent business demanded Mr Fielding's return to Rye. 'He lives in Church Square, quite close to my own house. We see a lot of each other. In fact, I was thinking of returning with him. London is so hot and I heard rumours yesterday that several cases of plague had been reported in Southwark.'

She paused. 'You also intend to leave town soon, I believe?'

'I go to Melcombe next week.'

Jane nodded. 'Country air is so much better for one at this time of year.' Her gaze flicked hopefully to his face.

'Oh, indeed,' Lysander had replied and smoothly changed the subject without issuing the invitation she was so obviously angling for.

He had no desire to invite Jane Godolphin to Melcombe. Not yet.

'So, what does Corinna have to say about your wooing?' The King's voice recalled Lysander's wandering attention.

'She approves the match,' he replied.

'You must bring her to court again before you leave for Melcombe.' Charles had a soft spot for Lysander's sister.

'Unfortunately, she has not been well these last few days. In fact, I may have to postpone my departure.'

'Pray give her my best wishes for a speedy recovery.' Concern tinged Charles's voice.

Lysander nodded and, ignoring the lightning and the rain drumming noisily upon their flimsy shelter, Charles proceeded to engage him in a discussion about his plans for Whitehall. Lysander, who shared the King's interest in the sciences, knew Charles wanted a proper laboratory to house his experiments.

'What do you think about constructing a Physic Garden? It could provide plants for my experiments and even medicines.'

'I think it an excellent idea, Sire.'

Such blameless pursuits might divert his attention from Barbara Palmer! Their relationship was already the subject of much gossip, scandalising many ordinary folk, but the Court only laughed.

The reckless, dissolute pursuit of pleasure had become the hallmark of most courtiers. It was now fashionable to laugh at virtue in any form. Wit was prized above hard work and honesty. Lysander had heard more brilliantly amusing jokes in the last few months than he'd heard in all his years of exile, but the humour was often cruel, mocking fidelity and honour.

It was strange, he thought, almost as though in achieving their goal of restoring the old order they had lost a lodestar to believe in. The horrors of war and exile had scarred everyone's soul, but he found it disturbing that so many were determined to wash away the past in a tidal wave of excess.

Jack had often accused him of being cynical and hardbitten, but Lysander knew in his bones that he could not be content in this new London for long. To spend an occasional night gaming and drinking until dawn was amusing. To spend every evening in such meaningless pursuits would bore him senseless!

The shallop was nearing Temple Stairs.

'Shall we drop you here or do you want to come back to Whitehall?' Charles asked.

'Another time, if I may, Sire.' Lysander was suddenly aware of having been gone all day.

Charles nodded. 'If Corinna is not feeling any better,' he

said, guessing what lay behind Lysander's polite refusal, 'let me know and I shall send my personal physician.'

Lysander thanked him and Charles ordered the boat to pull in.

Lysander disembarked with a lithe agility that made light of the slippery, mud-coated stairs and, with a final wave of farewell, set off for home.

'Thank God you are come!' Matthew greeted him the instant he stepped inside the house.

Shrugging off his wet cloak Lysander glanced at him sharply. 'What's wrong, Matt?'

''Tis Lady Corinna. She was took sick after dinner. Fainted clean away, she did.' Matt's homely face wore a look of anxiety.

'Where is she?' Lysander thrust his wet hat at Matthew.

'In her chamber. Mrs Barton is with her.'

Lysander nodded and sprinted up the stairs.

Tamsin answered his gentle knock. Laying a warning finger to her lips, she whispered, 'She is asleep,' and ushered him into the room.

Lysander stared down at his sister's sleeping form. Her face was pale, but she was breathing easily and seemed to be comfortable. Beckoning to Tamsin, he moved away from the bed.

Out of earshot, he halted. 'What happened?' he asked quietly.

'After dinner Lady Corinna said she wanted to do some embroidery. She went into the parlour and sent Marie to fetch the new silks we bought yesterday.'

Lysander had escorted them on this shopping expedition to Westminster Hall. Tamsin had thought it strange to find stalls and booths there sharing the ancient building with the law courts. However, there appeared to be a roaring trade in books and luxury goods and Corinna had found exactly the right shades of embroidery silks that she required.

'Then Marie came rushing into the kitchen to tell us that she had returned to find her ladyship on the floor.' Tamsin's mouth tightened involuntarily. Marie had been worse than useless! Wailing and carrying on fit to wake the dead instead of helping her mistress!

Tamsin had been forced to banish the Frenchwoman from the parlour. 'I think that Lady Corinna must have fainted. She came round again after a minute and Matthew helped me get her upstairs and into bed.'

'Did you send for a doctor?'

Tamsin shook her head. 'She would not hear of it, saying she would be better presently if we didn't fuss.'

Lysander frowned. Corinna shared Matthew's fervent dislike of physicians.

'I didn't like to insist,' Tamsin murmured apologetically.

Once she recovered her senses Corinna hadn't seemed ill. She had no fever or headache and complained only of tiredness.

'Don't worry. You have done well.' Lysander was swift to reassure her. 'Tomorrow I shall try to persuade her to change her mind and see a doctor. We cannot leave for Dorset until she is up to the journey.'

'May I ask how long you will be away?' Tamsin said timidly. 'Dinah and Luke are worrying, you see, if you wish to keep them on.'

'Tell them their jobs are safe. I mean to return to London quite soon. This visit to Dorset is merely by way of a reconnaissance to discover what damage has been done.'

Matthew, of course, would accompany his master, but Tamsin wondered what on earth she was going to do with herself in Lysander's absence. Even if she kept busy cleaning every inch of the house and furnishings, there would still be too many empty hours left in which to miss him.

'You look tired.' Lysander noticed the little frown between her dark copper brows and misinterpreted its cause. 'Go and get some rest. I'll sit with her for a while.'

Tamsin smiled, appreciating his concern. 'I'm not tired, sir,' she said quietly. 'But I ought to go and check that preparations for supper are running smoothly.'

He nodded, but as she turned to go added impulsively, 'Will you sup with me?'

Tamsin hesitated. The arrival of the Comtesse had prompted her to eat her meals in the kitchen. The decision to do so had been hers—she had not wanted to intrude on his time with his sister. In a sensible corner of her mind she knew she ought to make some excuse now and refuse his renewed invitation.

Enjoying his company was a dangerous delight! It would be folly to lose her heart to a man who could never be hers.

'I hate eating alone.' There was a persuasive note in his deep attractive voice. 'And I have missed our tête-à-têtes.'

Until he had met Tamsin Barton, Lysander had subscribed to the usual cynical view that the last thing one expected or, indeed, wanted in a pretty young woman was an interesting mind. It had been enlightening to discover that he could actually enjoy a conversation with her.

It was odd, but the many differences between them simply didn't matter. Their minds were in tune, almost as if they had been friends for a long, long time.

'I should be glad to share your supper.' The words sprang unbidden to Tamsin's lips and she realised with a little inward shiver that she didn't *want* to be sensible!

Like a moth to the flame, she thought ruefully, but she knew that she counted the risk well worth it.

The next morning Corinna was well enough to insist on attending church. 'I don't need a doctor,' she laughed, dismissing Lysander's suggestion as she rose from the breakfast-table. 'I merely over-ate at dinner and, since I did not think to loosen my stays, paid the consequences for my greed!'

She seemed so much recovered, with a bloom in her cheeks that had been missing for many a day, that Lysander dismissed his forebodings.

Corinna ordered Marie to fetch her best cloak. While they were waiting for the maid to return, Tamsin came into the parlour to check on the fire which had been lit earlier to ward off the damp chill which lingered in the air after last night's storm.

'Come with us to St Dunstan's, Mrs Barton,' Corinna invited on impulse.

Tamsin hesitated. Her benefactor had invited guests to dinner and she was anxious not to let him down. She had got up very early to begin preparations and had been busy ever since.

'How are things going in the kitchen?' Lysander asked, guessing the reason for her hesitation.

'Everything is under control, my lord,' Tamsin murmured.

'Then come with us.' Lysander endorsed his sister's invitation with an encouraging smile. 'The walk will do you good and I'm sure Matthew will keep an eye on everything while you are out.'

'You can rest your feet while you listen to the sermon,' Corinna added with a grin.

Delighted at this unexpected chance to be in Lysander's company, Tamsin nodded assent and ran upstairs to remove her apron and brush her unruly curls.

'Why did you invite her, Corinna?' Lysander asked. 'Do you like her?'

He was surprised to discover how much her answer mattered to him!

'Her company pleases me,' Corinna replied. 'Unlike Marie, she is cheerful!'

Her maid was homesick and her constant sighs were getting on Corinna's nerves. 'If Louise had not left my service to get married just before I decided to visit you, I would not have brought Marie at all,' she informed Lysander.

'Louise was your waiting-woman, was she not?'

'Aye, and a dear friend. I did think I might look for her replacement while I was here in England. It would be pleasant to have someone about me who spoke my native tongue, but there isn't much time to find the right person.'

Corinna shrugged. She didn't want to choose in haste and then regret it. Everyone knew that a waiting-woman occupied a special place in her mistress's household. Her successful candidate would have to act as a companion and confidante, secretary and maid all rolled into one. Louise had played the virginals and was skilled at cards and Corinna had treated her almost as an equal, buying her handsome gowns and providing her with a generous dowry when she had married.

Tamsin's return to the parlour was the signal for them to set off for the church of St Dunstan-in-the-West, Lysander's preferred place of worship, a short walk away. Tamsin, who did not share her aunt's extreme religious views, enjoyed the Anglican service with its hint of ceremonial and the sermon, which had the additional advantage of being shorter than the ones she was used to at home.

The service over, they walked home to Wych Street and Tamsin hurried back to the kitchen. To her relief, nothing had gone wrong with her elaborate menu during her absence.

A little after noon Lysander's guests arrived and to his surprise, Mistress Godolphin was accompanied by his cousin, Lord Fanshawe.

'Uncle Edward presents his apologies,' Jane announced with a pretty smile as Tamsin helped her remove her cloak. 'He has the earache.'

Mr Fielding's ear was painful and swollen and, fearing he would cast a damper upon the party, he had urged his niece to choose another escort.

'I was sure you would find your cousin's company agreeable so I asked him to take Uncle Edward's place.'

'You don't mind, do you, coz?' Jack enquired with a slightly nervous look.

Knowing Jack would never dream of trying to cut him out with the wealthy widow, no matter how much he liked her, Lysander told him not to be such a gull-finch.

Jack grinned at this insult and handed his cloak to Tamsin with a friendly wink and a jovial demand to know what she was cooking. 'The smells coming from your kitchen are delicious, ma'am!'

Tamsin laughed. 'I hope you will not be disappointed, my lord.'

Jane's eyebrows rose at their banter. She hadn't realised that Lysander's housekeeper was so young or so pretty! She also appeared to be on the best of terms with both men. In fact, her manner was altogether too friendly, in Jane's opinion, almost as if the wench thought herself their equal!

'Shall we proceed, gentlemen?' she murmured, a slight edge in her normally dulcet tones. 'I'm sure Lady Corinna is wondering what is keeping us.'

'Of course.' Reminded of his social obligations, Lysander offered her his arm. 'She's in the drawing-room. Let's go on up.'

Jane threw Tamsin a cool smile as she swept past, but Tamsin had the distinct impression that Mistress Godolphin did not like her.

Which is strange, she thought, since we've only just met!

Tamsin had heard a lot about the rich widow from Nat, who knew all the latest gossip.

'On the catch for another husband, so they say,' the coachman had said. 'And guess who she's set her sights on?' He'd tapped the side of his nose and winked at Tamsin, who had stared back at him in puzzlement.

They had been interrupted at that point in their conversation and she had never got around to asking him what he meant, but all of a sudden she had a horrible feeling she knew.

'Lack-wit!' she muttered to herself as she stamped back into the kitchen. Why hadn't she realised it before? It was as obvious as the nose on her face! The question was, did Sir Lysander reciprocate the lovely widow's interest?

Master Cooper was waiting on table and Tamsin had no chance to observe her benefactor's behaviour towards his guest. Busily arranging food on their best dishes, she tried not to think about what was going on in the dining-room.

'Don't look so worried, Mrs Barton,' Dinah said as she helped Tamsin add last-minute garnishes to the second course. 'They must like what you've cooked for 'em. See, most of them dishes is empty.'

Matthew had removed the first course and the used dishes returned to the kitchen bore witness to Dinah's encouraging remark. The fricassee of rabbit and the roast chickens had all been eaten and there were only scraps left of the ox tongue and the beef pie.

Scattering a handful of blanched almonds over a dish of sallet, Tamsin schooled her expression to cheerfulness and thanked Dinah for her encouragement.

When she had sent the final sweetmeats up to the dining-room, Tamsin collapsed on to one of the kitchen-stools. 'Thank heavens!' she muttered, stretching her stiff back.

She was hot, sticky and exhausted. 'Luke, broach that new barrel of small beer in the pantry. I think we all need a drink.'

Luke rushed off happily to obey, leaving his sister to slip off her shoes and rub her aching feet.

'I'm glad the master don't have fancy dinners every day,' Dinah declared.

Looking at the mountain of washing-up which had to be tackled, Tamsin nodded in heartfelt agreement.

She was halfway through her mug of beer when Master Cooper came in. 'Sir Lysander wishes to thank you all for your efforts,' he announced. He smiled at Tamsin. 'He wants you to come up to the dining-room, Mrs Barton, to receive the congratulations of his guests.'

Tamsin blushed. 'I don't think that's necessary,' she demurred.

'Go on, Mrs Tamsin,' Luke and Dinah chorused. 'Don't be shy, you deserves their praise.'

'Aye, lass.' Matthew nodded smiling agreement. 'You've worked like a Trojan. Come and accept the appreciation which is your due.'

Heartened by their support, Tamsin laughingly removed her stained apron and allowed Matthew to usher her upstairs.

'Tamsin!' Lysander leapt to his feet at their entrance and came to draw her forward to join him at the head of the table.

'You have excelled yourself,' he declared. 'That was the best dinner I've eaten this year.'

'Aye, so say we all!' chimed in Jack, thumping rousing affirmation on the table-top.

There was a distinct slurring in Lord Fanshawe's voice, but Tamsin was so delighted by the warmth of Lysander's smile that she scarcely noticed it.

'Congratulations, my dear. Everything was perfect,' Lady Corinna added her thanks with a little nod of approval.

Still holding her by the hand, Lysander picked up his glass, a reckless light in his green eyes. 'A toast! To the prettiest cook in London!'

He took a deep swallow of his wine, his eyes fixed on her face. Unable to tear her gaze away, Tamsin could feel her heart pounding.

Lysander smiled down into her eyes. 'Will you join—'

'I fear I have spilt some gravy on my dress,' Jane spoke up loudly, interrupting him before he could finish. 'Could you sponge it clean it for me, Mrs Barton?'

Ignoring the dark look cast her way by her host, Jane stood up and continued coolly, 'Now, if you please, before the stain sets and becomes impossible to remove.'

'Of course, ma'am.' Tamsin hid her annoyance and inclined her head politely.

Lysander was still holding her hand. For an instant his grip tightened as she sought to remove her fingers, then he released her.

Jane sailed out of the room and, with a last smile for the rest of the company, Tamsin followed her.

Jane had halted outside the withdrawing-room and was waiting for her. 'Come in here,' she ordered crisply.

Puzzled, Tamsin obeyed. To her surprise, Jane closed the door after them.

'Your dress, ma'am,' she began, a strange unease possessing her at the sight of Jane's cold expression. 'I may need water to—'

'Never mind that now,' Jane snapped and Tamsin blinked at the anger in her voice.

'I didn't bring you here to attend to my gown,' Jane continued in the same hard tone and Tamsin realised she couldn't see any stain disfiguring the glowing peacock lutestring. 'I wanted a word with you in private.'

'Indeed, Mistress Godolphin?' Tamsin struggled to maintain a polite expression, but inwardly she was seething. What was the matter with the wretched woman? She had been giving her cold looks ever since she arrived and now, after all Tamsin's hard work, she had deliberately spoilt her little moment of glory.

'I do not like the way you ape your betters, Mrs Barton. You put yourself forward too much, particularly around the gentlemen. You are a servant and I would have you remember it.'

Tamsin's mouth fell open. Was the widow so proud and puffed-up with her own importance that she couldn't abide anyone else enjoying attention?

'I'm sorry if my behaviour has given you offence,' she replied spiritedly, 'but I cannot see what need I have to apologise.'

'Don't be insolent!' Jane glared at her. 'I've seen the way you make sheep's eyes at Sir Lysander.'

Tamsin gasped, but before she could deny this ridiculous accusation Jane's hard voice hammered on. 'I am willing to make an excuse for you this time since you are young and obviously foolish, but in future you will remember your place or I shall have you dismissed.'

Tamsin stiffened. 'You speak very boldly, ma'am,' she retorted, anger lending her courage. 'However, it is Sir Lysander who decides my employment, not you.'

A sharp burst of laughter escaped Jane. 'If you think you can compete with me, you are even more naïve than I imagined. Little idiot, he may have a fancy to you, but your pretty face will hold no sway if I call him to heel.'

Her narrow grey gaze raked contemptuously over Tamsin.

'Behave yourself and I'll let you stay on until I am married to Sir Lysander, but I will not tolerate any further attempt on your part to ingratiate yourself with him.'

Married? Had he asked her to marry him?

'Make no mistake, he wants me for his wife,' Jane warned, reading her expressive face. 'And when I am mistress here, I don't intend to house any would-be rival so take this as fair warning of dismissal!'

Gemini, she was jealous!

Tamsin could scarcely believe it. Shakily, she strove for composure, her thoughts whirling.

'You are wrong, Mistress Godolphin,' she managed at last. 'I…I am merely grateful to Sir Lysander for his kindness, nothing more.'

She was lying and they both knew it. In spite of all her efforts to contain her feelings, she had fallen in love with Lysander Saxon.

Jane gave a disbelieving shrug. 'Deny it if you will. Just don't imagine that his behaviour today meant anything. He might not show it, but he drank as much as Jack and the smiles and compliments of a man flown with wine have no substance.'

She patted her elaborate ringlets into place and gave Tamsin a faintly malicious smile. 'I suggest you save your maidenhead for another man, assuming you still possess it, of course.'

Tamsin paled. 'You insult me, mistress! I have no intention of…of…'

'If you don't want to bed him, then you should take care not to give him and everyone else the impression that you do,' Jane cut across Tamsin's outraged protest, her voice as cold as ice.

A stricken look spread across Tamsin's expressive face and Jane's harsh tone softened a little. 'You may think yourself in love with him, but heed my advice and forget such folly before it is too late. He is out of your league and you will only get hurt.'

'Why should you care what happens to me, ma'am?' Tamsin asked, trying to hide her consternation.

'You mean nothing to me, I just don't want you causing trouble,' Jane responded promptly with a frankness that was more convincing than any flattering evasion. 'And you seem too young and green to realise that his current attraction won't last.'

Was it just jealousy speaking or was there a core of truth in Jane's warning?

'Believe me, he will not want you once he has satisfied his desire.' Jane gave a worldly little laugh. 'Why should he? Men are fickle and pretty faces are ten a farthing in London.'

She gave Tamsin a pitying glance. 'Don't you see? You have nothing else to offer him. It is inevitable that he will throw you out once your novelty wears off. At best, he might compensate you with a fat purse, but there's no guarantee you'll get so much as a penny.'

Tamsin stared at her, hot words of protest dying unspoken on her lips as her shocked mind struggled to assimilate exactly what Jane was saying.

Much as she longed to throw Jane's brutal verdict back in her face, she was horribly afraid that the older woman was right about one thing at least.

Falling in love with Lysander was a serious mistake!

Chapter Nine

'Mrs Tamsin! Come quick! It's Lady Corinna, she's fainted again.'

Tamsin shot out of the kitchen at the sound of Luke's anxious cry. By the time she got into the parlour Corinna, who was lying on the floor by the couch, was already coming round.

'Help me get her back on to the couch,' she instructed Luke.

With his assistance this task was soon successfully accomplished. 'Thank you, Luke. Now could you please go and ask Dinah to heat up some milk? I shall come and make a posset for her ladyship in a minute.'

With an audible sigh of relief, he hurried off.

Tamsin picked up a book which was on the floor. *Argenis,* a satirical romance by John Barclay. Corinna must have been reading it before she had fainted. Putting it safely out of harm's way she said, 'How are you feeling, ma'am? Shall I send for a physician?'

Weakly Corinna shook her head. Her smooth complexion was the colour of whey and there were dark circles under her eyes.

'Is there any way I can make you more comfortable? Would you like a cushion for your head?'

'Don't fuss,' Corinna murmured.

'You really ought to consult a doctor—'

'I won't see one so there is no point in badgering me,' Corinna interrupted, her voice growing noticeably stronger. 'I shall be perfectly all right in a minute.'

Tamsin bit her lip. She had no love for doctors herself, but surely something must be wrong or why else would an otherwise healthy young woman like the Comtesse keep fainting? 'If you don't mind my saying so, I think your brother will be angry if you refuse to seek proper medical advice this time, my lady.'

Corinna sighed. She knew Tamsin was right. Lysander would be furious with her intransigence. 'I know you mean well, Tamsin, but, please, just let it rest.'

She softened her refusal with a smile. 'Go and brew me one of your reviving possets, my dear.'

Tamsin dipped an obedient curtsy and quietly left the room.

Returning to the kitchen she made the strengthening hot drink, which she sweetened with honey, adding a little cinnamon and nutmeg. 'Take this to the Comtesse, Dinah,' she instructed, suspecting that Corinna might prefer the younger girl's attentions for the moment.

Tamsin had no wish to upset Lysander's sister. Corinna had been kind to her, often inviting Tamsin to go shopping with her or sit with her while she did her embroidery.

Perhaps she feels sorry for me, Tamsin mused. A stab of discomfort made the skin between her shoulder-blades prickle as she remembered Mistress Godolphin's abrasive behaviour a few days ago. Her dislike must have been obvious to everyone, she thought miserably.

Although she had done her best not to brood, Tamsin couldn't help worrying about the harsh warning Jane had thrown in her face. While it was clear that the lovely widow had a low opinion of men, she had far more experience of the world than Tamsin. In her heart Tamsin felt sure that Lysander would never behave in the cruel way Jane had described, but uncertainty plagued her.

What if she was wrong?

It would be foolish to dismiss Jane's advice out of hand. She *had* to try and keep her feeling for her benefactor in check! If she allowed herself to surrender to the desire that tormented her whenever he was near...

Tamsin's cheeks flamed. What was the matter with her! How could she even think of wanting to lie with him! Wasn't it shaming enough that she had let her wanton attraction become obvious? She had been so embarrassed by this realisation that she had spent the last few days trying to avoid him, an impossible task.

In one way, Tamsin was glad that Lysander was planning to go down to Dorset tomorrow, but how was she going to cope if Lady Corinna's sudden relapse prevented the trip? She could barely look him in the face now without remembering Jane's scornful words and blushing to the roots of her hair.

Desperate to confide in someone, Tamsin had set out yesterday morning to visit Martha, but her former nurse had not been home. She had been on the point of disconsolately returning to Wych Street when it occurred to her that there was still time to call on Molly.

Walking quickly, she went north and left the city via Aldersgate. Within moments she had reached Duck Lane; to her relief, Molly answered her knock.

'Tamsin! I wasn't expecting you until Friday.' Molly greeted her with a surprised smile.

'Have I come at a bad time?' Tamsin asked apologetically. 'Shall I go away?'

She had visited Molly twice since that day at St James's Fair and they had also gone on a picnic to the water meadows of Chelsea. Their friendship had grown stronger with each occasion, but Tamsin didn't want to impose on Molly's generous good nature.

'Don't be silly. You are always welcome.' Molly took Tamsin's arm and drew her inside. 'I've got to leave for the theatre in an hour, but that allows us plenty of time.'

She waved Tamsin to take a seat on the big shabby couch which dominated the untidy parlour and began to rummage hopefully amongst the clutter decorating her sideboard for a couple of clean mugs. 'What brings you here?' she enquired, glancing at Tamsin over her shoulder. 'I thought you said you would be too busy to get away until Sir Lysander had left town.'

Tamsin swallowed hard. 'I…I need your advice.'

'*My* advice?' Molly chuckled. 'That's a new one! Nobody's ever taken me for an oracle before!'

Triumphantly locating the desired pewter cups, she gathered up a jug of ale and brought everything over to where Tamsin was sitting. Setting the ale and mugs down on the rickety-legged table which stood close by the couch she swept a pile of clothes off the nearest stool with one casual flick of her hand and sat down in a rustle of orange taffeta skirts.

A faint grin touched Tamsin's mouth for a moment. That careless gesture—indeed, the whole chaotic two-room apartment—faithfully reflected Molly's extravagant personality.

Furnished with an odd mixture of her landlord's solid old-fashioned cast-offs and cheap bargains Molly had acquired, the small parlour was cosy and inviting. Molly had little money, but she had skilfully added colour and a touch of glamour with some bright rugs, silk cushions and a big gold-lacquered mirror.

In the tiny bedchamber which lay beyond the parlour, Molly had brightened up Master Wintershall's shabby old oak furniture with vivid crimson and gold striped bed-hangings and curtains. Here, too, the same comfortable confusion reigned. Her brilliant gowns, dazzling paste jewellery, cosmetics and bowls of fresh flowers had been scattered around by Molly's liberal hand until the bedroom was like a scented treasure-cavern glowing with light and colour.

It was as far removed as could be from the stiff formality of Whiteladies where Aunt Deborah's insistence on pristine neatness had been beaten into her dependants. Once she had got over her initial shock, Tamsin thou͏͏͏... home she would have liked for herself.

Tamsin had only felt this comfortable be͏͏... closet, which shared the same inviting atmos͏͏... Lysander and Molly's personal tastes were ver͏͏͏...

Thinking of Lysander, she was reminded insta͏͏... her problem and her face fell.

'Here, get this down you and tell me why on earth you think I can help,' Molly declared in her rich contralto voice, handing Tamsin a mug of ale.

'I want your advice because you know so much more than I do about men,' Tamsin began earnestly.

Molly grinned. 'Marry, come up, I could take that the wrong way!'

Tamsin flushed and bit her lower lip so hard that Molly immediately abandoned her joking tone. 'I'm sorry, it's not fair of me to tease you. Please, continue.'

'I'm not sure you'd be interested,' Tamsin murmured, her confidence wavering.

'Of course I will! Mind you, I can't promise my advice will help. I've never had much luck with men.' Molly's dark eyes twinkled suddenly. 'Lots of fun, aye, but nothing lasting. Actors promise you the moon, but you always end up paying for their supper as well as your own!'

During their earlier conversations Molly had been eye-poppingly frank. Although she was barely four years older than Tamsin, she had already had several lovers and Tamsin had been both shocked and fascinated by her tales of the theatre and the raffish world that lived on its fringe.

Independent by nature, Molly had left her dull village in Kent when she was fifteen to seek her fortune in London. While working in a tavern in Clerkenwell she'd met an actor who performed at the nearby Red Bull Theatre and discovered a whole new way of life.

Plays had been officially banned in 1642, but in practice clandestine performances had continued. Molly had gradually wormed her way into the Red Bull company carrying out

...ever menial task was handed out to her. Thanks to a rich lover who had taken a fancy to her a few months ago, she'd been able to abandon her tavern work completely and set herself up an orange-girl there.

Tamsin thought she was one of the happiest people she had ever met.

'Ask away,' Molly urged, breaking into Tamsin's musing. 'I promise I won't interrupt.'

'Well, you know Lysander had guests on Sunday and I was to cook a special dinner?' Thus encouraged, Tamsin launched into an explanation of all that had happened when the meal was over. 'I wouldn't mind so much, Molly, but I didn't realise my feelings for him were so transparent!'

'There's no shame loving him,' Molly declared firmly. 'Question is, how does he feel about you? I could see for myself that he likes you, but does he want more than friendship?'

'I...I think so,' Tamsin replied shyly. Smoothing her blue skirts nervously, she continued hesitantly, 'Do you think Mistress Godolphin is right? Should I try to forget about him?'

Molly frowned thoughtfully. 'I wish I could advise you to take no notice of that spiteful cow,' she said slowly, 'but it ain't so simple. She holds all the cards. Even if he prefers you to her, you can't compete with her money or rank.'

'I know.' Tamsin sighed.

Molly took a swallow of her ale. 'We are both alike, Tamsin. All we've got going for us is our looks and personality.' A self-mocking grin touched her sensual mouth. 'I ain't as respectable as you, but, let's face it, neither of us are the kind of girl a noble gentleman offers to marry.'

Tamsin nodded and took a deep gulp of her hitherto untouched ale. 'You're right, it's time I stopped burying my head in the sand,' she murmured. 'I must find other employment and move out of Wych Street.'

'Whoa! Hold your horses, who said anything about giving him up?' Molly's black eyes glinted with wicked amusement. 'You might not be able to get a wedding ring out of him, but there's nothing stopping you from becoming his mistress.'

Tamsin stared at her.

'Don't look so shocked.' Molly laughed, setting down her empty mug. She cocked her raven head at Tamsin and gave her a knowing grin. 'You *do* desire him, don't you?' she demanded.

Too honest to deny it, Tamsin nodded. 'But it's a sin!'

Molly shook her head firmly. 'Your canting Puritan relatives may think so, but you don't have to conform to their rules any more. Forget their sermons. What harm could it do to enjoy yourself for once?'

She reached forward and laid a reassuring hand on Tamsin's knee. 'There's little enough pleasure to be had in life without throwing away a chance of happiness. It might not last forever but, from what you've told me, he sounds like the kind of man who would treat you right.'

She grinned suddenly. 'Think of it! You could have fine gowns, jewellery, maybe even a house of your own.'

'But…but he's going to marry Jane Godolphin,' Tamsin spluttered desperately.

'So? Since when were husbands expected to be faithful?' Molly's tone was cynical. 'Anyhow, I reckon he'd tell her to boil her head if she threatened you again.'

Temptation shimmered before Tamsin's eyes and for one glorious instant she allowed herself to imagine the bliss of lying in Lysander's arms. Then she shook her head firmly.

'I can't, Molly. I wish I could, but it would be wrong and I would feel guilty.'

The despair in her friend's tone prevented Molly from telling her she was a fool. 'Then what are you going to do?' she asked gently. 'I know *I* couldn't resist temptation in your position!'

'I'm going to do what I should have done in the beginning.' Tamsin's expression was bleak. 'I'm going to move in with Martha and forget all about Sir Lysander Saxon.'

'Don't be so hasty! At least talk to him first. Find out how he feels.'

'What's the point? He's going to marry her and there's no place for me in his life.' Tamsin sighed. 'I can't even pretend that he needs my services any more. Matthew has fully recovered and Dinah and Luke are sufficiently well trained to work without my supervision.'

'He might not need your help, but what if he wants you to stay?' Molly regarded her with unaccustomed seriousness. 'You might make him unhappy by leaving and you'll certainly be miserable.'

'Not half as miserable as if I stay!' Tamsin had retorted shakily.

Staring into the heart of the kitchen fire, Tamsin replayed this conversation in her head. She had been so sure that the best course was to leave Wych Street as soon as possible, but she hadn't reckoned on Lady Corinna falling ill.

What was the right thing to do? Was it fair to leave when she might be needed or was she merely groping for another excuse to stay?

'The Comtesse said to tell you she is feeling better,' Dinah announced, coming back into the kitchen.

Tamsin swung round from the fire. 'Good,' she said briskly, determined to suppress her anxiety. 'I hope she drank all the posset?'

'Nay, she didn't fancy it.' Dinah placed the barely touched drink on the kitchen table. 'Said she wanted to rest, so she's gone upstairs. Marie is with her.'

Tamsin frowned. 'I wish she would see a doctor.'

Dinah grinned. 'Don't reckon that's necessary. Doctors can't do much to help what's wrong with her.' Seeing Tamsin's look of incomprehension, Dinah's grin broadened. 'She's breeding. A couple of months gone, if I know aught about it.'

'You mean she's having a baby?' Surprise lifted Tamsin's voice.

Dinah nodded. 'Mam was just the same when she was

having our Ruth. Fainting, always feeling queasy and off her food most of the time.'

'She's never said anything,' Tamsin murmured.

Dinah shrugged. 'Maybe she wants to be sure before she tells anyone.'

Just at that moment the kitchen door opened and Lysander walked in. His deep voice was cheerful as he greeted them both. 'Matthew tells me you wanted to see me, Mrs Barton.'

Oblivious to anything but his nearness, Tamsin drank in his immaculate appearance. He was dressed for the Court in his black velvet suit and his newly washed hair curled to his shoulders in glinting rings of gold.

'I've finished saying my farewells at Whitehall,' Lysander continued easily. 'However, there is still some packing left to do for tomorrow and I have to pay a visit to Mistress Godolphin, so, if you could be brief...'

Lysander drew out the last word with a look of enquiry, wondering why his efficient little protégée seemed to be wool-gathering.

Tamsin bobbed an apologetic curtsy. 'I beg your pardon, my lord.'

She waved Dinah to leave them and, when the girl had gone, took a deep breath to launch into the prepared speech she had sweated over last night. 'I must inform you, sir, that—'

Lysander stared at her in puzzlement as she ground to an abrupt halt. 'Tamsin?'

Tamsin hesitated. She had been nerving herself all morning to tell him that she wanted to leave his house but, if Dinah was right, things had suddenly changed.

'Lady Corinna fainted again while you were out,' she blurted, wondering whether she was foolishly clutching at straws in the hope of putting off the evil moment of departure. 'Dinah thinks she might be with child.'

Lysander let out a low whistle. 'I suppose Dinah ought to know the signs,' he murmured, echoing Tamsin's own thought.

'She wouldn't let me send for a doctor.'

'I'll speak to her.'

A broad grin appeared on Lysander's face. If true, it was the best news he had heard since the day they'd learnt that General Monck had thrown his support behind restoring Charles to his throne!

It would necessitate a change of plan, however. 'Assuming Dinah's supposition is correct, Corinna ought to stay here in London and rest, not jaunt about the countryside with me.'

'So you still mean to go to Melcombe?' Tamsin asked quickly.

'I must.' Lysander's brow creased in thought. He could delay his departure perhaps, but he would be failing in his duty if he abandoned the trip. 'I need Matthew, but I'll leave Nat here. You might require his services and he can also perform any heavy jobs you want doing.'

'I wish you weren't going,' Tamsin exclaimed, forgetting to guard her tongue.

An expression of surprise appeared on his handsome face and she hastily explained that she knew nothing of babies. 'I am not sure how to look after the Comtesse.'

'Just carry on in your usual sensible fashion, kitling.' He smiled at her. 'I'm sure you will cope splendidly.'

Tamsin remained silent and he reached out and brushed her cheek lightly with one long forefinger. 'Corinna likes you and I shall feel better knowing you are here to look after her in my absence.'

The shadow of anxiety in her lovely eyes remained and Lysander's smile faded. 'You are really worried, aren't you? I know you have already done a great deal to make this household run smoothly, but if you feel this new responsibility is too—'

'Nay, I want to help,' Tamsin interrupted firmly, setting aside her own plans.

This was not the moment to try and explain why she ought to leave. She owed him too much to refuse to do as he asked.

* * *

To Tamsin's surprise Lysander's absence passed more quickly than she had anticipated. Confined to the house on the advice of the midwife who had confirmed her pregnancy, Lady Corinna was bored and demanded entertainment. Lucinda Elliot, Jack Fanshawe's widowed sister, was a stalwart visitor, but the main burden fell on Tamsin, who, delegating various duties to Dinah, spent hours reading aloud to Corinna and discussing all the latest news and gossip which she brought home from her trips to market.

Corinna also decided to teach her some card games so that they could play together. Tamsin was initially reluctant, but once Corinna had promised that they would only gamble for bean counters she relaxed and discovered an aptitude for gaming that would have horrified her Puritan relatives.

Then, as the end of August approached, Corinna's queasiness and excessive fatigue suddenly ceased to plague her, just as the midwife had predicted. One bright morning she summoned Tamsin to the parlour and announced that she wanted Tamsin to act as her waiting-woman.

'I am tired of lying a-bed. Now that I am feeling better, I want to go out and enjoy myself, but Marie is so homesick that simply looking at her miserable face depresses me!'

Tamsin was happy to oblige. Although Corinna occasionally behaved in a high-handed and spoilt manner, more often than not she was good humoured and kind. She was also generous and insisted on buying Tamsin a pretty new gown.

'Pray accept it as a token of my thanks,' she urged, sweeping aside Tamsin's embarrassed protests. 'I am grateful for all your care of me, *petite*.'

Corinna smiled at her. 'I didn't believe that I could possibly be with child, you know,' she confided. 'My *mois* have never been regular and I put their absence down to the upset of travelling. Now I am so happy I want everyone to share my good fortune.' Her dark hazel eyes twinkled at Tamsin. 'Besides, I cannot have you looking shabby when you accompany me on our outings!'

The new dress was in amber moire with a cream silk pet-

ticoat beneath. Cut in the latest style, it had full billowing
skirts, elbow-length sleeves decorated with ribbons and a
tight, pointed bodice with a round neckline which was lower
than anything Tamsin had ever worn before.

'Gemini, my aunt would have a fit of the mother if she
saw me in this!' she exclaimed on viewing her reflection in
the long mirror which graced Lady Corinna's bedchamber.

Corinna laughed. She knew about Aunt Deborah for Lysander had revealed the truth of Tamsin's history before he
had left for Dorset.

'Take care not to mention that you know how she was
tricked by Mrs Cole,' he had warned. 'She is embarrassed
about landing up in a brothel.'

Corinna, who had every sympathy with Tamsin's plight,
had readily agreed.

'It suits you. You are developing a very pretty figure, Tamsin,' she now reassured her, privately deciding that it was
high time the girl had a little fun.

Tamsin was almost scared to wear it, but there was no
denying it was the most beautiful gown she had ever
owned...or that Corinna was right about her burgeoning
curves! She had grown taller since she came to London and
her old clothes were all getting too tight.

'We must do something about your hair too.' Corinna eyed
Tamsin's neatly braided coil with disapproval. 'Come here,
petite.' With a couple of quick movements she released the
unruly apricot-gold mass and, after exclaiming how lucky
Tamsin was to possess such thick, abundant curls, skilfully
arranged them into two fashionable bunches on either side of
Tamsin's head. A few of her own pearl-headed hairpins secured the remaining back hair into a high knot, leaving Tamsin's nape bare.

A new pair of soft leather shoes, the loan of Corinna's
velvet cloak, a fashionable muff to guard against the chilly
wind which had ushered in the arrival of September and Tamsin was ready to accompany the Comtesse to the Mulberry
Gardens.

It was the first of many such outings. Plunged into a whirl of activities, such as partaking of a dish of syllabub at the World's End Inn or joining in the early evening parade of carriages in Hyde Park, Tamsin was both shocked and beguiled by her taste of fashionable life.

Lysander had been gone almost a month when they had a letter from him. Corinna read out parts of it to Tamsin.

'He says that he encountered Lord Treneglos at the house of a mutual friend. Did you ever meet Tom?' Corinna asked.

Tamsin shook her head.

'He's a nice man.' A little smile touched Corinna's mouth. She had fond memories of Tom's visits to Melcombe when she had been a little girl.

'Apparently, Tom is visiting his elderly uncle, who is dying. That means he stands to inherit a very large fortune.' She glanced back at the letter. 'Sadly, he has not been so lucky in his quest to find his missing daughter.'

Tamsin wasn't listening. Her mind had slipped off into a daydream about Lysander. She had learnt to control her wayward thoughts for the most part, indulging in thinking of him only when she was alone in the privacy of her bedchamber, but listening to his letter made him come vividly to life and she longed for his return.

Not that it would do her any good, of course! She would have to leave Wych Street when he came back. Martha, who disagreed violently with Molly's suggestion that she ought to become Lysander's mistress, insisted that she must come and live with them.

'You can share Nelly's room,' she'd said. 'It'll be cramped, but it's better than following in that brazen trollop's footsteps and losing your good name!' The angry look on her plump face at the thought of Molly Heron faded and a sigh escaped her. ''Tis a pity you've had no answer to your advertisement about your father.'

Tamsin had posted a carefully worded enquiry at several

points in the city, but so far she hadn't heard any news concerning the whereabouts of Mr Penhaligan.

'I cannot rely on finding him,' she said ruefully. It had been childish of her to imagine that he would appear like a prince in a fairy-tale and make everything better. In all likelihood, he was dead. 'I must look for a new position.'

'Aye, ask Lady Corinna to give you a reference,' Molly suggested eagerly. 'She seems to hold you in regard and her word will carry weight.'

Tamsin nodded. It was a good idea, but she would have to ask her soon. 'I think she intends to return to France when her brother comes home.'

'Then you must be ready to leave the minute she does,' Molly had exclaimed and in her heart Tamsin had known her old nurse's advice was right.

'Lysander thinks he might be home by the middle of the month,' Corinna remarked, recapturing Tamsin's wandering attention.

She folded up the letter. 'I do hope he isn't delayed. I cannot leave London without saying goodbye to him.' She sighed. 'I'm sorry I missed the chance to visit Melcombe, but I want to go home.'

Tamsin nodded. It was only natural that Corinna should find it difficult to contain her impatience now that she was well enough to travel. She had written to the Comte to tell him she was returning shortly, but she was keeping the news about the baby to herself until she could tell him in person.

'Never mind.' Corinna's voice regained its cheerfulness. 'I can see Melcombe on my next visit and, in the meantime, what say you to amusing ourselves with a trip to the theatre?'

Tamsin hesitated. 'I'm not sure Sir Lysander would approve of my visiting a theatre, my lady,' she hedged.

Corinna demanded an explanation and then exclaimed, 'But it is a different matter entirely if you go with me! Lysander might not trust you with Mrs Heron, but he knows you will be perfectly safe with me. I shall hire a box and invite Jack Fanshawe to accompany us.'

Lord Fanshawe had often acted as their escort. Lysander had asked him to keep an eye on them and Jack, who was fond of Corinna, was happy to oblige.

Tamsin struggled with her conscience. Aunt Deborah had always maintained that theatres were the haunt of the Devil, but she had castigated many of the pursuits Tamsin now enjoyed.

'I'm certain you would find it interesting to see a play, but I won't force you, Tamsin,' Corinna said gently. 'It is up to you to decide.'

'May I think about it?'

'Of course.' Corinna smiled and turned her attention to thinking up other amusements.

She succeeded so well that Tamsin began to worry Corinna might over-tire herself in spite of her apparent bloom.

'I shouldn't fret. She has more energy than the pair of us,' Jack remarked when she asked for his opinion.

He had just arrived with his sister Lucinda for a visit to the Folly, a floating restaurant moored opposite Somerset House, and they were waiting for Corinna to finish her toilette.

The Folly was crowded when they arrived, but they were shown to a good table. Tamsin enjoyed her dinner, the food was excellent and there were musicians to entertain the customers, but she was scandalised by the bill, which was extremely high.

'Ah, but you are also paying for the pleasure of being seen in a fashionable setting,' Jack cheerfully informed her.

Tamsin emitted an unladylike snort. 'Aye, through the nose!'

Corinna shushed her and Tamsin obediently subsided. She had no wish to embarrass her companions, but later that evening she confided her indignation to her cousin Sam in the letter she was writing to him. It was her second letter, the first, sent some weeks ago, being merely a brief note to say that she had arrived safely.

Chewing the end of her quill, Tamsin strove to put the

strangeness of her new mode of life into words without giving details that might betray her whereabouts to her aunt if she should happen to find the letter.

Sam would understand how alien the concept of idle luxury was to her…and how seductive! When she wasn't being shocked witless, Tamsin was enthralled by the feel of silk smooth against her skin, the richness of honied sweetmeats on her tongue, the excitement of winning at cards and all the other fun and entertainment on offer.

But I don't think I should wish to live without purpose forever, she wrote.

Tamsin put down her pen. Aunt Deborah's influence was too strong to be ignored. She *needed* to feel useful!

She had always imagined she would find her fulfilment in becoming a wife and mother, but the man she wanted was out of her reach. The only way she could have Lysander Saxon was to offer to become his mistress.

Tears sprang to Tamsin's eyes. She dashed them away impatiently.

If she could be sure he loved her, she might have been brave enough to forsake virtue, but she had no idea if he really felt anything other than desire for her.

Even if he did, Jane would be the central figure in his life, Jane would have the home and babies Tamsin longed for. If she bore him children, they would be bastards, just like herself!

An icy shiver chilled Tamsin's spine. She couldn't stand the torture of sharing Lysander with anyone else. It would be too painful!

The only sensible course was to leave when he returned from Melcombe. She wouldn't be able to repay the rest of the money she owed him, but at least she had done her best to work off the debt.

One last conversation, one last glimpse of his wonderful smile, then she must steel herself to say goodbye to him for ever.

* * *

'Welcome home, sir.' Dinah let out a squeak of pleased surprise as she opened the front door. 'We weren't expecting you until tomorrow.'

'We made better time than I anticipated.' Lysander crossed the threshold and took off his travel-stained cloak. Handing it to Dinah, he asked after his sister and was reassured to hear that Corinna was in excellent health.

'Is she in the drawing-room?' Lysander turned to mount the stairs.

'Nay, sir.' Dinah turned from greeting Matthew, who had followed Lysander into the hall. 'She and Mrs Barton have gone to see a play.'

Lysander's brow quirked in surprise. 'Do you know which playhouse?' he asked thoughtfully.

Dinah nodded. 'The Cockpit, sir.'

Lysander pulled out his gold-cased pocket watch and consulted it. Almost six. The performance would have probably begun at half past three. If he were quick to change his dusty clothes, he might be able to catch the end of the second act and escort them home.

Asking Dinah to bring him up some hot water and a mug of ale to slake his thirst, he headed for his bedchamber. Fifteen minutes later he was walking swiftly down Drury Lane towards the theatre.

Lysander had visited the Cockpit several times before. John Rhodes had managed to obtain a licence to act from General Monck not long before the Restoration and his company still continued to perform at the Cockpit, much to the annoyance of Sir William Davenant and Thomas Killigrew, who were trying to create a monopoly for their own companies. They had recently used their friendship with the King to secure exclusive rights to put on plays in London, but Lysander suspected they would not find it easy to eliminate the competition.

The flag on top of the theatre was flying to show that a performance was in progress. It was the custom to allow late-comers in to see the last act without payment, but Lysander

generously tipped the doorkeeper a half-crown, the full price
of a seat in the pit.

He strolled into the crowded auditorium and a strong smell
of orange peel mixed with old perfume, candle-grease, sweat,
tobacco and dust hit his nostrils. Seeing that little space remained on the benches of the pit, he decided to remain standing, which afforded him an excellent view of the stage.

It was lit by a large chandelier and extravagantly costumed
actors stood declaiming their lines. Lysander, who hadn't
taken any notice of the playbills posted outside, recognised
the text: *The Woman's Prize,* Fletcher's comic sequel to
Shakespeare's *Taming of the Shrew.* An amusing piece, but
he hadn't come here to watch the play.

His gaze swept the boxes above the pit. There was sufficient light in the auditorium to examine the occupants clearly
and he soon spotted his sister. Corinna was wearing a vizard
mask, but, helped by the fact that she was sitting next to Jack
Fanshawe, he swiftly recognised her.

Lysander stared hard at the masked woman seated on his
sister's other side. Could that really be Tamsin? God's teeth,
it was!

The climax of the play arrived, signalled by a stirring flourish from the musicians playing in the fenced-off part of the
pit below the stage. Lysander scarcely noticed. His gaze was
riveted to the dainty figure who was leaning forward over the
edge of Corinna's box, her whole attention fixed on the actors. A riot of apricot-gold curls had fallen forward to shade
her masked face, but he could see the tops of her breasts
exposed in the low neckline of her fashionable gown.

Lysander caught his breath. How could he go on pretending she was still a child!

Corinna had seen him. She waved her fan in delighted
recognition and nudged her companions. Jack raised one
hand with a broad grin and Lysander returned the salute while
continuing to watch Tamsin.

She had straightened abruptly at Corinna's whisper and

was sitting very still, but he could see that the fan she held in one clenched hand was quivering.

The play ended and over the applause Corinna called out to him that they would meet him outside the entrance. Waving aside a pretty seller of tobacco who offered him 'a penny a pipe, sir' with a flirtatious flutter of her eyelashes, Lysander shouldered his way out through the sudden throng, who had also decided not to stay and see the short farce which concluded the playbill.

'Lysander!' Corinna flung herself into his arms with a fine disregard for decorum. 'I'm so pleased to see you home.'

Lysander returned her hug and enquired after her health. 'Though I scarcely need ask. You are positively blooming.'

'You may thank Tamsin here for that.' Corinna chuckled. 'She has taken excellent care of me while you were away.'

Lysander inclined his head in Tamsin's direction, acknowledging her presence for the first time. 'Mistress Barton.'

'My lord.' Tamsin swept him a graceful curtsy.

Lysander's brow quirked. He recognised his sister's hand, but why had she taken it upon herself to transform his drab little duckling into this exquisite swan?

'For two reasons,' Corinna informed him quietly as they set out on the short walk home. 'Firstly, I was bored and it amused me, but, more importantly, I have decided to offer her the position of my waiting-woman.'

'You want to take her back to France with you?' Lysander felt a sudden chill down his spine.

'Hush, not so loud!' Corinna scolded. 'I haven't told her yet.' She flicked a glance over her shoulder to where Tamsin walked in the rear, escorted by Lord Fanshawe. They were busy laughing over something and Corinna decided that they mustn't have overheard Lysander's exclamation.

'You have no objection, do you, dear heart?' she asked him. 'I know it is unkind of me to deprive you of such an excellent housekeeper, but it will be a good opportunity for her. Besides, when you are married, I'll warrant Mistress Godolphin will wish to select her own staff.'

Lysander, who had noted Jane's hostility, nodded slowly. 'I suppose so.'

Sensing his reluctance, Corinna let the matter drop and began to ask about Melcombe.

When they arrived home, Jack accepted an invitation to stay for supper. 'Come up to the drawing-room, Jack, and tell me what you thought of Kynaston's performance tonight. He makes such a pretty girl!' Corinna held out her hand to him.

'Aye, but if the rumour I've heard that Davenant is going to hire actresses is true, then Kynaston's days taking female parts may be numbered,' Jack replied, tucking her hand into the crook of his elbow.

Together they mounted the broad staircase and Tamsin could hear them still discussing the scandalous notion of real women acting on the stage as they disappeared out of sight.

Left alone with Lysander, Tamsin felt giddily breathless. The impact of his presence on her senses was overwhelming. In her dreams she had almost forgotten how tall he was, how devastatingly virile!

'What? No word of welcome for me, kitling?' Lysander's deep voice was gently teasing.

'It is good to see you home, my lord,' Tamsin murmured, struggling against the paralysing shyness which knotted her tongue. She could feel the heat stealing into her cheeks and kept her gaze modestly downcast to avoid having to meet his eyes.

A string of unusually fine pearls graced her slim neck. A loan from Corinna, no doubt, their glowing beauty was enhanced by a black pearl pendant. It offset the creamy perfection of her skin…which his fingers itched to touch!

'That's a very pretty gown you are wearing,' he said hastily. 'I swear you have grown, I scarcely recognised you.' Lysander tried for a jolly avuncular note…and failed.

Alarmed by his sudden silence, Tamsin risked an upwards glance and, encountering his gaze, saw the look of desire blazing in his eyes.

Unable to look away, Tamsin's heart began to pound so loudly she was sure he must hear it.

'You look lovely, sweetheart,' Lysander spoke at last, his voice hoarse as he broke the taut silence.

He took a step towards her and Tamsin panicked.

'Pray excuse me,' she gabbled, backing away from him. 'I must go and change, sir, and then start preparing supper.'

'Of course.' Regaining his self-control, Lysander let her go with a faint smile.

But Tamsin was acutely aware of his gaze following her as she fled up the stairs.

Tamsin set down her basket on the kitchen table and drew her arm across her forehead. Gemini, but she was hot! The day was unseasonably warm for mid-September and the market had been crowded.

It had also been full of rumours that the Duke of Gloucester was dead. The King's youngest brother, who seemed a very good sort of man, had caught smallpox a week ago and it was said his doctors were fools.

Tamsin hoped the rumour was false. There was always gossip about the royal family circulating. The King's dalliance with Mrs Palmer was the subject of many ribald jokes and lately folk were saying that his brother James, the Duke of York, had got Anne Hyde, daughter of the Chancellor, with child. There was even talk of a secret marriage!

Thank the Lord that the house was quiet and she could catch her breath for a few minutes. Sir Lysander had gone out early to see his goldsmith on a matter of business and Corinna had taken Marie to an operator for the teeth who practised near the Mitre tavern in Wood Street. The little Frenchwoman had a pain in one of her back teeth which had not responded to the oil of cloves Tamsin had furnished. She had awoken in agony this morning, but she was so scared of having any treatment she'd fallen into a fit of hysterics. In the end, Master Cooper had offered to accompany Lady Corinna, who thankfully accepted his escort.

Which meant that, since she had given Luke and Dinah permission to pay a visit to their mother, Tamsin was, most unusually, alone. Unpacking the provisions she had purchased, she sighed. She wasn't sure she wanted time to think!

Her task finished, she drew herself a mug of small beer and sat down to drink it. There was no use dodging the issue. After last night, she couldn't pretend it was all her imagination and she was making a fuss over nothing. The desire between them had been almost palpable.

Lysander Saxon wanted her and he was a man who got what he wanted!

She had been conscious of his eyes on her all the time she was serving supper. Suspecting he might seek her out afterwards, she had pleaded tiredness and gone early to bed.

But she couldn't keep avoiding him. She had to tell him she wanted to leave before it was too late!

Tension clawed at her scalp and she could feel the beginnings of a headache. Rising swiftly, she went and drew a bucket of cool water from the well and splashed her face.

It helped and, determined to ignore the nervous butterflies swarming in her stomach, she picked up a willow basket. There were wild blackberries growing in a corner of the garden. Rather than waste them, she could mix them with some apples and bake them in a tart for dinner.

Tamsin stepped out into the garden and promptly dropped her basket with a gasp of surprise.

'I didn't know you were here!' she choked, staring in dismay at the man who stood in the middle of the grass-walk, wielding a sharp scythe.

Lysander stopped cutting the grass at her exclamation. Straightening to his full height, he said, 'I got back half an hour ago.'

Her expressive face told him that she found his present occupation unusual and he laughed. 'Did you think me too fine a gentleman to get my hands dirty?'

Tamsin shook her head in hasty denial. She couldn't tell him so, but what actually disturbed her was the fact that he had taken the practical step of stripping to the waist for the task!

She stared in fascination at his naked torso. The only man she had seen thus uncovered was her cousin, but Sam was just a boy. His upper body was thin, pale and hairless. Lysander's skin glowed with a bronze sheen in the sunlight and a scattering of fine golden hairs adorned his broad chest.

Sleek firm muscle rippled as he moved to set down his scythe and Tamsin swallowed hard. Suddenly, she felt all hot again!

'Since that pesky gardener is neglecting his duty, I thought I'd make myself useful.' Lysander stretched his arms wide to ease his stiff shoulders.

'I shall leave you in peace, then.' Tamsin took a step backwards.

'Nay, don't go!' Lysander picked up the shirt he had discarded earlier and pulled it quickly over his head. 'I'm just about done here.'

He had hoped the exercise would cool his blood, but the fever which had burned in him last night had broken into fresh flame at the sight of her. She had braided her hair into its old severe style and was wearing her simple blue gown, but now he could not forget that this plain guise hid glossy curls and sensuous curves.

Looking back, he realised that the process had begun even before he went away, but the shock of seeing her dressed as a lady of fashion had opened his eyes to the fact that she had changed a great deal in the last three months. An easier mode of life and a richer diet had promoted a spurt of physical growth while freedom from her aunt's tyranny and success in her self-appointed task as his housekeeper had given her a new confidence and serenity.

She was no longer the frightened little waif he had rescued from that brothel. She was a lovely woman…and he wanted her!

'There's no need to go.' Lysander walked towards her. 'And, besides, I must talk to you.'

The nearer he came, the faster Tamsin's breathing became. She couldn't drag her eyes from his powerful body and a wicked longing to touch him tormented her. 'I have something to say to you too, sir,' she gasped.

'Indeed?' Lysander halted a scant few inches away. 'Is it important?'

Tamsin nodded frantically. 'I…I want to…I *must* leave this house before…' Her voice trailed off in miserable confusion.

Surprise flickered over his handsome features, swiftly followed by understanding. 'Before it is too late and our feelings get the better of us,' he said softly, completing her unfinished sentence.

A bright betraying blush coloured her cheeks. 'Aye,' she whispered hoarsely.

'But it is already too late, sweetheart.' Lysander looked down into her lovely eyes and a faint bittersweet smile touched his mouth.

'Much too late,' he continued and drew her firmly into his arms.

Chapter Ten

For an instant Tamsin resisted and then, as their lips met, all conscious thought dissolved and she yielded to Lysander's embrace, allowing herself to be swept along on the tide of desire rushing through her veins.

His lips caressed hers with seductive warmth and pleasure exploded in the pit of Tamsin's stomach. Her hands clutched at his broad shoulders and she pressed herself against him. With a low growl of delight, Lysander deepened the kiss. Obeying a primitive instinct, Tamsin's lips parted to his demand and waves of heat swept over her as his tongue began to explore her mouth with a skilful expertise.

Her senses reeling, Tamsin clung to him. The new sensations he was arousing in her body were so exciting she could scarcely breathe. A strange sweet ache was making her tremble and a tiny moan of pleasure escaped her as his hand moved upwards to cup her breast.

Tangling her fingers in his hair, she kissed him back with all the enthusiasm at her command. Encouraged by her ardour, Lysander began to stroke her breast through the fabric of her gown. Tamsin's spine arched in rapture even as her mind registered the shock of this intimacy.

In a far-off distant corner of her brain, she knew she ought to stop him, but she couldn't bring herself to pull away.

'You are so beautiful,' Lysander whispered against her mouth.

His hand slipped inside her bodice and the battle between modesty and desire was lost as the rising tide of hot excitement flooded over Tamsin, leaving her powerless to resist the spell he was weaving.

She gasped as his exploring touch found her tender nipple. He caressed it gently, rolling it between finger and thumb until it grew hard and swollen with excitement.

Dimly, Tamsin wondered if it was possible to faint from sheer pleasure.

'Damn your eyes! Make way there!' A loud shout, accompanied by a clatter of carriage wheels from somewhere beyond the garden wall, intruded into their idyll, shattering the silence.

Recalled to his senses, Lysander reluctantly released her and stepped back. 'This is madness,' he muttered, his breathing hoarse.

For a moment Tamsin gazed at him in bewilderment, her eyes cloudy with passion. 'I don't understand. You said that—'

'I know what I said!' Lysander interrupted savagely. 'But I was wrong!'

The last traces of pleasure-drugged haziness cleared from Tamsin's wits. 'You have thought better of it,' she murmured.

'You cannot remain here,' Lysander affirmed roughly. 'Not now.'

The look of hurt in her eyes cut him like a knife. 'It isn't a matter of what I want. If it were—' Abruptly, he bit off what he had been about to say. The situation was difficult enough! 'I am in no position to offer you anything, kitling. My future lies with Mistress Godolphin and I will not insult you by pretending otherwise.'

'You want her money for Melcombe.'

Lysander gritted his teeth. 'I *must* restore Melcombe. My parents sacrificed everything for the royal cause and now I have the chance to set things right. To fail my duty would dishonour both myself and their memory.'

Tamsin swallowed hard. How could she argue?

There was silence for a moment and then Lysander spoke. 'What happened just now…the fault was all mine.' A dull flush stained his impassive face and his voice was gruff. 'I had no business kissing you. Pray accept my sincerest apologies.'

The sun was still shining, the warm breeze still wafted the perfume of roses, even the gentle droning of the bees in the herb-bed was still the same, but to Tamsin it felt as if the world had suddenly turned cold and dark.

'I shall leave as soon as I have packed my things,' she said, striving to control her trembling voice.

She started to turn away.

'Wait! There is something you must know before you decide on your future.'

Gathering her courage, Tamsin slowly turned round to face him once more.

'Corinna wants you to go to France with her as her waiting-woman.'

Tamsin's eyes widened in surprise.

'It is a good opportunity.' Lysander shrugged awkwardly. 'And you have always wanted to travel.'

Tamsin bit her lip. What he said was true, but a shaft of pain lanced her heart. He wanted to be rid of her. She was an embarrassment to him!

'I will accept the offer.' There was nothing to keep her in London. She'd heard no word concerning her father and it didn't seem likely she ever would.

At least in France she wouldn't run the risk of bumping into Lysander and making a fool of herself by embarrassing him with her unwanted affections!

Exile.

Tamsin began to understand the true meaning of that hateful word as the short winter days dwindled into a blur of unhappiness. At first, the novelty of travel and then settling into her new home had taken the edge off her misery. The *Hôtel de Montargis,* situated on the Faubourg Saint-Antoine, was a pale stone mansion of fairly recent construction. It was magnificently furnished and possessed tall windows, wrought-iron balconies and a front courtyard large enough for the Comte's carriage to turn a circle. At the back was a beautiful garden with orange trees in tubs and formal, well-tended beds.

Paris, she soon discovered, was a lively city and there were many diversions. She had walked with Corinna in the Tuileries gardens and they'd taken carriage rides along the Cours-la-Reine. Soirées and parties of every sort had taken place most evenings, but as the autumn turned to winter Tamsin's determined effort to keep up her good spirits faltered. By the time December arrived only the necessity of preserving appearances prevented her from sinking into utter despair.

You've got too little to do, she scolded herself one frosty morning as she knocked on the door of the Comtesse's bed-chamber. Corinna, who was in her seventh month and grown very large, now tired easily. Their hectic social life had been curtailed and she spent much of her time resting, which meant that Tamsin's duties were light.

The amount of free time on her hands had, however, furthered her education. The Comte de Montargis had inherited a splendid library from his father, which contained books in several languages, and he had kindly given her permission to read whatever she wished. He had also taken a hand in improving her French.

'You have a quick mind, *petite,*' he'd said, borrowing his wife's nickname for her. 'It gives me pleasure to assist your efforts.'

Tamsin, who had been relieved to discover that she had the knack of picking up a foreign language without too much difficulty, was grateful for his generous help. Now approaching forty, the Comte's dark hair was streaked with grey and his once slim figure was beginning to show his fondness for food, but he had merry brown eyes and a charm that was quite beguiling.

Both he and Lady Corinna had been very kind to her. She had been given an elegant bedchamber and showered with gifts, including three winter gowns.

All the same, she thought to herself, as Corinna bade her enter, she would have gladly swopped her luxurious new life for the kitchen of Wych Street if only Lysander had wanted her there.

'Come and sit down.' Corinna greeted her with a smile. 'I have some news which will interest you.'

She resided cosily on a red velvet couch before a roaring fire. Tamsin noted she was wearing a new dressing-robe made of the finest wool. As the babe had grown in her womb Corinna preferred loose comfort to fashion, ignoring the barbed comments made by her husband.

Taking her place opposite the couch on a stool padded in the same red velvet, Tamsin reflected that the Comte's initial joy at his wife's return had faded. While there was no mistaking his pride at the thought of becoming a father, it was noticeable that he now spent far less time in Corinna's company than he had done previously and there was an edginess between them that Tamsin did not understand.

She had overheard them arguing the other evening when Corinna refused to accompany the Comte to Court.

'I will not attend the King's *levée* with you tomorrow!' Corinna had stormed. 'You know that Louis takes no account of feminine weakness and will extend no mercy to any woman in my position. I should be expected to stand for hours with no hope of refreshment or rest.'

'Other women manage,' the Comte had retorted sharply.

'Then they must care more for their own advancement than they do about carrying a child successfully to term.'

Corinna's scathing retort had silenced her husband's protests, but Tamsin feared he was still resentful.

Unlike his English counterpart, Tamsin had learned, King Louis was a man who valued formality. He enjoyed elaborate ceremony and liked to surround himself with his courtiers. To be absent was to lose his favour so, although her sympathies lay with Corinna, Tamsin could understand Pierre's anxiety.

'From Lysander,' Corinna announced, waving a letter and immediately capturing Tamsin's wandering attention. 'He writes to tell me that Mistress Godolphin has returned to town at last, her uncle having recovered from the ague which kept her so long in Sussex.'

Corinna lifted her eyes from the page and directed a mischievous glance at Tamsin. 'I wonder at her patience in nursing Mr Fielding. I should have thought she would have been anxious to return to the hunt.'

'Perhaps she did not deem it necessary, ma'am.'

There was an unusually waspish note in Tamsin's gentle voice and a flicker of guilt assailed Corinna. London seemed so far away she had forgotten that she had once suspected her young companion of having a *tendre* for Lysander, a *tendre* he might have returned in other circumstances.

'Well, it seems that you are right, *petite*,' she said carefully. 'For Lysander writes to say that he has asked her to marry him. Their betrothal will be formally announced on Christmas Eve.'

For all the warmth of the fire blazing in the hearth, an icy chill settled over Tamsin and it took all her self-control not to start crying.

Lack-wit, she admonished herself silently. You knew this was bound to happen!

To her relief, Corinna soon dismissed her, saying that she intended to take a nap before dinner. Tamsin sought refuge in her own bedchamber, but, unable to sit still, she finally flung a cloak around her shoulders and fled to the Picture Gallery where she paced up and down its great chilly length, her thoughts in turmoil.

'If you desire some exercise, *petite*, why don't you come for a ride with me? I was just about to take that new chestnut of mine out, but I shall gladly wait while they saddle up Mignonne for you.'

The Comte's voice interrupted Tamsin's dismal musing and she sank into a graceful curtsy. 'Thank you, *monseigneur*,' she said, knowing that Corinna would not require her services for a while. 'I should enjoy some fresh air.'

'Good.' The Comte's dark-complexioned face broke into a broad smile. 'Go and put on your riding habit and I shall meet you in the courtyard.'

Tamsin hurried to obey, grateful for the diversion.

When she had first arrived in Paris the Comte had treated her with haughty indifference, but his attitude had changed. He had even suggested that Tamsin should take dancing lessons and polish up her rusty riding skills.

'You will not always be with child,' he'd said, brushing aside Corinna's surprise. 'Such accomplishments in your waiting-woman may serve you well in the future.'

Tamsin had been glad to add to her skills and even more glad of the distraction. It helped take her mind off Lysander.

Stop thinking about him, she scolded herself as she scrambled into her black-velvet riding habit, yet another present from Corinna. You have a lot to be thankful for! So get on with your life and forget about Lysander Saxon!

But, somehow, it was impossible to take her own advice!

Three days before Christmas, Corinna slipped on a patch of ice in the garden and fell. To everyone's relief the baby did not appear harmed, but, unfortunately, Corinna was not so lucky. She had severe bruising and a badly twisted ankle.

'I'm sorry, *petite*,' she apologised to Tamsin on Christmas Eve. 'I had hoped we would be out enjoying the festivities.'

Her normally vivacious face wore a depressed expression and Tamsin hastened to reassure her that she didn't mind missing the entertainments Corinna had planned to attend.

'Anyway, I am used to a quiet Christmas,' she asserted stoutly. 'My aunt refused to allow any special celebrations. She thought them pagan nonsense.'

In spite of her cheerful smile, a pang of regret smote Tamsin as she spoke. The memory of Lysander saying that they must ensure she celebrated Christmas properly this year was as crystal sharp as the frost lacing the gardens outside Corinna's bedchamber.

Corinna sighed. She would have liked Pierre's company tonight, but any form of physical weakness revolted him and he found the sight of her unlaced figure distasteful.

He had, of course, paid a dutiful visit to her room for a few minutes each morning and he had been generous with gifts, but he spent much time out with his friends.

Corinna's ankle mended as January progressed and her spirits improved. The Comte's frequent absences no longer seemed to trouble her and Tamsin suspected she had become too wrapped up in the coming baby to worry about her husband's thoughtless behaviour.

Then one morning in early February, just after Tamsin's seventeenth birthday, another letter from London arrived.

'Do put down that sewing and listen, Tamsin,' Corinna commanded. 'This is from my cousin Lucinda to confirm that she will arrive next week as planned, but you'll never guess what else she has to say.'

Tamsin obediently set aside the baby smock she was hemming.

'Lysander's betrothal party on Christmas Eve was cancelled!'

Tamsin's eyes widened. 'Why?'

Corinna scanned the letter. 'Lysander decided it would be in bad taste to celebrate because of Princess Mary's death.'

The Princess Royal had married William of Orange, but had never been happy in Holland. Widowed at an early age, she had been delighted by her brother's restoration and had come on a visit to London the previous autumn. Sadly, she had fallen ill just before Christmas. Her doctors could not decide whether it was spotted fever, measles or smallpox, but after only five days her mysterious illness became fatal.

'I didn't realise she actually died on Christmas Eve,' Corinna exclaimed. 'The news we had was so garbled I thought it half-rumour!'

'Perhaps Sir Lysander will hold the party on another date soon,' Tamsin replied in a carefully controlled voice.

'Lucinda seems to think he is dragging his heels!' Corinna's expression held astonishment. She perused the letter again. 'She says Jack told her that the lawyers are arguing over the betrothal contract. Perhaps that is why.'

Tamsin knew that the signing of a betrothal contract was regarded as binding as an actual wedding ceremony so it was sensible to make sure all the conditions were fully met. It didn't necessarily indicate Lysander had changed his mind about marrying Jane.

All the same, her heart gave a queer little lurch.

'It is all very odd.' Corinna frowned. Lysander had not written for several weeks, which was unusual in itself. He had always been a regular correspondent, even in the days when he had been on campaign.

'Perhaps we shall learn more when Mistress Elliot comes to visit us,' Tamsin suggested.

Corinna's face brightened. 'I am looking forward to seeing her. Her manner reminds me of my mother, you know.'

It had been arranged that Lucinda, who was her closest female relation, would come to stay with Corinna in time for the baby's birth, which was expected some time towards the end of February. Corinna did not care for her husband's relatives and did not want them in attendance.

To their relief, the weather, which had been very cold with strong winds, relented and Mistress Elliot's journey was not delayed. She arrived on the eve of St Valentine's Day and, after greeting her, the Comte said, 'Come, Tamsin, let us leave my wife and her cousin together so that they may enjoy a comfortable talk.'

After receiving a little nod of assent from Corinna, Tamsin allowed the Comte to whisk her away.

'Put on your cloak, *petite,* and we will take a walk in the gardens.'

Outside, the sun was shining, bestowing its faint warmth upon them as they paced the immaculate gravelled paths. Tamsin lifted her face up to the pale sky and took a deep breath. 'I can smell spring in the air,' she said happily and gave a little skip.

She became aware that the Comte was watching her intently and she coloured. He must think her simple! How was she to explain that the sunshine and the hope that Lucinda might have news of Lysander had banished her inner gloom?

'Your pardon, *monseigneur*,' she murmured.

'For what?' The Comte gave a hearty laugh. 'I like to see smiling faces about me, *petite*. There is not enough jollity in this house.' He came to a halt and, beckoning Tamsin closer, pinched her cheek playfully. 'You are a pretty little thing. It distresses me to see you shut away like a nun. You should be out enjoying yourself, not mouldering away because my wife wishes to be a hermit.'

Tamsin blinked at him in surprise. 'I am very happy to serve Lady Corinna in whatever way she wishes. She has always been kind to me.'

'Bah!' He shrugged dismissively. His smile broadened. 'I would like to be very kind to you, *chérie*.'

A frisson of alarm dried Tamsin's throat. Was it her imagination, or was he *flirting* with her?

'Ah, I see you are surprised!' He chuckled. 'I thought you might have guessed how I feel since I've made my fondness for you so plain.'

He slipped an arm around her waist and squeezed it. 'You are a tempting little morsel, *petite!*'

Gemini, her imagination hadn't run mad!

'Come, admit it! You feel the same attraction, I've seen the way you smile at me.'

A wave of revulsion swept over Tamsin. It was on the tip of her tongue to retort that he was sadly mistaken, but common sense prevailed. She couldn't afford to offend him!

'Now that horse-faced Elliot woman has come, my wife

will not have so great a need of you and we may spend more time together.'

Frantically, Tamsin struggled for a diplomatic reply.

The Comte gave her waist another squeeze. 'Ah, you are overcome by the honour I pay you.' He released her. 'Let us finish our walk. I can be patient a while longer.'

Tamsin allowed him to tuck her reluctant hand into the crook of his elbow.

Maybe her aunt was right. She had wanted to lie with Lysander and for that sin, God, or the Devil, had sent the Comte's lust to be her punishment!

In England it was the custom to take the first person of the opposite sex you saw on St Valentine's morn to be your Valentine, so Tamsin did her best to avoid the Comte. Unfortunately, he was not so easily thwarted and, after breakfast was over, insisted on giving her a handsome gold ring set with turquoises as a Valentine's day present.

'The stones match your beautiful eyes,' he announced, slipping it on to her finger.

As he leant forward to kiss her, Tamsin saw Corinna's startled face over his shoulder and inwardly cursed.

Twisting aside so that his lips merely grazed her cheek, she thanked him coolly and made haste to sit next to Lucinda.

The Comte scowled and withdrew. After a moment Corinna excused herself and followed him out of the room.

The sound of voices raised in anger could be heard and after a moment of awkward silence Lucinda Elliot coughed. 'I fear the Comte is prone to infatuations, my dear,' she said with the frankness she was noted for. 'His interest rarely lasts, but his current attentions put you in a difficult position.'

'I wish he would leave me alone! I swear I have done nothing to encourage him!' Tamsin dragged the ring from her finger.

The last thing she wanted was to upset Corinna and she was about to hurl it to the floor when Lucinda caught her hand and took it from her. 'Allow me,' she murmured, slipping the ring into her pocket.

Tamsin stared at her and she gave a little shrug. 'When you have been as poor as I have, my dear, you learn never to waste anything, even an unwanted gift. I shall keep this safe for you until you decide what you are going to do.'

'I've already decided,' Tamsin replied jerkily. 'I'm going to go back to England.'

'I think that is probably wise, although I would suggest you wait until the baby is born.'

Tamsin hesitated. Much as Corinna must hate the sight of her own husband making sheep's eyes at Tamsin, she would probably be distressed if Tamsin ran off. 'We have grown close,' she admitted. A sigh escaped her. 'Perhaps if I had been ugly, the Comte would have left me alone.'

'Very likely,' Lucinda answered with a hint of asperity.

Tamsin bit her tactless tongue.

The Comte had contemptuously referred to Lucinda as horse-faced and, although cruel, the description was apt. She had unfortunately large teeth with a yellowish tinge to them and a plain-featured long face. Her tall figure was equally bony and her mouse-brown hair lacked any hint of fashionable curl.

Her only attractive feature was a pair of fine dark eyes, which now smiled at Tamsin. 'I long ago accustomed myself to the sad fact that my younger brother inherited all the looks in our family,' she said humorously. 'And I console myself with the knowledge that I shan't suffer the usual disappointment as I grow old!'

Tamsin reflected that, apart from men like the Comte who never bothered to look beneath the surface, it was obvious to everyone why Mistress Elliot had many friends. She might be poor and plain, but she had an engaging sense of humour and a kind nature to go with her sensible disposition.

Jack had once mentioned that his brother-in-law had adored her and their happy marriage had made light of the hardships of war. When Master Elliot had been killed in battle, Lucinda had struggled on alone to run their small estate until poverty had finally driven her to join her brother in exile, although she swore she would find herself another home when he married.

'Did you have a chance to read your letters yet?' Lucinda asked, diplomatically changing the subject.

She had brought several messages with her from England and two of the letters had been for Tamsin, much to Tamsin's surprise.

For a rapturous moment she had allowed herself to imagine that they might be from Lysander, but one had been from Molly Heron and the other from Martha. Both had been penned by an amanuensis and both contained interesting news.

Molly's was that she had got a job as an actress with the King's Company, an ambition she had been nurturing since last December when women had finally appeared on stage. Her friend's delight shone through the stilted phrases and Tamsin, although shocked at the very idea, couldn't help but be pleased for her.

Martha's letter was even more surprising.

There has been a reply to your advertisement for news about your father, she'd written. *Shall I pass on your new address? Please send instructions as soon as you can.*

Dizzy speculation had joined her concern over the Comte's worrying behaviour rendering Tamsin's night sleepless, but now in the clear light of morning it was all suddenly quite simple.

She would tell Corinna and her husband that urgent family business required her presence in London. It was true, after a fashion, and it would enable her to leave without offending the Comte or inventing a foolish excuse that would further humiliate Corinna.

Unfortunately for this plan, Corinna's pains began that evening.

'It is not seemly that you stay,' she murmured, dismissing Tamsin from her presence.

There was a note in her voice that stilled Tamsin's protest.

Unable to settle to anything, she eventually fled into the gardens when the taut silence was rent by screams, screams which became ever louder and more frequent.

It was very dark in the garden with only an occasional glimpse of the moon, which was playing hide and seek with the high, scudding clouds. Her breath steamed in the chilly air, but Tamsin barely noticed the cold.

Corinna hadn't wanted her near. She must blame her for the Comte's behaviour!

The sound of footsteps on the gravel made her whirl round with a little gasp. 'Who's there?'

'Do not be alarmed, *chérie.*' To Tamsin's dismay, the Comte materialised out of the darkness. He walked towards her. 'It's nearly midnight. You should be abed.'

'I could not sleep,' she replied curtly.

'Ah, my poor wife, but it is the lot of women to suffer.' He shrugged. 'Let's discuss more pleasant things, *chérie,* like how your lovely eyes rival a peacock's feather in colour.'

'Pray do not talk such nonsense, *monsieur.*' Angrily, Tamsin turned to walk away.

'Wait!' A shaft of the moonlight revealed his affronted expression. 'You do not have my permission to withdraw.'

Reluctantly Tamsin paused.

'You don't seem to understand the honour I do you. You are a nobody. By rights I should have maintained a distance between us as I did on your arrival.' He smiled caressingly at her. 'Instead, I befriended you, *petite.*'

'I never sought your favour, *monsieur,*' Tamsin retorted, her voice shaking. 'You are a married man.'

'What has that to say to anything?' Genuine astonishment widened the Comte's eyes. 'Fidelity is for the bourgeoise, *chérie.* Surely you cannot think otherwise?'

Tamsin made a small noise of disgust in her throat. How different he was to Lysander! 'If you loved your wife, *monsieur,* you would not wish to insult her by consorting with her own waiting-woman.'

He had the grace to look ashamed for an instant. Then he gestured airily. 'She has the compensation of my wealth and rank. Her position is assured. It would be ridiculous of her to expect me to remain faithful, particularly when her condition denies me her bed.'

Tamsin's mouth tightened and, abandoning diplomacy, she tried to leave, but he grabbed her by the arm.

'I would advise you to forget me, *monsieur*,' she spat at him furiously, wrenching free of his hold. 'I do not return your affection.'

'How dare you speak to me in such an insolent manner!' Rage darkened the Comte's face.

'I dare because it is the truth,' Tamsin declared passionately. 'Instead of propositioning me you should be paying attention to your wife!'

'Be silent!' he snapped. 'You forget your place, *mademoiselle*. One more word and I shall dismiss you.'

'That won't be necessary. I am leaving. I have urgent business to attend to in London.'

'You want to go?' Surprise punctured the Comte's anger. '*Chérie*, I spoke in haste, do not—'

'Please, *monsieur*, I am grateful for all your kindness, but let us agree there has been an unfortunate misunderstanding,' Tamsin interrupted hurriedly, hoping to avert disaster.

The Comte rubbed his chin thoughtfully. 'Perhaps it might be awkward if you stayed.'

Tamsin watched him turn over what she had said in his mind. She suspected that he did not want a breach with Corinna and that, although she was currently angry with him, Corinna felt the same.

'Say nothing of this conversation to my wife.' He waved dismissal with one well-kept hand. 'You must tell her that you are leaving us because you are needed in London.'

'Of course, *monseigneur*.' Tamsin swept him a deep curtsy and withdrew.

With any luck, once he had got over his injured pride, he would endeavour to make amends to Corinna!

*   *   *

'I shall miss you, Tamsin.' Corinna smiled. 'Be sure to write.'

'Aye, we shall rely on you to keep us up to date on all the London gossip,' Lucinda chimed in.

'I shall do my best,' Tamsin promised.

They were standing in the courtyard where the carriage that was to convey Tamsin to the coast waited. Outriders had been hired to provide her with safe escort and the Comte's agent had arranged for her to travel on board ship with a respectable married couple who were bound for London.

Her luggage, far more than she had arrived with, had already been loaded. All that remained was to say the final goodbyes.

Tamsin pressed one last kiss upon Henri-Charles's downy little head. He was a lovely baby and at three weeks old had already captured his father's heart. Pierre's obvious adoration had gone a long way to soothing Corinna's anger and her generous response had set the seal upon their reconciliation.

Delighted that the Comte seemed to be taking her advice, Tamsin had kept discreetly out of his way and been rewarded by the eventual return of Corinna's affection. Nothing more was said of the events of St Valentine's morn and Tamsin had quietly dropped the gold and turquoise ring into the poor-box of the nearest church.

'Are those the letters you want me to deliver?' she asked Lucinda, who handed them over with a nod of thanks.

Tamsin tucked them into her fur muff. Lucinda was going to stay in France to keep Corinna company and Tamsin half-suspected that the visit might be a prolonged one. It might even become permanent. The cousins were fond of one another and there was nothing to keep Lucinda in London.

And at least Corinna could be sure that the Comte would not make not advances to her new waiting-woman if Lucinda accepted the post!

'As you know, my husband is at Court this morning. He asked me to apologise for his absence and say his farewells,' Corinna announced calmly.

'Please thank him for his hospitality,' Tamsin replied with formal courtesy, secretly pleased that the Comte had shown consideration for his wife's feelings and stayed away.

The marriage seemed on a better footing now and, hopefully, their newfound harmony would last!

Tamsin took her place in the coach.

'Give my love to Lysander,' Corinna requested, stepping back.

'I will,' Tamsin answered, her heart beating faster at the thought of seeing him.

She leant out of the window and waved as the carriage set off. 'Goodbye and God bless.'

It pulled out of the gates and she sat back, settling herself upon the seat, a queer mixture of exhilaration and trepidation filling her.

Hopefully, there would be news about her father, but she hadn't the least idea of how Lysander would receive her. He might even be angry, but she didn't care. She *had* to discover why he hadn't signed the betrothal contract!

Lucinda had not been able to tell her. 'Everyone knows that he wishes to marry Mistress Godolphin,' she'd said in answer to Tamsin's cautious enquiries. 'Perhaps the lawyers are still arguing. Which, I suppose, is why he has kept on the house in Wych Street since any wedding plans must now perforce wait until after Easter.'

The marriage could not be solemnized during Lent, which still had another month to run. There was ample time to discover whether Lysander's hesitation had anything to do with her. If it had, she was determined to convince him they had a future together.

Molly was right. She couldn't marry Lysander, but it didn't mean that she had to give him up. These last few months in exile had taught her that life without him was no life at all. She had been so miserable that nothing could be worse, not even having to share him!

Buoyed up by a determined optimism, Tamsin found the journey flew by. At Dieppe she boarded the *Papillon*, a merchantman bound for the port of London with a mixed cargo of wine, silks and lace. Fair winds ensured an easy passage and a week after setting out from Paris, a hackney deposited her outside the house in Wych Street.

'Mistress Tamsin!' A wide grin of welcome lit Luke's face as he opened the door.

'You are looking very well, Luke.' Tamsin crossed the threshold with a smile. 'I hope Dinah and the rest of your family are all in such good fettle?'

'Aye,' he nodded. 'And I've got a new baby sister too,' he added with another grin.

Controlling her impatience, Tamsin politely asked after the latest addition to the Finch household as she removed her heavy travelling cloak.

'Mam named her Tamsin. After you,' Luke said proudly.

'I'm flattered,' Tamsin laughingly replied, resolving to send Mrs Finch a suitable gift for the child.

'Let me take that for you, mistress.' Luke relieved her of the cloak.

'Is his lordship home?' Tamsin's tone was carefully casual.

'Aye. Master Cooper's gone out, but Sir Lysander is in his closet. Shall I go and tell him you are here?'

'It's all right,' Tamsin said quickly. 'I shall announce myself.'

She mounted the staircase, her heart beating like a kettledrum.

'Come in.' His well-remembered voice answered her knock and, taking a deep breath to steady her nerves, Tamsin opened the door.

'Good God!'

Lysander dropped the pen with which he had been writing and stared uncomprehendingly at the apparition who had appeared on his threshold, his expression betraying sheer disbelief.

'Here's a fine welcome,' Tamsin exclaimed with a little

chuckle. She carefully closed the door behind her. 'Is that all you can say to me, my lord?'

Lysander leapt to his feet. Two hasty strides brought him round the desk. 'Kitling,' he said thickly. 'It *is* you!'

She moved towards him and melted into his arms as he seized her. Holding her in a crushing embrace, he kissed her fiercely and Tamsin responded with an answering fervour.

She had flung her arms around his neck; when he at last raised his head to draw breath, she tenderly smoothed back a dishevelled lock of hair from his brow.

'I thought you were a ghost, conjured up out of my desperate imagination,' he whispered shakily, devouring her face with his eyes.

Tamsin smiled lovingly at him. The depth of longing in his husky tone banished her remaining doubts. 'So I take it that you missed me,' she murmured with a hint of mischief sparkling in her eyes.

Lysander gave a laugh that was almost a groan. 'Little minx!' His deep voice turned the words into a caress.

He kissed her again, his arms tightening possessively around her. Delight coursed through Tamsin's veins and she clung to him, kissing him back until they were both giddy and breathless.

Reluctantly, Lysander lifted his mouth away from hers. He stared down into her upturned face. Her eyes were closed and she was breathing fast, a beatific smile curving her lips.

For an instant his unguarded expression revealed his innermost thoughts and then, abruptly, he released her.

Tamsin's eyes flew open. She watched him take a step backwards, visibly seeming to recollect his scattered wits.

'Lysander—?'

'Forgive me.' He flung up one hand to interrupt her anxious query. 'Your unexpected arrival took me by surprise.' He essayed a polite smile. 'Where did you spring from, by the way?'

'Do you mean you wouldn't have kissed me if you had known in advance?' she demanded, ignoring his question.

'You know damn well I wouldn't,' he replied almost angrily.

Tamsin gritted her teeth. In spite of his rapturous welcome, it seemed nothing had changed!

'Aren't you going to invite me to sit down?'

He waved her to a chair, but he remained standing. 'Why have you come back, Tamsin?'

She raised her brows at him. 'What a very uncivil question and here was I, thinking you were pleased to see me.'

A dull flush coloured his high cheekbones at the sarcastic edge to her tone. 'You know what I mean,' he said shortly.

'I suppose so.' She settled her skirts more becomingly and smiled at him sweetly. 'And, therefore, since it appears that we are about to have a dispute, perhaps you would be kind enough to offer me a glass of wine? I haven't had a thing since a hasty breakfast snatched before we docked and my throat is parched.'

He jerked his head in assent and, moving with a stiffness that betrayed his tension, went to pour two glasses from a squat green bottle standing on the tray kept on the small oak dresser.

He handed one glass to Tamsin.

'Thank you.' She took a few small sips. 'My compliments, sir. A very pleasant claret.'

Lysander reflected wryly that once upon a time she would not have known what wine she was drinking. Nor would she have dared remind him of his manners with such cool confidence.

He gazed at her intently. She had changed in other ways too. The alteration from skinny little waif into a lady of fashion, which had begun last autumn, was now complete. She would never be a tall woman, but her dainty figure was delightfully curved in all the right places. Her glowing hair had been skilfully arranged into a fashionable mass of ringlets and she wore her expensive travelling costume of golden-brown velvet with all the assurance of one born rich.

Apart from the lack of paint and patches upon her clear-skinned face, she could have been any noble lady of the court!

Tamsin, who was well aware of what he was thinking, tilted her head on one side and with a flirtatious flutter of her eyelashes, murmured, 'You were saying, sir?'

'Don't play games with me, Tamsin,' Lysander growled. 'You may have learnt society manners in France, but I am not going to oblige you with polite fencing. I want the truth. Now answer my question: why have you come back to England?'

A tiny thrill of excitement shot through Tamsin. There was a dangerous glint in his green eyes that made her heart thump…and her innards contract with desire!

'Very well.' She set aside her wine. 'You want the truth? I came home because I missed you so much I thought I would die of it.'

Shaken by her reply, Lysander took a swallow of his wine. 'I thought you must have quarrelled with Corinna,' he muttered, knowing he was cravenly prevaricating.

Tamsin shook her head impatiently. 'We are on excellent terms.'

This was not the moment to try and explain about the Comte's unwanted infatuation!

'It grieves me that you were unhappy in France. I had hoped you would settle down and—' Lysander bit off what he was about to say. He could not bring himself to utter the trite platitudes he knew were proper.

'God's teeth, Tamsin, you should have stayed in France! What good can it do either of us to resurrect the past? I told you before that I must fulfil my duty.'

'Even though you hate the very thought of marrying for money?'

He winced. 'Jesu, but you have acquired a sharp tongue!'

Tamsin tossed back her curls. 'What do you expect? I am no longer a child and I won't meekly do what I am told.'

Lysander gave an unwilling laugh. 'I can see that,' he retorted drily, finishing the last of his wine and putting the empty glass down on his desk.

A faint blush crept into Tamsin's cheeks. 'Oh Lysander, don't let's quarrel,' she begged.

His expression softened. 'That's the last thing I want, kitling,' he said quietly. 'Perhaps it was high-handed of me to send you off with Corinna, but I truly thought it was for the best. There is no future for you here.'

'But there is!' Tamsin rose to her feet and walked slowly towards him.

'Sweetheart, you cannot stay here with me.' Exasperation and barely concealed regret roughened Lysander's voice. 'You are much too beautiful and I'm no monk!'

'I'm not asking you to turn monk.' Ignoring his angry expression, Tamsin laid her hand on his chest. Beneath its covering of dark green moire she could feel his heart thumping wildly. 'All I am asking is that you take me as your mistress.'

Chapter Eleven

For the second time that morning Lysander Saxon lost the power of speech.

Tamsin hid a smile at his incredulous expression. 'Believe me, I have thought long and hard about our situation and it would be the perfect solution.'

'You have been learning some very strange notions in France, my girl,' Lysander declared wrathfully. He removed her hand from his chest. 'Of all the pea-brained ideas…do you really think I would take advantage of your youth and innocence in such a manner?'

'Will you stop talking such nonsense? I know what I want, what we both want.'

'It would compromise my honour.'

'I don't see how.'

'Then you do not understand what honour means.' Lysander's tone was stiff.

Tamsin took a deep breath. Why was he being so stubborn? She could see the longing in his eyes. He wanted her, she was sure of it!

'Tell me that you don't care about me, tell me that you love Jane and I will go,' she said softly.

She had found his weakness. 'I cannot,' he replied hoarsely.

Tamsin stepped up close again, her eyes searching his face.

'I know we cannot wed, but if I am willing to take the risk, why won't you?'

'Because it would be unfair on you.' Lysander's eyes flashed angrily. 'You think you could handle being my mistress, but I know you, Tamsin, and you are more of a Puritan than you think. The shame of it would spoil things between us in the end.'

A flicker of fear danced over her face and then she shook her head firmly. 'Being together would be worth anything,' she murmured, putting her arms around his neck and lifting her face up to his.

Lysander struggled with his conscience. The temptation to kiss her and throw honour to the winds was unbearable!

'And what about Jane?' he growled, removing her arms and taking an abrupt step back. 'How does she figure in these plans of yours?'

'You haven't made a public announcement of your betrothal.' Stung by his action, Tamsin's tone was angrily defensive.

'The contract has not yet been signed.'

'Because you don't really want to marry her!'

'Perhaps.' Lysander acknowledged her shrewd hit with a rueful nod.

'However, enough people know of my intentions for her to be ridiculed if I suddenly abandon her.' He folded his arms tight against his chest. 'Which I have no intention of doing. As you pointed out, I need her money.'

'Many married men keep mistresses.' A note of desperation crept into Tamsin's voice.

He quirked his eyebrow at her. 'I find it odd that you approve of adultery.'

'I told you before that I was a reluctant Puritan,' she said shakily.

She looked so distressed it was all Lysander could do to stop himself from folding her into a comforting embrace. 'Kitling, I have given my word to Jane,' he said softly.

'Would you have me insult her by parading you as my mistress before we are even wed?'

Tamsin bit her lip, trying to still its trembling. 'So you want me to leave?' she whispered, hardly able to believe she had lost.

Lysander crushed the denial that sprang to his lips. 'It would be best,' he replied heavily. 'I shall order Nat to bring the coach round. We can collect your luggage on the way to Mistress Croft's. I assume it is still aboard ship?'

He was sending her away. Tears rose up in Tamsin's throat to choke her. Swallowing them, she muttered, 'Thank you, but there is no need for you to escort me to Martha's. I can get a hackney.'

'Don't be stupid,' he said roughly, hating himself. 'It is the least I can do.'

Tamsin felt too devastated to argue. Her whole world had fallen down about her ears and only pride prevented her from weeping.

She'd been wrong. Oh, she could not deny his arguments were sound, but when it came down to it, he didn't care for her as much as she'd thought. If he had, he would have put love, not honour, first. Just as she'd been willing to count reputation well lost for his sake.

A useless, unwanted sacrifice it seemed.

'What can I do, Molly? Lysander won't listen to me and I cannot think of a way of changing his stubborn mind. He would rather see us both miserable than stain his precious honour.'

Molly Heron gave a rich chuckle. 'Here, have another cup of wine.' She poured more Rhenish into Tamsin's beaker. 'What you fail to understand, Tamsin, is that men aren't like us. They've got no common sense. They think foolish abstract ideals will keep 'em warm at night! Hah! Half the trouble in the world is caused by their damn stupid honour and pride.' She shook her raven head. 'Do you see women fighting duels and starting wars? Nay! Because we know what is important and learn to compromise.'

They were sitting in Molly's new apartment. April sunshine filtered into the room, rendering its cosy fire almost unnecessary and raising a dazzle of coloured sparks from the jewelled combs decorating Molly's hair.

'I wish Martha shared your views,' Tamsin murmured, sipping her wine. 'She keeps telling me I am foolish! All she cares about is finding me new employment now that this news about my father has come to nought.'

This second blow had fallen in quick succession to Lysander's rejection. Tamsin had contacted the person who had enquired about her advertisement, only to discover that the man was a lawyer, acting as agent for another.

'I'm afraid I am not at liberty to divulge any information about my client,' he'd replied in answer to her eager questions. All he would admit was that he had been ordered to find one Mrs Barton, a seventeen-year-old who originally hailed from the West Country.

'From what you say, I believe you are the woman in question, mistress,' he'd finally conceded and Tamsin had then demanded to know when she could speak to his client in person.

'Unfortunately, he is away from London at present. I shall send word to him and contact you in due course.'

Feeling puzzled and frustrated, Tamsin had gone back to Martha's crowded little house to inform her former nurse that, for now at least, they were still in the dark.

'I reckon your father hired that lawyer,' Molly now declared. 'Who else would want to find you?'

'It could be Master Hardy,' Tamsin said darkly.

'The man your aunt wanted you to marry?'

Tamsin nodded.

'I doubt it. You said he's a skinflint and this fellow must be willing to part with his money. Aye, and rich too. Lawyers don't come cheap.'

'I suppose so.' Tamsin felt a comforting glimmer of re-assurance at Molly's pronouncement.

She'd been worried that Gideon Hardy might be seeking revenge for the humiliation of being jilted.

He deserved it, he knew I didn't want to marry him, she thought defiantly, pushing away the uneasy realisation that she had demanded Lysander should treat Jane Godolphin with almost the same lack of consideration.

'What's wrong? You are squirming like a louse thrown on the fire.' Molly eyed her askance.

'I've got a headache,' Tamsin fibbed hastily.

Molly grinned. 'I'm not surprised. How many times did that brat wake you up last night?'

Martha's youngest was teething and there was no peace in the house for anyone. 'It's not his fault,' Tamsin protested. 'Besides, it was very good of Martha to take me in—'

'But you wish you could get a good night's sleep and she'd stop treating you as if you were still in the nursery,' Molly cut in with brutal honesty.

Tamsin gave a wry laugh. Moving into Martha's hadn't worked out as well as she had anticipated. Martha was indeed inclined to fuss over her, Ned refused her assistance in the shop, Cousin Nelly resented her if she tried to help with the children and the overcrowding was getting on her nerves!

'It's the constant noise and having to share a bed with Nelly that I find difficult to bear.' She sighed wistfully, re-membering the peaceful garden and her lovely spacious bed-chamber in Paris.

It didn't help, of course, that she was depressed about Ly-sander's rejection. Every night for the last two weeks she had lain awake for hours listening to Nelly's snoring before fi-nally managing to cry herself to sleep. She couldn't stop thinking about him and wishing there was something she could do to change his mind.

'You could always come and live here, you know.'

Molly's unexpected offer jerked Tamsin from her unhappy

reflections. 'But...but what about your new gallant?' she spluttered.

Molly shrugged. 'If he don't like it, he can go hang.' She touched one of the jewelled combs in her hair. 'He's generous, I'll grant you, but he ain't paying enough to tell me how to run my life.'

A group of court gallants had recently attended one of Molly's performances and the young man in question had taken a fancy to her. After a great deal of flirting she had decided to accept him as her latest lover.

'It's kind of you, Molly, but I don't want to get in your way,' Tamsin said shyly.

'I usually visit him.' Molly grinned. 'Anyway, I'm rarely at home.' Actresses were much in demand and Molly, with her good looks and rich voice, had become instantly popular. 'You can have the second bedroom and Sally can sleep in here.'

Molly had gone up in the world since she lived above Master Wintershall's. She now rented three large rooms in St Martin's Lane and employed a little maid to look after her.

Tamsin thought about it. 'Done,' she said. 'But you must allow me to pay you a fair rent.'

They bickered over this amiably for a couple of minutes and then Molly said, 'You'll need a job. You can't live off the French money you saved forever.'

Tamsin agreed. Living in London was expensive and, as well as insisting on paying her way at Martha's, she'd bought several presents for the children. 'What do you suggest? Housekeeping or a waiting-woman's post would require me to live in, but I don't want that.'

Corinna had given her a glowing reference, but Tamsin was in no mood to tie herself hand and foot to another employer. She was too angry and unsettled.

Molly nibbled one fingertip thoughtfully. 'I know. Come with me to the theatre this afternoon and I'll see if I can get you taken on as a player.'

Tamsin's eyes widened. 'But…but, Molly, I should never be able to get up in front of all those people and speak!'

'You won't have to,' Molly laughed. 'Not at first, anyway. All you'll have to do is stand there and be part of a crowd.'

'But why would Killigrew want to hire me? I have no experience.'

'You are very pretty and he's keen to get the better of Davenant's company of players. Attractive girls bring in audiences.' Molly shrugged. 'He's a hard bastard, but once you've got experience the wages are good and I'll be there to protect you.'

A variety of emotions played across Tamsin's expressive face.

'You're not still worried about hellfire?' Molly exclaimed. 'I thought you enjoyed the theatre now.'

'I do.' Tamsin had been often enough with Corinna to lose her initial nervousness. She liked being a spectator, but an actress? To be part of that raffish world?

'I don't know if I could cope,' she said frankly.

Molly shrugged lightly. 'It was just a thought.' She smoothed her satin skirts. ''Course, it would annoy the hell out of Lysander Saxon.'

Tamsin directed a suspicious glance at her and saw a gleam of mischief in the coal-black eyes.

'Well, don't you want to get your own back?' Molly demanded with a wicked giggle. 'S'death, he might even be angry enough to change his mind. After all, if you are destined for a life of sin, he might decide he may as well be your protector as some other man.'

Tamsin gulped. 'That's blackmail!'

'Nay, it's using your brains,' Molly retorted in a firm voice. 'Which is what you have to do to get what you want if you are a woman. We can't afford to let fancy principles get in our way—this is a man's world and we have to use whatever weapons we've got to hand.'

Tamsin's conscience told her what Molly proposed was wrong, but she asked herself bitterly what good had her Pu-

ritan scruples done her. It might be unfair to try and manipulate Lysander in such an underhand manner, but she was
tired of letting others order her fate.

'You're right, Molly,' she declared rebelliously. 'Why
shouldn't I go after what I want? Lysander doesn't care that
he has broken my heart, the Comte didn't give a fig when
he turned Corinna against me and even my father probably
abandoned me because it suited him!'

She took a calming breath. 'I never thought I would say
this, but if being an actress can bring me the kind of independence you enjoy, then I'm all for the idea.'

Grinning, Molly refilled their wine cups. 'Let's have a
toast,' she cried. 'To your new career. May it bring you your
heart's desire or, failing that, at least provide you with a little
fun!'

Tamsin raised the beaker to her lips. 'To love and fun,'
she echoed defiantly and drank deep.

'Beg pardon, my lord, there's a woman here to see you.'
Dinah stuck her head round the parlour door.

Lysander, who was about to leave the house, frowned. 'Did
she give her name?'

Dinah nodded. 'Said she was Mrs Croft.'

'Show her in.' What the devil was Tamsin's former nurse
doing here?

A respectably clad plump figure entered the room. Her
expression was shy, but her voice was clear as she rose from
her polite curtsy.

'I am sorry to bother you, sir, but I thought you ought to
know that Mistress Barton has left my house and gone to live
with that Molly Heron.'

'Has she, indeed!' Lysander bit back an expletive.

'And I've had a letter come for her, but I don't know that
hussy's address so I can't send it on.' Martha's chin wobbled.

'Please don't cry, Mistress Croft.' Lysander forced himself
to sound calm.

'Oh, sir! She says she is going to become an actress! She wouldn't listen when I tried to talk sense into her.'

'Don't worry. She'll listen to me,' Lysander replied grimly.

'Then you'll find her, sir, and put a stop to this nonsense before it is too late?' Martha's doleful expression brightened.

'Leave it to me, Mistress Croft.' Lysander smiled at her. 'When I find her, I'll send you word, but now I must beg you to excuse me. I have an appointment to keep.'

Martha dropped a grateful curtsy and Lysander showed her out.

He left the house a few minutes later, his brisk walk concealing the angry thoughts whirling in his head.

'Lysander! Do you intend to ignore me, man?'

'Tom! I didn't know you were back in town!' Lysander slowed to a halt, a pleased smile breaking out on his face as he recognised the man who had hailed him.

'I got back from Cornwall yesterday.' Lord Treneglos shook Lysander's hand warmly. 'It is good to see you.'

'Aye, it's been too long.' Lysander paused and then decided to risk enquiring how Tom's search for his daughter was going.

'She is alive and, what's more, she's here in London! I am off to see the man I hired to help me now, he has an office in Bow Street.'

Lysander, who was on his way to visit Jane, suggested they walk along together and listened with interest as Tom eagerly explained that his agent had arranged a meeting for the pair of them today.

'I'm so damn nervous I'm shaking,' he confessed. 'When I failed to find her last autumn I was sure she must be dead. It's hard to believe that I am really going to see her after all this time! And, since coming into my uncle's fortune, I can give her all the things she's missed!'

'You deserve your good luck if ever a man did, Tom,' Lysander answered with sincerity.

They reached the corner of Bow Street and Lysander bade Tom farewell. 'You must invite me to meet your daughter as soon as you've had some time together,' he added with his final good wishes.

'I will,' Tom promised and Lysander strode off down the Strand, whistling cheerfully.

By the time he reached Lady Court, however, the beneficial effect of meeting Lord Treneglos had worn off and his thoughts had returned to the problem which Martha Croft had brought to his attention.

'You are late, sir.' Jane, who was dressed very finely in a new gown of purple taffeta, hurried into her hallway to greet him. 'Had you forgot we are to join Lord Fanshawe and the others?'

Lysander restrained a curse. They were due to meet Jack at Marylebone Gardens, a notable place of entertainment with a fine bowling green that they had intended to try if the day was fine.

'I pray you will excuse me, I am not in the mood for bowls.'

Jane's expression hardened into annoyance and, with an impatient swish of her skirts, she turned on her heel and stalked into the parlour. Lysander followed her, trying to stem his own irritation. She deserved some sort of explanation, he supposed, but he had rarely felt less like pandering to her whims!

'It seems to me, my lord, that you are seldom in the mood for any enjoyment these days.' Jane went on the attack the minute he closed the door behind him. 'You have had a face as long as a fiddle for nigh on a month now. Is there something wrong that you have not told me of?'

Lysander shook his dark blond head. How could he explain that he wanted Tamsin so much it was crucifying him to hold to his resolve!

An impatient sigh escaped Jane's compressed lips and then, visibly trying to contain her displeasure, she said, 'I understand from my lawyers that an agreement has been reached and the betrothal contract is now ready for signing.'

'Aye,' Lysander replied shortly.

Jane stared at him indignantly, affronted by the lack of enthusiasm in his tone. She had been about to suggest that they go and see the lawyers since their plan to spend the day in the village of Marylebone had gone awry, but the signing would keep. 'Since you do not appear to be in the mood for my company, sir, I suggest you say farewell.'

Lysander pulled himself together. It wasn't fair to inflict his foul temper on Jane. 'I beg your pardon,' he said gruffly. 'I have just received some bad news and my wits are gone a-begging.'

Jane's expression softened. 'I am sorry to hear it,' she murmured in a gentler tone. 'Is there anything I can do to help?'

He declined, thanking her gracefully.

'Very well.' She hesitated. 'Should you mind if *I* joined Jack and the others?'

'Of course not. There is no reason for your outing to be ruined because I must deal with a matter of urgent business.'

Mollified by his reply, Jane did not seek to detain him further and they parted on good terms.

However, watching him stride down the street from the parlour window, a little sigh escaped her. More and more often of late, she had begun to wonder if she had been wise to accept his suit.

Still, it was too late for regrets and, her expression brightening at the thought of Jack's amusing company, she hurried to put on her cloak.

Lysander's mood deteriorated as the day progressed. His visit to Duck Lane to question Master Wintershall yielded no results. Molly Heron had not left a forwarding address with the stationer and he was forced to continue his search. Abandoning thoughts of dinner, he tracked down a couple of her acquaintants only to draw a similar blank before finally deciding to try the theatre in the hope that she might be performing that afternoon.

By the time he arrived in Vere Street it wanted barely half

an hour to the start of the performance. The doorkeeper admitted that Mistress Heron was acting in the play, *The Scornful Lady,* but was reluctant to let Lysander go backstage.

'Wait until after the performance is done, my lord,' he begged. 'You'll be welcome in the tiring-room then.'

Hungry and thoroughly out of temper, Lysander was in no mood to be denied. 'Here!' He thrust a coin at the man, who smiled, bowed unctuously and escorted him to the women's tiring-room.

Inside, it was hot, noisy and crowded. A strong smell of stage-paint, powder and frangipani perfume assaulted his nostrils. His gaze roved sharply over the room. Women in various stages of undress jostled for position before the looking-glasses, struggling to paint their faces and arrange their hair.

Someone glanced towards the doorway and saw him standing there. Her gasp of surprise and accompanying ripe curse made several pairs of eyes swivel in his direction.

Lysander, who had just spotted Molly Heron's raven head, ignored them and strode towards the dressing-table where she was seated. Molly, who had been busy outlining her eyes with black, looked up and let out a little scream of fright.

'Molly! Are you all right?' A slim, red-haired figure shot out from behind a dressing-screen, an anxious expression on her pretty face, and suddenly the question burning on Lysander's lips was made redundant.

'God's teeth!' He stared in horror at the tight, extremely low-cut gown clinging to her curves, its tawdry bombazine echoing the turquoise of her eyes.

A thick layer of paint hid her freckles and cheap, green ribbons decorated her apricot-gold curls. Coloured glass earrings dangled from her ears, their garish hue a sharp contrast to the genuine pearls glowing around her neck.

In one corner of his brain, Lysander noted they were the string with the black pearl pendant he had seen her wearing once before. Corinna must have presented them to her, a very expensive gift and totally wasted on this setting.

'You look like a two-penny whore,' he spat.

The insult restored Tamsin's power of speech. 'How dare you!' she raged. 'You have no right to come here and revile me. Go away!'

The angry frown on Lysander's face deepened. 'Get your things. We are leaving.'

'You must be mad! Why on earth should I listen to you?' Tamsin glared at him, her eyes snapping. 'I am not going to miss my first performance just to please you.'

Lysander grabbed her by the arm. 'I will not allow you to make a public spectacle of yourself,' he growled.

Tamsin tried to wrench free, but failed. 'It's none of your business what I do,' she hissed at him, horribly aware of their audience, who were listening with open-mouthed interest.

'I'm making it my business.'

'Why? In case you had forgotten, you told me to leave you alone.' Tamsin saw a flicker of misery in his eyes and a bitter triumph filled her. 'Now it's my turn to say the same, Lysander.'

'Aye, get out,' Molly chimed in, coming to stand next to Tamsin. 'You are not wanted here.'

Still keeping hold of Tamsin's arm, Lysander turned his head in her direction, his eyes narrowing with a cold ferocity that made Molly fall silent.

'As for you, Mistress Barton,' he continued, his icy gaze swinging back to Tamsin, 'you are coming with me whether you like it or not.'

Without further ado, he seized her by the waist and flung her over his right shoulder.

'Put me down!' Tamsin pummelled his back with her fists.

Ignoring her screams of protest and a chorus of gasps and nervous giggles from the other women, Lysander marched out of the tiring-room.

Startled heads turned in his direction as he headed for the theatre's exit, but such was the expression on his face that no one dared stop him.

Tamsin found herself being tossed into a hackney. Lysander yelled something at the driver, jumped in after her and the vehicle immediately set off at a wicked pace.

Breathless from her unceremonious landing, Tamsin struggled into a sitting position and made a grab for the door handle.

'Don't be a fool, you'd break your stupid neck!' Lysander's arm shot out to prevent her escape.

'You have no right to do this.' Rage cracked Tamsin's voice.

'I will not allow you to ruin your reputation.'

Tamsin glared at him and, unable to think of a way to escape, turned her face away.

She was acutely conscious of his nearness, but she managed to keep up her pretence of ignoring him until the hackney arrived in Wych Street.

'I am not coming with you,' she declared, suddenly aware that she was still dressed in her stage-costume.

'Yes, you are.' Lysander hauled her out of the coach and, despite her struggles, Tamsin was powerless to prevent him from carrying her into the house.

Master Cooper, who had opened the door, goggled at them and for an instant Tamsin was reminded of that first night when Lysander had brought her home from Mrs Cole's.

But there was no tenderness in his expression now and he waved Matthew aside with a curt, 'Not now', when Matt tried to tell him that Lord Treneglos had called.

'But he said it was urgent he speak with you, my lord!'

Matt's plaintive cry followed them up the stairs. Ignoring it, Lysander strode into the withdrawing-room and kicked the door shut behind them.

'Let me go!'

'What did you think you were playing at?' he demanded furiously, setting her down.

'Why shouldn't I become an actress if I want?' Tamsin's face wore a rebellious look.

'You know the answer to that! Or are you so hellbent on ruining your reputation that you imagine you would enjoy running with that crowd? Damn it, Tamsin, you are a fish out of water there and you know it!'

Tamsin opened her mouth to deny it, but no words came out. Innate honesty told her he was right. She had found the world backstage both strange and frightening with its hard-bitten atmosphere and cynical striving for success. Without Molly's support she would never have got through this week of rehearsals.

'And what concern is it of yours, pray?' she countered, unwilling to admit her doubts.

'I promised Martha I would stop you going on stage.'

Tamsin's eyes flashed. She might have known! Honour again!

'Well, you can go right back and tell her to stop worrying. I don't need her fussing over me. I can look after myself.'

'You ought to be grateful that she cares, you spoilt brat!' Lysander exclaimed.

'And you ought to keep your nose out of my affairs, you great bully!' Tears of rage sparkled in Tamsin's eyes. 'You've made me look a complete laughing-stock!'

'Tamsin.' Lysander laid a hesitant hand on her shoulder.

'Don't!' Tamsin knocked his hand away. 'I don't want to hear your apologies.'

'I wasn't going to apologise!' Lysander lied, his temper flaring up at the look of disdain she gave him. 'You don't deserve an apology. You are behaving like a foolish child unable to see the consequences of your actions.'

'Stop calling me a child!' Utterly incensed by this remark, Tamsin's hand flew up and made violent contact with his cheek.

'Why, you little—' Grabbing her by the shoulders Lysander was about to retaliate when the urge to shake her abruptly vanished. Beneath his hands, she felt delicate and fragile...and wholly desirable!

Breathing hard, he stared down into her face, trying to shore up the barriers he had erected to control his feelings, but it was too late. His defences had crumbled.

Tamsin sensed the change in him. She too had been trying
to hide behind anger. Now, she saw her own desire reflected
in his eyes.

Her slap had left a vivid red mark on his cheek. Timidly,
she reached up and touched it gently.

Turning his head, Lysander pressed a kiss into her palm.

A tiny sigh of satisfaction escaped Tamsin and, slowly, his
hands slid from her shoulders down to her narrow waist.

'God's teeth,' he muttered and pulled her into his embrace.

Their lips met hungrily and Tamsin pressed herself close.
Through the thin cheap fabric of her gown she could feel a
growing hardness at his loins and wondered why it did not
shock her. Without thought, her mouth opened under his and
their tongues entwined.

His hand cupped her breast, stroking it gently before slipping inside the low neckline. Tamsin gasped with pleasure
against his mouth as his skilful fingers investigated her nipple, rousing it delicately until it stood proud and hard.

'Sweetheart!' Lysander swept her up in his arms and carried her over to the couch. He sank down beside her, bearing
her back against the cushions. He kissed her again and Tamsin responded eagerly. She felt his hands upon the bodice of
her gown, untying the laces which held it closed. It fell open
and Tamsin felt cool air upon her skin.

She caught her breath as Lysander's lips left hers and travelled slowly down her throat. He rained delicate butterfly
kisses across the upper curve of her breast and she sighed
with delight.

His hair trailed against her skin, tickling softly. Hesitantly,
Tamsin reached up to touch him, her hand sliding caressingly
across his shoulders. His mouth found her nipple and the feel
of his tongue, hot and wet against its sensitive flesh, sent
tremors of arousal through her entire body.

'I can hear your heart beating like a little drum,' Lysander
whispered, raising his head and gazing into her eyes.

Tamsin gave a tiny choke of laughter. 'It wouldn't surprise
me, my lord, if they could hear it in the street!'

Lysander slid back up the couch. Taking her face between his hands, he smiled at her. 'You are entirely adorable,' he murmured and set his mouth on hers once more.

It was a long deep kiss and they were both so lost in passion's thrall that neither of them heard the door open.

'Lysander, I must speak with you!' Lord Treneglos's urgent voice shattered the silence.

Reacting without thought, Lysander shot up into a sitting position and Tom let out a gasp of dismay as he realised his *faux pas.*

'Forgive me, I didn't realise you…' His voice trailed off as his gaze took in the dishevelled girl lying on the couch. An expression of stunned disbelief appeared on his plump face and with a roar of anger he leapt forward.

'Unhand my daughter, you damned blackguard!'

'Take off those pearls and look at the clasp if you do not believe me.' Lord Treneglos's voice trembled. 'The words *semper amamus* are engraved there.'

Tamsin's hands were shaking so hard she found it difficult to undo the necklace, but at last it came loose and she stared at the gold clasp.

Our love is forever.

Her eyes flew to Tom's face. It was true. He was her father!

'I gave those pearls to your mother on our wedding day.' Tom sighed. 'Not that I need any further proof of who you are. You were named after me, but you are her image, Thomasina.'

'My mother was a blonde,' Tamsin replied carefully.

A faint smile touched Tom's mouth for a fleeting instant. 'In my youth, my hair was much the same colour as yours.'

Lysander broke his deliberate silence. 'You say she was named after you, but her name is—'

Tom turned to glare at him. 'Tamsin is the Cornish pet form of Thomasina,' he interrupted coldly.

Tamsin had often daydreamed about her first meeting with

her father, but never in her wildest imaginings could she have envisaged anything as disastrous as this!

For the first few minutes after Lord Treneglos had burst in on them she had been too embarrassed to take in what he was saying. Fumbling to fasten her bodice, she'd heard him rage at Lysander, screaming of treachery and deceit without understanding what he meant.

Now she knew. He thought Lysander had been deliberately hiding her, an accusation which left Lysander ashen-faced with horror and disbelief. He'd attempted to deny it, but too furious to listen, Lord Treneglos had continued to hurl allegations of lechery and seduction at his head.

An answering anger had erupted in Lysander and for one awful moment, Tamsin had thought they might come to blows. Screwing up her courage, she'd quickly stepped between and intervened by demanding to know why Lord Treneglos thought she was his daughter.

'A Mr Penhaligan was my father,' she had declared and, behind her, heard Lysander catch his breath.

'Penhaligan is my family name,' Lord Treneglos had replied gently. 'I only inherited the title after my marriage.'

Tamsin still could hardly believe it!

'So Aunt Deborah really did deceive us,' she murmured, her stomach twisting as she stared down at the pearls in her hand.

'Aye.' Tom's answer was heavy with disgust. 'She tried to defend herself when I visited Whiteladies by claiming that the lack of proper communication led to confusion, but I believe her motive was spite.'

'And you have been looking for me all this time?' A wondering note crept into Tamsin's voice.

He nodded. 'You are my nearest flesh and blood.'

He held out his hand to her and Tamsin slowly put hers in his. Drawing her gently towards him, he kissed her forehead. 'I am desperately sorry for this bad beginning, my dear, but I hope to make it up to you. I want to wipe out the past and all its misfortunes, if you will let me?'

Tamsin nodded and attempted a smile. It came out crooked, but her fingers tightened on his.

He returned the pressure for an instant and then turned to Lysander, his smile abruptly fading.

'I assume you know what reparation you must make?' he enquired with a deadly formality.

Lysander inclined his head. He was very pale and a muscle twitched by the corner of his mouth, but he bowed to Tamsin with exquisite grace. 'Madam, will you do me the honour of accepting my hand in marriage?'

Tamsin choked.

'She will.' Lord Treneglos answered for her. 'My lawyers will attend on you tomorrow, Saxon.' He glanced at Tamsin. 'Come, Thomasina. There is no further need to linger here.'

Tamsin recovered her voice. 'Lysander cannot marry me!' she gasped. 'He is betrothed to Jane Godolphin.'

'My understanding is that the marriage contract has not yet been signed.' Tom's expression was implacable.

Tamsin wondered how he knew and just as quickly realised he must have already heard the latest town gossip. She gave him an imploring look. 'There is no need for such drastic measures, sir!'

She stole a glance at Lysander and her heart sank at his icy expression. If only he *wanted* to marry her! But he didn't. He had pledged his word to Jane and honour meant everything to him!

'There is every need!' Anger crackled in Tom's voice. 'Half the town knows that you once lived unchaperoned in this very house with him.'

'I was housekeeper here,' Tamsin protested.

'No one will believe that, not after today. I was told that Saxon was bound for the theatre so I followed him there. You had mentioned to my agent that you had once worked in this house and I wanted Saxon to clear up the puzzle. However, when I arrived the whole place was buzzing with talk of how he had abducted an actress.' Tom took a deep breath, striving to contain his feelings. 'I didn't realise, of course, that you were the girl involved.'

Tamsin winced. 'What…what you saw just now…I can explain,' she began, blushing to the roots of her hair. 'I mean, I—'

'Hush, my dear. I do not blame you.' Tom threw Lysander a dark look. 'It is unfortunate that Mistress Godolphin must suffer, but I cannot allow her needs to take precedence over yours.'

'But…but—'

'Enough, daughter. You are overwrought and in no condition to think clearly.' Tom removed his cloak and wrapped it around her, hiding her wanton gown. 'Come. My carriage is outside.'

Reluctantly, Tamsin allowed him to lead her away, but at the door she could not resist glancing back at Lysander.

He stood motionless and the expression of frozen despair on his face made Tamsin wish she had not looked back.

In spite of the splendid comfort on offer at the White Horse Inn, Tamsin passed a sleepless night and rose early. She wanted to try and convince her father that he was making a mistake, but Lord Treneglos would not listen.

'There is no point in further discussion, my dear. Saxon took advantage of you and now he must pay for it.'

'Without his help I should have been in a worse predicament! He saved me from Mrs Cole!'

'Thomasina, I beg you will never mention that woman's name again!' Tom shuddered.

Over supper last night Tamsin had confessed all that had happened since she left Whiteladies and he had been horrified. Riddled by guilt that he was to blame for her misfortunes, he was determined to put things right.

'My dear, Lysander Saxon knows as well as I do that marriage is the only way to silence the gossip and save your reputation. He may not want to marry you, but he has no choice,' he declared, unintentionally rubbing salt into Tamsin's wounded pride.

'And what if I do not want to marry him?' she asked tightly.

Tom lifted his brows. 'From what I saw yesterday, I rather hoped you did.'

Tamsin blushed. 'Not unless he is willing.'

'Don't fret. I shall give you a dowry that will enable him to restore Melcombe. He will not be able to reproach you.'

He had misunderstood her. She wanted Lysander to love her, not feel trapped!

'Come, let's have some breakfast; then, when Petroc returns from Mrs Heron's, we shall go shopping to find a present to send to Master Latham to thank him for his kindness to you.'

Tom had dispatched his trusted manservant, another Cornishman who had been with him for years, to collect Tamsin's belongings from Molly's. He had forbidden Tamsin to see the actress, but had allowed her to send a final message of reassurance and farewell.

Molly would understand why Tamsin had to break off their friendship. She wasn't the type to bear resentment and Tamsin hoped that one day they might meet again, for she would miss Molly's cheerfulness and her devil-may-care attitude, which had always appealed to her own streak of rebelliousness.

She wouldn't miss the raffish world backstage, however. She was not cut out to be an actress. It was probably the Puritan in her!

You should have listened to your conscience earlier, she scolded herself as they sat down to breakfast in the private parlour her father had hired. Then you wouldn't feel so guilty!

She had hated the stage, but had continued in the hope that it might persuade Lysander to change his mind and take her for his mistress. For all her anger, a part of her had been relieved that he had stopped her performing yesterday, but just look at the mess her attempted manipulation had landed them in!

He must hate me, she thought miserably, and the bread she was attempting to eat turned to sawdust in her mouth.

If Tamsin had but known it, Lysander was making equally poor work of his morning draught.

Besotted with one woman while tied to another! Was it any wonder he felt furiously guilty at gaining his heart's desire at the expense of his honour?

Abandoning the dining-table, he screwed up his courage and set out to visit Jane. The interview which followed was harrowing and, after taking one look at his white face, Matthew hurried to fetch him a large glass of brandy on his return.

'I'm afraid Lord Treneglos's lawyers are waiting for you. I put them in the withdrawing-room,' he murmured sympathetically.

'Thank you,' Lysander replied. He downed the brandy in one swallow. 'I think I may have need of this!'

The two men rose at Lysander's entrance. Bowing politely, they presented a list of Lord Treneglos's terms for his perusal.

'You will want to consult your own lawyers no doubt, my lord,' the senior man said when Lysander had finished reading the document.

'Aye, but everything looks straightforward enough,' Lysander replied in a slightly surprised tone. Tom's terms were remarkably generous.

Had his understandable anger cooled? Lysander fervently hoped so. He had known Tom for too long to want to quarrel with him.

'Then, if you are agreeable, Lord Treneglos suggests that the marriage contract be signed tomorrow.'

Lysander's startled expression prompted the junior lawyer to speak up. 'Our client sees no point in delay.' He coughed delicately. 'Unless…will there be any difficulty with Mistress Godolphin, do you think?'

'Mistress Godolphin intends to travel home to Rye for Easter. I doubt if she will return to London for some months.' Lysander's voice was perfectly toneless.

The two lawyers exchanged satisfied glances. 'In that case, Sir Lysander, may we tell Lord Treneglos that you will present yourself at our office in Mincing Lane at eleven o'clock tomorrow?'

'You may.'

They bowed themselves out and Lysander took a deep breath.

By tomorrow noon he would be as good as married!

Having taken the precaution of practising her new signature earlier that morning at their Lombard Street inn, Tamsin was able to sign her true name on the betrothal contract without faltering. She stared at the wet ink. Thomasina Penhaligan. How strange it looked!

Soon, very soon, she would have to learn another new name, she thought with a flicker of panic as she lifted her eyes from the parchment and met Lysander's brooding gaze.

The lawyers produced a bottle of wine and the customary toasts were drunk. The atmosphere, however, remained strained and Tamsin found it hard to thank everyone for their good wishes.

It was a relief to leave the small dark office behind, but the ordeal was not yet over.

'May I beg the favour of a word in private with your daughter?' Lysander asked with formal politeness as his companions were about to enter their coach.

Tom shook his head. 'I think not.'

Lysander's mouth tightened.

'We shall see you in church.' Tom ushered Tamsin into the coach, ignoring her frantic look of appeal.

It drove away and, muttering a curse beneath his breath, Lysander went in search of Jack.

He ran him to earth in the Sun Tavern in Threadneedle Street, one of his cousin's favourite haunts. Jack, who was about to sit down to dinner, immediately invited Lysander to join him.

They found a free table in one of the smaller rooms where they could be assured of privacy and gave their order to the potboy, who brought them a bottle of sack and a plate of oysters.

'Your eel pies will be along in a minute, gentlemen,' he told them before disappearing off to serve another customer.

'I shall be glad to be done with Lent,' Jack remarked in a deliberately jovial tone. 'My stomach aches for a proper bit of beef.'

Lysander, appreciating his kind intentions, managed to raise a smile. 'Perhaps my luck would have been better if I had kept the proper observance,' he answered ironically and, fixing his cousin with a direct look, asked him if he had heard the rumour about him abducting an actress.

Jack took a fortifying swallow of his wine. 'Aye,' he nodded. 'But I don't believe it,' he added stoutly.

'You should,' Lysander replied and proceeded to lay out the full truth for Jack's inspection.

'Poor Jane!' Jack exclaimed involuntarily. 'How humiliated she must feel!'

Lysander winced and, realising his lack of tact, Jack hid his concern for Mistress Godolphin and hastily asked when the wedding was to take place.

'At the end of next week.' Lysander had agreed to procure a special licence to save time calling banns. 'Will you be my groomsman?'

'Of course I will,' Jack responded.

He was agitated on Jane's behalf, but he didn't blame Lysander. His cousin had been caught between the devil and the deep blue sea. There was no way he could behave honourably to both women!

'With any luck, with Easter and the forthcoming Coronation, people will be too busy to go on paying attention to us,' Lysander continued with a pretence of optimism.

'Aye,' Jack agreed, but silently he doubted it. The story was too sensational!

'I can still hardly believe that little Tamsin is Treneglos's missing heiress,' he murmured, taking one of the oysters. 'As for the idea that she was going to appear on stage...' He swallowed the morsel of seafood and spread his hands wide in a gesture of amazement. 'What could have prompted her to think up such a crazy scheme?'

'Oh, I have a good idea,' Lysander replied curtly and his expression darkened ominously.

Chapter Twelve

Rain beat against the windows of St Mary Woolnoth and Tamsin was shivering as she walked down the aisle on her new husband's arm. But it was not the chill permeating the old church nor the gloom of the afternoon which affected her.

Lysander's deep attractive voice had been coolly impersonal as he took his vows. He looked magnificent in a new suit of bronze-coloured farandine, but she couldn't tell what he was thinking from his imperturbable expression.

On leaving the church they repaired to the White Horse, where Lord Treneglos had made provision for the wedding feast. Removing her wet cloak, Tamsin shook the creases out of her deep cream lutestring skirts and saw several water marks. The rain had dampened her gold lace petticoat as well, but somehow it no longer seemed to matter if her lovely dress spoiled.

She had done her best to look beautiful today. A fashionable hairdresser had been summoned to arrange her hair in artful ringlets, her clothes were the finest money could buy and her father had given her a pair of exquisite pearl earrings to match the necklace that had once been her mother's.

But Lysander didn't seem to have noticed her efforts.

'Let me welcome you into the family, cousin!' Jack appeared at her side and, with a broad grin, kissed her cheek.

Heartened by his cheerful chatter, Tamsin took her place at

the table. Too nervous to eat, she could barely touch any of the elegant dishes her father had ordered.

Glancing sideways, she noted that while Lysander's appetite seemed similarly affected, he was drinking steadily.

She signalled for her own wineglass to be refilled. Her father, who was seated on her other side, whispered, 'Is that wise, my dear?'

'Pot valour,' Tamsin whispered back with a wry smile.

The long meal came to an end and the guests began to depart, for Lysander had flatly refused to countenance any of the usual bedding ceremonies. Tamsin was relieved. Such traditional romps as the untying of her garters and the flinging of bridal stockings would have been too much of an ordeal for her strained nerves.

Tamsin slipped into her bedchamber when all the guests had gone. With a tiny sigh she picked up her silver toothbrush from the dressing-table. The irony of choosing it for herself all those months ago had hit her when Tom had finally presented it to her last night. If only he had found her earlier, she might have been able to win Lysander's love fair and square!

Crushing this useless speculation, she dropped the toothbrush into the elaborate dressing-case, which had been Lysander's wedding gift to her.

There was a knock at the door and her father entered. 'I wanted to say goodbye to you in private.' He smiled at her awkwardly. 'And ask if I might call on you soon?'

Tamsin reassured him. 'I don't blame you for forcing this marriage, Father.'

Tom's face lit up and he kissed her cheek. 'Thank you for your understanding, my dear.' He paused and then, gazing at her anxiously, added, 'Tell me I am right in thinking that you care for Lysander?'

Tamsin bit her lip and then nodded abruptly.

Tom let out a sigh of relief. 'I swear to you that I would not have wed you to him if I had believed otherwise.'

Seeing her surprised expression, he coughed. 'I may have cursed Lysander Saxon to hell and back, but I have known him since he was a child. He has his faults, but my suspicions were unworthy.'

'Perhaps you should tell him you have forgiven him.' Tamsin suspected her father's coldness had cut Lysander to the quick.

'I shall,' Tom nodded. 'But our reconciliation can wait.' He picked up her cloak and put it around her shoulders. 'You must go. He is waiting for you downstairs.'

They went out to the coach and Lord Treneglos placed her hand in Lysander's. 'I pray you will find happiness together,' he said formally and withdrew.

The ride to Wych Street was conducted in an uncomfortable silence. Tamsin opened her mouth several times to break it, only to find that her courage had deserted her. She half-suspected Lysander of doing the same, she could feel the tension coiled in his lean frame, but the interior of the coach was too gloomy to be sure.

She was touched to find Martha and her husband lined up in the hallway with Master Cooper, Dinah and Luke to congratulate them.

'We all came to the church to see you wed,' Luke piped up as she thanked them for their good wishes.

Matthew produced a tray of glasses filled with wine and a toast was drunk to the bridal couple.

Martha drew Tamsin on one side as the others returned to their duties and her dark eyes were misted with tears. 'Your mother would have been so proud of you today.'

Tamsin swallowed the lump in her throat. Etiquette had forbidden her to invite a lowly shopkeeper's wife to the wedding-feast, but she had missed Martha. 'Thank you,' she whispered.

'I know you were angry with me for interfering, but it's all turned out for the best, my lamb.'

Tamsin murmured agreement, surreptitiously crossing her fingers for luck.

When Ned and Martha had gone, Lysander politely offered her his arm to escort her up to the withdrawing-room.

'I told Matthew that he and the others could have the evening off,' he announced as she seated herself. 'They will leave a cold supper for us in the dining-room. I hope this arrangement meets with your approval?'

Tamsin nodded carelessly. 'Someone may as well celebrate.'

Lysander paled. How bitter she sounded! 'I thought this match was to your liking,' he began, an unusual note of hesitation in his deep voice.

'Well, it certainly isn't to yours!' Tamsin interrupted hotly, losing control of her wine-influenced tongue. 'You have made that plain enough!'

'Do you blame me, ma'am?' Lysander could feel his own temper rising. 'Thanks to you, I was forced to reject the woman to whom I had pledged my word. My honour has been compromised and my name has become a laughing-stock.' He glared at her. 'What's more, I strongly suspect you planned your ridiculous début at the theatre merely to manipulate me into changing my mind about your wanton offer!'

Tamsin's heart sank. Oh God, he hadn't forgiven her!

Lysander moved to the marble fireplace and leaned against it casually, resting his arm on the mantelpiece. His heart was thumping as if he had been in action against the French! Observing her stricken expression, his flash of temper vanished.

'Do you really dislike the notion of being married to me?' he asked, hoping his negligent pose concealed the tension tightening every nerve as he waited for her answer.

'You are not my idea of a good husband,' Tamsin retorted, recovering her composure.

He quirked one eyebrow. 'You did not seem so indifferent to me before.'

'I do not deny there has been desire between us,' Tamsin snapped. 'But I am not such a child as to confuse lust with love. I wanted to be your mistress, not your wife.'

To her satisfaction, his well-cut mouth dropped open in astonishment.

'No woman of sense wants to get married,' she said coolly.

'Men use their wives worse than a dog. They think them fit for nothing but breeding heirs. Mistresses, on the other hand, get gifts and attention.'

Tamsin knew she was quoting Molly to hide her hurt feelings. If he didn't want her, she was damned if she was going to admit to wanting him!

'Thanks to you, I have lost my freedom,' she continued sharply, echoing his hateful words. 'You cost me the chance to select my own husband at a time of my own choosing. And, I'll warrant you, I should have chosen a very different kind of man.'

She smiled at him with poisonous sweetness. 'Your brother-in-law has an excellent library. I read in one of his books that your namesake was a Spartan general, a man noted for his arrogance and pride. I see those traits in you and I do not admire them.'

Lysander felt as if she had kicked him in the stomach. In spite of all that had gone wrong, he had assumed that they could patch up their differences. 'Are you saying that you now hold me in distaste?'

The note of incredulity in his voice infuriated Tamsin. Of all the conceited… 'Of course!'

The lie burnt her tongue, but stubborn wilfulness kept her expression indifferent.

'Then it seems to me, ma'am,' Lysander said slowly, 'that this marriage is a farce.'

Tamsin stared at him warily. 'What do you mean?'

Before he could answer there was a loud knock and Dinah came hurrying in without waiting for permission to enter.

'Well?' Lysander rounded on her impatiently.

'Beg pardon, my lord, but it's the King!' Dinah's eyes were round with awe.

Tamsin barely had time to jump up from the couch before Charles strolled in. She had a brief impression of immense height, rich clothing and a swarthy face surrounded by curly dark hair before sinking into a hasty curtsy.

'Please forgive the intrusion, Lady Saxon.' Charles extended a hand to raise her to her feet. 'I promise I won't stay above a moment.'

His voice was rich and pleasing, but a cold shiver ran down Tamsin's spine. Did Lysander want her to be his lady?

'Although I was prevented from attending your wedding, I couldn't let the day go by without wishing you both well.' Charles handed Tamsin a silk-wrapped gift with a smile.

It was a smile that transformed his heavy features, she thought as she unwrapped the gift. Its warmth made her understand why all the ladies fell victim to his charm!

The gift was a small painting of the Dutch school set in a gilt frame. Lysander thanked Charles and asked him if he would take a glass of wine.

Tamsin set the painting down carefully. Her hands were shaking. The King's presence and his splendid gift only added to the sense of unreality which had haunted her all day. Any minute now she was going to wake up and find herself back in Paris, the last two months nothing but a crazy dream!

'I must go,' Charles eventually announced with a flattering reluctance. 'I am expected at Whitehall.'

Tamsin knew that he had created several Knights of the Bath earlier in the day, which was why he had not accepted an invitation to the wedding, and she surmised that some form of entertainment was scheduled to conclude the ceremonies.

They escorted him with correct formality to the front door. 'Bring your wife to Court soon,' Charles added to Lysander as he bade them farewell.

'I think not, Sire.' Lysander's voice was cool.

A little startled, Charles cocked his head enquiringly.

'Mistress Penhaligan agrees with me that our marriage was a mistake.' Lysander shrugged, his expression inscrutable. 'The obvious solution is to seek an annulment.'

Tamsin gasped and even Charles Stuart, who was noted for his *sang-froid,* looked shocked. 'Are you quite sure, my friend?'

'Quite.' Lysander glanced at Tamsin. When she remained

silent, he continued lightly, 'It should be simple enough to arrange, I imagine.'

Charles gave him a sardonic look. 'You intend to claim it is a marriage contracted *per verba praesenti,* but which *nisi accedat copula carnalis?*'

'Exactly so, Sire.' Lysander inclined his head.

The Latin phrases revolved dizzily in Tamsin's brain. 'Would one of you mind telling me what you are talking about?' she asked faintly.

'It means that the marriage is strictly on paper,' Charles replied quickly.

Tamsin's gaze flew to Lysander's face. 'You mean…'

'I do not intend to consummate this marriage.'

His green eyes were stormy, but he bowed to her with exquisite grace. 'Until the ecclesiastical courts are done with us, we will have to live together, but rest assured that I will do all in my power to grant you the freedom you so evidently desire.'

Tamsin stuck her head out of the coach window. They were coming to the end of a long driveway which had wound its way through woodland and thick shrubbery and she could now see the house.

Melcombe Manor stood firmly planted on a slight rise, dominating the scene with effortless grace. Roughly L-shaped, its mellow local stone seemed to have caught the warm July sunshine.

'It's beautiful,' she said to her father, suddenly understanding why Lysander was so attached to his birthplace.

The coach came to a halt. 'Are you sure this is what you want?' Tom asked, laying a restraining hand on Tamsin's arm. 'It's not too late for you to continue on to Cornwall with me.'

Tamsin shook her head. 'I must see Lysander,' she said firmly.

She descended from the coach and surveyed the house. Seen more closely, there was evidence of damage and neglect to both the stonework and roof. But repairs were under way and she wondered how Lysander was financing them since he hadn't touched a penny of her dowry.

She had barely seen him since their wedding day three months ago. When they met he was civil, but distant. Bewildered and furious, Tamsin had retaliated by refusing to retract her hasty words and treating him with the same cool politeness. No matter her heartache, she would not beg him to keep her as his wife!

That he was being discreet about the annulment Tamsin knew from the lack of gossip and, since it was unfashionable to hang upon each other's arm, their largely separate lifestyles occasioned little comment.

At the end of May, Lysander had announced he was leaving for Melcombe. 'I don't know when I shall return,' he'd informed her, coolly adding that she had his permission to live with her father if she wished.

Pride kept Tamsin from following his suggestion, but when Lord Treneglos visited Wych Street on Midsummer's Day and found her in tears, Tamsin was forced to confess the truth.

Shocked, Tom had urged her to seek a reconciliation. Tamsin had refused.

Then, a few days ago, a summons had come from Whitehall and Tamsin found herself enjoying a private audience with the King.

'You realise, my dear, that the annulment of your marriage is proceeding?' he asked, after waving her to a seat in his closet. 'These matters are confoundedly slow, but I suppose you know that?'

Tamsin nodded, ignoring the fierce cramping of her stomach.

'It is likely that the final decision will rest with me.' Charles's harsh features wore a kindly smile. 'Which is why I asked you here. Are you sure you don't want to change your mind?'

Tamsin gazed at him, her tongue frozen.

'You see, it occurs to me that this match is extremely suitable if the pair of you could only be brought to realise it.' His dark eyes held a perceptive awareness as he waited for her answer.

There was a short silence, filled only with the ticking of the many clocks Charles kept in his closet. 'I'm…I'm not sure, Sire.'

'Then perhaps you ought to discuss it with your husband,' he suggested gently.

Tamsin struggled with the pride and anger which had sustained her for the last few months. In her heart she knew she didn't want to let Lysander go. 'I will, your Majesty.'

Lord Treneglos had insisted on accompanying her to Dorset. 'I intend to spend several months in Cornwall's good air, my dear,' he'd said, brushing aside her objections. 'It is no trouble to visit Melcombe Regis first.'

Realising that he needed to know the outcome of her attempt, Tamsin had gladly accepted his escort. The summer roads had been dusty and rutted, but the long journey was over at last.

Giving her blue cambric skirts a determined shake to free them of dust, she marched towards the front entrance.

A servant admitted them and they stepped into a vast hall with ancient wooden beams that betrayed its Plantagenet origins. Tamsin noted that the far end of the room was still under repair with workmen busy with buckets of plaster.

'I wish to speak to Sir Lysander,' she said, raising her voice above the workmen's din.

'The master is not at home, ma'am.'

'Then where is he?'

'I do believe he be at the quarry,' the woman answered.

Tamsin shot a puzzled glance at Tom.

'We will speak to Sir Lysander's steward,' Tom announced and the maid showed them into a parlour off the hall. It overlooked the garden and the scent of roses drifted in through an open window.

Too restless to sit, Tamsin walked over to the window and stared out at a bed of irises, phlox and delphiniums, but her attention was concentrated on listening for footsteps.

To her disappointment, the man who came hurrying in was a stranger. 'I was hoping to see Master Cooper,' she exclaimed.

After taking the precaution of hiring one of Nat's cousins to act as her new manservant, Lysander had taken Matthew with him.

'Master Cooper accompanied Sir Lysander to the Isle of Portland, ma'am.' The steward, a heavy man in his thirties, bowed politely and introduced himself as John Easton. 'They are supervising work at the quarry.'

'I remember now,' Tom chimed in. 'Lysander's mother came from Portland and her family owned a large stone quarry there.' He frowned. 'I thought it was disused.'

'Sir Lysander has opened it up again.' There was a note of pride in Master Easton's voice.

Tamsin nodded impatiently. 'Can you send a message asking him to return?'

'The only means of reaching the Isle is by boat. I doubt if he could be back here before morning.'

'Then we will wait. Please prepare bedchambers for us.'

Seeing the man's startled look, she explained who she was.

'I beg your pardon, my lady. I had no idea you planned to visit us.' Master Easton paused uncertainly.

Tom put him out of his misery. 'We can see that the house is at sixes and sevens. Just do your best, man.'

Over supper, Tom explained to Tamsin that the Isle belonged to the Crown and had always been loyal. 'Even though the Parliamentarians held most of this area, including the town of Melcombe Regis.'

'They used this house as a garrison, didn't they?' Tamsin glanced around the dining-room. The wooden panelling was scarred and broken in places.

'Aye. Damn near ruined it, too!' Tom sighed, remembering the house in all its glory before the War.

'I suppose Lysander's family have lived here forever,' Tamsin said wistfully.

She felt like an interloper, aware of the covert stares of the servants, who plainly wondered why their master had left his new bride behind in London.

'Actually, it was bought by Lysander's grandfather,' Tom said, surprising her. 'He was a local lad made good. A son of minor gentry, he went up to Court and had the luck to marry a Scots heiress who came to England as a lady-in-waiting to Queen Anne when James took over the throne. He then bought this house from the original family, who were sadly impoverished, and set about extending it.'

Lord Treneglos smiled at his daughter's amazed expression. 'Lysander's father possessed the same passion for improvement. When I first came here he was in the middle of building the library. He installed handsome panelling and a wealth of fine furniture and paintings in every room.'

He shrugged. 'It was all sold to raise money for the cause.'

'If Lysander can make a success of this quarrying, do you think he will be able to restore his fortunes?'

Tamsin had discovered from Tom that Portland's fine white limestone was highly prized. Indeed, Inigo Jones had used it in constructing the great Banqueting Hall at the Palace of Whitehall.

Tom nodded thoughtfully. 'It would be damned hard work and I believe there is a tax levied on every ton of stone exported, but it could be a most profitable enterprise. There is much new building going on in London now.'

So he would not need her dowry after all!

'Why didn't he decide on this scheme earlier?' she burst out. 'He need never have approached Mistress Godolphin!'

'Gently, my dear!' Tom patted her shoulder soothingly. 'I expect it has taken him this long to get the quarry in good order and set up the right contacts in London, to say nothing of the difficulties of arranging the necessary sea-transport. The whole business is outside the usual scope of a gentleman, after all.'

There was a note of admiration in her father's tone and Tamsin reluctantly conceded that he was right. Instead of taking the easy option like his grandfather and using a rich heiress's wealth, Lysander was forging his own path.

She swallowed hard. Which meant, of course, that she had lost one of her bargaining counters!

Contrary to her expectations, Tamsin slept well in the scantily furnished chamber assigned to her and she hurried downstairs the next morning in a fever of impatience.

'A letter has come for you, my lady.' Master Easton handed her a note, which bore Lysander's seal, and discreetly melted away.

Tamsin ripped it open and, seeing her turn pale, Tom asked her if anything was wrong.

'He won't see me.' She raised stricken eyes to Tom's face.

'Surely, we can persuade him to change—'

Tamsin shook her head. 'He makes it very clear that he doesn't want anything further to do with me. Look—' she waved the letter '—he has even ordered me to leave Melcombe "as soon as I am sufficiently rested"!'

'Come and sit down,' Tom urged anxiously, afraid she might faint.

'No!' Tamsin took a deep breath, her fingers straying involuntarily to her mother's pearls which she had worn for courage. How ironic the motto engraved upon their clasp seemed now!

She attempted a brave smile. 'Let us go. We have a long journey ahead of us to Cornwall.'

Music floating out onto the frosty December air alerted Lysander Saxon to the fact that he was late and the evening's entertainment in the Vane Room had begun. He lengthened his stride and, in the gloom of the Matted Gallery, would have hurried past a couple going in the same direction if a well-known voice had not hailed him.

'Coz! Where have you sprung from? It's been months since you were at Whitehall!'

'Jack! It's good to see you.' Lysander shook Lord Fanshawe's hand. 'I've just returned from Italy,' he continued, answering his cousin's question.

'Where, no doubt, you have been busy learning techniques to further your successful venture of stone-cutting,' Jack's companion said.

There was amusement in the lady's voice. Lysander stiffened, suddenly recognising her.

'Mistress Godolphin.' He bowed, his expression wary.

Jane laughed. 'Pray do not look so worried, sir. I promise not to scream abuse at you.'

She exchanged a secretive glance with Jack. 'I long since recognised we were not suited and therefore, my lord, you are forgiven.'

Lysander hadn't realised how much he needed to hear her say so until now. It felt as if a great weight had rolled off his conscience!

He took the hand she held out to him and raised it to his lips. 'I should be very glad to be your friend,' he said simply.

'Then I hope you shall come and dance at my wedding next month,' she replied with a mischievous smile.

Lysander glanced from her to his cousin's proud face and let out a pleased chuckle as Jane removed the embroidered glove from her left hand to show off a diamond ring that sparkled in the dim light.

He congratulated Jack and, turning back to Jane, said, 'You have chosen the better man, my dear.'

'I know.' Jane's tone was smug.

Jack had followed her to Rye and his admiration had been balm to her bruised feelings. Truth to tell, she had always found his company easier than Lysander's. He didn't possess the fine estate she had once thought necessary, but this no longer seemed important.

She had come to care for him. What's more, unlike Lysander, he shared her preference for town life and was so amiable that she knew she would always get her own way.

Life with Jack would be agreeable and if on occasion she ever sighed for a little of that dangerous excitement which

Lysander's stormy green gaze could inspire, she was too much of a realist to regret his loss. Let that apricot-haired hussy have him and good luck to her!

'Tamsin is back in London too,' Jack announced as they resumed walking. 'I saw her the other day at the Royal Exchange. She is looking prettier than ever.'

'I hear she is living with her father,' Jane murmured.

It was hard to be sure in the poor light, but she thought she saw Lysander's jaw clench.

'The lease is almost up on the house in Wych Street,' he replied neutrally, which, as Jane noted, was no answer at all.

They reached their destination. After the chilly gloom of the gallery, the King's withdrawing-room was an explosion of bright colour and warmth, lit by hundreds of wax candles. Satin-clad Cavaliers and their jewel-bedecked ladies strolled or stood in little groups, their loud chatter drowning out the music provided for their entertainment.

Lysander parted from his companions and went to pay his respects to the King, who greeted him with a friendly smile and an enquiry after his travels. They spoke of Italy for a while and then Charles said, 'The documents you requested are ready for signing.'

His shrewd dark eyes noted how Lysander stiffened. 'Your wife is here tonight,' he added casually. 'Why don't you bring her along to my closet later and we'll conclude the business?'

Lysander nodded assent, aware of the curiosity on the faces of the courtiers who surrounded them.

It was hardly surprising, he reflected grimly. While couples at court rarely lived in each other's pockets, his absence from his wife's side had been prolonged enough to occasion comment.

If it hadn't been for his vow to set her free... Lysander forced the thought aside. He couldn't afford to weaken now, not with the end in sight!

He retired from the royal presence and went to search the throng for Tamsin. He found her talking to a dark-haired young gallant clad in scarlet moire and for an instant could not resist feasting his eyes upon her graceful figure. She was wearing a gown of leaf-green silk, looped back to reveal a pale lemon petticoat and her lovely hair tumbled in a mass of artful ringlets about her white neck.

She looked like the personification of spring, fresh, young, beautiful and heartbreakingly innocent!

Gritting his teeth, Lysander stepped forward.

Tamsin broke off her conversation, her eyes widening. 'My lord.' She sank into a deep curtsy. 'I did not expect to see you here.'

To her relief, there was no trace of the shock she felt in her voice.

Lysander heard the coolness in her polite greeting and his spirits plummeted. For a moment, he had been sure there was a flash of joy in her eyes, but now her face was a blank mask.

He bowed. 'I trust I find you well, ma'am?'

'Very, sir.' Tamsin fanned herself idly with her fan, praying that he would not notice her hand was shaking.

In truth, with her father's protection and the King's friendship, she had been shielded from the usual cruel speculation surrounding a neglected wife. It was only her heart that had suffered.

'La, my angel, you are living proof that a woman gets on better without a husband to bother her!' The painted and patched gallant at Tamsin's side tittered.

Lysander turned his head slowly and allowed his gaze to rake the younger man up and down. 'And who might you be, sir?'

The coldness in his voice caused the gallant to take a precautionary step away from Tamsin, but he answered haughtily, 'Antony Blackwell, at your service, my lord.'

'Lord Blackwell's son?'

Antony nodded.

Lysander's mouth thinned. Blackwell was a notorious womaniser and drunkard and he had heard that his son was cut from the same cloth for all that he had barely attained his majority.

'Antony has been acting as my escort these last few weeks since I got back from Cornwall,' Tamsin said sweetly. She laid her hand on Mr Blackwell's sleeve and fluttered her long eyelashes at him. 'He is such entertaining company.'

'Indeed,' Lysander replied tightly.

God's teeth, was she deliberately trying to provoke him?

'Do you intend to remain in London long, sir?' Emboldened by Tamsin's hand on his arm, Antony's light voice held an insolent note.

Lysander shook his head. 'When I have concluded an urgent matter of private business,' he said, itching to plant his fist in the middle of Mr Blackwell's painted face, 'I mean to keep Christmas at Melcombe.'

'Great Jupiter, you will risk travelling so far at this season?' Antony gave a theatrical shudder. 'Rather you than me. You will be shaken to pieces!'

The smile on his rouged lips told Lysander that the young man found this idea pleasurable. 'I'm sorry to disappoint you, but I intend to travel by sea.'

'Even worse!' Antony fluttered the embroidered handkerchief he carried in one hand. 'All that tossing about and cold winds!' His gaze sought Tamsin's. 'Don't you agree, my angel, such a journey is simply too horrible to contemplate?'

Tamsin was silent, her mind racing. What did he mean by urgent private business?

'Surely, you cannot approve of such a barbarous mode of travel?' Antony persisted.

'Actually, I quite enjoy it,' Tamsin replied lightly, striving to dismiss the conviction that Lysander was referring to their annulment.

It was so hard to think straight with him standing close! For months she had nursed her anger and tried to ignore her anguish, telling herself that she no longer cared for a man who could use her so vilely. She thought she had succeeded.

Fool! The very sight of him tonight had set her ablaze with all the old longing!

'Corinna told me what a good sailor you were,' Lysander

said unexpectedly. 'She said you were the only passenger on board who did not succumb to seasickness on the way over to France.'

'You have seen her?'

Lysander smiled at her excitement. 'Aye, I visited Paris on my way home from Italy.'

Tamsin knew he had been abroad. He had, very properly, sent word of his intentions before leaving England. Angry though she was, she also had to acknowledge that he had continued to pay her allowance, which was more than generous enough to maintain her in comfort.

'She sent you her best wishes and I am to tell you that they are all well and happy.' Lysander grinned. 'My nephew has not yet mastered the art of walking, but not for the want of trying as my aching back could tell you!'

Tamsin laughed. 'I wish I could have seen you helping him walk!' she exclaimed, forgetting to guard her tongue.

'Tamsin, I—'

Mr Blackwell yawned noisily. 'Oh, pray forgive me!' he begged insincerely. 'Such a charming family anecdote, but I must remind you, my angel, that we promised to play a hand of gleek with the Earl, who is over there waiting for us.'

'Very well. Pray excuse me, my lord.' Tamsin crushed a flicker of irritation.

She had found Antony Blackwell's admiration flattering at first. Dazzled by his wit and his fashionable manner, she had accepted his attentions, but lately she was beginning to suspect he was nothing more than a beribboned dandiprat whose hollow compliments masked a selfish nature.

How could I have thought him agreeable? she marvelled to herself, her eyes involuntarily straying towards Lysander, who was wearing the black velvet suit laced in silver, which had always been her favourite.

Against him, Antony looked insignificant for all his gaudy satin and jewels.

'I will speak to you later.' Lysander fought the impulse to

ask her to stay. After tonight, she would be free to enjoy the company of whatever fop she chose!

'Of course,' Tamsin murmured politely, inwardly resolving to avoid another encounter at all costs. She couldn't afford the pleasure of his company, she thought bitterly, as she allowed Antony to lead her away.

The rest of the evening passed in a hectic whirl as she tried to convince herself and everyone around her that she was enjoying the party. She had just finished dancing the allemande with Antony as her partner when a servant came up to them and quietly told her that the King wished to speak to her.

Tamsin's heart thudded against her breastbone. She could only think of one reason why Charles might want to see her in private.

Brushing aside the servant's offer, Antony insisted on escorting her to the King's closet. To Tamsin's surprise, however, the room was empty.

'You need not wait, Antony. I'm sure that the King will be along in a minute.'

His pale gaze fixed on her speculatively. 'Why waste an opportunity?' he said and grabbed her by the waist.

'Are you mad, sir?' Tamsin was indignant.

'If you are going to whore for the King, my angel, I don't see why I shouldn't sample your charms first.' He attempted to plant a kiss on her unwilling lips.

'How dare you imply such a thing?' Tamsin managed to free one hand and slapped his smirking face.

He rubbed his cheek and glared at her. 'Why else would he invite you here?' A jeering laugh shook his somewhat plump frame. 'If you think you are safe just because your husband is his friend, you are even more innocent than I thought.'

'You disgust me, sir. The King's friendship towards me is genuine and not prompted by lust, as yours seems to have been!' She struggled in his hold. 'For God's sake, try to remember you are a gentleman and let me go!'

He ignored her protest and renewed his efforts to kiss her.

Tamsin twisted her head aside, but fear coiled in the pit of her stomach as he began to roughly paw her breasts. 'Stop it! You are hurting me…oh, thank goodness!'

Suddenly the cruel hands were snatched away and, half-dazed with fright, Tamsin watched her husband's fist crash into Antony's jaw, sending him reeling to the floor.

'Get up!' Lysander growled.

The fierce light in those green eyes convinced Antony to remain where he was. 'I…I don't think brawling in the King's apartment is a good idea,' he stammered.

Contempt flared Lysander's nostrils. 'If you won't defend yourself, then apologise to my wife and get out!'

Antony staggered to his feet and, after mumbling a few disjointed words to Tamsin, edged away holding his aching jaw.

'One last thing,' Lysander added softly as he reached the door. 'If I hear you have breathed a word of this to anyone, I shall take great pleasure in slicing your miserable hide into small pieces. Understood?'

Antony nodded and hastily fled the room.

Lysander turned to Tamsin. 'Are you all right?' he asked gently.

She nodded. 'I always knew he was a fop, but I didn't realise he was a coward,' she said, attempting a shaky smile, but her chin began to wobble and she burst into tears.

'Sweetheart!' Without conscious thought, Lysander gathered her into his arms. 'Don't cry. He isn't worth it.'

'I'm…I'm not crying over him, you great fool!' Tamsin sobbed.

'Then why—' Lysander stopped abruptly, his heart hammering. Was she, *could* she, be crying over their estrangement?

'Please. I should like to wipe my face.'

Lysander released her as if he had been burnt and Tamsin brushed the back of her fist across her tear-streaked cheeks.

'Here. Use this.' He handed her his handkerchief.

'I thought these things were only for show,' she quipped, desperate to defuse the familiar attraction she could feel spiralling between them.

He smiled, that wonderful warm smile which had first captured her heart, and she knew it was no use.

No matter how he had hurt her, no matter how she tried to
deny it, she loved him and she always would.

Tamsin finished wiping her face. 'Thank you. I shall return
this to you once it has been laundered,' she said, tucking the
handkerchief into her pocket. 'When do you intend to leave
London?'

Her coolly indifferent expression ripped Lysander's bubble
of hope to shreds. 'In a day or two,' he answered, trying to
match her tone.

There was an awkward little silence.

'The documents of annulment are ready for us to sign.'
Lysander broke it abruptly. 'That's why Charles asked us both
here.'

Tamsin swallowed hard. 'I suspected as much,' she said
rather unsteadily. She brushed back a stray curl that had escaped its pins during her struggle with Antony and prayed for
courage. 'I wonder what is keeping him?' she continued with
false calm.

'Are you so anxious for our marriage to be over?' Lysander
burst out, his deep voice ragged.

Tamsin stared at him in astonishment. She had never seen
him look so uncertain! 'Aren't…aren't you?' she stammered.

'No!' Lysander ran his hand wildly through his hair, struggling to regain his composure. 'Forgive me. Of course I shall
do as you wish and sign the papers.'

Tamsin gazed up into his face. 'You think *I* want this annulment?' she asked falteringly.

'You told me you I wasn't your idea of a good husband
and that if you had been given a choice you would have chosen a very different kind of man.'

Hearing the pain in his voice, Tamsin regretted her foolish
words more than ever. 'I was angry with you. I didn't mean
what I said.' She swallowed hard. 'I knew you didn't want
me for your wife so I told you that I wanted my freedom to
save my pride.'

Lysander took a deep breath. 'Let me get this straight,' he said slowly. 'Are you saying that you lied to me to protect yourself from rejection?'

Tamsin hung her head. 'You seemed to care more about Jane than you did about me and I wanted to hurt you,' she muttered.

Lysander put out his hand and gently tilted up her chin so that she could not avoid his gaze. 'I regretted breaking my word to Jane,' he said quietly. 'I did not regret breaking the betrothal.'

'But you blamed me for compromising your honour,' Tamsin retorted with a flash of resentment.

'Aye and it was unfair of me,' Lysander admitted.

He released her and shook his head ruefully. 'I think my wits were addled by the shock of finding out you were Tom's daughter!'

Tamsin bitterly regretted that she'd been too ashamed of her supposed illegitimacy to ask him to help find the mysterious Mr Penhaligan.

'I never guessed, you know.'

Tamsin nodded. 'My father realised his mistake a long time ago.'

'I am glad to hear it.' A smile touched his mouth and Tamsin found she could not drag her eyes away.

Lysander's breathing deepened and she saw an answering desire leap into his eyes. 'Kitling,' he said and reached for her.

Controlling herself by an effort of will, she took a step backwards. 'Wait,' she said shakily. 'I want no more misunderstandings between us, Lysander.'

Gathering her courage, she gazed into his eyes and said, 'I love you. I think I have since the night we first met, but you were trapped into this match. For the sake of my own self-respect, I need to know if you feel anything at all for me.' A little smile trembled on her lips. 'Apart from lust, I mean.'

Lysander took both her hands in his. 'You did not trap me into marriage,' he said firmly. 'My feelings were fixed long before your father caught us *in flagrante delicto.*'

A wild rose colour bloomed in Tamsin's cheeks at the memory of lying in his arms and he smiled down at her with a wicked laughter in his eyes that set her pulse racing.

'When we quarrelled on our wedding day,' Lysander continued more soberly, 'I thought you wanted to be rid of me. I'll admit I was angry, but I also knew I had little to offer you. As a rich heiress, you could make a better match if I set you free.' He lifted her hands to his lips and pressed a swift kiss against each one in turn. 'But I can't, sweetheart. When I saw you in that fop's arms I realised I love you too much to let you go.'

A choked sob escaped Tamsin and she flung her arms around his neck with a little cry of happiness.

He bent his head and his lips found hers in a tender kiss that swiftly changed to passion as she opened her mouth to him with a sigh of voluptuous pleasure.

Their breath mingled and excitement raced along Tamsin's veins in a white-hot flood. She clung to him, delighting in the feel of his strong arms around her.

Aeons later, Lysander reluctantly lifted his mouth away from hers. 'You'll never know how much I have longed to do that these last few months,' he said unsteadily.

She smiled at him as contented as a cream-fed cat and, safe in the shelter of his embrace, felt the last remaining remnants of past anger and pain fade away, but she could not resist one final question. 'Why wouldn't you see me when I came to Melcombe looking for you? All this time I thought you had deserted me because you cared more for your honour that you did for me.'

He shook his head vigorously. 'Sweetheart, I was afraid that if I came anywhere near you my resolve would crumble and I wouldn't be strong enough to give you your freedom.' He stroked her hair gently. 'I knew Tom would look after you.'

She nodded. 'He did, but I was so unhappy. All I wanted was to see you again.'

Lysander understood. 'I went to Italy to put more distance between us and thereby avoid the temptation of throwing myself at your feet and telling you that I loved you. Gathering knowledge about stone-cutting was just an excuse.'

'But I came to Melcombe to tell you I was sorry for behaving so shrewishly and that I wanted to be your true wife!' Tamsin gave a laugh that was almost a groan.

'What a pair of deluded fools we were!' Lysander's arms tightened around her. 'To have wasted so much time so needlessly!'

'Then let's not waste any more.' Tamsin grinned at him saucily and lifted her face for his kiss.

Lost in enchantment, they did not hear the door quietly opening.

Charles Stuart smiled at the scene that met his eyes and soundlessly withdrew.

Strolling back to the Vane Room, he paused to throw the sheaf of papers he held on to the nearest fire before continuing on his way with a jaunty whistle.

On the eve of Christ's birth snow began to fall on the countryside around Melcombe Regis, gently wrapping the cold fields in a silent blanket of white.

'Lysander, look!' Tamsin finished hanging the last evergreen garland and ran to the window to gaze out at the dancing snowflakes.

'Thank God, the repairs to the roof are finished!'

Tamsin laughed. 'You are very practical, sir, in the face of such beauty!'

'If it holds, we can have a snowball fight tomorrow,' he offered repentantly.

'I accept your challenge!' Tamsin grinned. Then her expression sobered. 'I hope it won't prevent my father from arriving.'

'If I know Tom, nothing will thwart him from spending Christmas with you,' Lysander answered.

His prediction proved correct. Lord Treneglos arrived shortly before dusk. Tamsin was busy in the kitchen helping prepare food for their neighbours, who had all been invited that evening to partake of the first hospitality the newly restored Melcombe had to offer. When she heard the carriage, she dashed outside to find Lysander greeting Tom with a hearty handshake.

She smiled, glad that their quarrel was over.

'My dear!' Tom kissed her cheek as she joined them. 'You are looking radiant!'

Tamsin laughingly thanked him for the compliment and begged him to come in out of the cold. They retired to the winter-parlour with a jug of mulled ale and Tom admired the changes that had revived the old house's beauty. 'You must have been very busy since your return.'

'Even busier than before we left London,' Tamsin affirmed.

Prior to taking ship, they had closed up the house in Wych Street as they intended to make Melcombe their home and only visit London occasionally. Tamsin had even managed to find new employment for Dinah and Luke, who wanted to stay near their mother. She had been sad to part with them, but her new servants seemed pleasant and willing to please.

'I have something for you. It came after you set sail.' Tom presented Tamsin with a letter, which proved to be greetings from her cousin Sam.

'Do you think we could invite him to visit us soon?' Tamsin asked Lysander shyly.

'Of course.' Lysander smiled at her. 'It will be good to meet him at last.'

Sam had been helping a neighbour with hay-making when Tom had arrived last year at Whiteladies in search of Tamsin and Lysander couldn't help wondering what would have happened if Sam had told him then of her whereabouts.

Still, it was profitless to dwell on the past. And, no matter how convoluted their path, love had triumphed in the end!

'Speaking of visitors,' he said with a glance at the new tortoiseshell clock which stood on the mantel-shelf, 'I must go and check the wine for tonight.'

'Let me help you,' Tom offered and, remembering the mince-pies in the oven, Tamsin jumped up too.

A few hours later the great hall, which Tamsin and the maids had decorated with glossy green ivy and red-berried holly, was filled with laughter as their guests sat down to a supper of venison and turkey and plum-porridge before playing traditional games of hunt the slipper and hoodman-blind.

Collapsing on to a stool before the hearth where a huge Yule log blazed, Tamsin gladly accepted a cup of mead from one of the servants, who were carrying round trays of drinks.

'I don't think I will have any energy left for dancing,' she laughingly told Lysander, who, dressed in his garnet-red finery, came to join her.

'No?' He quirked one eyebrow at her.

'Well, in a minute or two perhaps,' Tamsin grinned, smoothing her silken skirts.

He sipped at his tankard of lamb's wool. The hot ale with roasted apple and spices was a winter favourite and Tamsin's special recipe, like her delicious mince-pies, had attracted many compliments. 'You have made quite an impression to-night,' he murmured. 'And not just because you are the most beautiful woman in the room.'

Tamsin coloured with pleasure. She had been nervous about playing hostess for the first time and worn the leaf-green gown which was Lysander's favourite and her mother's pearls for luck, but her fears had proved needless. 'Our neighbours are pleasant folk,' she said, finishing her mead. 'I shall enjoy their company.'

'So long as they do not take up too much of your time.' Lysander gave her a burning glance. 'I want you too much to share you, my reluctant Puritan.'

Tamsin's blush deepened at the passion in his eyes. In their marriage-bed she had found joy beyond imagining.

'After the dancing, I thought we would sing carols and send the wassail-bowl and cakes round to end the evening.' Lysander, who treasured her uninhibited response to his lovemaking, took pity on her confusion and ceased his teasing to make this suggestion.

Spiced Christmas ale and gingerbread. 'That would be lovely,' Tamsin agreed with a sigh of content.

He set aside his empty tankard and took her hand in his. 'I once told you that I wanted to give you the chance to celebrate Christmas properly. Does this—' he waved his free hand to encompass the hall '—live up to your expectations, kitling?'

She nodded silently, her glowing smile more eloquent than words.

The musicians he had hired struck up a lively tune and he raised her to her feet. 'Come, my lady wife, by tradition we must open the dancing.'

As they moved to take their places Tom called out to Lysander to look up; when he did, he saw that they were standing under a kissing bough of mistletoe. Stretching up, he plucked one of the white berries and to the cheers of the crowd drew Tamsin into his arms and kissed her soundly.

'Merry Christmas, sweetheart,' he whispered as he released her.

Tamsin smiled. It was going to be a wonderful Christmas, the first of many they would enjoy together.

Semper amamus. Their love was forever.

* * * * *

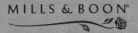

MILLS & BOON®

Historical Romance™

THE RAKE
by Georgina Devon

A Regency delight!

Compromised in an attempt to save her father's
life, Juliet Smythe-Clyde's only hope of saving her
reputation is to marry Sebastian, Duke of
Brabourne. But Juliet has no intention of being the
neglected wife of a womaniser…

THE MAIDEN'S ABDUCTION
by Juliet Landon

Isolde Medwin's decision to throw herself on the
mercy of Silas La Vallon, a long-term enemy of her
father, had ended with her being compelled aboard
his ship to Bruges. She was in potential danger, so
why should she suddenly find herself fighting a
growing attraction for her abductor?

On sale 5th January 2001

FREE

2 BOOKS
AND A SURPRISE GIFT!

We would like to take this opportunity to thank you for reading this Mills & Boon® book by offering you the chance to take TWO more specially selected titles from the Historical Romance™ series absolutely FREE! We're also making this offer to introduce you to the benefits of the Reader Service™ —

- ★ FREE home delivery
- ★ FREE monthly Newsletter
- ★ FREE gifts and competitions
- ★ Exclusive Reader Service discounts
- ★ Books available before they're in the shops

Accepting these FREE books and gift places you under no obligation to buy; you may cancel at any time, even after receiving your free shipment. Simply complete your details below and return the entire page to the address below. **You don't even need a stamp!**

YES! Please send me 2 free Historical Romance books and a surprise gift. I understand that unless you hear from me, I will receive 4 superb new titles every month for just £2.99 each, postage and packing free. I am under no obligation to purchase any books and may cancel my subscription at any time. The free books and gift will be mine to keep in any case.

HOZEC

Ms/Mrs/Miss/Mr ....Initials ....
BLOCK CAPITALS PLEASE

Surname ....

Address ....

....

....Postcode ....

Send this whole page to:
UK: FREEPOST CN81, Croydon, CR9 3WZ
EIRE: PO Box 4546, Kilcock, County Kildare (stamp required)

Offer valid in UK and Eire only and not available to current Reader Service subscribers to this series. We reserve the right to refuse an application and applicants must be aged 18 years or over. Only one application per household. Terms and prices subject to change without notice. Offer expires 30th June 2001. As a result of this application, you may receive further offers from Harlequin Mills & Boon Limited and other carefully selected companies. If you would prefer not to share in this opportunity please write to The Data Manager at the address above.

Mills & Boon® is a registered trademark owned by Harlequin Mills & Boon Limited.
Historical Romance™ is being used as a trademark.